Susan's Hope

JOANNE LEHMAN

Susan's Hope
by Joanne Lehman

Library of Congress Control Number: 2025945422

International Standard Book Number: 979-8-89674-027-8

Masthof Press
219 Mill Road | Morgantown, PA 19543-9516
www.Masthof.com

Dedicated to
Taylor, Logan, Jorian
& Amilyana

ACKNOWLEDGMENTS

After I'd drafted *Leah's Faith*, I imagined what might happen to the beautiful, supportive, and spirited Susan now that her sister had found love and healing. I wondered how long Fannie could continue to run her floundering quilt shop. Was it true that she and Hank had a little romance going on between them? By now, these women were my friends, so I jotted down blurbs for my next two books, called it the Benville Community Series, and sent my ideas to Liz Petersheim at Masthof Press.

Talk about small but mighty! My publishing experience with Masthof Press has been incredibly positive, and Liz's covers and page design have given me so much joy. Emails are answered quickly, and marketing materials arrive at my door within a day or two of reviewing a proof. Thanks for everything; you're the best, Masthof Press!

Once again, I must thank my two critique partners, Nanette Littlestone and Pamela Raleigh. Some years ago, we were perfectly matched by the Women's Fiction Writers Association. Without these two southern belles (Pam is from North Carolina and Florida, and Nanette is from Georgia), my characters would be emotionless marionettes ambling across pages of calm descriptions. Pam and Nanette show me the way as they shower me with positivity.

Thanks to my faithful Amish sensitivity reader, Sue Weaver, who has brought the finer points of Amish life to my attention with her careful reading and thorough feedback. Sharon Dean stepped in to help me with publicity and found me a launch team. A big thank you to Sharon and the team. Thanks also to my beta readers: Delores Ivan, Carita Keim, Colette and Doyle Mosier, and Rita Miller. Your thoughtful reading and comments made this book better.

Thanks to my extended family for being there when I was looking for character names. Whether it's Albert and Elma (my late grandparents), uncles Myron and Ray, a couple named Richard and Mary, or my nephews Aaron, Jacob, Andy, Adam, or Caleb, please understand that all my characters and their actions are purely fictional.

Speaking of names, thanks to EdenKeepers LLC for letting me borrow yours. It's perfect. Thanks to Reuben and Carol King, owners of our Sarasota home away from home on Searcy Avenue, for inspiring Eva Good's home and neighborhood. I'm indebted to all the creative upcyclers and crafters who, like me on occasion, enjoy getting messy and taking on a challenge. Finally, I've been so blessed by several spiritual mothers and guides. And, while *Dawdi* is a fictional character, his personality springs from the DNA of a handful of fathers and grandfathers who have nurtured me since childhood.

Acknowledgments usually include mentions of family, so thanks to our son Jeremy, who is a lot like Luke, a naturalist who points out things in the woods that I would never notice. He knows what a "rattle can" is and how to use it. Our daughter-in-law, Ana, came to mind when I invented Band Ana because her karaoke parties can entertain us for hours.

Thanks to my son-in-law, Michael, who, with our daughter Laura, grows more than one hundred native plants in their postage-stamp-sized "yarden." Michael's Saab, Wasabi, isn't a convertible, but I must credit him with that clever car moniker. Thanks to Laura for designing and regularly updating my author's website and for sharing my fiction writing adventures.

Our grandchildren, Taylor, Logan, Jorian, and Amilyana, are a vast source of inspiration and pride as they find their way in the world. I love you, and I'm blessed to know you and learn from you.

Finally, I would like to thank to my husband, Ralph. He's the man I once dreamed of. Long ago, in our Susan and Luke stage of life, we found each other. And now, we've made it all the way to here—these satisfying years we still get to enjoy together.

What else can I say? I've been blessed beyond measure. Thanks be to God!

SUSAN'S HOPE

"For I know the plans
I have for you,"
declares the Lord,
"plans to prosper you
and not to harm you,
plans to give you hope
and a future."

JEREMIAH 29:11 (NIV)

CHAPTER 1

October in Ohio was as shiny as a new copper penny, but not today. For most of the month, it had been overcast and rainy. Yesterday, it rained so hard that Salt Creek had risen to a foot below the bridge. Susan Troyer looked down into the swirling, clay-colored water and urged Jasper, her new buggy horse, onward. The gelding balked and stood resolutely on the road at the edge of the bridge. He tossed his head, and the harness slapped his neck. Susan repeated the slap using the reins in her hand. Nothing. She was stuck. *Thanks, Jasper.*

A car pulled up beside her and roared to a stop. Susan suspected, knew without looking, who had come to her rescue. She stuck her head out from the side of the buggy. It was Amos Maust in his nasty car. Would she never be free of this loser? A week ago, she'd told him she was done. And now he was following her on this rugged little buggy road, ready to help in her hour of need.

"Looks like Jasper needs some horse sense. What's his problem?" Amos asked.

"The creek spooked him," Susan said. The trace of annoyance in her voice was as much for Amos as for Jasper.

Amos pulled his rusty old sedan off the road and into the weeds and let it idle. Exhaust fumes wafted across the damp, crumbling asphalt, mixing with the scent of fresh horse manure. Susan remained on the buggy seat, determined not to interact with Amos more than necessary.

Amos, her friend—not her boyfriend—was the lost sheep of Benville. Bishop Maust's oldest son remained unsure of his future long after most of his peers had settled down. He worked on a construction crew, wasn't in the church, but wasn't entirely out, either. His father and others regularly prayed for his redemption. They had no idea how much it was needed.

Amos strode toward Susan, and a wave of despair swept over her. "It's okay. Jasper is new. He's just a little stubborn, that's all."

"Stubborn like his owner," Amos shot back. "Playin' it safe on this side, rather than go the whole way over."

"That sounds more like you," Susan jabbed back.

Amos took hold of one of the wooden hames attached to the horse's harness. With his other hand, he reached for the bridle and gave a yank. Jasper remained planted. After another couple of tugs, the horse finally yielded, and Amos walked alongside as the gelding grudgingly plodded across the bridge. When they had safely crossed, he let go and walked back toward Susan, who remained seated in the buggy.

"Thank you," she said. Her voice was cool. "This horse has a few things to learn."

"You bet!" said Amos. "See you around!" He strode back to his old rattletrap. Susan heard the familiar scrape of the door opening and the slam of it shutting. He revved the engine, but instead of careening around her like she expected, he slowed to buggy speed and followed Susan up the next hill and around the bend. Her anger flared, then sputtered into the ever-present hopelessness—a hallmark of her emotions during this season of life. Last week, she'd thought—unrealistically—that she'd seen the last of Amos, but now here he was.

Amos pulled alongside Susan's buggy on the deserted road. "Your last fling with me is next weekend! Red Hawk Country Fest.

No arguments! You owe me!" he shouted over the car's engine. Susan glared at him. But there was that grin, that little twist in his smile that melted her heart despite the knowledge that had become clear. Amos wasn't husband material.

"We're done, Amos. I told you last week. It's over." She tried to make her voice reflect serious finality. But habit made it sound like a tease, a hesitant reversal of resolve, too flirtatious, and not at all final.

Amos was a teenage crush that should have ended long ago. But he was nearby. He was cute, with a mop of curly hair. He was fun. And lately, it was his availability as much as anything. Most young men and women in the Benville, Holmes County, Amish community had joined the church. Her friends and cousins were married and settled before they were twenty. Only a few in Susan's age group were still unattached. Susan was twenty-one, and her friend Ruthie soon would be. Amos was a couple of years older.

"I insist. Red Hawk Country Fest, Saturday night. You know you don't want to miss it. I'll pick you up around 7:00." He pitched a flyer out his car window, and it fluttered to the ground.

Susan retrieved the flyer and glanced at it. He knew how to get to her. It would be fun to go to Red Hawk Country again. She'd been there every year since she was seventeen. What could it hurt to go with him one more time? It was an *Englischer* event and there was always a big friend group that sat together. Jasper threw his head impatiently, as if trying to rid himself of the harness that kept him in his place. She understood the discomfort of being held too tightly. And like Jasper a moment ago, she felt powerless to move on. How could she when there was nowhere to go?

For a couple of years now, she'd enjoyed the little parties in someone's shop that Amos always seemed to know about. Someone showed a movie or played music. There were tacos or pizza, and sometimes a few too many drinks. But lately, running around with Amos wasn't as fun. She was tired of him and his rowdy friends with their craft beer obsessions and country music preoccupations. Susan was determined to move on. After the coming weekend.

"Wear the blue hoodie and bring a blanket. It might get cold. Remember, if it wasn't for me, you and Jasper would still be sitting at the bridge."

Not true. Susan was perfectly capable of guiding Jasper, just as Amos had. But something was appealing and romantic about their moment on the roadside. The way Amos had come to her aid right when she needed him. Letting go of their relationship wasn't as easy as she thought it would be. Old habits. The way of least resistance.

"Okay," Susan said. She'd be rid of him soon enough. "Just for you, one last time. Against my better judgment." Appeased, Amos sped off.

Susan and Jasper turned onto the larger road that led into town, where she would shop for the groceries on *Maemm's* list. She'd remember to grab a package of the large-sized disposable diapers for her sister Leah's twins. They'd run out of the healthy Costco brand she usually kept on hand. As *Maemm* requested, on the way home, she would stop by Crestview Orchard to pick up three bushels of yellow delicious apples they'd ordered. Yellow Delicious was *Maemm's* favorite, which she used to make fifty half-gallons of canned applesauce every year.

Might as well have some fun Saturday night. After all, I'm going to be up to my elbows in applesauce between now and then.

CHAPTER 2

At Hofstetter's, the little general store, Susan grabbed a cart and made her way through the aisles gathering things they needed to keep the Troyer household running. Two of Susan's three younger brothers were teens. Adam was close behind Andy and Jake. Their *Daett*, Albert, liked to joke that his three sons each had a hollow leg. Susan was sure the other leg was filled with applesauce. She reached for a ten-pound bag of sugar and dropped it in the cart, then added a bag of flour and a fresh bottle of cinnamon for the apple dumplings they were sure to make this week. She collected a few boxes of canning jar lids and topped off the cart with more essentials. At least this morning, she was out of the house instead of digging potatoes or harvesting remnants in the cabbage patch.

As she rounded the end of the cereal aisle, her cart bumped into another customer's going the opposite way. "Oh! Sorry!" A familiar laugh greeted her apology. "Ruthie!" Susan stared into the grinning face of her best friend.

"Watch your speed, or you'll get a ticket!" Ruthie lived on a farm with her parents, and like Susan, she was still single. She was an Amish anomaly—an only child. She was also a little chubby and not at all shy. She was prone to laugh loudly in a fake-sounding way, although it was completely genuine once you knew her.

Bumping into Ruthie interrupted Susan's gloomy thoughts. She'd become increasingly depressed as she filled her cart with various sundries and miscellanea. Mindless chores were now her role in life. She had little to look forward to but more of the same.

Susan and Ruthie parked their carts alongside the aisle. "*Maemm* sent me here for sugar. We're getting the apples this week," Susan said.

"Us, too. How many are you planning to do?" Ruthie asked.

"Three bushel. Picking them up on my way home."

"Just one for us. Hey! Let's get ice cream at the Heifer Creamery when we're done here," Ruthie proposed.

"Sure. Why not? Let's make it large. Have an ice cream dinner," said Susan.

The two went their separate ways down different aisles of Hofstetter's and checked out at separate registers. They pushed their carts through the doorway and out into the cool October morning. Susan loaded her groceries into the buggy, while Ruthie packed hers into the cart attached to her E-bike. Clouds still blanketed the sky, and Susan looked forward to eating ice cream and chatting with her best friend.

The Creamery was decked out in a style Ruthie had once described as "early cow barn." Tin wainscoting topped with weathered boards rimmed the small dining room. Painted wooden cutouts of cow faces and rustic signs with words like "moo" and "Drink Milk" were scattered on the walls, and glass milk bottles stuffed with sunflowers graced the tables. Antique milk house equipment in one corner completed the look.

Susan ordered two scoops of butter pecan, and Ruthie requested an equal serving of cookies and cream. They settled into a corner booth and picked up where they'd left off. They always had so much to talk about. Susan imagined marriage like that, only more so. But lately, it felt like a hopeless daydream. Where was the man who would share her days, light up her life, and love her for the complex mess she had managed to become in just twenty-one short years?

Once settled in their booth, Ruthie, as usual, began with the weather. When you live on a farm, as Ruthie did, the weather is always top of mind.

"Can you believe all this rain we're having? It's so unusual for October," Ruthie said.

"The water is so high, Jasper balked at the bridge today," Susan said. "He's not the horse *Daett* thought when he bought him for me at the auction barn."

"Auctions aren't the best place to get a horse," Ruthie said. Her *Daett* was a farmer, not a woodworker like Susan's *Daett*.

"Well, anyway, Jasper did go across the bridge. Help showed up just in time."

"Let me guess...the devoted boyfriend, Amos Maust, came to the rescue."

"Yeah. But he's not my boyfriend. We're just friends now—not that we were ever anything else," Susan added quickly.

"Sure, you are...just friends."

"We are, as of a week ago, Saturday. It's not working—it won't ever work. He's got problems I can't fix, despite everyone wishing I could settle him down."

"Yeah! His *Maemm* thinks if you two were married, he'd join the church," Ruthie said. "Because you would join, wouldn't you?"

Susan nodded. But if Anna Maust thought Susan was her son's salvation, she was wrong.

"I'm glad you're finally seeing it," Ruthie said. "I don't like him. He's not good for you, even as a friend. You're better off without him."

Ruthie didn't like Amos. But he was charming. And until lately, they'd had fun together. Maybe she was outgrowing him.

"I like Amos," Susan said. "He's a free spirit." She pictured the long brown hair that curled around his ears and spilled over his shirt collar. What would Ruthie think if she knew that an hour ago, Susan had agreed to go with Amos to the Red Hawk Country Fest? But Ruthie didn't need to know *that*. Anyway, there was still a chance Susan would change her mind.

"I get tired of his attitude," said Ruthie. "Amos and his friends are up to no good, living in that icky Massillon apartment."

"Lots of guys do that," Susan said. "It's convenient to meet up with the crew when they work for the construction company." The three young men shared a dingy apartment above a bar. Susan had been there once. It was dark inside and had old, creaky floors.

"He still comes home to his mother for a home-cooked meal," Ruthie said.

Susan knew Amos' parents welcomed him whenever he stopped by. They prayed for him, just as she knew her parents prayed for her.

"He drinks and smokes," Ruthie said with disgust. "Why go with a guy who does that?"

Ruthie had a point. Susan hated the smell of cigarillos, those rattail smokes Amos and his friends liked. They made his car stink even when he held them out the window. She'd reminded him more than once not to smoke while he was driving.

"The bad habits bother me. I think he's addicted to that stuff," Susan said.

"You're right. He is." Ruthie stood, threw the plastic ice cream dish into the trash, and came back, settling into the booth.

"Seriously, Susan, you shouldn't give Amos one bit of attention, let alone riding around with him," Ruthie said. "It could be dangerous if he's drinking. How do you know he doesn't drink before you ride with him?"

Susan didn't answer. She knew he liked his beer. And she'd shared one or two in a weak moment. She valued Ruthie's opinion. Why did she have this soft spot for Amos when she knew their relationship was going nowhere?

They sat a while longer, and the conversation finally drifted past Amos.

"How's your neighbor Ben Keim these days?" Ruthie asked.

"Oh, I have news!" Susan said. "Did you hear what Ben's doing now?"

"No. What? He isn't getting married, is he?" Ruthie sounded anxious.

Susan suspected her friend was interested in Ben Keim. In their district, he was one of the few young men who was still unattached.

"You and Ben would be good together," Susan said.

Ruthie shrugged. She refused to admit interest in Ben. Or that he could be interested in her.

"Anyway, there's still time. I don't think he's ready to settle down just yet," Susan said. "He came over to talk to Leah and Aaron when I was helping with fall cleaning." For more than four years, Susan's older sister had been married to Ben's brother, Aaron, and they had four *kinnah*. "Ben told us he'd applied to work at an organic farm in Vermont."

"Really? Vermont? I don't think I ever knew anyone who went to Vermont."

"It's up in New England. Pretty far away," Susan said. "I guess he hopes to own a farm someday. He said you can make a lot more if you become certified organic, but he doesn't know the first thing about it."

At one point, Susan had hopes that she and Ben would become more than just good friends. But ever since Leah and Aaron's wedding, Ben had been cool. She didn't know why, but it made her sad. Maybe the fact that his brother had four *kinnah* scared Ben. It *was* hard to believe her sister already had four children—twin toddler girls, a two-year-old boy, and a baby boy named Michael. Susan envied Leah, who had settled down in Benville with a good husband and her own family. She'd have a comfortable life as part of the Keim family, who owned a large shop where they made hardwood furniture.

"I know Ben likes farming," Ruthie said. "He came over to talk to *Daett* about farm stuff—intensive grazing of cattle, where to get a good team of Belgian work horses—that sort of thing. But after he left, my *Daett* said, 'He's a long way from owning a farm.'"

Susan nodded. "Maybe Ben came over to see you," Susan said. "You could do worse than ending up with Ben Keim."

"Don't get any ideas. He's just like that—always wants to talk with the farmers."

Susan didn't push it further. "Aaron isn't happy about losing Ben's help at the woodshop, but he's a farmer at heart. Always has been. Ben and Aaron used to argue about it a lot."

"I'd say if he wants to do something different and get out of Benville, Ohio, he should do it," Ruthie said. "Too many of our young people just settle down without thinking about all the interesting things they could do."

Susan thought Ruthie had a point. She'd heard the excitement in Ben's voice before he'd left. She admired his ingenuity and the way he'd planned a legitimate escape from Benville, the little town named after his ancestors, a place that surrounded them and held them too close for comfort sometimes.

"I think he was surprised when that organic farm emailed to say they had work for him." Susan stirred the melted ice cream left in her dish. She had a fleeting memory of good times with her childhood neighbor. His easy banter still warmed her heart, but they had drifted into young adulthood separately. When Susan and Ben met now, it was by chance. Most often, they met at Leah and Aaron's chaotic household, where an infant and three toddlers were the center of everyone's attention.

Ben's coolness was just one more loss in the unraveling of her childhood. Susan's older sister, Leah, was so caught up in being a wife and mother that she barely noticed Susan's social life, or the lack thereof. Susan had been relegated to the roles of auntie, babysitter on short notice, errand girl, and unpaid housecleaner. She had no life of her own except for the one she shared with Amos. And that would soon be over.

CHAPTER 3

Susan left town and followed the township road to Valley View and Crestview Orchard, owned by her uncle Aden Weaver. He greeted her with his trademark boisterous "Hello!" Susan climbed down from the buggy and tied Jasper to the hitching rail. She stepped into the dark shed where wooden crates of apples were stacked on tables, and pallets covered most of the floor. The sweet scent of apples was overpowering. The afternoon sun had emerged, and a shaft of gold streamed through a gap where a piece of siding had blown off in a storm. Dust sparkled in the sunbeam. *Maemm* had called in their order, and Aden had three wooden apple crates lined up and tagged with Albert Troyer's name. Susan pulled out the fifty-dollar bill *Daett* had left on the table that morning for the apples.

"How is your sister Leah doing these days?" Aden asked. The familiar question, in one form or another, followed Susan everywhere she went. A few years ago, her older sister had surgery in Cleveland to correct scoliosis, a birth defect that would have caused her to become disabled. She was somewhat of a celebrity because a famous doctor had performed her surgery at no cost. It was a miracle for Leah, who had been gentle and dependent on her younger sister, Susan. *Maemm* protected Leah by giving her simple chores, while Susan did the more difficult garden work.

It was wonderful that Leah could live without a disability. But everything changed between the sisters after Leah's surgery. Before that, Susan was the beautiful, popular, fun-loving sister with a bright future. But now Leah was the shining star who had overcome her suffering, married the well-to-do Aaron Keim, and gave birth to twins a year later.

Meanwhile, Susan had run out of options. Now, even Amos Maust wasn't an option. Susan couldn't explain all of that to Uncle Aden, but his question reminded her of how their two lives had changed in just a few years. All the attention on Leah made Susan fume inside, but she didn't show it.

"Leah is doing so well," Susan assured their uncle Aden. "She's as strong as I am. She works hard and she's so terribly busy with the new baby, their little Matthew, and the twins, Rachel and Rebecca."

"I imagine so. It seems not long ago that Lydia and I had little ones. Now they are all in school."

Susan nodded. She remembered helping Lydia when the children were small.

"It's so good to see Leah and Aaron making a life together," Aden said. "They are such a fine couple. Wonderful family! Tell them I said 'hello' when you see them. We might come up there for a visit again one of these Sundays."

"*Maemm* would like that. We all would," Susan said. She picked up a crate of apples, and Aden picked up a second one. They walked to Susan's buggy, and she moved the grocery bags to make room for the crates. It was going to be tight. Aden returned to the shed and brought the third crate.

"I'd better get going. *Maemm* might want to start in on these yet today."

"Enjoy your apple dumpling supper," Aden said as Susan backed away from the hitching rail.

"How do you know we're having apple dumplings?"

"Hey! I'm married to your *Maemm's* sister. It's hereditary. The day you get the apples, you have apple dumplings for supper. And probably not much else," Aden warned.

Susan hadn't noticed, but now that Aden mentioned it, she was sure he was right. *Maemm* would make apple dumplings for supper. And to make matters worse, Susan had eaten only ice cream at noon.

The trip home was smooth, and Jasper crossed the bridge without paying any mind to the muddy water. The sunshine that usually lifted Susan's spirits didn't do anything to ease the dull ache in her chest. Aden's comments about her sister didn't help.

Everything changed after that summer six years ago, when Leah had surgery at Cleveland General. The community was thrilled with Leah's transformation, as she now stood straight and tall. She radiated confidence and happiness, and her fear of being disabled disappeared. Aaron Keim had started dating her even before she was fully recovered. By the following fall, they were married.

"You're next," Aunt Lydia had said that day. But now, some years later, Susan was still alone.

CHAPTER 4

"I don't know why we peel all the apples," Susan complained. "Most everyone uses the Victorio strainer for applesauce anymore. It goes so much faster than coring, peeling, and *schnitzing* them."

The Victorio was a stainless-steel wonder that they clamped onto the edge of a table. It was perfect for making tomato juice, grape juice, and applesauce. It prevented hours of tedious work.

Maemm paused briefly, her paring knife still in the air, as slices of peeled apple dropped into the cold saltwater on the stool beside her. "We might do that for the next bushel. But *Dawdi* likes chunky applesauce. *Daett* doesn't say much, but he does, too."

Susan nodded. The men should be satisfied it was homemade, but *Maemm* catered to their whims. Susan kept her thoughts to herself, but inside, her annoyance grew. Maybe someday she would get to decide things—even if only whether to strain the applesauce. She would tell the men that chunky sauce was too much work. Susan and *Maemm* continued in silence, the ticking clock on the wall the only accompaniment to gentle plops as peeled sliced apples fell into the salted water that kept them from turning brown.

After a few minutes, *Maemm* broke the silence. "Don't forget that we're going out to Delaware this weekend to the Weaver cousins' reunion. Then, we will probably go to the beach that evening for a little while. *Daett* always enjoys birdwatching on the beach. But it's going to be a quick trip. We'll be back Sunday night."

"Oh, is that this weekend? I forgot when it was."

"We leave on Friday at noon, so all three bushels need to be taken care of by then. They're pretty ripe already." *Maemm* wiped her hands on a dishtowel and went to the stove to put on another kettle of peeled apples to cook.

"You know I'm not going along to Delaware," said Susan. "I have plans with Ruthie and a couple of others. We're going shopping at the mall."

Maemm frowned. "You can find nice things a lot closer to home. Why go running around like that when you don't need to?"

Susan stifled her bitter thoughts. She wanted to shout back. *Why go to Delaware? There are plenty of Weaver cousins closer to home. Why not make applesauce the easy way? Why not get Leah and your boys to help peel apples?* But Susan held her tongue. She knew her place. She had no more influence over what happened here than she did when she was ten years old.

At least they weren't making her go to the reunion. The shopping trip was a lie. The real plan was to go with Amos to Red Hawk Country Fest. There wasn't a need to hide this from *Maemm,* but Susan wanted some privacy, something to call her own within the narrow confines of Benville. Until recently, she'd looked forward to parties with Amish youth from different communities. There were volleyball tournaments and singings, and little adventures with Amos. But now that she was twenty-one, she knew it was time to "put away childish things," as the scriptures said. Susan knew her parents hoped and prayed for her to join the church. But she liked being in control of her life, at least for a few hours on a weekend.

By Thursday afternoon, the three bushels of apples had been turned into gleaming, sealed half-gallon Mason jars of applesauce. They covered the entire kitchen table. The boys carried them to the basement, where Susan lined them up on the fruit cellar shelves. She couldn't deny the feeling of satisfaction. By the third bushel, *Maemm* was ready to cook unpeeled apples and strain them through the Victorio. What a time-saver that had been.

On Saturday evening, Susan found her Gap jeans in a dresser drawer with the other clothes she wore on weekends when she went out. She had turned down an invitation to have supper with her brothers at Aunt Fannie's house. She looked through a stack of folded T-shirts and picked one with the words "Do Something Wild." It was from a local nature reserve and showed a forest in the background, a lake, and a great blue heron in flight. It was the flying part she wanted to remind herself of. *After tonight, I'll be free of you, Amos.*

Susan took off her *kapp* and let her hair down. Standing in front of the bathroom mirror, she brushed her hair fiercely until it shone. Then she fussed with makeup and lipstick she'd bought at Sephora. It wasn't as exciting as it used to be to pretend she was *Englisch*. It was time to "put away childish things." She thought of *Dawdi* and his recent words about joining the *Gmay* and taking her faith more seriously.

She grabbed a blue hoodie and a fleece throw on her way out to meet Amos. He waited impatiently for her to get settled, then spun out in the gravel as they departed, leaving a cloud of dust trailing behind them down the lane.

"How's my girl tonight? Ready for a fun time?" The car careened around the corner and onto the road.

"Yikes! Look out! And I'm not your girl, remember? We're done after tonight." Susan lurched against Amos' shoulder, and he wrapped his right arm around her. She pulled away, scooted over, shrugged into the hoodie, and threw the fleece blanket across her lap.

"The car heater isn't working. I was only trying to keep you warm," Amos said.

"I'm fine, thank you. And you know this is the last time I'm doing this, right?" she said. She'd had some fun times with Amos, but that part of her life was over. Tonight was her chance to make that clear, and she vowed to do just that.

"Last time for what?" Amos asked.

"Us. I'm only going with you because you helped me get Jasper across the bridge last Monday," Susan reminded him. "I need to get serious about my life. Even if you aren't ready yet."

"I know. I know. After tonight, you're going to settle down and be a good Amish girl—your last hurrah with ole' Amos before you get baptized."

Amos reached out to turn up the radio. It was the one thing she would miss—listening to his car radio. He sang along to the latest country song, turning his head to look at her while keeping one eye on the road. Dry cornstalks in the fields flew past as they traveled across the county, slowing down to admire the ridiculous, over-the-top Halloween decorations in the small towns they passed through. He was taking the scenic route.

They had attended the Red Hawk Country Fest at the Stone Barn for the past three years. Amos and Susan drove through Holmes and Ashland Counties on narrow township roads. Fall leaves swirled to the ground all around them. The fall rain had freshened the landscape, giving it a polished shine under the clear, periwinkle evening sky. Traffic slowed to a crawl as vehicles gathered on County Line Road, which led to a long gravel lane and eventually to a pasture field where stakes marked the entrance to a rough parking lot. They bumped along over the uneven grass, in a line of mostly pickup trucks and vans, with one dingy car among them.

Amos and his buddies looked forward to this music festival, which featured a lineup of local bands and craft beers. Susan remembered to note where Amos parked. One year, they wandered in the dark for what felt like an hour, trying to find Amos' car. She made a mental note of her surroundings and tried to estimate how far they were from the barn and the main stage for the concert. They grabbed lawn chairs and blankets from the back seat and walked with other concertgoers toward the gate.

"If you have the cash for admission, I can grab our sandwiches and drinks," Amos said. Susan wanted to remind him that this whole thing was his idea, but she nodded and reached into her purse. "It's thirty dollars each, right?"

"Yeah. This looks bigger than before." Someone was selling program booklets, and Amos gave a dollar so they could read about the performances. The back cover featured a full-page ad for this year's Red Hawk IPAs from three Ohio microbreweries. "Sweet!" Amos said, pointing to one of the featured selections. "They have the Derecho IPA. Fourteen percent lager. I've been waiting for this. It's a microbrew take-off on Hurricane. You might like this one—it's fruity, slightly sweet."

Amos was always urging her to try a new brew. He considered himself a beer expert, and Susan was confident tonight would be no different. Most IPAs were overwhelming. She didn't like the taste of beer to begin with. It would be a relief to be done with Amos' obsession with drinking.

She had to admit Derecho was a clever name, even if it was a copy of a beer called Hurricane. They had seen evidence of the actual derecho, a destructive straight-line windstorm that swept through Ashland County and snapped trees in half as if they were matchsticks during a thunderstorm. Months later, broken tree trunks could still be seen along the roadside here and there.

They wandered the grounds, exploring the food trucks. The program indicated that all guests should buy their drinks at the on-site bar. Susan followed Amos into the barn, where the lower-level animal stalls and dairy stanchions had been replaced with a long, shiny bar made from a live-edge plank. The stools, crafted from the seats of discarded farm equipment, looked uncomfortable.

Amos ordered two Derechos. He handed one to her. "Do they have Dr. Pepper? That's more my speed."

"Come on, live a little. You're not gonna get a chance much longer," Amos said.

Does he always make fun of me? Why do I pretend not to notice? He constantly mocked her dislike for his beer. The more he mocked her, the less she wanted to cooperate with him. But he ordered a soft drink and handed it over, keeping both bottles of beer for himself.

They shifted their blankets and folding chairs so they could carry the drinks. "We can order food later when the lines aren't so long," Amos said. "Let's find the guys and settle in."

Susan figured it would be the usual older Amish group, his two housemates, Bob and Josh, and their girlfriends.

"My buddies told me to look for them on the hill. Do you see any maple trees? They said they'd be near the second one." Susan and Amos stopped walking and paused out of the traffic flow while they examined the grounds.

Above them, the hillsides sloped downward and came together, forming an amphitheater with the old barn at the bottom. A temporary stage was set up on the wide lawn just in front of the barn. Several instruments were already in place for the evening's first performance, and the hillsides were filled with people mingling or settling onto blankets and folding lawn chairs.

While Amos scanned the crowd for his friends, Susan examined the program. "This is quite a line-up of performers. Did you expect such a big crowd?"

"It's like Woodstock," Amos said.

"What does that mean? 'Woodstock'?" Susan asked.

"Don't tell me you've never heard of Woodstock? Little innocent Susan. 'What's Woodstock?' she asks. She's never heard of Woodstock," Amos mocked her. A flash of irritation caught her off guard. She was done with his disrespect that he pretended was a joke.

Amos continued: "Back in the sixties, there was a huge hippie party on a farm in New York with music, beer, and weed. It lasted three whole days. Thousands of people attended. Three days of peace and music, or beer and music."

"Thousands?" Susan asked.

"Thousands."

"Well, I don't think there are a thousand here," Susan said. "Maybe a few hundred, though." She wasn't sure how the loud music of Red Hawk Country could create peace. For her, it was the opposite, a respite from the overly peaceful life of Benville. *If only there was some in-between place.*

Susan closed the program booklet and helped Amos look for their group. "Over there, up at the top of that hill. I think that must be the tree they meant." Susan pointed. "I see Bob's white cowboy hat."

They made their way up the hill from the barn, then followed the upper rim until they found the group and set up their chairs beside Amos' housemate Bob. He'd brought his girlfriend, Zoe, who greeted them. "I have a bag of snacks and wine spritzers I can share later," she said.

"Thanks. I'm good for now." Susan raised her plastic cup of Dr. Pepper.

It was a perfect fall evening, but cool enough that Susan had already put on her hoodie. Amos had put on his Carhartt jacket earlier to avoid carrying it. Josh stood up to greet them. "Hey, Amos, Susan. You made it to the Stoned Barn." Amos and the guys laughed, and Susan pretended to smile at the not-funny joke. Their banter annoyed her. Would they ever grow up and talk about something serious?

"I brought my little buddies from down in Hayesville. They need some new experiences." Josh gestured toward a younger Amish group, guys who were only fifteen or sixteen, lounging on a blanket. Their Amish haircuts were partly hidden under ball caps. They wore navy sweatshirts and new blue jeans. Amos knew Ray and Myron, who worked with a roofing crew.

Amos and Susan greeted everyone and made small talk with the others before settling into the folding lawn chairs, ready to listen to the Band-Ana Boys, a local country cover band featuring four guys and a lead singer named Ana, dressed in a short, figure-revealing cowgirl outfit. She pretended to dance with her microphone, and the sequins sparkled under the lights. The crowd quieted, and Amos drank his beer quickly. Susan sipped her soft drink and felt embarrassed for the woman on stage. It wasn't the Amish way to call attention to herself. But onstage, that was the point.

Amos urged her to try the second bottle of Derecho. She swallowed her reservations. The beer was bitter and burned her throat. She handed it back after one sip, and Amos rolled his eyes in disgust.

They sat listening, most of them holding a beer in one hand. She sipped the Dr. Pepper until only melting ice remained in the cup. Amos drank the second bottle, excused himself, and said something to Bob before walking over to the bar. Susan was worried about the young guys. They were underage and probably didn't understand the effects of alcohol. They shouldn't be drinking at all, especially those IPAs.

The sun was setting, and floodlights flickered around the amphitheater. Amos returned with a cardboard six-pack carrier filled with doubles of the three craft beers listed on the back of the program. He grabbed one and passed it around to everyone, including the underage boys, Ray and Myron.

"They're too young to drink," Susan reminded Amos. "You shouldn't give it to them."

He scoffed. "Give me a break. Everyone here drinks—except maybe you."

Susan thought about mentioning that she was drinking a wine spritzer but decided against it. Amos would make fun of that, too.

Before intermission, Bob and Zoe left and returned with a bag full of sausage sandwiches and another six-pack of beer. The food and drinks circulated, and Zoe handed out bags of chips. They ate, sipped, and listened to more music. During intermission, some of the guys returned with reinforcements, ready for the main musical act. By then, their group was relaxing, drinking, and talking loudly. Ray and Myron helped themselves to more beer. The older guys had been drinking for years already. Susan didn't like it, but they were experienced. The younger guys probably weren't. Ray looked unsteady and spaced out. Myron spilled ketchup on himself, which he wiped up with a wad of napkins.

The main acts of the evening started, and Susan forgot everything except the music, which drew her in with its lyrics telling stories of life, grief, and loss. Her heart beat in sync with the sound as she tuned out everything else. The set shifted again, and below them on the hillsides, a few people stood or packed up to leave. The rest stayed quiet and subdued. But on the upper hillsides, where they sat, noisy interruptions popped up here and there, making it hard for Susan to focus on the final performance.

The darkness, music, and food eventually took over again, relaxing her into a mellow mood. It was getting late, and Amos leaned back in his chair as if he were asleep. Susan worried that he might be drunk. She hoped not. She wasn't planning to ride home with him if he was. Bob and Zoe snuggled together under a blanket beside them. At least Amos didn't expect her to do that. She draped her fleece throw around her shoulders for extra warmth against the cool, damp evening.

Out of nowhere, a police officer appeared and aimed a flashlight beam at their group. A few uniformed officers were making rounds, looking for someone or something. Susan wasn't sure what. They passed by Susan, Amos, Bob, and Zoe but stopped in front of the younger boys, asking to see their IDs. They were checking the crowd for underage drinking. Myron jumped to his feet immediately, and the officer asked for ID, which he didn't have. Susan's heart pounded. She'd been afraid that something like this might happen.

Why hadn't Ray reacted? He was still on the ground, lying on his back with his eyes closed. Some concert-goers did that while they listened. She hadn't thought much of it until now. Had he passed out from drinking too much? Susan elbowed Amos, who opened his eyes and watched the officer lean over and tap Ray's shoulder. He still didn't move.

By now, everyone around them was fully awake. The band began a new song. People nearby were standing, either to see what was happening or to avoid the crowd at the end of the concert. Susan saw some gathering their things. A few watched with worried looks as the officer took Ray's pulse.

Amos stood up and mumbled, "What's up, people?" He swayed.

Susan saw Bob and Zoe quickly pull her bag under a blanket. They folded their chairs. "We gotta go," Bob announced. "Cinderella here needs her beauty sleep." The officer paid no attention to them. He was radioing for backup.

Others in the group vanished into the darkness, and panic tightened in Susan's chest. Anyone she might have asked to drive her home was out of sight and heading toward the parking lot. She had no idea who Myron and Ray had come with. Whoever they were, they had fled the scene, leaving Susan and Amos, who was drunk, to handle questions. Amos thought their last name was Hershberger. Susan remembered hearing someone say the boys were from Hayesville. That's all they knew.

"Is he okay?" She pointed at Ray, who still hadn't moved. Her legs felt weak, and she shivered as she wrapped the fleece around her like a shawl.

When an EMT arrived, she checked Ray's vital signs again. Another EMT came with a stretcher. The officer and the EMTs helped Ray, who still hadn't moved. Susan froze, digging her heels into a patch of grass. Her chin trembled. She understood the dangers of too much alcohol. And she knew Amos wouldn't pass the breathalyzer test waiting for them. She had been through this before with him, months earlier. He had barely passed that time. As for Myron, she was pretty sure he wasn't of legal drinking age, and they'd each had at least two Derechos, or a similar brew—possibly more.

The officer put away his flashlight and focused his attention on Susan, Amos, and Myron, who was crushing his ball cap between his fists. "Gather your things and follow the path to the cruiser parked behind the shed." From behind them, he shone his flashlight on the gravel. Amos swayed, corrected his balance, and they walked single file down the gravel path toward the flashing lights behind a farm outbuilding in a small gravel parking lot. Susan clutched her fleece, wrapping it tightly around herself to stay warm. The emergency vehicle began moving away from them, onto the lane, heading for the hospital.

The officer told Myron to get in the front seat of the cruiser. He left Susan and Amos standing nearby. The rhythmic beat of the last set's encore continued, but it was now just background noise. Susan's chest tightened as she thought about her situation. She had cash in her wallet and a picture ID showing her age and home address. Amos had a driver's license. Myron was probably from one of the nearby Amish communities, an inexperienced teenager.

As she expected, the officer asked for identification, which she and Amos provided. He kept hold of their IDs as he questioned them. Susan told the officer what she knew about Ray and Myron. She honestly admitted that she had tasted Amos' Derecho, drank a Dr. Pepper, and later had a wine spritzer. Still, the officer tested her. Susan blew into the breathalyzer. "You're good," he said. "Get in the cruiser." She obeyed. Myron was sobbing quietly in the front seat.

"It'll be okay," Susan said. She felt so sorry for him. "That Derecho was too strong for anyone."

"B-b-but Ray. What if...?" Myron let out an audible sob.

"Your brother is on his way to the hospital, where he can get help. That's the important thing," Susan said.

The officer guided Amos into the back seat. They sat in silence, listening to exchanges between him and another officer. Amos slouched against the door and seemed unaware of anything. A wave of despair washed over Susan as she watched the long line of vehicles

leaving the premises while they still sat in the cruiser, waiting for…
she didn't know what. It must be at least eleven o'clock.

Finally, the officer turned to Susan. "Amos is the only licensed
driver in your group, and he's not legally allowed to drive." Susan
nodded slightly. The lump in her throat was about to choke her.

"I'm holding his driver's license, but here's your ID, young
lady." He passed it across the seat, then looked at Myron. "I'd ad-
vise you, young people, to watch who you associate with in the future. Riding with a drunk driver or being escorted in a police cruiser
aren't the most effective ways of finding your way back to where you
belong. I'm taking you to the Ashland sheriff's office. Once you're
cleared, we'll let the folks there decide how to get you home.

CHAPTER 5

By the time the car reached the Ashland County Sheriff's Office, Susan had a moment to realize just how much trouble she was in. Amos was in worse trouble than she was, but she'd never thought she'd be taken in for questioning or see a medical emergency. Would she have to go to court? Would her family find out what happened? Amos was still too drunk to be questioned or to fill out paperwork. The officer inside led him down the hall and into what he called "a secure location."

Myron and Susan sat beneath the harsh lights in a no-nonsense room. A deputy handed them clipboards with information forms to fill out and return to the desk. They did as they were instructed, then waited as the minutes passed. Near midnight, the frowning receptionist directed Susan to a different waiting area. As she stood to follow, Susan looked toward Myron. That was the last time she saw him. He looked at her pleadingly, but she only gave a slight nod. She felt sorry for him, but she had her own problems to deal with.

"You can wait here," the receptionist said. Fluorescent lights glared overhead. "I'll get the Behavioral Health Officer. Stay put."

Susan sat down on the hard plastic-covered armchair that the receptionist offered her. The woman then turned quickly, leaving Susan alone in the empty room.

Any exhaustion she might have felt at this time of night was replaced with a racing pulse and gut-churning fear. How had this happened? How had things gone so wrong? Her clammy hands gripped the fake wooden arms of her chair as she surveyed the dull waiting room where she waited alone for...what? A behavioral health officer, the receptionist said. What did that mean? Trying to distract herself, she studied the safety posters on the wall. She swallowed a wave of nausea, a reminder of the sausage sandwich, chased with Zoe's wine drink she'd consumed before the evening turned sour.

Susan reflected on the events that brought her to a sheriff's office at midnight. It had been two weeks since she told Amos she wouldn't date him again, but she still agreed to go to the concert. She had noticed warning signs that Amos was a problem drinker but chose to ignore them. She was either too slow to act or too honest to run like Bob and Zoe had. She knew those boys were underage and shouldn't be drinking at all, let alone enjoying IPAs. Why didn't she warn them when she saw what they were doing? She had told Amos, but he didn't care. She wasn't used to speaking up. She'd told herself she didn't know those kids. But they were part of her community, they were Amish kids, and she didn't try to warn them. Now, Ray was in the hospital, and Myron was sitting in the county sheriff's office.

Susan took a deep, shaky breath and tried to feel comfortable in the too-tight jeans she wasn't used to wearing.

After about twenty minutes, a young woman not much older than Susan approached. She wore a badge, and her long, dark hair was held back with a large plastic hair clip. Her clothes almost resembled a uniform, but they were plain office attire—a simple dark shirt and crisp khakis. "Hello, I'm Angie. I'm associated with the drug and alcohol agency assigned to this office." She smiled warmly. "I'm going to ask you to do a drug and alcohol assessment. Hopefully, this won't be too painful." She smiled again.

Susan hadn't expected kindness. She tried to smile, but inside she still felt sick to her stomach.

"It's my job to gather information and make recommendations to law enforcement concerning your situation. If you'll follow me down the hall, we can do the interview in my office where it's a little more private." She led the way and gestured for Susan to enter in front of her.

A set of brown upholstered chairs faced Angie's desk, and Susan sat in one. "Can I get you some coffee or water before we start?" she asked.

"Coffee please."

"Help yourself to a granola bar, too. It might have been a while since you've had something to eat," she said, gesturing toward a basket filled with snack packages. Susan unwrapped a bar. Angie returned and held out a cup of coffee. "It's from the Keurig. Be careful. It's super-hot."

Susan's hands trembled as she took a cautious sip. She nibbled on a granola bar, hoping the food would calm her unsteady stomach. Angie settled herself behind a cluttered desk and rummaged through a drawer. She pulled out a yellow legal pad and a sheaf of printed forms.

The coffee burned going down, and Susan took another bite of the granola bar. She tried to calm herself, setting the food and drink on a nearby table and clasping her hands in her lap.

"I want to evaluate you for substance abuse, but I'm also curious about any information you can share regarding underage drinking among the Amish. I understand you're of legal age, but there was a young man in your group who was a victim of alcohol poisoning. Any details you provide could help us protect the community." Angie looked directly into Susan's eyes. Her intense gaze made Susan lower her eyes to her hands. She fidgeted and looked at the ripped threads in her jeans, which were meant to conceal her Amish identity.

Angie filled out the form with the basic information: name, address, phone number, birth date, and age. She moved on to "previous arrests" (none) and other details about Susan's alcohol use. Susan tried to answer each question as honestly as she could. Angie handed Susan an additional four-page questionnaire about alcohol consumption. She checked boxes for "Always, Sometimes," or "Never" and felt a little better when she realized her answers mostly leaned towards "Never," with only four "Sometimes."

"I think I've got what we need here now," Angie's tone became more professional. "Remember, heavy drinking can lead to addiction. It can also lead to death. This is serious. We don't want another incident like this to happen among your people—or any young people anywhere." Susan picked up her coffee cup, giving herself a moment to gather her thoughts. "I don't know much about it," Susan answered honestly. "My boyfriend—well, he isn't my boyfriend now—just someone I know from Benville. He asked me to go to Red Hawk Country Fest. I didn't know those kids sitting with us. I didn't think anything bad would happen." Susan felt disconnected from herself, ashamed as she listened to her lame excuses.

"Something bad did happen," Angie said. She paused, letting the weight of her words hang in the air. "Someone died, maybe from alcohol poisoning, out there," Angie added. She shuddered, and Susan saw her eyes fill with tears.

"Ray," Susan said softly. Her voice was hushed, and tears welled in her eyes. "I don't know him, but I knew it was serious. He wasn't breathing. The officer called the EMTs." She shuddered at the memory of realizing the teen's condition and the terror in his brother Myron's eyes.

"Alcohol is a dangerous drug. Many people don't realize how risky it is. Moreover, the teenagers at that concert and the adults giving them beer were breaking the law." Angie's earlier kindness faded as she confronted Susan. "It's illegal to drink alcohol if you're under age twenty-one. You understand that, don't you?"

Susan nodded and felt her stomach tighten at the truth of Angie's words. "And it's illegal to serve it to them. Did you offer it to them? Can you tell me more about what you observed?"

"I didn't buy any beer there. But Amos, the guy I came with, did. I think the guys just passed it around, and the younger ones took it."

If my parents found out I was there when this happened, they'd be so upset. "I know some were drinking the hard stuff. I just had a Dr. Pepper, and maybe some wine." Susan felt light-headed. There was a slight tremor in her hand as she sipped the coffee again, hoping her comment would be enough to end Angie's questioning.

Amos would be questioned once he sobered up. He'd have to answer for what he did.

Angie continued, "Our agency is doing some outreach with various Amish groups, trying to put education into the hands of those who are at risk. If you know of young people who need help, or if you ever need assistance, we're here for you," Angie said. "From what you've told me, we're lucky you didn't get caught up in heavy drinking tonight. But now you understand what can happen. I hope you'll speak up if you see something like that again. Don't let teenagers drink. We saw tonight how this can end."

It seemed like the interview might be over. Susan waited, hoping she was right. Angie didn't push for anything more.

"Since you're over age twenty-one—looks like your birthday was just last month—you can't be arrested for drinking. But even so, I'd like you to consider attending substance abuse prevention classes at the agency closest to your home in Holmes County." Angie gave Susan another long look.

"Your boyfriend will probably need to attend, I'm sure. You can go with him. Does that sound like a plan?"

"I broke up with him. I doubt we'll get back together," Susan said. She couldn't imagine explaining a regular appointment with a substance abuse support group meeting. Or even how she would tell her brothers why she wasn't at home tonight. At least *Maemm* and *Daett* were in Delaware visiting relatives. Her younger brothers were sound asleep in their beds by now. She'd come up with something to explain her absence—car trouble, helping someone stuck in a ditch, or a detour that got them lost. As for those classes, she'd decide later what to say, or maybe she'd skip them altogether.

"Is that the right time?" Susan gasped as she pointed to the clock on the wall above the filing cabinet. "Is it 2 a.m.?"

Angie shifted her gaze. "Yes. That's correct. I can release you now if someone can pick you up. I'll give you this form to sign, indicating I've advised you to attend the classes starting in two weeks."

Susan scribbled her name on the page and waited while Angie copied it and handed it back to her.

"I don't know anyone to call at this hour," Susan said. "Maybe I can get a ride home in the morning. I don't know." The adrenaline from the last few hours was gone, leaving Susan feeling exhausted, weak, and alone.

"Tell you what," Angie said. "I have a couple more interviews to do, then some paperwork. If you want to wait outside in the waiting room, I can take you home after work. I live in the Fredericksburg area; it won't be far out of my way." She smiled again and shoved all the papers into a fresh file folder.

"Thank you. That would really help me out," Susan said. Inside, she breathed a sigh of relief. With a little careful thought, she could cover her tracks, and no one at home would ever know what happened tonight. She'd deal with the guilt somehow on her own. That was the best thing to do.

———————

"You ready?" Angie stood in front of Susan, who was startled awake by her greeting. "So much for another week of night duty for me," Angie said. "It's after 7:00. I think you were sleeping."

Susan stood up too quickly and felt herself sway. "I guess I did sleep some." She was disoriented and weak.

"This way," Angie said.

Susan followed Angie, who walked briskly down the hallway and out the back door. When they were both outside, she pulled a set of keys from her large purse and locked the door. "I'm over here," she said.

Susan followed her to a tan Toyota. The inside was dusty and cluttered with fast food bags, children's toys, and a box of brochures about substance abuse. She lifted the box from the front seat and tossed it to the back. A few papers fluttered to the floor.

"I'm down in Fredericksburg, off 201. Where should I drop you?" she asked.

Susan had come up with a plan during her naps in the waiting room. "Can you drop me off at my friend Ruthie's house? It's right on your way. That saves you the trip over to Benville," Susan said.

Everything went smoothly, in fact, better than expected. When she reached the end of Ruthie's long lane, Susan saw her friend coming down the lane driving her mother's horse and buggy. Perfect. Susan got out of the car. "Thanks for the lift. And thanks for everything." She meant it. Angie had done what she needed to, but hadn't pushed for more information than Susan could give.

Angie drove away, leaving Susan standing by the mailbox. Susan pulled her cell from her pocket and called K & T. Her brother Jake would be at work soon, so she'd leave him a voice message. "Hi! It's Susan for Jake." She adjusted her voice to sound more normal. "Just wanted to let you know I'll be home by noon or so. I'm over at Ruthie's. Staying here for a little while yet." Nicely done. No one's the wiser. I didn't lie because I didn't say I stayed the night. But it kind of sounded like it.

Ruthie pulled up next to Susan. "What are you doing here? Where's your bike? How'd you get here?" Susan hoped Ruthie wouldn't mention the jeans and T-shirt, but that wasn't to be.

"You're still in your weekend outfit, I see. Must have been a wild night." Ruthie pointed to the "Do Something Wild" shirt and laughed. "How wild was it?"

Susan tried to fake a hearty laugh. "Okay, I guess. But I'm done with Amos. Forever. That should make you happy."

"Tell me all about it," Ruthie said, patting the seat next to her.

"That depends. Where are you headed? The thrift store, maybe? I need a dress."

Ruthie looked at her friend, who was still wearing the jeans and had her hair twisted in a plastic clip. "We can do that. I was headed to Miller Machinery to pick up a part for *Daett*. He didn't think it would fit in the bike trailer, in case you're wondering why I've got *Maemm's* horse." She paused. "But you're on notice. No more rescue missions. After today, you're on your own. I'm going to Florida."

Susan climbed into the buggy and didn't comment on the "no more rescue missions." Amos was finished, and last night marked a turning point. No more drinking. No more jeans. That was all behind her now. And no one would be the wiser. The thoughts raced through her mind. "Wait. Florida?"

"Yep. I'm turning twenty-one next week, and when my parents asked what I wanted for my birthday, I told them I wanted a Pioneer Trails bus ticket." Ruthie glowed as she shared her news. "I'm pretty sure they got it. I'll find out Tuesday when they give me the usual cake and card."

As the horse trotted down the township road, Ruthie filled her in. It was more than a quick trip to the beach. She'd decided to "relocate" for a while and live in Sarasota with a Mennonite relative on her mother's side. Get a job there, even. Maybe meet someone.

Ruthie's eyes lit up with excitement as they always did when she got a big idea. "You should come with me. That would be so fun."

Susan's mind started racing with the possibilities Ruthie had put in front of her. She couldn't tell Ruthie about last night's incident. Not right now, at least. But her best friend had unknowingly offered her an escape from everything.

"Say you'll do it!" Ruthie demanded. "*Maemm's* Mennonite cousin, Eva Good, has spare bedrooms. She lives there year-round and is alone since her husband died. She told *Maemm* I can stay as long as I want."

"Really? Do you think I could stay with her, too?"

"I can ask her. I'll call her today. She said there are plenty of jobs in restaurants and hotels. She was a hotel manager, I think. She's retired now, though."

Susan considered the possibility of accepting Ruthie's offer. She could leave Benville and Amos, who clung to her like a burr.

"Come on. Do it. We'd better travel while we can. The way we're going, next thing we know we're going to be part of the 'old girls club,'" Ruthie said.

"I'm starting to think I'm turning into Fannie the Second," Susan said. "The last thing I want is to be an aging single woman like my Aunt Fannie Troyer, living out my days in Benville and running the Cozy Corner Quilt Shop."

"You're a long way from that," Ruthie said. "We're only twenty-one."

"I know, but still...." In Susan's mind, she was already packing a suitcase she didn't own.

"You're invited. Come on, it would be so much fun!" Ruthie sounded excited. "It would be a great adventure. We can go together." She threw her arm around her friend and gave Susan a side hug.

"Well, I *am* of age, and then some. I guess my *Maemm* and *Daett* don't have much to say about it if I decide to go with you," Susan said. "How much is a ticket?"

"I believe it's around $200 one way."

"I've got that. No problem."

They rode in silence for about a mile. The beautiful fall colors, which usually caught her attention at this time of year, were set aside as Susan imagined the possibility of starting fresh. She could build a new life somewhere else—leave all her problems behind. She had heard many stories about Sarasota. Amish people from across the country found their way there—some just for the winter, others, like Ruthie's *Maemm's* cousin, for a lifetime.

"I think I want to be a waitress at a big restaurant. Like Yoder's," Susan said.

"Well, I want to go to the beach," said Ruthie. "While people here are firing up their woodstoves and shoveling snow, we will be sitting in the sunshine, walking on the beach, and eating chocolate peanut butter pie at Yoder's Restaurant."

"Or working there," said Susan.

Everyone talked about the amazing desserts at Yoder's, but the pie was really just an excuse to tell your friends about your trip to Florida.

"I looked online at the library for jobs in Sarasota," Ruthie said. There are plenty of places where we can work. "You can work. I'm going to the beach." They both laughed at Ruthie's lame joke.

When they arrived at the thrift store, Ruthie tied the horse to the hitching post, and Susan sank back into the plush seat. "I got you," Ruthie said. "Sit tight." Susan didn't argue. She was exhausted from the roller coaster of last night's trauma and this morning's brilliant escape plan.

Susan was almost asleep when Ruthie returned about half an hour later with two large, rolling suitcases: one black canvas and the other pink, hard-sided. "Take your pick," she said cheerfully.

"Which one do you want?" Susan asked.

"Here. This is yours," Ruthie said, handing her the black one. She stowed the pink suitcase in the back of the buggy. "Open it," she commanded Susan. Susan unzipped it and reached inside. Her fingers brushed against something soft, and she pulled out the pink fabric.

"I found you a dress. There's a scarf in there, too. Now go put it on so you look decent. You can change in the porta-potty. Make it quick," Ruthie said.

"Don't worry. It will be quick. It's a porta-potty. Ugh!" Susan hurried across the parking lot, clutching the pink dress. It looked like it might fit, even if the color wasn't great. She didn't think she deserved a friend like Ruthie, who always supported her. Susan peeled off her T-shirt and pulled the pink knit dress over her head. She smoothed the skirt. It wasn't a perfect fit, and the fabric was snagged, but it would work for now. She wriggled out of the too-tight jeans that had been irritating her inner thigh for hours.

Susan shoved the jeans and shirt into a large thrift store dumpster right next to Ruthie's buggy. "Florida here I come!" she exclaimed as she climbed into the buggy and carefully tucked the new dress around her legs. It felt good to be herself again.

And now she and Ruthie came up with a grand plan.

CHAPTER 6

At 2:00 on a Wednesday afternoon, the first day of November, Susan and Ruthie stood with their suitcases on the south side of the Wooster Minit Mart, holding their Pioneer Trails tickets. The private shuttle company transported passengers between Sarasota's Pinecraft area and Amish communities in Ohio and Indiana. Ruthie's ticket was round-trip because her parents wanted her to come home for Thanksgiving. But since they'd decided to stay in Sarasota for the winter, Susan had purchased a one-way ticket.

Along with Susan and Ruthie, four other travelers waited with them at this final pick-up point before the bus headed to Columbus and beyond. They didn't know the *Englischer* couple or the Amish couple, who were from a different district. But they knew they would reach Cincinnati and the Ohio River before suppertime.

This trip was a fresh start, a chance to begin again, and perhaps even find the elusive husbands they both hoped for. Susan's parents understood when she explained that she needed a change and that Ruthie wanted her support. No one argued with her. After all, she was old enough now to make her own decisions. If anything, her parents had encouraged her. While they didn't know the full story, Susan sensed they were pleased she was leaving Amos, who wasn't a good influence. *Maemm* had said years ago that he wasn't husband material for anyone. And Susan was finally convinced her parents were right.

Susan felt like a servant, even though the family paid her for some of her work, and Fannie paid her for the occasional days she worked in the quilt shop. But Susan didn't have much to call her own. Jealousy grew in every direction as Susan and Ruthie watched their friends get married and start their adult lives. The other young women in their group had all settled down with good Amish men and joined the church. The men began their careers making furniture, farming, or working in small factories. The women had given birth to children, or in Susan's sister Leah's case, four children. Susan wanted her own life, even if it wasn't what she'd once imagined.

Susan's thoughts were interrupted as the bus roared up Route 250 toward them. Her heart pounded with the realization that she was finally leaving. She shivered in her lightweight jacket but decided there was no point in packing a down-filled one for Florida. And she was leaving more than just a jacket behind. *Goodbye forever, Amos. You'll wonder where I am when I don't show up at that substance abuse education—or will you be sitting in jail awaiting a murder trial?* She blamed Amos for Ray's death. She also blamed herself. She would never forget the sight of Ray's lifeless body being lifted onto the stretcher by the EMTs that night at Red Hawk Country Fest.

The Daily News published a story about Ray's death, mentioning an "ongoing investigation" and increased efforts to monitor and educate Amish youth about drugs and alcohol. Susan's brothers discussed the article, and Susan clenched her fists beneath the dinner table. She wasn't about to admit she had been there. It wouldn't be long before rumors about Ray's death started circulating, but Susan's family believed her when she said she and Ruthie went to the mall that weekend.

Maemm had changed the subject and filled them in on the upcoming Thanksgiving plans. It was the Weavers' turn to host dinner this year for the extended family at their shop. Lydia Weaver was Maemm's sister, so she would need to help Lydia with cleaning that week. Lydia told her she needed to bring six pies. Thanksgiving would be different for Susan, though, and *Maemm* would have to find someone else to peel the apples this time. She couldn't imagine celebrating Thanksgiving in Sarasota, where it would be as warm as summer.

Her reverie ended when a typical charter bus with large, opaque windows pulled up near them. The air brakes hissed. The doors whooshed open, and the driver got out to stow their larger pieces of luggage in the compartment beneath the bus for the trip.

The seats were nearly full since this was the last pickup before the trip started. As Susan and Ruthie stood in the aisle waiting for the two couples to find seats and stow their belongings, Susan looked around. She didn't recognize anyone. Ruthie led the way, searching for two empty seats next to each other. Finally, at the back, they found two empty seats. They stowed a few of their belongings and sat down.

"I'm keeping my packed lunch with me. We might want to eat soon, don't you think?" Ruthie, always eager to make plans about food, had talked extensively about what they should pack. She settled into the crowded space next to the window and juggled a fleece throw, a small cotton-covered cushion, and her plastic lunch bag.

"I packed quite a bit. Snacks, too," Susan said. "We will have plenty of time to eat it." The thought of riding in these cramped quarters from now until tomorrow at noon suddenly struck her as a nightmare. They'd been told there were only two stops during the trip. In the meantime, they were stuck here waiting for the exciting future at the other end of the ride.

They were beginners but had heard second-hand stories about this trip. People said the key was to fall asleep and stay asleep as long as possible. Susan hoped she would sleep, but she was too excited right now to even think about napping.

"Welcome to your Pioneer Trails motor coach." The driver, a trim middle-aged man in a blue shirt and horn-rimmed glasses, greeted everyone after they were all seated. "I'm Dan Miller. I'll be your driver for the first half of this trip. Riding with us is Paul Erb, who will take over in the middle of the night when most of you are sound asleep."

"I hope so!" Susan whispered as she poked Ruthie in the ribs.

The driver continued by giving the make and model of the motor coach, which until now, passengers had referred to as a "bus." "In the rear of the motor coach, you will find a restroom for your use." Dan Miller pointed to the end of the aisle, just behind where Susan was sitting. Ruthie poked Susan in the ribs this time. "Good for you. No problem if you have to go." The two friends giggled as they fastened their seatbelts.

"We will arrive in Sarasota tomorrow, just in time for lunch," Dan Miller said. "We have only two scheduled stops on our trip. Around midnight, we will fuel up at a travel center, and you can go inside and buy a drink or snack. At that time, we will rendezvous with a north-traveling Pioneer Trails motor coach. Paul Erb and I will switch places with the drivers on the northbound coach. The replacement drivers will take you to your destination in Pinecraft, while Paul will drive the northbound passengers, me included, back to Ohio."

"Let's get going," Susan whispered. "Enough already."

"Your only other stop will be in Columbia, South Carolina, around 4:00 a.m., when you can order breakfast at Pancakes and More." That was an early breakfast! Susan and Ruthie both got up early, but neither of them had ever eaten breakfast at four in the morning. "That stop will be no more than an hour. Now, let's get on the road. Happy trails!" Dan Miller hung up the microphone he was speaking into and sat down behind the wheel. He released the air brakes, and the motor coach pulled onto the highway.

Susan and Ruthie shifted in their seats, watching the Ohio landscape turn into a blur of brown cornstalks. They were leaving behind rotting pumpkins, gray skies, chilly west winds, and snow flurries that had started just as they boarded their ride to a sunny paradise.

The passengers' voices rose and fell with the rhythm of the bus wheels that kept turning, hitting rough spots where the highway had been patched, dodging orange barrels marking construction, and gliding over long stretches before taking an off-ramp to another major highway.

Ruthie rummaged through her tote and pulled out a large plastic bag of popcorn. "So, tell me, how do you see our prospects for meeting a good Amish man in Sarasota?" Ruthie asked.

"I'm not sure we're heading to the best place for that. I hear Pinecraft is mostly old folks," Susan said. "Are you planning to marry a widower twice your age?"

"Remember, those old folks have visitors from back home. That's what I'm counting on. You'll meet lots of people if you work in a restaurant, but I'm not sure I want to do that." Susan didn't argue, but she hoped Ruthie would come around. It would be more fun to work at the same place.

"*Maemm's* cousin, Eva Good, knows everyone around there. She will help us find jobs once we're settled. She used to be Amish, but she met her husband Caleb in Sarasota years ago. He was a Mennonite, though—not Amish. He passed away a year or two ago. I remember him from the time they came to our reunion. He was a kind man."

"What kind of Mennonite is she?" Susan asked. She'd known Mennonites who dressed plainly but drove cars and had electricity, and others who didn't dress much differently from anyone else. Just like with the Amish, there were several types of Mennonites. They shared roots that went back to Europe when Anabaptists were hated by both Catholics and Protestants because of their radical beliefs.

"I don't think Eva's Plain. But she's a Christian like us and involved in her church, from what *Maemm* said. Eva and Caleb worked for Mennonite Disaster Service, repairing homes after hurricanes and floods. They owned a motorhome that they stayed in while Caleb directed some projects in Texas. That was before he got sick," Ruthie said. "We knew some Amish kids who went to work with them once. They said Eva was the best cook. That was her job. While Caleb directed the work crews, Eva led a crew of volunteers who made all the food for them. Before they did that, Caleb worked in construction and Eva managed a hotel. I think they are well off. That is, Eva is probably well off since they owned a business, and she worked, too. They never had any kids."

Susan looked forward to meeting Eva. "It will be fun to stay with her. Sounds like she'd have a few stories to tell us. And it makes me feel better knowing she used to be Amish. Seems like she'll understand us."

"I don't know. Maybe. She left the Amish at a young age to marry Caleb. He was from Ohio, too. Her Christmas letter was filled with how much she misses Caleb. They did everything together. It must be hard to live with someone for all those years and then lose them."

The bus slowed to a crawl as they approached Cincinnati. Ruthie kept up her chatter about Eva, who would help them find jobs in Sarasota. "*Maemm* used to be close to her when they were young, and they stayed in touch. When Eva found out I wanted to visit, she called to talk to me and said she'd be happy to have us stay with her. She said it's too quiet since Caleb passed, and it would be good to have some company."

Susan and Ruthie stopped talking and watched the city through the windows. It was nearly sunset when they crossed the Ohio River into Kentucky around 7:00. "I say we eat supper. What do you think?" Other passengers were pulling bags of food from the overhead compartments, so Susan stood and grabbed her lunch bag. They kept talking as they ate ham sandwiches and baby carrots. The bus grew quiet as the passengers relaxed to the steady hum of wheels on the pavement and the dim overhead lights. Susan and Ruthie realized they couldn't talk nonstop. After a while, they each withdrew into their thoughts. Ruthie pulled out a dog-eared paperback she'd bought at a thrift store and read by the light of a small clip-on book light.

Susan tipped back her seat and adjusted it. The driver turned off the lights, and all was quiet except for a few snores. Susan dozed off. True to his word, just after midnight, Dan Miller pulled into a truck stop and parked next to another Pioneer Trails bus. Some passengers stayed asleep or tried to, while others got off to stretch their legs and grab a cold drink. Susan and Ruthie waited in line for the ladies' room and didn't buy anything. When they returned to the bus, they were greeted by a different driver who nodded hello. Once everyone was settled, he took a headcount and announced that the breakfast stop would be at 4:00 a.m. in Columbia, South Carolina.

———————————

The air brakes hissed loudly, waking Susan, who had been asleep. Her neck was at an awkward angle, resting against a small pillow Ruthie had wedged between them. Ruthie sat upright, and the pillow dropped to the floor. She came out from beneath her fleece throw. "What's going on?" she asked.

"I don't know. I guess I was sleeping. What time is it?" Their eyes both took in the lighted screen above the driver's head. It was 4:05 a.m. "Four o'clock. Is this our breakfast stop?"

Ruthie looked out the window. "We're stopped on the highway. I don't see a pancake restaurant out there. Do you?"

There was only a guardrail and the dull interstate scenery below the lighted stretch of highway where they had stopped. A passenger across from them lifted the window blind, revealing a similar scene. "I think we're stopped on the road. There are lights, so we must be close. I don't know what's going on," Susan said.

Just then, sirens wailed as police cars and ambulances with flashing lights sped past the bus in the next lane. By now, everyone was awake and talking. The bus driver was on his cell phone. He stood and waved his hand to quiet the group. Susan was too far back to hear anything he said over the muffled whispers of other passengers. The sirens continued, and a chill ran up Susan's spine. Memories of the incident at Red Hawk Country Fest bristled under her skin. She felt cold. Then hot. Then scared.

"There must be an accident," Ruthie said. Her innocent comment only intensified Susan's focus on the trauma she had recently endured. She still hadn't told Ruthie about Ray's death, only that she had been out most of that night and regretted her decision to go with Amos again.

The bus driver turned on the lights, and Susan squinted until her eyes adjusted. People shifted in their seats. Sirens continued as the bus driver stood and took the microphone from its holder. "We're very close to our breakfast stop, but unfortunately, there's a bad accident directly in front of us. We were first on the scene, and it will be at least an hour until everything is cleared. The highway patrol gave us clearance to walk to Pancakes and More, our breakfast stop.

We have permission to walk on the grassy strip alongside the road and into the restaurant parking lot. Please walk single file." The bus driver paused and looked across the group of passengers, who now all had their eyes glued to the front of the bus. "If you prefer, you can stay on the bus with our second driver, Harold. The restaurant offers carry-out if you want to send someone from your party while others stay. This is our final stop before Sarasota." With that, he clicked off the microphone and stood beside his seat.

Most of the passengers collected their belongings, and Susan stood to the side so Ruthie could get out. "Let's go. No way am I staying here," Ruthie said.

"It will feel good to go out and walk. I was sound asleep, how about you?" Susan asked.

Ruthie nodded. "Me, too."

They exited the bus. A female officer, holding a large flashlight, urged everyone to line up single file. Some people had their own flashlights, and a few used their smartphones' flashlights. Susan and Ruthie got in line. The sirens had stopped now, but red and blue lights flickered in the darkness just ahead of the bus.

The officer paced back and forth, giving instructions. "There's been a three-vehicle accident, possibly alcohol-related. Personnel are tending to the seven victims, so please stay clear of the scene as you make your way to the restaurant parking lot."

Ruthie squeezed Susan's hand and moved ahead of her in line, while Susan clutched her purse tightly and pulled her lightweight coat around her. Out of the corner of her eye, she noticed an officer testing someone with a breathalyzer. She shivered again, remembering how she knew what it was.

The group silently crossed the road, climbed an embankment, and paused at the top to look toward the scene of the accident. The officer's words echoed in her mind: "*...alcohol related....*" The words repeated in her head in sync with her steps: "*...alcohol related...*" step "*...alcohol-related....*"

She gasped in the cold night air. The mangled cars sat on the highway at strange angles. EMTs dressed in hazard gear lifted what appeared to be a young man from one of the vehicles. They strapped him to a bodyboard while Susan stared at his bloodstained shirt. His face was also covered in blood. He was quiet and still as the medical team placed him on a gurney. Susan looked away and kept walking. She felt lightheaded. Her stomach clenched with nauseous cramps. "I'm out of breath," she gasped. "I'm not used to walking so fast."

Susan's stomach lurched, and she leaned over, heaving into a nearby shrub. Ruthie wrapped her arm around Susan's waist. When she straightened up again, Ruthie said, "Let's get you inside where we can clean up and get some water. I think I'm going to order us both a bowl of oatmeal. That should go down okay."

Susan coughed and nodded her head. The thought of oatmeal made her feel like hurling again. She took a deep breath and said, "I'm okay. I'll be okay. I shouldn't have looked at that accident."

CHAPTER 7

Ruthie's Aunt Eva loaded their luggage into her shiny purple Volvo station wagon and then navigated the car around the hundred or more bicycles that crowded the streets near the bus parking lot. There were no horses anywhere in Pinecraft, Sarasota's Amish settlement. Susan took it all in. *No problem. I'm fine if I never drive another horse and buggy, ever.* Young and old alike rode two- and three-wheeled bicycles. *I could get used to this.*

Eva's home was in an allotment off Bahia Vista Street. The houses were ranch-style and sat low to the ground. She turned into the driveway of a house painted a deep brown. A brick sidewalk led to a doorway flanked with large, low pots of cacti and beds of flaming orange foliage. Eva pressed a button inside her car, and the garage door opened.

"Now you girls just take some time to settle in," Eva said. She opened the back of the station wagon, and they unloaded their bags. Eva helped them and led the way inside. A large painting of a beach sunset in the foyer caught Susan's eye as she passed it. Eva led the two young women down a hallway. "You two can just rest a bit while I get some lunch ready," Eva told her guests. "I'm putting you in the guest room. The dresser is empty. When you're ready, you can unpack your things. You can hang your dresses in the closet; it's empty."

Susan rolled her large suitcase into the bedroom. Bright sunlight streamed through the slatted blinds, casting a pattern on the pale green bedspreads. Everything smelled fresh and clean. A vase of lavender sprigs sat beneath an antique ceramic lamp decorated with a Victorian scene.

Ruthie threw herself on the bed furthest from the door, claiming it for herself. "I'm exhausted," she said with a huge sigh.

"Me, too." They were both so tired but relieved to have arrived that neither said another word. Susan sat on the bed across from her friend and thought about what had just happened—the packing and hurried goodbyes to her family, the long bus ride, the accident, and finally arriving in Sarasota, a busy city with streets several lanes wide, then settling into Eva's quiet home on a street lined with closely spaced houses. So much had happened in such a short time, and thoughts of home and the troubles she'd left behind seemed far away. She planned to keep it that way.

Soon, Eva called them and they took seats around the small kitchen table. Eva bowed her head and said a short prayer, thanking God for the food and "traveling mercies" for "these adventurous young women." She had made barbecue beef sandwiches and a green salad, and offered tall glasses of iced tea with lemon from a colorful glass pitcher. "I made us an apple cake for dessert. It's an old recipe from back home. My favorite. I hope you like it." The meal reminded her of home, and the cinnamon topping made her think it was fall, despite the warmth of the Florida sunshine.

"This is just perfect," Susan said. "I didn't realize how hungry I was."

"Yes," Ruthie agreed. "The last time we ate anything was hours ago when the bus stopped at a pancake place in the early morning hours."

While the women ate, Eva engaged in small talk, trying to fill the silence. The two weary travelers nodded at the right moments but were so exhausted and hungry that they barely responded. After each had eaten a generous slice of the streusel-topped cake, Eva excused herself and cleared the dirty dishes. "Now, you girls go settle in; take a nice shower or bath. There's plenty of time to nap. I'm sure you're tired and need to rest. I'm going to run a few errands. I'll pick up some roasted chicken for dinner." Eva wiped her hands on the apron she'd wrapped around herself, then motioned as if to shoo them out of the room. Almost as an afterthought, she added, "After dinner, I want to tell you about a big decision I made this week. Then we'll discuss your goals and plans. I'm here to help you both, but I'd love to hear what you expect from your time in Sarasota."

Susan gulped and swallowed her apprehension. This didn't sound like a conversation she wanted to have. She was used to running from her discomfort. And she had no goals she wanted to discuss. Did Eva know she was avoiding her mistakes? Did she think she could somehow change her? Why did she even care whether her two young visitors had goals? And what did Eva's big decision have to do with her?

While Ruthie soaked in the tub, Susan unpacked her bag. She hung her dresses on hangers in the closet, neatly arranging her eight homemade dresses in order of color, like a rainbow, from pale pink to vivid purple. She placed her underclothes in the second drawer of the dresser. Susan closed the bedroom door and lay down on the bed. When she woke up, it was getting dark. She smelled food and heard Ruthie and Eva laughing in the kitchen. Susan quickly got up and carried fresh clothes with her to the bathroom. She showered and brushed her hair, pinning it securely under a clean scarf. She'd keep her *kapp* for work or church.

Wide awake now, Susan wandered into the living room she'd only glimpsed on her way into the house. She took in the details of Eva's tidy home. She looked at photos displayed on shelves, admired hand-quilted pillow covers, and observed how everything in Eva's home was attractive and thoughtfully arranged. Back in Benville, their home was set up mainly for utility and convenience. Eva's rooms were furnished with beautiful, soft rugs, landscape paintings of sunsets and the ocean, and chairs with leather upholstery. Her bookshelves were artfully arranged with a mix of plants and books stacked among pottery vases, miniature statues, and woven baskets. There were touches of glass and crystal, floral plates hanging in a holder on the wall, and a crocheted throw tossed over the sofa. Susan sank into a small, soft chair that fit her body perfectly. She had never sat in such a luxurious chair. She relaxed into its comfort and absorbed the warmth she felt here.

Dinner chatter was much livelier than during their earlier meal. Both girls had rested and felt more at ease. Eva offered another slice of apple cake, this time with a scoop of vanilla ice cream. She brewed a pot of decaf coffee, and they sipped it from pottery mugs that Eva said she'd bought from the potter she'd met when she and Caleb had been on one of their many trips.

Susan had forgotten Eva's mention of a conversation about goals announced at the previous meal. But Eva hadn't. "Let's take our coffee into the living room and get comfortable," she said. "I thought it would be a good idea to talk about a few things, so we all understand each other."

Susan's heart somersaulted, but she stood and picked up her coffee. Ruthie followed. Susan reclaimed the leather chair and placed her mug on a coaster within arm's reach on a side table.

When everyone was seated, Eva's voice adopted a more formal tone as she started the conversation. "When Ruthie's mother asked if I would look out for you, I agreed. I thought it might be good to have some company. It gets so quiet here now that Caleb has passed."

"We're so happy you agreed to let us stay with you," Ruthie said. "We'll try to help out and not be a bother."

"I'm sure you won't be. I'm happy you're here. I just had some questions for you, that's all."

"What questions?" Susan asked. Her voice sounded strange, a little strained and too high-pitched.

"Well, you might not know this, Susan, but I was once Amish myself, and I understand how that feels. The reason I wanted to discuss your goals is that I want to help you both in any way I can. That's easier for me if I know your plans and what you want right from the start."

"I'm not exactly sure what you mean by goals," Susan said.

"I just want to be upfront about everything," Eva said. "I know some Amish girls come to Sarasota to get away from their parents or to make a fresh start. Maybe they're looking for a husband, or want to earn some money. I'm just curious what you two have in mind."

Ruthie glanced at Susan, who was looking at her hands in her lap. Had Eva heard gossip from back home? She hoped not. But gossip spread.

"I think for me, I just wanted to go on an adventure," Ruthie said. "At first, I considered staying for a week or so, but then I thought, 'why not stay all winter and get a job, maybe even longer if I can afford to rent a place to stay?'" Ruthie took a breath and looked at Susan, waiting to hear how she would answer.

"I guess I'm the same," Susan said. "I was starting to feel like a fifth wheel at home. My sister Leah has four *kinnah*. I helped her with them and her housework, looked after our *Dawdi* who isn't well, and helped *Maemm* besides. I felt like I didn't have a life of my own."

"They relied on you and needed you, but I can understand how you would feel in that situation," Eva said. Her smile was reassuring.

"Susan's boyfriend dumped her, and that's what made her decide to come with me to Sarasota," Ruthie said.

Susan had hoped to avoid even thinking about Amos. Ruthie was a good friend, but sometimes she spoke before she thought.

"Well, something like that," Susan said. Amos hadn't dumped her. *She'd* dumped *him*. But she wasn't going to correct Ruthie and risk explaining more. Enough talk of boyfriends.

CHAPTER 8

Eva ignored the comment about Amos. She took a sip of coffee and seemed ready to talk about something else. "I might not be as young as you two, but I have goals and plans, too—and maybe jobs if you want to work for me. I haven't told you my big news yet." Her eyes shone with anticipation.

"Ruthie, your *Maemm's* letter arrived just when I needed it. I didn't expect everything to turn out this way, but I might be able to hire you myself. I'm the owner of a brand-new business. I just purchased a badly neglected property outside Sarasota. I can hardly believe I own an inn. But I do—such as it is."

"An inn? I thought *Maemm* said you were retired," Ruthie said.

"Well, I thought about it, but I guess I have goals, too. Even at my age."

Susan was beginning to like Eva. She had a lot of energy for an older woman.

"I wondered how in the world I'd ever get the place cleaned up by myself," Eva continued. "Now, you two are here. Perfect timing. When I agreed to host you, I didn't know I would end up buying that inn. It's a lot for me to take on, having two houseguests and renovating an inn at the same time. But I can't question God's timing or God's plan."

Susan's stomach twisted. She had her own plans, and they didn't include being part of a clean-up crew. When she imagined life in Sarasota, she envisioned herself in an apron with small blue flowers, serving mashed potatoes and roast beef to tourists. She expected to live in Pinecraft, where young Amish men came to visit their grandparents in the winter. And those grandparents took the family out to eat at Yoder's or Dutch Kitchen. Where a glowing young Susan would serve a giant wedge of pie to someone named Reuben from Nappanee, Indiana. Reuben would give her an appreciative glance, leading to a conversation, then a trip to Siesta Key, and eventually courtship and marriage, and....

Susan refocused her attention on Eva. "They keep us women in the dark, you know? I had no idea how much money my dear Caleb had tucked away. All those years he worked so hard. He started out as a teenager on a roofing crew, and by fifty, he owned the business with over thirty employees. I never once thought about what he was worth—I mean, in terms of money." Eva reached across the sofa where she and Ruthie sat and patted Ruthie's hand.

"We never had any children. God knows we tried." Eva laughed, and Ruthie's face turned red. Susan wanted to remember this moment. She and Ruthie could giggle about Eva's joke later. She had never heard a grown Amish woman say such a thing. But by now, it was clear that Eva had long since left Amish life behind.

The personal history continued. "I kept busy working at different hotels and inns around Sarasota. That's how I learned the hospitality industry. I had to stop working when Caleb took sick, of course. Thank goodness he'd already sold his business. I never could have managed all of that on my own.

"Somehow, after Caleb died, I didn't get around to returning to work. Then one day, Caleb's investment advisor called and asked me to stop by...." Eva took a deep breath and wiped away her tears as if they might overflow. But she recovered for a moment. "I'll spare you the details, but Caleb left me well off. That's all I'll say."

"Is that how you bought the inn then?" Ruthie asked.

"Yes. I'm going into business for myself. I never dreamed I could do this. But why not? I'm happy to let you both stay here for a couple of months, maybe longer if all goes well. I can surely use your help and pay you to help me get the inn ready." She looked back and forth between them, then added, "Unless you have other ideas about the kind of work you want to do. It's going to be tough working out there at the inn. I'll show you tomorrow."

Had Eva read her mind? "I don't know," Susan said. "All along, I was thinking I wanted to be a waitress at one of the restaurants. I'm not a good cleaner like Ruthie is. Do you know if any restaurants are hiring?" Susan said.

"Sure. If you want restaurant work, I can help you find it. There's a lot of staff turnover, and they're busier in the winter. So, chances are good you could get a job at Yoder's or Dutch Kitchen. Is that what you were thinking?" Susan's anxiety eased when she realized Eva wasn't bothered that her guest preferred working at a restaurant rather than at her inn.

"I'm fine with helping you at the inn," Ruthie said. "I like to clean, and it sounds fun to remodel it and get it ready for visitors. If it's out of the city, it might feel more like home to me—only different."

"Whatever you decide is okay with me. I can hire cleaners if you want to work somewhere else." Eva sounded reasonable, and Susan felt relieved.

"You girls are at a stage in life when many important decisions must be made. The choices you make now will shape the entire direction of your life. When I was about your age, I met Caleb. It was a huge decision to leave my Amish life behind, but for me, it was the right choice. I needed trusted adults I could talk to back then, and I found people to help me. I want you to know I'll always be here for you if you need someone to talk to."

Susan pondered Eva's words. She had never thought about not being Amish. It was her entire world. That must have been so difficult for Eva. Had Ruthie ever thought about leaving the Amish? They had never discussed that possibility. Had Ruthie thought about doing what Eva had done? Leaving Amish life behind? Is that why she hadn't joined the church yet?

Ruthie smiled at Eva. "Thank you. We appreciate your hospitality. It's so good to know we have someone to talk to about important things—besides my best friend, of course." She shot a smile in Susan's direction.

Susan smiled back. "Right now, I just want to have a life of my own. It was such a relief to hear from Ruthie that I could come here with her. And I want to see the ocean."

"I'm sure we can arrange for you to get to the beach." She grinned at them. "I just wanted to say right up front that I'm here for you. In MDS, I met young girls like you, and I'm a good listener. You can always talk to me. If there's something you need or some way I can support you, I'm here for you." Eva smiled in a way that made Susan believe she meant it.

"I don't want any smoking or drinking going on here. And no parties. You both seem like nice girls. I probably don't even need to say that," she added. "While you're here, I expect you to keep your room clean, pick up after yourselves, and pitch in at mealtimes and clean up, just like you did back home. You can stay here rent-free until after Christmas. By January, you'll both have jobs, and if you want to stay longer, I should be able to rent you a suite at the inn."

Eva explained the best times to do laundry, where they might want to shop if they needed anything, and finished by inviting them to attend the Mennonite church on Sunday if they wanted to join her. Then she stood.

"We'll clean up the kitchen for you, Eva," Ruthie said. "We'll try not to be a bother and stay out of your way."

"That's great. I'll let you do the dinner dishes while I go out on the lanai. Caleb put a television out there before he got sick. We always watched Wheel of Fortune and Jeopardy together after supper. It makes me feel closer to him when I sit out there." She opened the back door and left Susan and Ruthie to the dishes.

In the kitchen, the young women filled the sink with hot water, ignoring the unfamiliar dishwasher. They put the leftovers away and talked quietly, making sure they couldn't be overheard by their host. "She's something else, isn't she?" Ruthie asked.

"What do you mean?" Susan asked. She didn't want to criticize her best friend's relative, who was being quite generous by letting them stay in her guest room.

"Goals? What are our goals?" Ruthie smirked. "What did she expect us to say?"

"She wanted to find out if you're searching for a husband," Susan teased.

"And if he has to be Amish, or if any kind of man will do," Ruthie laughed.

"Whatever. I'm just glad we got here and have a place to stay."

"Yes. That's so good for us. I think I'll help her at the inn. Are you sure you don't want to do the same?" Ruthie asked.

"I was really set on working at a restaurant. I think I'll try that first and see how it goes. If it doesn't work out, I can always fall back on Eva's offer. You understand, don't you?"

Ruthie kept drying dishes and didn't answer for a moment. "I guess so. I hope it works out if that's what you want."

Susan felt a sense of relief. Finally, she was going to decide something for herself. It felt good to know she could make her own choices, for once.

CHAPTER 9

"How about a little drive in the country? I can't wait to show you the inn," Eva asked the following morning at breakfast.

"I can't wait to see it," Ruthie said.

"It's not much to look at right now, but with a thorough cleaning and new furnishings, it will be beautiful. It has good bones but needs some major updates. You'll see what I mean."

Susan had been considering taking a walk and checking out the restaurants near Pinecraft, maybe filling out some applications, but there was plenty of time for that and she did want to see the inn where Ruthie and Eva would be working.

"I have a contractor ready to remodel the kitchen. That's my biggest priority right now," Eva said. "I need to take another look before I have him draw up the plans."

They got into Eva's Volvo in the garage, with Ruthie in the front seat and Susan in the back. They made their way through the allotment where tall palms shaded the streets. Through the open car windows, Susan heard the rustling of dry palm fronds, reminding her of the brittle cornstalks they'd left back in Ohio. Left for good.

The low, flat homes with stucco exteriors were similar, but each had slight differences. Masonry arches and walls kept mounds of unrecognizable plants from taking over. Back in Ohio, the gardens were all put to bed, and everything was brown under gray skies. But here, awnings shielded sunny windows, and spiky grass grew in random clumps among decorative stone. The pure blue sky contrasted with the bright carpet of rough green grass watered by built-in sprinklers. Red flowers bloomed along the street and in front of many homes. Susan didn't recognize these plants but occasionally caught a glimpse of foliage like the familiar houseplants back home.

If Ruthie noticed these things, she didn't bring them up. She was kept busy answering Eva's questions about relatives in Ohio. Susan tuned them out, happy to soak in the scenes from the car window where everything was lush, green, and bathed in sunshine.

The car turned onto a dusty gravel road, with fields opening up on the side. Cattle grazed inside fences, but there were no red barns, white silos, or white plastic-wrapped hay bales. Eva finally paused for a moment, wiped sweat from her neck, and stole a quick glance at Susan in the rear-view mirror.

"I guess this looks a little different from home to you, girls," she said. "Ruthie, I'm so glad you're here. I can still hardly believe I own an inn. I figured I'd have to hire a company to do all this cleanup, but knowing you're here to help me, I think we might be able to handle this ourselves."

Susan was worried. Was Eva trying to get her to join her cleanup crew? When she thought about living in Sarasota, she imagined renting a house in Pinecraft with Ruthie. She pictured both of them working at a restaurant. But Ruthie had already agreed to work for Eva before even seeing the inn, leaving Susan to find a restaurant job on her own.

Finally, Eva turned down a narrow lane leading to her property. "Welcome to Saw Grass Inn!" she said grandly. She stopped near a once-elegant concrete fountain that was now crumbling in places, filled with blackish water, and overgrown with spiky grasses. They got out of the car and stood there, looking at the neglected property Eva had taken on rather than give in to early retirement.

Susan surveyed the rambling, rundown motel with wings that spread out at odd angles. The central section was two stories and faced the driveway. It looked even older than the rest. The roof, covered in red tiles, was strewn with debris from the surrounding trees. Arches framed the second-story porch. Spanish moss hung from mismatched electrical torch lights, some of which had broken glass. The faded doors were different colors, with chipped, peeling paint.

"I'm seeing 'vintage Florida' with a bohemian vibe," Eva said. She laughed. "You girls must wonder what I was thinking to buy this."

Susan was speechless. She had no mental picture of "vintage Florida." And the words "bohemian vibe" might have been spoken in a foreign language for all she knew.

Ruthie must have been just as confused. "You will be a great innkeeper. I know you can do it," she said.

"I've been managing inns for most of my life. But this feels different. It's mine. It feels like a big adventure to me. And now you're here to share it with me."

Eva sounded pleased with herself. "I heard about this place, and I asked myself 'Why not?' I have the money. I have the skills. I have plenty of good years ahead of me yet."

Ruthie's face lit up. "It's exciting. Susan, are you sure you don't want to help Eva?"

"Now Ruthie," Eva said. "We heard her say she wanted to work in a restaurant. If you and I can't get things cleaned up ourselves, I'll hire a service. Neither of you should feel obligated to help me. Let's go inside and take a look."

They walked across the sandy ground between the driveway

and the front door of the rundown old hotel, kicking aside pinecones and navigating around vegetation that had grown during the years the place had been empty.

"This is such a beautiful setting, close to a stream and not far from the old celery fields that are now a lovely sanctuary for nature. Eventually, Saw Grass Inn will be seen as an extension of that. But first things first, let's go in and take a look."

Eva produced a key and, with some effort, opened the front door, pushing aside a mound of dried grasses and pine needles before motioning for them to enter. "No one has stayed at this inn for a couple of years. It was listed with the agent for far too long. It needs quite a lot of TLC before I can start booking guests."

Eva stopped talking and looked around. They stood in the main lobby where sunlight streamed through the dirty windows. Cobwebs on the exposed beams of the lobby caught her attention. "Goodness! I need to bring my long-handled webster. I hope it will reach that high.

"All of this has to go," Eva said, gesturing toward the wooden benches upholstered in orange and brown plaid. "I haven't done much yet. But I did clean up two rooms that make up a little suite. It's that part over there." Eva pointed to the smaller wing.

"When I get this in better shape, you two could stay here if you want to. You'd each have a private room. I'd feel better knowing someone is on the grounds while it's undergoing renovations," Eva said.

Susan gulped. All along, she'd wanted to live in the city. She wasn't sure how to tell Eva, but this wasn't going to work for her at all. No way.

"It's so huge," Ruthie said. "I can see why you need help. But I like staying at your place in Sarasota. At least for now."

Thank you, Ruthie. We need to talk this over.

"Oh, I wouldn't think of having you stay here now," Eva said. "I meant after it's all done and we're open to guests. The suite could be like a little apartment for you two. As for now, if you decide to pitch in for the next few weeks, I'll hire you, Ruthie. And Susan, you're going to be working at a restaurant. And you're both my house guests for now. It's going to be weeks until Saw Grass Inn is habitable."

They moved single file through a narrow hallway into the kitchen, dodging drywall scraps and exposed wires. The place smelled damp and musty. "At least the demo crew was here. I hope they're finished soon," Eva said. "Follow me. This is kind of a maze." She pushed aside a set of swinging doors and led them from the kitchen into a dining room. The furnishings had long since gone out of style, and the floor was covered with stained carpet. The dirt-encrusted windows let in very little light. More cobwebs were visible as Eva flipped the light switch. They dripped from rustic wagon wheel chandeliers. "I was hoping they'd get that old carpet out of here. And those light fixtures. I've got to go back to the kitchen and make some notes, maybe call the contractor and tell him what I'm thinking so he can draw up the plans. He came out here yesterday when I was busy getting you two settled."

Susan and Ruthie wandered through the rest of the inn, giggling and holding their noses as they poked their heads into guest rooms and a broom closet. They checked out the suite that Eva had pointed out. It was clean but empty of furniture. They circled back to the kitchen again, where Eva was now on the phone, and exited through the back door, walking past dumpsters and around the shorter wing of the inn.

"Your aunt is a sweet person. I like her. But I sure don't know why she wants to own this place," Susan said.

"I know. *Maemm* said she was always kind of different. I didn't get what she meant. But I guess she's creative. We might be surprised how good this place looks in the end."

"Maybe. But I'm glad I won't be working here."

"Or sleeping here." They laughed at Ruthie's joke and went back to the fountain, where they sat on the edge, waiting for Eva and soaking up the inviting, if unfamiliar, Florida sunshine.

That Friday and Saturday, Susan and Ruthie explored the businesses around Pinecraft. They walked to the post office to buy stamps and stopped at a thrift store to look for used books. At a dollar store, they each bought a pre-paid cell phone. Amish people on bikes and tricycles were all around.

They had heard about Pinecraft from people who had visited here. Now they could see it for themselves. Susan and Ruthie wandered through the narrow streets where Amish folks sat chatting outdoors on folding chairs. It was strange to think that they knew no one, even though everyone they saw in Pinecraft was Amish.

At noon, they went to a restaurant for soup and salad, then sampled the pie. "I thought I wanted to work at a restaurant, but the waitresses look exhausted," Susan said. They shared a thick slice of peanut butter cream pie. Her imagination had pictured good-looking Amish men, not the busy tourist scene of their current lunch spot.

"They work hard," Ruthie said. "Ours forgot to bring us water even after we asked twice. I'd have trouble keeping track of everything." She dug her fork into the creamy center, splitting the slice in two. She slid her piece to the edge of the plate they shared.

"I was watching her," Susan said. "With a little practice, I think I could get the hang of it," she added as she licked whipped cream off the tines of her fork. She savored the crumbly peanut butter sprinkled on top of the pie. "The day would go fast if you were busy. Did you see the big tips some people left?"

"Not really," said Ruthie.

"On one table, I saw a twenty-dollar bill. The waitresses get to keep that money. Tips could add up fast," said Susan.

"I guess if you're good at it, but I've agreed to help Eva at Saw Grass Inn. After all, she's my relative, and I think I owe it to her. It's a little different for you. You're not related to Eva, but if you decide to join me, it would be fun working together."

They finished their pie in silence, then left the table so those waiting in line could sit down. The thought of being around so many new people and meeting someone, an Amos replacement, was never far from Susan's mind.

CHAPTER 10

Partway through the following week, Eva came home from a church meeting with some good news for Susan. "A friend in my Mennonite women's group is one of the owners of a little place called Sugar N Spice. She's putting in a good word for you with the manager."

Susan's heart raced, knowing the job she'd hoped for might be within reach. *Can I do it? Ruthie's right, they hustle. Could I keep up?* But she was ready for the challenge. After all, she'd come to Florida to have an adventure, try new things, and meet new people.

"They're always looking for help and often hire Amish women," Eva said. "My friend will give the manager a heads-up. She said we should go over there tomorrow, mid-afternoon, when it's less busy. I can go along, show you where the place is, and make introductions."

"Oh, thank you! I was still getting up the courage to ask about applications at a couple of places," she told Eva. It was a relief to know Eva would be there to help her land the job.

"I know you were hoping to work at those big Amish-style restaurants where all the tourists go, but this might be a better place to start. It's not as busy or well-known, but they have home-cooked food. The locals tend to eat there," Eva said.

"I know. Those places are so busy. I wondered if I could keep up, so this might be a good place to start," Susan said.

"I agree," Ruthie said. "That sounds better. You're going to do great." She gave Susan a thumbs up.

The next afternoon, Eva pointed to a bicycle in the garage. "You can ride Caleb's old bike to work. It's close by, so I won't need to drive you there. If you can pump the tires and adjust the seat, I'll show you the way."

Susan got the bike ready, and they set off. Eva bicycled through several quiet streets Susan hadn't been on yet. She breathed in the warm, humid Florida air, happy to be back on a bicycle. Eva pointed at the street signs when they made a turn. Susan tried to memorize street names and landmarks but quickly gave up. Everything looked the same to her. *Help! How am I going to do this without Eva leading the way? Maybe this isn't a good idea after all.*

"Here we are," said Eva. She pointed to a restaurant tucked into a small shopping plaza, surrounded by a few other off-the-beaten-path businesses. They locked the bikes to a bike rack out front. Susan noticed a blue and white sign hanging over the cracked concrete sidewalk. Black plastic urns beside the door were filled with dusty silk flowers that had seen better days.

Once inside, the scent of fried potatoes, meat, and gravy surrounded them, assuring them that the place must serve good food. A gray-haired woman in a blue gingham apron greeted them. She was dressed simply and wore a white scarf pinned to her hair, which made Susan feel like they might share something in common.

"Clara, this is Susan. She's here from Ohio and is looking for work. We heard you were hiring," Eva said.

"Yes. I'm short-staffed again. I just lost two people last week," she said curtly.

Clara looked Susan over, starting at the top with her white *kapp* and finally resting her eyes on Susan's clunky white Nikes. "You're wearing the right shoes, at least." She gave Susan a tight smile. "We don't have a special uniform here, but comfortable shoes are a must."

Susan blushed. She wasn't used to such obvious scrutiny. Her eyes shifted toward a glass case near the entrance, just inside the door. Different kinds of cream pies—chocolate, peanut butter, and coconut cream—topped with mounds of whipped cream—made it clear this restaurant met her expectations. The pies looked just like the ones she and Ruthie had sampled at the other restaurant.

Clara led them to an empty booth near the back of the restaurant. "You can sit here. I'll give you this application to fill out. Go ahead and get started, and I'll be right back. I need to go over a few details with you." The seats of the dark-stained plywood booths were hard. The booths lined both sides of the restaurant's walls. Simple wooden tables and chairs filled the center area of the floor.

Susan's heart sank as she took in the faded gingham curtains at the bay windows in front, along with the half-dead plants on the windowsill. Pale, blue-striped wallpaper above paneled walls displayed framed pictures and vintage kitchenware. The furnishings looked shabby and faded. She'd hoped to work in a more bustling, modern place with a gift shop and crisp, bright, quilted wall hangings, not a forgotten-in-time hole in the wall. But they were hiring, and Eva thought this was a good place to start.

Carefully, Susan filled out the application. Occasionally, when she didn't know what to write, she asked Eva for help. In answer to the question about wait staff experience, Susan wrote "None." But she mentioned working at her Aunt Fannie's Cozy Corner Quilt Shop under "Previous Retail Experience." In response to the question "Why should Sugar N Spice hire you?" she paused for a moment, trying to think of how to answer.

"Looks like you're stumped," Eva said.

"I don't know how to answer this question," Susan said, turning the page so Eva could read it.

"Maybe just mention that you're new to the area but have experience working with food. You have a lot of relevant experience that will transfer to waitressing." Eva's gift was encouragement.

Susan remembered the afternoons spent canning tomatoes and peeling peaches in *Maemm's* kitchen. She had learned to make cakes, pies, and pudding from scratch. She often baked bread when *Maemm* was busy with other things. Most mornings, she'd prepared *Dawdi's* breakfast for him.

In the end, Susan wrote a short essay about food that spilled onto the back of the page. She read it a second time, and hope grew inside her. She was one step closer to landing a real job at a restaurant.

Clara returned and slipped into the booth next to Eva. Susan felt nervous around Clara at first but soon got caught up in Clara's stories about the restaurant's history, the regulars who came for breakfast and lunch, and the owner's emphasis on fair hiring practices. She seemed to think Susan was an ideal employee, even though she'd never worked in a restaurant. "I'm sure you know how to work," she said. Susan nodded in agreement.

"We open at 6:00 a.m. for breakfast, and I need you to arrive ten minutes early so you're ready to go."

"I'm used to getting up early. That won't be a problem." At home, she was often up at five and in the garden before six.

"I'll be here with you on the first day and show you what to do," Clara said. "We'll start you off with easier tasks and work up to waiting tables."

"I was hoping I could do that right away. I'm sure I can handle it," Susan said. "I learn fast. But whatever you need me to do is okay." She added the second part, conscious of making a good impression.

"We'll start you out making breakfast plates. That's a little slower than later in the day. And we need help with the pies. We get those from a bakery at one of the other restaurants." Clara turned over the page to read what Susan had written on the back.

"I haven't worked in a restaurant before, so on the application, I just wrote about kitchen things I did at home," Susan explained.

"Let's get you started and see how you do with serving breakfast plates. It might take some time to build up to waitressing. Your pay will increase later when you work as a waitress because then you'll get tips."

Not receiving tips was disappointing, but Susan didn't say anything to Clara.

"My most important advice to you starting out is that you must be able to follow directions; that's the main thing," Clara said. She was all business.

Susan hid her disappointment and gave Clara a shy smile. She knew how to follow directions. She'd done that all her life.

Several times, Clara excused herself and went to speak with one of the workers who was clearing tables or waiting on customers.

"She's quite the hands-on manager," Eva observed. "I hope this works out for you."

Susan wasn't sure what she meant by that, but it didn't sound positive. "What did she mean about the pies?"

"Your guess is as good as mine," Eva answered. "Just be sure to ask questions if you don't understand something. Most new jobs are kind of tough at first, and you don't always get to do exactly what you want right away. You learn what the manager expects of you and then try to meet or exceed those expectations."

Eva was proving to be a great help to Susan. She had found her a place to work, attended the interview, and offered valuable advice. Susan was determined to be a good employee at Sugar N Spice and make Eva proud.

———————————

The first day at Sugar N Spice passed in a blur of minor mistakes, followed by manager-produced anxiety, and ending in a sigh of relief when it was time to go home. Clara was detail-oriented and expected her workers to be the same. There was a certain way to do everything, whether it was pouring water, placing toast on a plate, or wiping down a countertop. Clara put on a friendly face for the customers but switched it off the moment she was directing her employees, especially the new one.

She was all business as she instructed Susan on her various duties. "First thing, when you get here, you are to sweep the steps and the sidewalk out front. Then wipe down the door handles and polish the window in the front door. If you happen to see fingermarks during the day, take a moment to wipe them down again. That front door is their first impression. Cleanliness is next to godliness."

Susan stole a glance at the faded curtains that must have been hanging at the windows since the place opened. She eyed the dusty plants with dead leaves that needed to be pinched off. Was there a certain time or way to water them, she wondered? But Clara didn't mention the plants, which weren't included in the morning routine or any routine.

The dank-smelling utility closet held a collection of cleaning supplies, including a filthy, worn-out, yellow broom. As she swept the concrete steps, Susan wished for *Maemm's* plastic kitchen broom.

Even the old one at home was so much better. She thought about mentioning the need for a new broom to Clara but decided not to risk offending the boss on her first day.

As breakfast started, Susan learned how to read the hastily scrawled order slips that Clara and the other waitress clipped to a line above the cook's counter. The cook's black-dyed hair was covered with a mesh hairnet that framed her oily, round face. She was all business. Susan's job was to help the cook assemble the plates of food and deliver them to the tables. "What's that white stuff on this plate?" she asked the cook. It looked like cream of wheat but thicker.

"That's grits. Don't you know what grits is, girl?" The cook scowled at her, and Susan blushed with embarrassment. She'd heard that people in the South ate grits, but she'd never seen them. Susan gave the harried cook a weak smile and wiped her brow with her hand.

Clara appeared just then with another warning. "Don't just stand there. When the cook hands you a plate, you should have the toast already buttered and ready. Don't waste time standing around. The food must be hot when it gets to the table." Susan darted to the toaster and dipped a brush into the melted butter. "Don't do it like that," Clara said. "Hold the toast over this tray so you don't splash butter on the customer's plate."

"Okay. Sorry," Susan said. Her hands trembled as she followed Clara's instructions. Clara stood too close, watching Susan's every move as she fumbled with the slippery brush. A pool of melted butter dripped onto the tray.

Clara grabbed the plates and took them into the dining room, leaving Susan standing there with a lump in her throat and tears forming in her eyes. The cook hollered "Table 10!" and Susan grabbed three plates at once. The pancake platter was heavier than she expected, and as she juggled the plates like she'd seen the others do, a pile of bacon slid from one and fell to the floor.

At that moment, Clara walked into the kitchen. She said nothing, but her face hardened. She seized the plate and handed it back to the cook, who replaced the bacon. Clara motioned for Susan to take it, but still said nothing.

With her heart pounding, Susan once again balanced three of them in her two hands, ready to carry them to the dining room.

"When you have that many orders, you need to use a tray," Clara said. "Don't you have any sense at all?"

Susan placed the plates on a tray as directed and carried them to table ten. As she served the guests, she felt the tray teeter under her hand but somehow managed to keep it steady. The guests barely glanced at her as they unfolded napkins and poured syrup. With her heart pounding, Susan hurried back to the kitchen and grabbed the next order. Her feet were starting to hurt, and she felt hot and sweaty, but Clara said nothing about taking a break, and the other employees kept working.

When the breakfast crowd thinned, Clara called Susan to the back of the kitchen where a table was filled with several freshly baked pies that had been delivered from a nearby bakery. "We cut these into seven pieces to make them go further. Make sure every piece is the same size. That's not easy."

"We had seven people at our table at home. I think I can handle that," Susan said. Some of her skills learned in *Maemm's* kitchen would be used at Sugar N Spice, after all.

"Plate one or two pieces of each kind of pie. When the tray is full, take them to the front and put them in the display case. Your job is to ensure that the case is always stocked. People are more likely to order pie if they see it as soon as they walk in. Before doing that, you'll need to tidy up the case."

Clara returned to the kitchen where the cook was cleaning the grill and preparing for the lunch crowd. "Susan, we need a mop bucket over here. Cook has a greasy mess on the floor."

Susan blinked and wiped her eyes, hoping no one noticed the tears she brushed away while she grabbed the mop from the closet. So far, Sugar N Spice was anything but nice. Eva had told her it might be tough at first, but Susan hadn't expected it to be this hard. Still, it was her first day. It had to get easier each day, right?

Eva wrote down directions for biking to the restaurant, and Susan never got lost on her way to work. She learned the names of the streets: Searcy, turn left at the large cactus in front of the blue house, Wood Street, and Lockwood Ridge. Go straight when you reach Phillipi Creek. She arrived early and remembered to do everything exactly as Clara wanted. Still, there were always new things that went wrong, and Clara consistently caught and reprimanded Susan for each minor mistake. The rest of the staff received occasional positive comments from Clara, but never Susan. The others looked at her with pity but said nothing, as if befriending the new girl might somehow get them in trouble.

Every afternoon, Susan watched the clock, feeling relieved when her shift ended at three. As she rode back to Eva's, passing beneath the spreading southern oaks dripping with Spanish moss and the palm trees with their spiky leaves, she tried to make sense of the situation. She reminded herself that she knew how to work; she was strong and capable. Eventually, she'd learn everything—wait tables, get tips—and Clara would be happy with her. She had to be patient and work as hard as she could. She was determined to stick it out no matter what.

In the meantime, Susan bottled up her problem. She refused to tell Eva and Ruthie that she was struggling with the job she'd so badly wanted. *Why doesn't anything ever go my way? Is God punishing me for not preventing Ray's death back in Ohio? Maybe I'm like Jonah in the Bible. I ran away, but I still have to answer to God for my mistakes.*

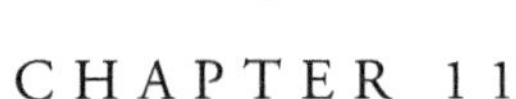

CHAPTER 11

"**I**s everything okay?" Ruthie asked Susan one evening as they were getting ready for bed. "You don't seem like yourself lately." She unpinned her *kapp* and released the large tortoise shell barrette underneath. Her long, wavy hair flowed down her back. She whipped it forward and began brushing vigorously, all the while giving Susan a penetrating stare. "Are you homesick? I know I am...a little."

"No. Everything's fine. Just fine. I don't miss Ohio's overcast skies that last for days on end." Susan kept her voice firm and convincing. "I'm still getting used to my job. I'm just tired from being on my feet all day." Susan began brushing her hair as the two faced each other, their brushes moving rhythmically in the humid air of their small bedroom.

"How is your job going? Do you like working for Eva at the inn?" Susan had already heard so much about their adventures as they uncovered new horrors day by day—mildewed carpet, leaky shower heads, peeling paint around windows that needed far more attention than just cleaning with blue spray and a lint-free cloth. Susan knew Ruthie enjoyed working with Eva, who was caught up in a dream becoming reality. Susan steered the conversation away from her own job. She couldn't admit that she was struggling and starting to lose hope in her plan to be a waitress.

Ruthie had no trouble talking about Saw Grass Inn. "It's a real mess out there. Today we found cockroaches under a bathroom

81

sink." Ruthie made a face and pretended to gag. "Every day when we get there, I wonder if we'll ever get the place clean. Eva found some junk guys who came over today and took all the old furniture. The rooms look a lot bigger now that they're empty."

Susan half-listened as she mulled over her personal work troubles that seemed far worse than cockroaches.

If Eva noticed Susan's low mood, she didn't let it show. Susan didn't have the heart to tell Eva what was going on at Sugar N Spice. Since Susan and Ruthie had settled in, and Eva had started renovating the inn, she seemed happier. She talked about Caleb less often and couldn't stop sharing her plans for Saw Grass Inn. Her dinner chatter was a pleasant distraction from Susan's work problems. For Eva and Ruthie, there was always another adventure, another problem to solve.

Eva described ideas for the lobby and the décor she was already collecting as she and Ruthie stopped nearly every day to load the station wagon with thrift store finds. "Florida is a gold mine when it comes to thrift shopping," she told Susan and Ruthie. "The snowbirds die, and their kids can't be bothered to move all their stuff back up north. They don't want their parents' old stuff."

Ruthie grimaced when Eva said that.

"But it's their loss," Eva said. "Things were higher quality back when I was young." She paused for a moment, as if realizing her two young guests might be offended. "I know you girls wouldn't be like that. I'm talking about spoiled rich kids." Having reassured them, she continued unfolding her plan.

Eva continued. "I have the best idea for the Saw Grass Inn's dining room. I'm collecting tableware, a mishmash of patterns. It will cost a fraction of ordering new dinnerware. If it breaks, there's always more at a thrift store. Maybe a row of teapots on a sideboard—all different kinds." She sounded excited and hopeful, even joyful. She didn't seem to mind the hard work, the long days, or the frustration when workers didn't show up on time. Her high spirits weren't dampened, even after another day of deep cleaning revealed yet another major flaw—another leaking faucet needing repairs. Susan noticed all this, and it puzzled her. Susan's trials dragged her down and increased her doubts about the choices she'd made. *Where does all that joy come from? Why can't I feel that way?*

Again, the next day, Susan biked to Sugar N Spice. She now had a habit of leaving the house very early to enjoy the freshness of the day. She stopped at Locklear Park and took in the sweet-smelling air. She examined the unfamiliar plants noted the colors of the beaks and legs of the waterbirds so she could check them later in Eva's bird book.

When she dreamed of working at a restaurant, she hadn't expected the feeling of being trapped that started the moment she put the broom away, washed her hands, and began serving breakfast. Once again, Clara arrived late this morning, without an apology. Susan's heart pounded, her hands grew clammy, and her face flushed. Her boss' presence always had that effect whenever she appeared. She seemed to sneak up on Susan without warning, as if she were just waiting to catch her making another mistake.

Susan's mind flitted back and forth, reviewing Clara's many commands, but there was always another one within an hour of the manager's arrival. Had she checked the cooler to make sure there were five flats of eggs? Why hadn't she rinsed the microfiber mop yesterday? Remember to wipe up after you brew a new pot of coffee. She'd been there for three weeks. Surely, she'd get the hang of everything soon.

"We're closed on Thanksgiving Day," Clara announced that

Monday. "But it's our busiest week of the year. We offer Thanksgiving-To-Go. We order twice as many pies and go through eight gallons of stuffing." Susan smiled, recalling the day Eva mentioned stuffing, and Ruthie pointed out that in Ohio, they called it "dressing." Whatever it was called, it was on the menu this week at Sugar N Spice.

It was hard to imagine Thanksgiving even happening here in Florida. At home, the snow flurries had started, and calls from *Maemm* and letters from her sister, Leah, mentioned holiday plans that Susan would miss this year. Susan didn't care much about missing the family Thanksgiving. At home, she'd felt out of place as one of the only unmarried cousins her age. It was fine with her that she'd celebrate differently this time. Eva had invited Susan and Ruthie to a dinner at her church. It was open to anyone who wanted to join—a potluck followed by board games and hymn singing.

But that was still three days away. In the meantime, Sugar N Spice was busy with people coming in to eat turkey and mashed potatoes as if they couldn't wait one more day to stuff themselves with dressing and the rich sweet potato casserole Sugar N Spice was offering as a weekly special. Everyone, it seemed, wanted a piece of pumpkin pie until there was none left, and they settled for pecan or Dutch apple.

Clara emerged from the back of the restaurant just as Susan reached for the last piece in the case. "The pie case is empty again, Susan. Right away."

"I'll handle it. This one goes to table seven."

Clara grabbed the pie from Susan's hand, and Susan hurried to the back room. She was skilled at cutting a nine-inch pie into seven slices. If Clara had noticed, she didn't say anything, maybe a sign she was doing at least one thing right.

Susan took a dozen pies out of their boxes and began slicing and placing portions onto serving plates. The lunchtime crowd was thinning, but the early bird dinner would start in half an hour. She carefully plated each piece, ensuring no crumbs or whipped cream smudges were left behind. Then, she found the largest tray and loaded it with a nice variety.

What happened next was something she kept thinking about long afterward. The floor was uneven at that spot. She'd known that and had carefully walked over it a thousand times by now. Did she slip on a greasy cake frosting spill? Was her shoe untied? Were her shoelaces too long? Or was she just *doppich?* Clumsy?

As she hurried out of the back room carrying the large tray filled with fresh servings of pie, she tripped on the uneven floor. Eight full plates of perfectly cut pie tilted, and everything tumbled. Plates shattered, with shards mixing into a child's finger painting. Berry, lemon, pumpkin, and lime colors blended on the floor. Everyone in the restaurant heard the crash. There was a brief, elongated silence. Then the noise of customers' voices resumed.

Susan briefly looked up at the restaurant ceiling. Without thinking, she muttered a barnyard word, an unladylike Amos-word she despised. But now it slipped from her lips just as Clara stood over her. Susan scrambled to her feet and reached for the tray leaning against the counter. Her dress, apron, and shoes were smeared with pie and whipped cream. Clara snatched the tray from Susan's clenched hands. "I think you're done here," Clara said. Her voice carried a finality Susan didn't expect. "And watch your mouth." She paused, and Susan managed a weak apology.

"I'm sorry. I...." Susan stammered, unsure of what more to say. But Clara didn't wait to hear more.

"This isn't working out," Clara said. "For me. Or for you, for that matter." Clara's posture was perfectly straight, and she showed no hint of apology or help. She scowled at Susan, who was standing there trembling. The breakfast cook, who was leaving soon, started cleaning up the pile of smashed pie with a wad of paper towels. Someone else rushed in with a mop.

"You're finished here. Go clean up. I'll give you the rest of your pay, minus the cost of three pies, at the front register," Clara said.

Susan's face changed from hot pink to white when she realized she was being fired.

"That's okay. Forget the pay. It's just a few hours." Her hopelessness showed in her trembling voice. "That's only fair considering the ruined pies." She couldn't bear to have any more interactions with Clara, not even to pick up her final paycheck.

Susan bent over to wipe pumpkin custard from her shoes. Then she hurried to the bathroom to wash her hands. Her heart pounded, and her weak hands used damp paper towels to wipe stains from her skirt hem and shoes. She took off her apron, which had caught most of the mess, and rinsed it under running water until only a faint red berry stain remained. The cool water on her wrists felt soothing. She peeked out the door, and when the way was clear, she quickly gathered her belongings, stuffed the damp apron into her bike pack, and slipped out the back door. She mounted her bike, feeling shaky and out of control.

Susan judged that it was a little past two o'clock, still two hours before Eva and Ruthie would be home. She rode through the streets, up one and down another, trying to let the breeze cool her face, willing the rhythmic pedaling to soothe her shattered nerves. *What will I tell everyone? I'm so ashamed of myself. How can I ever face Eva, who got me this job? What will Ruthie say?* Telling them what happened and how unhappy she'd been at Sugar N Spice seemed unthinkable right now. *I'll figure out what to say. Maybe I don't have to tell them everything. Maybe I can say I decided I'd rather help Eva at the inn.*

Susan let her body take over then. She rode aimlessly, not caring if she got lost. And she was lost for a while. At the end of Lockwood Ridge, the boardwalk to Locklear Park appeared, and Susan dismounted to walk her bike across the wooden bridge. Here, she could let her feelings settle and gather her thoughts amid the spell of massive southern oaks draped in Spanish moss. She lingered near the boardwalk to watch an ibis dip its beak into the dark water. Susan swallowed back the hopelessness as the white bird seemed to do.

She noticed picnic baskets and coolers on the tables under a pavilion. They seemed to belong to a group of Plain Mennonite men and women who were playing bocce ball on the hilly lawn. Several games were happening at once. The teams spread out, calling back and forth to each other. Susan imagined they were here on vacation, a big joyful family, playfully competing.

She stood watching for a while, noticing how the men wore plaid shirts and looked quite normal, like anyone on the street. The women wore long dresses they had sewn from pastel prints. Their white head coverings were smaller than an Amish *kapp* and pinned to their upswept hair with bobby pins. A few younger women wore denim skirts and canvas shoes. But their community seemed just as strong as any Amish group playing volleyball back home or shuffleboard at the Pinecraft park here in Sarasota. What would it be like to belong here, to be part of them?

Susan sank onto a park bench, watching and reflecting on what had happened. Dropping a tray of pie was a costly mistake. But most of Clara's complaints were minor—a dish towel folded instead of unfolded to dry. A cup with a chip she hadn't noticed. A table left waiting half an hour because she'd forgotten to tell a customer they'd run out of lemon-grilled chicken for the zesty citrus salad.

An overwhelming loneliness swept over her. She was no better off here in Florida than at home. At least at home, she had the safety of her family, a place where she belonged. Even though Amos wasn't right for her, and he'd led her down the wrong path. She could even blame him for making her leave everything behind to start over. And then there was Clara, whom she hadn't liked from the very beginning. Susan would never be good enough for Clara. Maybe she'd never be good enough for anyone—maybe not even for herself. Tears filled her eyes and streamed down her cheeks. She brushed them away with her fingers.

It had seemed so easy to move to Florida and start fresh, but nothing had really changed. She was still alone; she'd been fired from the job Eva had kindly helped her find. Life was tough, and she had nowhere to turn.

Nowhere? A small voice inside her questioned that desperate assumption. *What about God?*

Two older women from the Mennonite group walked by. One looked at her.

"Are you okay? Is everything all right?"

Susan nodded and offered a nervous smile, feeling self-conscious that they'd noticed her sitting there all alone.

God hadn't been in Susan's mind much lately. *God, I need help. I'm lost,* doppich, *alone. I've disappointed everyone. Especially myself. I just got fired from my first real job. I ran away from home, but all my problems came with me. Help me.*

Susan stood up from the bench and walked around the lake, watching black ducks nearly hidden in the water plants. They dipped their heads and then stretched them above the plants, bobbing here and there. The walk calmed her. Her mind let go of the mess that had become her life, and she took a deep breath. She noticed everything—the gray-green Spanish moss dripping from tree branches, the scrub palms growing wild, the long-needled pines, clusters of ferns, and even a now-dormant wild grapevine.

The weight of her suffering fell off her like an unnecessary Ohio jacket in Florida. When she finished circling the pond and got back to her bicycle, the bocce ball players were gone. *Susan, my beloved daughter, I have plans for you.* That inner voice was speaking again. *Stay hopeful. A better future is on the way.*

Susan might have begged for more explanation, but since it came from inside her own self, she let the promise linger like a flicker of hope. Then, she got back on her bike. It was time to return to the house and tell Eva and Ruthie what had happened. The entire story. With nothing held back.

CHAPTER 12

A few drops of rain started to fall as Susan hopped on her bike. As she pedaled up Lockwood Ridge toward Searcy Avenue, the rain turned into a heavy downpour that washed away the leftover pie and berry stains on her skirt and shoes. Battling the relentless rain drained all her energy. The day's worries dissolved into the puddles along the curb. Susan steered around them and pedaled faster.

She burst into the kitchen through the garage and stood dripping on Eva's spotless, cream-colored rug. In her rush to escape the rain and get home, Susan had lost track of her imagined conversation with Eva and Ruthie. Now, Eva was exclaiming over her.

"My goodness, Susan. You should have called. I could have come over to Sugar N Spice and picked you up." She turned away and pulled a hot casserole from the wall oven.

"We're having an early supper—something I had in the freezer. You'd better get dried off and changed right away. I'm heading out on an important errand afterward. I can tell you all about it while we eat."

Relief washed over Susan. Maybe she could put off telling Eva about getting fired. It seemed this wasn't the right time.

When they sat around the supper table, Eva offered a brief evening prayer. She thanked God for the "blessings of this day." Susan felt her stomach tighten at the thought of what surely couldn't be a blessing. Eva had no idea how terrible the day had been.

When the prayer was finished, Eva served a generous pile of noodles with tomatoes, hamburger, cheese, and more cheese onto each of their plates. As usual, she started sharing the latest news about Saw Grass Inn.

"I always knew that the inn is right behind the furthest part of Celery Fields where they are beginning a re-wilding process," Eva said.

Ruthie paused her fork in mid-air, her mouth open. "What is Celery Fields? What is re-wilding?" The same questions crossed Susan's mind, but she was also still trying to decide whether to reveal her secret failure and come clean to her two housemates. This hurried supper felt like bad timing for sharing her sad story.

Eva ignored Ruthie's question. "If I give the Audubon Foundation an easement of forty feet for a right-of-way, some of my property can be designated as a wildlife refuge. It's great for me—a big tax write-off and a draw for my guests. Celery Fields is a great birding area."

Eva paused, and Susan asked Ruthie's question again. "What is re-wilding? I've never heard of that."

Susan decided not to tell Eva and Ruthie about her day just now. It wasn't the right time.

"You probably heard about the Amish farmers of long ago who came to this area to grow celery in the muck out there. That's how Pinecraft began. It was a bog back then—rich, dark soil that resulted from the draining of the swamp." Eva paused and took a bite of her casserole. "This needs salt," she said. "Could you pass the salt?"

Susan handed her a saltshaker, and Eva sprinkled it onto her noodles and ground beef.

Eva continued. "Now they've reversed that. It seems that nature needs places for water to collect, especially these days with all the streets, buildings, and parking lots."

"Re-wilding is a strange term, isn't it?" Eva mused. "I thought

so, too, when I first heard it. I guess it means they reintroduce native plants and remove those that didn't originally grow here in
Sarasota."

Susan thought about all the unfamiliar plants and birds she'd
seen since she arrived. Almost everything here was different from
home—even the natural world.

"I need to pick up some information and documents at Celery
Fields about the stormwater facility and its impact on the inn. Since
Thanksgiving is coming, I want to do this tonight. If you girls want
to come with me, we can walk along the boardwalk and watch the
sunset. That's why we're eating so early."

Ruthie, who looked a bit pale, said, "I don't think I should go.
I'm on my period right now and I have bad cramps."

Leave it to Ruthie to tell it like it is.

Eva gave a weak smile. She turned to Susan. "I hope at least
you will come with me. It will give us a chance to catch up. I'd like to
hear how your job is going. I guess you've been extra busy with the
holiday almost here."

Eva continued, "By the way, that reminds me, I won't be home
Friday evening. I was invited to dinner by some visitors to the area—
people Caleb and I have known for a long time. You could join us.
Ruthie will be in Ohio having Thanksgiving with her folks."

"It's okay," Susan said. "I'll find something to do." Eva had
already done so much for her; she didn't need to intrude on her social
life, too.

Susan felt a cramp in her stomach, caused by something different than Ruthie's. Maybe this was meant to happen. She could
confide in Eva about getting fired—get it over with and out of the
way. It wouldn't be as hard to tell Ruthie later. She could do that at
bedtime if Ruthie wasn't asleep when they got home. It was Eva she

was most afraid to tell. Susan couldn't bear to disappoint her. But the sooner she did it, the better.

"It would be nice to watch the sunset with you," Susan said.

As they made their way down Tuttle Ave., Susan considered how she might start a conversation with Eva. She needed to build up to her revelation, the sooner the better. But Eva was unaware that Susan had a confession to make. Eva shared her swirling thoughts aloud. "They're finally finishing the new phase of the stormwater sedimentation ponds. When I bought the inn, I never considered how close the property boundary is to Celery Fields and those ponds they built. Just think about it. There are fishing and kayaking opportunities nearby. Saw Grass Inn will be the go-to lodging for birders from all over. I could even have the Audubon Society give talks at the inn, schedule nature hikes."

Eva paused and took a breath. She glanced at Susan as if expecting her to offer a few ideas. Ruthie would certainly have done that. But given Susan's state of mind, she could only offer a bland comment.

"I don't know much about Florida plants and birds. I walk through Locklear Park and don't recognize a thing." Her voice sounded as dejected as she felt about her life right now. *Should I tell her about the extra time I spent there today after I lost my job? Correction: got fired.*

Eva was reassuring. "You've only been here a short time. Of course, everything is different, but you can learn. Keep looking. You'll eventually see some migratory birds you recognize. The longer you live here, the more you pick up." Eva stopped the car at a light, and several bicycles crossed the road. The riders were cruising down the Legacy Trail, built on the old railroad bed. Not so different from the bike trails back home in Holmes County, but here the trail went through the city.

"You've probably seen Phillipi Creek in our neighborhood," Eva continued. "Most of the time, there isn't much water in it, but as more areas are developed, the water needs a place to go." Susan nodded, happy to let Eva explain. "That creek can't handle all the water run-off if we have heavy rain. So, these ponds I'm talking about at Celery Fields, they're important for this sprawling city."

They had left the busiest streets of Sarasota and were now on a wide parkway. Soon, they turned into a gravel parking lot with only a few cars. Eva parked her station wagon and led the way to the park office building. "I'm supposed to check in with the front desk. I think they want to explain a couple of things in the packet, and then we can walk out onto the boardwalk over the water."

Eva walked over to the desk and asked for her contact person. Susan looked around the spacious lobby and was drawn to colorful boards with pictures and explanations of the wildlife found at Celery Fields. She moved slowly, examining several of them, trying to find plants and birds she might recognize. She wanted to learn their names. She remembered how her sister Leah once asked her, "Why does it matter if you know the name? Can't you just enjoy looking without giving it a label?"

But Susan enjoyed knowing the names of things—plants, birds, streets, and people, of course. She remembered telling Leah that she thought it was natural to care about names—after all, Adam and Eve were tasked with naming everything in the Garden of Eden. At the time, Leah wasn't convinced. Maybe she thinks differently now that she and Aaron have given names to their four children.

Susan continued studying the pictures, moving slowly around the room. When she reached the last display board, Eva came out of a door just to her left. She was holding an oversized manila envelope. "We can drop this in the car before we go for our walk. Looks like you had plenty to entertain you. Did you learn anything?"

"I recognized a couple of birds I've seen in Florida. I'm pretty sure I've seen a pelican. Also, a white egret." She pointed to the framed pictures hanging between the large windows.

"Very common around here. But probably not in Ohio. Let's get outside and see what we can find," Eva said.

After Eva dropped her package in the car, they headed toward a long boardwalk that stretched across the water where water plants floated. Spiky sawgrass grew in clumps. "Caleb and I used to sit out here and watch the sunset. Seems like such a long time ago," Eva said. "And in another way, it seems like it was just last week. I'm so thankful for all those good memories."

Susan listened but didn't have much to say. She was overwhelmed by bad memories—so many bad memories. Her mind drifted back to that dreadful night at the concert, when a young man had lost his life, and she and Amos ended up at the sheriff's office. What would Eva think if she knew? She had escaped to Florida hoping for a fresh start. And now, here she was, facing more failure—a failure she must confess to Eva.

They walked to the very end of the boardwalk where it widened into a large deck. Benches were built into the railing at regular intervals. Eva plopped down on one of them and patted the space beside her. "Have a seat, Susan. Let's rest here and watch the sun go down. I'd like to catch up with you. Seems I haven't seen much of you lately. How are things going for you at Sugar N Spice?"

Eva had arranged the perfect opening. Susan smoothed the soft knit fabric of her flowing skirt.

"Honestly, Eva, I have to tell you something about that. I'm not working there anymore. After today." Susan's breath escaped with a slight shudder.

Eva looked sideways at Susan, her face a mix of question and surprise. "Why? What happened? I thought you wanted to work in a restaurant. It seemed perfect for you."

"It wasn't going very well. Maybe I'm not cut out for it. I don't know."

"Tell me a little more," Eva said. "I had no idea you were having problems with your job. Of course, a new job always takes some getting used to."

"It just wasn't working out. Clara, she...." Susan's words trailed off. She shouldn't blame Clara for what happened.

"I don't know Clara very well, but she seems friendly enough."

"She's nice to most people, but for some reason, I just couldn't do things right. She made me so nervous." Susan watched a great blue heron glide across the marsh with an outstretched neck. This was a bird she *did* recognize, a picture of grace against Susan's angst.

"Today, I totally blew it. I dropped a whole serving tray full of pie," Susan's voice sank to a whisper. "It was awful. I feel so ashamed."

Eva took Susan's hand in her soft palm and gave a quick squeeze. "Oh, my dear girl. That's dreadful, but accidents happen. I'm sure you apologized and helped clean up." She half-turned her body, and Susan could feel compassion in the older woman's gaze.

"She...told me to leave, to get out. Right then. In front of everyone." Tears filled Susan's eyes, and Eva's grip tightened around her hand.

"I'm so sorry. That shouldn't have happened. You're still so new there. Accidents happen all the time. And she embarrassed you in front of others. There's no excuse. No one was hurt, and pie can be replaced. What was she thinking? Did you try to talk to her about it?"

"No, she told me to gather my things and leave. Some of the other workers helped clean up. It was a huge mess—broken plates, pie everywhere. My dress, my shoes. I just wanted to get out of there."

"I don't blame you. I'd have done the same. Do you think you'll go back?"

Eva didn't get it. Susan was done at Sugar N Spice.

"No. I'm never going back. She fired me. I can't go back. She doesn't want me. I don't think she even likes me. I couldn't do anything right. She was constantly picking on me and correcting every little thing," Susan blurted out everything. "I'm so *doppich!*" Susan swallowed a lump in her throat. She refused to cry in front of Eva.

"Goodness, Susan. I had no idea. Why didn't you say something earlier? I need to think about this. She doesn't seem like a very good manager to me." Eva paused. "Maybe that's why she has trouble keeping good staff. The restaurant owner told me they experienced a lot of staff turnover. Now I understand." Eva was still holding Susan's hand and gave it another gentle squeeze.

Susan felt strange holding the older woman's hand for so long, but Eva didn't let go. "I'm so sorry you had to go through this. Do you want me to talk to her? I could do that."

"I don't think so. And I couldn't even start to talk to her. It wouldn't do any good, anyway. Her mind is made up about me." Susan was sure no words could fix the bad blood between herself and Clara.

"You haven't had much work experience. Maybe this wasn't the right place for you. I'm sorry about this. I really am," Eva said. "In a way, I feel like it's my fault. I thought it might be better there than at those other places. They're so fast-paced. If you want to be a waitress, I'm sure you can find something else. There are hundreds of restaurants in Sarasota." Eva finally let go of Susan's hand.

Susan kept her eyes on the heron, which was now standing completely still, silhouetted against the red sky in the west. She spoke without looking at Eva.

"It's not your fault," Susan said. "It's me. Maybe it isn't for me. I don't know what I was thinking." Her voice dropped lower with each phrase.

"No, you wanted to try it, and I'm glad you had the chance. It wasn't a good fit. I don't think anyone's to blame. Don't be hard on yourself. Some jobs just aren't right for certain people. Keep dreaming. Something better suited to you will come along. I believe that."

Susan took another shaky breath and let her eyes rest on the water. The bird had flown away somewhere. A few ducks bobbed among the water plants, and the solar lights along the boardwalk illuminated the path back to land as Eva and Susan stood.

"Thanks for understanding," Susan said. "I hated to tell you because it was so nice the way you helped me get that job. I didn't want to disappoint you. I wish it had worked out."

"Don't you worry about it for a minute. I have a feeling there is something else you're meant to do. Don't lose hope."

"I'll try not to. Maybe I can help you and Ruthie at the inn for a while." As she said this, she felt a mix of resignation and relief. Why had she been so stubborn?

"I'd love for you to do that. And Ruthie will be thrilled," Eva said.

They went back to Eva's car, and she unlocked Susan's door before heading to the driver's side. She placed the packet on the middle of the front seat and got in.

"There's plenty to do over there." She pointed straight ahead, where the Saw Grass Inn was obscured by a stretch of palm scrub. "Once I get into the contents of this, there's going to be even more to do, trust me." She patted the big envelope on the seat between them.

"Thanks for understanding. I'll do my best to help you."

"I know you will, Susan. I think you might be just the person for one of the next things on my agenda." Eva reached over and patted Susan's shoulder.

They were the last to leave the Celery Fields parking lot. Eva drove through a bit of filtered evening light as they headed back toward town and home. Susan let her tired body relax into the Volvo's worn, comfortable seat.

It had been a long day, but it had ended well.

CHAPTER 13

Ruthie had left for her Ohio Thanksgiving. And now, on Friday evening, after Eva left for the restaurant to meet her friends, Susan went for a walk. She needed to burn off the extra calories she'd eaten at the Mennonite Thanksgiving potluck. It had been just as Eva said it would be. Eventually, she went into the kitchen to help Eva, who was on cleanup duty. She was starting to realize that many of the Mennonites at Eva's church were snowbirds who only lived in Florida part of the year. And the crowd was much older than Eva had mentioned when she talked about single men.

Now, Susan walked down the sidewalk, avoiding bicycles and people pushing strollers. It was a lovely evening with a cool breeze stirring the crimson bougainvillea that spilled over from lawns and nearly blocked the sidewalk in some spots. She took a deep breath of the warm air, grateful she wasn't in Ohio, happy she was finally on her own.

As she approached Harvest Home Church, the noise of people talking spilled out of the open windows and across the street. The sign outside announced that the service began at 7:00. "Everyone Welcome! Revival!" The conversation soon ceased. Susan stood on the sidewalk, watching the crowd of Plain people as they took their seats.

On an impulse, Susan entered and sat in the very back row. The wooden benches had backs, unlike the church benches at home. People were packed tightly against each other with little room left anywhere. Just then, a man rose to welcome everyone. The air was warm and humid in the simple, wood-frame church building. Mennonite and Amish people were dressed in clothing that to the uninitiated, looked uniform. But Susan Troyer could tell by the shape of a head covering, the number of pleats in a bonnet, or the style and fabric of a woman's dress whether she was from Indiana, Pennsylvania, or Ohio.

As the service started, Susan lifted a hymnal from its wooden holder on the back of the pew in front of her. The young song leader rose to greet the crowd. "Welcome in Jesus' name, from wherever you've come. Jesus is among us! Please open to number 246 in your hymnal. Let us sing together." His voice was strong and enthusiastic. He blew a pitch pipe and hummed the pitch. Everyone began singing.

The tune and words took her back to the Sunday night singings in Holmes County with the youth group. "*What a friend we have in Jesus, all our sins and griefs to bear; what a privilege to carry everything to God in prayer.*"

She'd sung this hymn so many times. But this time felt different. *Do thy friends despise, forsake thee, take it to the Lord in prayer.* The painful experience of getting fired by Clara, who wasn't a friend. Or having to leave Benville to get away from trouble, and Amos, who had proven himself unworthy of her friendship.

...everything to God in prayer...everything? She swallowed back a lump that had formed in her throat, skipping a few phrases until she'd regained composure, and the words became her prayer, another way to let go of life's recent troubles.

As the group finished the final verse, Susan kept her eyes on the song leader. He was incredibly handsome. His shiny black hair was slicked back from his face. The color reminded Susan of crow feathers. His deeply tanned skin had a reddish glow that practically shimmered against his crisp white button-down shirt. His eyes scanned the crowd as if searching for someone. She wished he would look at her, but she was hiding in this corner, and he was now announcing a second hymn.

"Please turn to number sixty-seven, 'Revive Us Again.'" He was warming up now and led with his whole body, swaying to the rhythm of the hymn. With his arm extended, he unified the voices of the congregation, drawing sound and breath from everyone present. He was lean and fit. Susan could imagine the muscles rippling under his sleeve as he directed with his left hand and easily held the worn hymnbook in his right. Around her, Susan heard four-part harmony burst forth, and she was swept up in the energy of the room. *Revive us again! Fill each heart with thy love, may each soul be rekindled with fire from above, Hallelujah, thine the glory, hallelujah Amen! Hallelujah, thine the glory, revive us again.*

Susan's contemplative mood lifted. She sensed that something was about to change. She could feel it in the air around her. The singing had boosted her spirits, as it often did. She wished for more, but it was time for prayer and scripture reading.

The visiting minister from Tennessee, known as Brother Jim, delivered a whole sermon about "...all have sinned and come short of the glory of God." His message was lengthy, and the room grew increasingly humid and stifling. At times, people nodded or whispered phrases like "Amen, brother," or "Yes, brother," but mostly, they stayed silent, listening closely to the rhythm of his words and the southern accent, which was noticeably different from Susan's ministers back home.

Children stood and walked out, sometimes holding their mothers' hands. Susan watched through a window as the sun slowly dropped behind the rustling palm trees. Street noises continued, occasionally punctuated by a siren a few blocks away. Susan felt sweaty and tired from sitting so long on a hard wooden church pew. She thought about leaving, but the idea of more singing at the end of the service held her back, restless and increasingly aware of her own sin, which felt more real with every sentence spoken by Brother Jim.

Finally, the service drew to an end. The handsome song leader once more rose to lead the congregation in an invitation hymn. His velvety voice soothed her, as he guided the gathered community to open the hymnal to number 80: *Just as I am without one plea.* Preacher Jim's voice became quieter, almost soothing, as he invited everyone to come to Jesus for forgiveness.

He asked the faithful to pray for those who were convicted of sin, and "for those among us who are lost to come to the cross. Everyone: bow your head and close your eyes as you prayerfully sing." Susan closed her eyes but then stole another look at the song leader, who now had *his* eyes closed. He was slowing the music, tamping down the sound, guiding the group to sing more quietly, as if in prayer.

Susan reflected on the guilt she had tried to push away—the sin she had come here to escape. Her thoughts floated into the preacher's words. She believed she had fallen far from God's grace and glory. How could God love her with all the lies and deception? Overlooking Amos' bad behavior, even when it led to someone's death? How could she ever admit to Brother Jim, or anyone else, everything that had happened between her and Amos? Brother Jim had listed it all—the alcohol, dancing, and worldly music. How could she ever confess publicly that she had been part of a group that drank so heavily that someone died? To escape all this, she lied to her parents about staying overnight with Ruthie. Then she bought a bus ticket. She ran away to Sarasota, claiming she wanted to avoid the winter cold and find a job—though she had already been fired from that job. She said she needed a change, a break from Ohio's weather. But deep inside, she wanted to forget it all. Still, she couldn't forget any of it. Her secret would stay safe if she never told anyone.

Her stomach twisted in a knot at the thought of standing and walking to the front of the church. Others were doing just that, lining up so Brother Jim could lay his hand on their heads or shoulders and pray for them. Susan sat still, impatient for the meeting to end. She wasn't about to do that even though she didn't know a single soul in the crowd.

She'd escaped Ohio, but the guilt followed her. She had been taught the words of scripture. But now, inside her, she understood the truth of it: "All have sinned and come short of the glory of God." And that included Susan Troyer.

Everyone had been standing during this song, verse after verse. She shifted from one foot to the other and stole a glance at the people nearby. They were singing with their eyes closed. No one noticed when Susan slipped to the door and carefully opened it. She eased herself outside into the cool evening breeze. She walked briskly up the street, trying to shake the emotional upheaval that had overtaken her during that meeting. She felt anything but revived. All she wanted was to return to the safety of Eva's home on Searcy Avenue.

CHAPTER 14

The long Thanksgiving week finally ended, and Eva had plans. "If I'm going to be ready to take reservations for next winter, we need to launch Saw Grass Inn by spring," she told Susan. The urgency in her voice spilled out as they sat sipping a second cup of coffee at breakfast. "I've managed inns and hotels long enough to know there are always bugs to work out. I sure don't want to do that during peak tourist season." She took a sip of coffee.

"Ruthie should be back on Tuesday," Susan said. "But I can help you today if you need me." Her body prickled from the inactivity of the past few days when all she'd done was eat, read a book, and of course, attend that revival meeting. She was used to working.

"I have a job in mind for you, but that's still about a week away," Eva said. "In the meantime, you can help me with painting furniture. We're going to paint some chairs today. There are a few dozen out there in the garage. Pick out some that aren't too wobbly and load them into the station wagon."

"What will I be doing next week?" Susan asked. "You keep saying you have a special job for me. What is it?"

"You did a lot of gardening back in Ohio. It sounds like you enjoy it, right?"

Susan hadn't thought of it as exactly enjoyable. But after being in the stuffy restaurant with people all around her, getting outside appealed to her.

Eva stood and carried her coffee cup to the sink. "Next week, we'll be hosting a team from EdenKeepers. They're the recommended company to get us started with the re-wilding process. I'd like you to be there working alongside them. I'm too busy, and let's face it too old, to be doing some of the heavy lifting and squatting I know will be part of that project. Bursitis." Eva laughed and slapped her hands on her bottom as she said this.

Susan gave a half-hearted smile and cleared away the remaining breakfast dishes. Sometimes she didn't know how to respond to Eva's goofy jokes.

"EdenKeepers will remove the unwanted plants that are taking over. Afterward, they bring in a truckload of new seedlings—the kind we want to promote in the area bordering the Celery Fields," Eva said.

Susan was lost in unwanted thoughts as she put the milk carton back in the fridge. She was still upset over that revival meeting. The preacher's words brought back all the bad memories of her times with Amos. Not just the concert, but many other times, too. The sneaking around, lying to her family, the drunken feeling, the nights they found a secluded spot to kiss—even though she knew their relationship meant nothing. And then, it all ended in disaster.

In her bedroom, Susan made the bed, and kept replaying the mix of inclination and hesitancy she'd felt at the end of that revival meeting. In her heart, she'd acknowledged her "sinful nature." She knew exactly what the preacher was talking about. But she'd been too cowardly, too shy, too embarrassed to have a stranger pray with her. They'd emphasized the need to confess her sin publicly. Maybe she'd feel different if she had gone forward.

Back in the kitchen, Susan swept the floor with a broom. She and Eva discussed ordinary topics—what to have for dinner, an update on the inn's window replacement schedule, when the painting crew would finish, what supplies Eva needed to bring to the inn, and what she needed from the garage.

Eva had been collecting cast-offs she planned to use as furnishings. Her vision of the place remained a mystery to Susan. Occasionally, Eva shared parts of her grand plan with Susan and Ruthie, more often with Ruthie, who worked with her and had joined her on thrift store and yard sale trips. "I'm going to combine the old and new creatively," Eva said. "Add some color and character. Make the place come alive." Her voice rose a bit with each sentence as she expressed her enthusiasm.

Susan entered the garage and looked up at the uneven stacks of dining chairs reaching the ceiling. She picked up a dark-varnished chair with a torn green and fuchsia upholstered seat. A similar chair beneath it lacked upholstery but appeared sturdy. There were two solid oak pressed-back chairs with tight spindles and sticky varnish, two bulky captain's chairs, and a stray arrow-back.

Susan opened the garage door and carried the chairs one by one to the back of Eva's station wagon. Old varnish flaked off, but the chairs were sturdy and heavy. The musty odors of old wood and past lives clung to Susan's hands as she lifted them and stacked them into the trunk and on the back seat.

Eva joined Susan in the garage and rummaged through paint cans and brushes. She filled a 5-gallon bucket with small plastic containers of paint, brushes, sandpaper, and putty knives. She was whistling a hymn under her breath as she grabbed a pile of rags and slid them into a paper shopping bag.

"I hope these are what you had in mind," Susan said.

Eva eyed the chairs and smiled. "Those are just the ones," she said. "I grabbed two or three of them from beside a trash can out by the street. Just slipped them into the back and went on my way. Roadside rescue." She laughed heartily, and this time Susan laughed, too. It felt good to laugh. As they drove, they listened to a Christian radio station Eva liked. She sang along with the songs while Susan tried hard not to breathe in the smells coming from the back seat.

Eva turned down the radio. "I guess I never told you about my plans for the dining room. That's what these chairs are for," she said. "I got some good tables from a restaurant that went out of business. They'll be delivered in a couple of weeks. My idea is to pair the old with the new—well, newer."

"So, these chairs will match the newer tables?" Susan asked.

"Exactly," Eva said. "And wait until you see my colors. You know, I've worked in hospitality my whole life, in the hotel business. However, to me, hospitality is more than just crisp sheets and white towels. People want to feel at home somewhere. Like they belong there. They want to experience something when they travel, have their imaginations sparked by surroundings different from home."

Susan thought she understood, but she questioned how the dusty chairs in the back of the car could fit into Eva's grand vision. "I think I get that," Susan said. "I feel so different here in Florida with the palm trees, the flowers—even in the winter. I feel like another person, sort of." Despite the misadventures at the restaurant, she was happy to be free of Amos, and away from her family, who always had another chore for her to complete. The bright sunshine lifted her mood.

"I remember feeling like that when Caleb and I first came to Sarasota. It was completely different here," Eva said. She stayed quiet for a moment, and Susan thought she might be recalling something about Caleb and those early years after they got married.

"Back to the chairs," Eva said. "You must wonder what in the world I was thinking when you loaded them up. But you'll see. You're going to be surprised when it all comes together."

"I guess I have to trust you on that one," Susan said. Despite Eva's strange ideas, she was drawn to her. She was so honest and real. And she was a living example of hospitality. She lived what she believed—the way she'd taken in Susan and made her and Ruthie part of her life. The past few weeks would have been far more difficult without Eva's help and support.

After unloading and Eva's guided update on the inn's progress, they began painting. However, Eva kept getting interrupted. A delivery truck arrived with bed frames and mattresses. The kitchen remodelers came in for a final walk-through with Eva to ensure everything was exactly as she'd ordered.

When she returned, Eva and Susan spread a large drop cloth on the floor where they planned to do the painting. "My idea is to have a cozy, colorful dining room that makes people feel like they are in their grandmother's kitchen," Eva said. "Each table will have a checked cloth in a different color—periwinkle blue, bay aqua, finch yellow, coral orange, and sage green. The tables will have an eclectic mix of chairs in some of those colors. We can paint those two pressed-back chairs sage green, maybe. And the captain's chairs, I'm thinking, periwinkle. What do you think?"

Susan forced a smile and said nothing. She thought about the beautiful solid oak and cherry furniture built in her neighborhood back home and the dull sheen of the stains, the flawless matte finish. She wouldn't consider painting over that beautiful wood. But these chairs had long ago lost their charm. They had been used and discarded. Why would Eva want these old things in her new dining room?

As if she'd read Susan's mind, Eva explained herself. "We're a throw-away society anymore. Everyone wants the newest, the shiniest, the best, the most expensive. But happiness doesn't come from stuff." She paused to let her words sink in. "Why not give these old chairs a second chance, a new life?"

Does Eva expect me to answer that question? No comment.

"Show me how you want me to do this," Susan said. "I've never painted a chair before. I don't know where to start."

"We're going to use chalk paint, so we won't need to strip off the old finish completely. A quick sanding and wiping them down, and we'll be ready to paint. I like to say it's a spiritual experience," Eva said. "I told you we are giving the chairs new life, didn't I?" Eva laughed again as she picked up a small power tool and applied a triangle of sandpaper to the flat surface. "I'm a big fan of this little mouse sander. We might want to wear safety glasses and masks, for protection from flying debris and these old varnishes."

They put on their safety gear, and Susan watched Eva use the small triangular tool, which was smaller than an iron and roughly the same shape. The tools in *Daett's* shop were much larger and more powerful. As the tiny, mouse-shaped sander came to life, Eva directed its nose into the crevices, smoothing out the rough patches. A few bits of varnish splattered around. Here and there, a patch of fresh wood peeked through the old varnish.

"Chalk paint is wonderful," Eva said. "It clings to the old finish and glides on like a breeze." Her voice was muffled beneath the mask she wore over her nose and mouth.

When Eva finished sanding the first chair, she dusted the crevices and larger surfaces, then wiped it down again with a tacky cheesecloth, creating a smooth, dust-free surface.

"You made that look so easy," Susan said.

"Here, give it a try. Follow the grain of the wood." Eva handed the mouse sander to Susan. It sputtered to life and quivered beneath her hand. She gained control, guiding it over the chair's legs, across the seat, touching up the chipped spots on the rungs, and then lightly polishing the back.

After tipping it up and quickly sanding the legs, Eva gave her a thumbs up. "Let's wipe these two down and then get them out of the dust," Eva said.

They carried them across the large dining room, which was still a work-in-progress, waiting for painters and new flooring in a few days. They placed the prepped chairs on a large, old table left by the previous owners of the inn.

"I use synthetic brushes for chalk paint. I prefer narrow ones, but a wider brush works, too." Eva placed several brushes on the table, and Susan chose one that was about two inches wide. Eva tipped her chair upside down. "It's easiest to start painting the legs and the rungs, on the inside, where no one sees. That keeps you from reaching over wet paint, too," Eva advised. They took turns dipping their brushes into the warm sage color. The paint glided onto the surface of the chair effortlessly. It soaked into the old varnish and clung to the sanded wood, smoothing everything.

"I like this color," Susan said. "It reminds me of one of the plants *Maemm* likes, dusty miller."

"You're right, it is just like dusty miller. I hadn't thought of that but it's the perfect description," Eva said.

Conversation flowed as Susan and Eva transformed the two discarded chairs into something new and different. Occasionally, they stepped back to admire their work. Susan continued cleaning and painting while Eva came and went, dealing with deliveries and making phone calls. After applying the first coat of sage green to the two chairs, Eva returned with pliers and began removing the old fuchsia brocade upholstery from the dark-varnished chairs. She sanded the pair and carried them across the room to the tables where Susan was painting. "What color should we use on these?" Eva asked.

"I vote for finch yellow," Susan said. "But the painted chairs look kind of dull. Are they finished, or is there another coat of something we'll add?"

"You guessed right," Eva said. "There is another step to the process. That was the base coat. After the second coat, we can distress them with a sanding block or the mouse sander." Eva gave a quick tutorial on the first chair that had already dried. She demonstrated how to use the mouse sander to remove paint in random areas, allowing the old finish to show through. "After that, we'll apply a wax and then buff them. I've also seen other techniques, such as stenciling, crackling, or adding a rough, chippy finish. For these chairs, we're going to keep it simple and distress them a bit, then wax and buff."

Despite her best effort to stay neat, by lunchtime, Susan's dress was splattered with sage and yellow paint. A large smudge on her arm would need a good scrubbing. The color scheme was starting to grow on Susan. By the end of the afternoon, all six chairs would have two or three coats of chalk paint in sage, finch, and coral.

At lunchtime, they washed up with dish detergent in the large sink. The kitchen was so new that the appliances and windows still had manufacturers' stickers on them. Eva pulled some sliced ham and turkey from the huge, nearly empty double refrigerator. They each made a sandwich and carried them outside on paper plates to some old Adirondack chairs under a cluster of palm trees. They drank hibiscus tea Eva had brought in a half-gallon Mason jar. It was the perfect time to ask Eva a question Susan had been wondering about as she'd painted the chairs.

"I keep thinking about something you said, Eva," Susan started. "You mentioned that painting those chairs is a spiritual experience, like we're giving them new life. I understand that but they're still old. Aren't we just covering up the flaws and dirt with a fresh coat of paint?"

Eva paused, and Susan felt silly for asking the question. But she had been thinking about Eva's comment all morning. Was it just a joke? Or did she mean something more?

"I'm glad you asked. It was probably just an off-hand comment on my part. But there's some truth in it, I think. Like a chair and its maker—if God is the maker, the creator—then what God made isn't junk. The goodness is still inside that chair—the sturdiness, the craftsmanship, the functionality. None of that has changed with time. But scuffs and wear happen. A refurbishment is needed for the chair to be useful again. It won't be new. But it will be renewed." Eva paused, giving Susan time to consider her words.

Susan took a breath. Eva was someone she trusted; someone she might be able to talk to about the things that had been bothering her so much lately. *Dare I tell her—ask her? Will she understand?*

"Ever since I got here, I've been thinking about a lot of things. I don't know if Ruthie told you, but I needed to get away from Ohio. Not just to find a job, but because I was heading down the wrong path. And my boyfriend was a loser. I had to get away from him, too." Susan flushed. She wasn't used to talking about personal things, but it was freeing to open up to Eva.

"Ruthie didn't say anything, but I could sense something was wrong," Eva said. "Sometimes a person just needs to get away. And sometimes, you need to make peace with what happened, with your past." Eva glanced sideways, and Susan met her eyes. They were filled with compassion. Susan hadn't expected to feel the surge of love rising inside her when she was with Eva. Her eyes welled up with tears; her chest swelled with emotion.

"I went to that revival meeting the other night," Susan said. "And I can't stop thinking about it." Her voice revealed her nervousness. "I was sitting way in the back and didn't know anyone. I felt terrible. Lonely. Like the sinner the minister kept talking about. 'All have sinned and come short of the glory of God.' I don't know how many times he said that. And every time, I just thought of all the bad stuff that happened between me and Amos. And how even after I got here, I didn't feel happy and nothing was going right, and...." Susan wiped tears with her fingers and smelled the lingering scent of paint and dish detergent. She looked out beyond the small grove of palms to a giant southern oak dripping with Spanish moss.

Eva paused quietly for a few moments. When she finally spoke, her words were calm and filled with kindness. "No matter what you've done, Susan, God loves you. That's the most important thing to remember. God loves you and forgives you. Did you go forward to confess and receive Jesus?" Eva's words were gentle but encouraging.

"No. I didn't. I wanted to. Kind of. But I was scared. I didn't know anyone. Now I keep wondering, why didn't I? I should have. Don't you think I should have? I mean, I did so many things I shouldn't have, but I was afraid. I feel so guilty. I'm so ashamed that I just sat there like that." Susan wiped more tears.

"It's okay that you didn't go forward for prayer. God knows your needs." Eva reached over and squeezed Susan's hand. "God loves you. God's grace will meet you where you are. Leave that guilt and shame in the past." She breathed softly and then continued. "It's like the scuffed finish and torn, faded upholstery on those chairs. Your guilt masks and mars the solid goodness inside you." Eva fingered the sweating half-full glass that sat on the wide arm of her chair. "You said you're sorry for what happened. God hears that confession and offers grace. Believe that. Move on. There's a good life waiting for you out ahead. I'm sure of it."

They sat quietly for a moment, sipping the sweet tea as Susan's mind wandered to a peaceful place in Eva Good's welcoming presence. *God, I'm so sorry. Please forgive me. I want to move on. Help me do better from now on.*

Eva stood and gathered the empty glasses and paper plates. "You go ahead and rest a bit out here. I have some computer work to do. I'll let you know when I'm ready to start painting the rest of those chairs."

Susan breathed in the fresh, sweet air and gazed up at the puffy clouds overhead. She listened and heard birds she was beginning to recognize. She was alone. But after talking with Eva, she didn't feel lonely anymore. She felt, heard, understood, and cared for with love.

CHAPTER 15

The day before Ruthie was due back in Sarasota, Eva and Susan took the remaining chairs to the inn. Each one was wobbly or loose. Eva's handyman would glue and clamp them so they would be sturdy and guest-ready. Now, as they waited in a parking lot for the Pioneer Trails bus to arrive, Eva said, "After Ruthie gets here, maybe we can go out to the inn. If all three of us work at it, we should be able to clean and paint the rest of the chairs today."

Susan thought of the "lesson of the chairs." She had given it a name. Inside, she felt good, clean, and renewed. "Eva, I want to thank you for helping me yesterday. Not just with the painting, but for helping me understand forgiveness and redemption. I've heard those words so many times in church and at school, but now I feel them. I know them."

Eva wrapped her arm around Susan's shoulders and gave her a side hug. "I'm glad I could help. Remember, always keep searching for answers. Be open. There are lessons all around us. Live with your questions until the answers come."

The profound words lingered in the air, which was still pleasantly warm even in late November. The bus roared into the parking lot and pulled to a stop right on schedule. Ruthie was one of the first passengers off. She looked surprisingly rested after spending the night on a bus. "I think I figured it out," she said when Eva noted her appearance. "I sat near the front and fell asleep early with the help of a dose of melatonin. Or maybe it's because I was alone, and

Susan's talking didn't keep me up all hours." Ruthie belly-laughed at her joke, as she often did.

Susan hugged her. "I missed you. But for the record, it was *you* who kept *me* awake on the last trip. Anyway, I'm glad you came back. I was worried you'd stay in Ohio."

"No way!" Ruthie said. "It's snaining up there."

Susan envisioned the wintry blend of snow and rain that caused so much misery.

"None of that here," she said. "Just another day in paradise."

They ate lunch at Eva's, and while they were eating, Eva brought her laptop to the table and played a "trash to treasure" video about painting chairs with chalk paint. "Ours look a lot better than the ones in the video," Susan said. "Much more colorful—you should see them. They're blue, yellow, green, and even orange."

"Make that coral," Eva added. "I've been rethinking the seat coverings. I might go with a tropical print if I can find the right colors."

Susan wasn't quite sure, and Ruthie hadn't even seen the new colors, but both nodded in agreement. They understood Eva might change her mind several times before choosing the perfect design.

"I'm a messy painter," Ruthie said. "I'm going to put on my oldest dress if we're going to be painting." She glanced at the computer, where the video had come to an end on the screen. "And, whatever you do, when we're painting the chairs, Eva, don't you dare make a video of me."

Eva laughed and looked back and forth between the two young women. "You two! What would I do without you?"

"You need us," Ruthie said. "And now you have both of us."

Susan felt the weight of her former job lift off her shoulders as she thought about the fun the three of them would have working together at Saw Grass Inn. Her time there with Eva had been more like play than work. And it sounded like there was more fun ahead.

On the way back to the inn, Ruthie shared the news from Benville. She blushed slightly when she casually mentioned that Ben Keim had returned home from Vermont for the holiday from his internship at an organic farm. "He came over to visit my *Daett* and get some advice about draft horses, equipment, and such," Ruthie said.

"Are you sure he didn't come over to see *you?*" Susan asked with a tease in her voice.

"I'm sure he didn't even know I was home until he came through the door. But he did ask about you. I went with him to the plow parts shop, and then he took me for a coffee. But don't get any ideas," Ruthie added. "We're just friends."

Susan let the subject go, but she was sure Ben had his eye on Ruthie and that they had exchanged phone numbers. Ruthie and Ben wouldn't be the first Amish couple to find each other only after leaving home to explore the world.

Ruthie, it turned out, had painted furniture before, but never in the colors Eva had chosen for these chairs. The afternoon flew by quickly with all three women sanding and painting the remaining dozen or so chairs, pairing them up, and choosing colors for each pair.

To improve their workflow, they set up an assembly line. Eva smoothed out the rough spots with her mouse sander, then wiped down the chairs. Susan carried them across the room and applied the first coat, followed by Ruthie adding a second coat of paint. Midway through the afternoon, they took a break to drink tea and wait for the paint to dry. Later, Eva played music from a small speaker attached to her phone, and the three women worked together, distressing the chairs with sandpaper and applying a wax glaze.

Susan's mind drifted to the days ahead when she would be at the inn with these two women. Why did she once resist working here? She'd given up her dreams of working in a restaurant—unless one day she could work in the dining room at Saw Grass Inn. But that was still a long way off, and Eva had other plans for her in the meantime.

By late afternoon, they were tired and dirty but finished. They put lids on the leftover paint and dropped the sticky nylon brushes into a container of water to soak. "Let's go home," Eva said. "I'm going to have a pizza delivered. I'm too tired to cook and too dirty to even go inside somewhere to pick one up on the way home."

On Saturday, they did their usual chores. While Eva made a list and went to buy groceries, Susan and Ruthie cleaned the entire house and did their laundry. In the afternoon, they went down to Pinecraft and got ice cream cones. Then they walked back to the park to watch people playing shuffleboard. Most of the lanes were occupied by gray-haired men, but two nearest to the fence had a sign above them saying they were reserved for women, and those playing appeared to be only slightly younger than the men in the other lanes.

An older man wearing an Amish hat and a short-sleeved button-down rode up on a bicycle and stopped beside the fence. He hooked his thumbs under his suspenders as he watched the competition. "Do you want to play?"

Ruthie was quick with a witty reply. "Goodness no. We're far too young to play shuffleboard," she said.

"Might be right," the man said. "Say, I haven't seen you two around here before, but you're welcome to come to church tomorrow. Visitors are always welcome at Harvest Home Church." He handed each of them a small card with the address and times. "We had a revival last week. Good meetings. And souls won for Christ."

"I went to one of those meetings," Susan said. "I know where it is. Right on Bahia Vista Street. Thanks for inviting us. We might come tomorrow."

"Wonderful! Wonderful! I'll look for you." The man pedaled away on his bicycle, and Ruthie shot Susan an incredulous look.

"You went to a revival meeting?" she asked. "By yourself?"

"I did." The feelings from that evening still overwhelmed her. The loneliness. The guilt and shame that troubled her during the invitation song.

"I don't think I've ever gone anywhere entirely by myself. I didn't know anyone there. It was a long meeting. But you were in Ohio, and Eva had dinner with some friends. I didn't have anything to do, so I went for a walk. And the next thing I knew, I was in the church. They had good singing."

When she reached the last part, Susan remembered the song leader—his black, shiny hair, his strong voice, and his presence. She thought about the rush of feelings and the confusion during that final song. Even now, it still made her feel queasy.

"They had a time at the end when you could walk up to the front, and they'd pray for you. I almost did that, but I chickened out." It sounded different when she explained it to Ruthie. Not as fraught with anxiety and guilt. Ruthie just nodded her head in agreement, as if to affirm Susan's decision.

"We could probably go on Sunday. Do you think we should?"

"My parents asked me if we were going to church while we're in Florida. I know they want me to," Ruthie said. "I guess we should. Don't you think? It'd be easier if we went together."

"Sure, let's go. Maybe the same song leader will be there, and you can check him out," Susan said.

"Sounds like you're the one who wants to check him out," Ruthie said.

The evening ended with a long game of Chase the Rat. Eva was excited to learn that both Susan and Ruthie had played and enjoyed it. "No one seems to play this anymore," Eva said. She took out the polished wooden board with the familiar indentations, and Ruthie and Susan sorted the marbles into color groups.

"Caleb made this board for me a long time ago. It was one of his first gifts to me. Playing with it again feels like old times. I'd almost forgotten about it."

"My Aunt Fannie sold these boards in her quilt shop after she started selling toys and games," Susan said. "I used to help her at the store whenever she needed me."

By 9:30, Eva had clearly won several rounds and announced that it was her bedtime.

"We need to turn in, too," Ruthie said. "Susan and I are going to Harvest Home Church tomorrow morning."

"I'm glad you're doing that," Eva said. "Of course, you're welcome to come to the Mennonite church with me anytime."

"Thanks for the offer," Susan said. "But a man over at Pinecraft Park invited us, and we told him we'd be there this week."

"Susan has her eye on a guy she saw over there," Ruthie blurted out.

Susan blushed and punched Ruthie's arm. "What do you know about anything?" she said.

Eva looked back and forth between them. "You girls! I'll let you two put the board away now. Unless you want to play again tomorrow afternoon."

The next morning, Susan put on her favorite dress. The pale blue fabric was soft and silky and the pleats in the skirt draped more smoothly than in most of her other dresses. Ruthie wore her favorite dress as well, a rose-colored one that highlighted her dark hair. When they were ready, they walked to church, where they were greeted by the man they had met at the park and his wife, who stood beside him near the door. Susan and Ruthie found a seat halfway up on the left side. "Is he here?" Ruthie nudged Susan just before the first song. "Is that him?"

Susan frowned. The song leader who stood to lead the first hymns was at least three decades older than the one she'd seen at the revival meeting.

"Nope," she whispered. "I don't see him anywhere."

Susan had already methodically studied the benches on the opposite side of the room, hoping to see the young man with the crow feather hair. But he wasn't there.

Monday morning at nine o'clock, the EdenKeepers trucks caravanned down the winding lane and parked in the circular driveway of Saw Grass Inn. The parade was led by a gigantic green dump truck, followed by a muddy pickup pulling a low trailer equipped with two small but sturdy-looking tractors, a miniature front-end loader, and a skid steer. Susan recognized all the equipment on the trailer from her time with Amos, who had worked on a construction crew.

The last truck in the lineup was an extended-cab pickup. Racks mounted on the truck bed held weed whackers and various dangerous-looking gas-powered tools. Workers stepped out of the truck and began removing some of the tools and a couple of chainsaws in orange cases. They lined up everything on the porch, against the side of the inn. Two men dropped a ramp from the trailer and started unloading the small tractors. One by one, they started them up and backed them down onto the driveway, parking them under a large, long-leaf pine in the side yard.

Eva, Susan, and Ruthie stood staring at the crew and the impressive array of equipment. The two acres of land next to the Celery Fields were overgrown with palmetto and vines, a jungle of useless overgrowth that would need clearing out as a first step.

"Goodness!" Susan said. "Did you know they were bringing all this?" Eva turned to her with a look Susan interpreted as dismay.

Before she could say anything, a tanned, muscular man approached them and extended his hand to Eva. "Good morning. I'm Jeff from EdenKeepers. I hope you're ready for us. I brought the whole crew this morning." Susan noticed that Jeff's workers wore faded jeans or khaki cargo shorts, but everyone had crisp, emerald green work shirts with the EdenKeepers logo—a yellow sunburst with a lime green palm frond sprouting from the center.

"Oh yes, we've been waiting for you. I reviewed the information provided by the wildlife conservation agency. I wish I knew more about native plants, but I guess that's why we hired you. It's a big undertaking." She paused to watch as the crew backed a small tractor off the trailer. "That's a lot of equipment."

"We won't use all this today," Jeff said, "but as we discussed earlier, we'll need to remove any plants listed as noxious weeds by the Federal government—invasives like turkey berry, two-leaf nightshade, and so on. If this is similar to the other re-wilding projects we've done, we'll need most of this eventually."

"This is such a mess. It hasn't been cared for in years." Eva pointed to the jungle that took over the area just beyond the inn's circular driveway.

"We'll park this dump truck somewhere convenient so we can haul off the stuff we're pulling out. Today, most of us will leave to finish our other job. My naturalist buddy, Luke, will stay here and assess the area. He'll tag plants we're removing—the invasives. Once the plants are tagged, I'll bring in the whole crew to rip out the overgrowth, and then we'll reintroduce the native species. It's a process, but the goal is to restore the area to its natural state before people changed it."

"What time frame are we looking at?" Eva asked.

"We should be finished in about ten days," Jeff said. "Will you be available to walk through the property with Luke so he can explain how this will work?"

"I plan to be around all week during working hours," Eva said. "Unfortunately, I've got a lot going on here. As I mentioned to you when we talked before, I'm going to put Susan on this project." Eva gave Susan a pat on the shoulder, and Jeff smiled at her. "She's worked in gardens back in Ohio and will be available to help with errands. She's going to keep me updated as you proceed."

Susan gulped. This situation was more than she had expected. *Maemm's* vegetable garden back home, bordered by a couple of rows of marigolds, was easy to maintain with just a few hand tools and a small rototiller.

Jeff seemed fine with Susan serving as Eva's liaison. "That's quite okay, Eva. Today might be a bit slow, but once we get going, Susan," he turned to her, "I can bring release forms for you to sign. That way, if you're willing, you can feel free to jump in and help with pulling and later with planting."

"My employees are covered under my policy," Eva said. She turned to Susan. "Are you okay with helping out with some of the grunt work?"

"Sure. I guess so. Whatever you need me to do."

Jeff's tanned skin puckered around his blue eyes, shaded by a wide-brimmed safari hat. "I hope you have a pair of tough gloves. You're going to need them."

The driver of the dump truck walked toward them. He wore tan canvas work pants and heavy lug-soled work boots. He, too, wore a khaki-colored safari hat, but his long strides and swagger suggested he was younger than Jeff.

"Luke, my man," Jeff said. "Come over here. Meet your new boss."

Luke joined the circle, and Susan got a clear look at his face. She stifled a gasp as Jeff kept making introductions. Her knees felt unsteady, and the sun shining down on them suddenly felt too hot for the start of a workday. Luke nodded politely to Susan and Eva, who then introduced Ruthie.

Susan would have remembered this face anywhere, but Luke, the song leader from the revival meeting, looked at her without recognition. After all, she'd sat in the back corner that night and left before the meeting ended.

Now, just to be sure she wasn't dreaming, she looked again. She'd memorized his face the night of the revival. She would recognize that crow feather hair anywhere. At that moment, as the introductions finished, Luke removed his hat. "Pleased to meet you." His dark eyes seemed to change, deepen, for a moment as palm branches swayed and the sun filtered through. He nodded casually as if his mind was elsewhere, but his words perfectly expressed Susan's thoughts about her new job. "Looks like this is going to be a great place to work for a week or two."

CHAPTER 16

Eva's cell phone rang, and she gestured to those nearby. "Sorry, I need to take this." She answered her phone while waving goodbye to Jeff, who turned and headed for his truck. That was a signal to the crew, and before long, Susan was left standing a few feet away from Luke. She took a step back and glared at Ruthie as if to say, "What's Eva thinking, leaving me alone with this guy?"

Ruthie wandered off, leaving a nervous Susan to handle things alone.

"Guess it's just us then today, huh?" Luke looked her over, as if he was a bit puzzled by her appearance—the light pink home-sewn dress, simple blue kerchief covering her hair, and sturdy brown flip flops. Susan felt self-conscious and brushed a stray hair from her forehead. Luke's shoulders squared as he turned toward her, and Susan's heart skipped a beat when she noticed hints of a muscular body beneath his emerald green shirt.

"So, how do you like working for Eva Good?" he asked.

"I haven't worked for her very long, but she's a very kind woman. She's related to my friend Ruthie. We came from Ohio for the winter, and she's letting us stay with her."

Luke smiled. "I feel like I've known her forever. For my first job, I worked in construction with her husband, Caleb," Luke said. "Back before I got my job with EdenKeepers. Nice of her to duck out on us, huh?"

"Ummm, yeah. I guess...." She realized too late that he was joking. She took in his tanned forearms, his square jaw, and his dark chocolate eyes. She crossed her arms, hugging herself to feel less vulnerable.

"This is something," Luke said, gesturing toward the inn and the land in front of them. "She's taken on a huge project." Luke paused, as if waiting for Susan to reply, but she couldn't think of anything smart. Her mind was in a jumble. *It's him, the song leader from the revival meeting. I'm going to be working with him. Can this really be happening?*

Luke continued. "I guess Eva wants you to learn about what we're doing on the property so you can keep things up between EdenKeepers' visits." He turned slightly and gestured a swath with his arm, indicating the area they'd be working in. "Once the area is cleaned out and we've reintroduced the natives, it's just a matter of watching the growth and keeping the invasives at bay." He took off his safari hat and brushed a clump of spiky black hair from his forehead, then clapped the hat back on.

Susan gaped, then managed a few words. "Eva," Susan stammered. "She...she, I don't know...." Her voice trailed off as her face reddened.

Luke nodded. "She's got her own ideas. Always has. Guess we have to humor her. Knowing her, she probably wants to cut down on landscaping costs. That would be Eva." He paused a moment. "Did she give you some boots, gloves? You could use some long sleeves, some pants underneath that dress. This is rough work." He looked at her closely, and Susan felt her face redden, as if she were half-naked, not just without boots and long sleeves.

"I'll go ask. Eva's probably off her phone by now," she said.

"Okay, see what you can find. I'll get my coveralls and the rattle can." Susan had no idea what he was talking about. It was a relief to have him send her inside to get protective gear. She made the errand last longer by going around the side of the inn and entering through the back door, giving herself time to gather her wits. She was quite sure Eva would be in the kitchen or dining room since that had been the focus of her attention the past few days.

Eva looked down from her perch on a ladder where she'd been using a razor blade in a metal holder to scrape a stubborn sticker off a tall window in the dining room.

"How's it going out there?" Eva asked. "Everything okay?"

"Yeah. I'm sorry to bother you," Susan said, "but Luke told me I need boots and stuff. I don't have anything like that here. What should I do?" Susan was having a self-confidence meltdown.

Eva descended the ladder. "I've got some boots you can probably wear. What's your shoe size?"

"Eight," Susan said.

"I thought we were about the same. Mine are eight-and-a-half. Of course. You're going to need something to protect your arms and legs from that jungle. I should have thought about that."

"You had a lot on your mind," Susan said.

Eva walked over to a shopping bag in the corner and rummaged through it. "I have a bag of thrift store clothes I brought for painting and such." She pulled out a wrinkled gray athletic shirt and a pair of leggings. "Maybe these will work in a pinch. What do you think? Will these fit? They aren't too thick; it's too hot to wear sweatpants on a day like today." She tossed the clothes to Susan, who caught them. "My gum boots are just inside the garage door. Use the socks inside them or they might rub and cause blisters."

In the empty kitchen, Susan pulled on leggings beneath her skirt and slipped her arms into the long-sleeved T-shirt that she tied around her waist. In the garage, she put on thick cotton socks and tall, sturdy rubber boots. She went back to Luke, who was dressed in khaki coveralls and tough construction boots. He glanced at Susan's outfit and smiled. "Well, you're not OSHA-approved, but that'll do in a pinch. But where's your machete?" Susan wasn't sure how to interpret his comment. Was he joking? She offered a weak smile and watched as he pulled a stake with a square green and white sign attached from the truck. He hammered it into the sandy soil at the edge of the jungle—Danger! Alligators and Snakes in the Area.

She shuddered and stepped back, her eyes wide with concern. "Is that for real?" she asked.

"Doubtful," he said. "But it keeps people out of our workspace. Honestly, I only saw one gator in the wild, and that was a baby in a conservation plot we cleared out a few months back. Confirmed our efforts to re-establish habitat, I guess." Luke stepped back a bit and cocked his head, admiring the sign.

"What about the other part, snakes?" Susan asked.

"Nothing to worry about here. If this were the Everglades, you wouldn't be following me into the swamp. Burmese pythons. But around here, we're more likely to see Eastern kingsnakes, rat snakes, or green and black water snakes—all harmless. You're not afraid of a harmless snake, are you?"

Susan thought about the nest of garter snakes she'd jumped away from when they slithered out from under the old well house back home. "My *Maemm* doesn't like snakes, but I guess we tolerate them. *Dawdi* told us they're a gardener's best friend."

"*Dawdi?* I haven't heard anyone use that word in a while. But *Dawdi's* right," Luke said. "They eat slugs and other pests, even small rodents. That old Bible story about the serpent—I think people go too far if they're chopping up a garter snake with their hoe. I'm an EdenKeeper. I'm not convinced that serpent was a snake."

"Maybe a serpent is something different?"

"I don't know. But whatever it was, I'm sure it wasn't a harmless, bug-eating, sun-loving snake like most I've encountered." Luke's dark eyes flashed as he grinned at Susan.

Luke opened the truck door and tossed in the mallet he'd used to put up the sign. He climbed up, grabbed the electronic tablet from its holder on the dashboard, and unplugged it. Then, he leaped down, landing firmly on both feet directly in front of her. "Before we get started, how about I give you a quick education on invasives?" He propped himself against the side of the dump truck, tapped the screen, and motioned for Susan to come closer.

She leaned in, catching a whiff of spruce and spearmint. They were both sweating in the midday heat and humidity. Susan's breath quickened as she felt the closeness of his body. He was a head taller than she was, and ruggedly handsome in a way that made it hard for her to focus on the screen.

Luke pulled up a website with pictures and descriptions of plants on the list of undesirables. "Without proper attention to growth, some plants can overtake an area. Often these are species that never belonged here in the first place," Luke said. "We call these 'invasive species' because they are prone to take over and choke out others that do belong here. Kinda like the Ohio tourists." Luke laughed. "Just kidding. You're fine. Glad you're here."

His joke made her feel more comfortable. She suspected he enjoyed showing off his plant knowledge. She was happy to listen. After all, she was trying to learn about Florida's plants and trees.

"We'll start with the trees," Luke said. "There are only a few types we eliminate, and we'll probably see just a couple of these on

Eva's property. I'm pretty sure I already saw melaleuca. That's no surprise since they're everywhere in this part of Florida. They take over the sawgrass marshes and disrupt water flow." Luke leaned in and held the screen closer so Susan could see pictures of the trees and close-up views of the leaves, flowers, and bark. It was hard to concentrate with him so close they were almost touching. He didn't seem to notice, though. "That's exactly what's happening here—obstruction of natural water movement." Susan read the description, stumbling mentally over the unfamiliar words.

"Commonly known as paperbark tea tree, or broadleaf paperbark, among other names such as punk tree, the melaleuca quinquenervia is a small- to medium-sized tree that belongs to the myrtle family. With its spreading branches, it can grow to seventy feet in height. Look for gray-green leaves that are egg-shaped and cream or white bottlebrush flowers in late spring to autumn."

Luke's face twisted into a scowl. "What a mess we've made here in Florida—really everywhere—by thinking we can change God's green earth with plants that have no business being here. Wrecking the ecosystem just because we want fancy ornamental plants in our gardens. There are so many thoughtless people doing what they call 'landscaping.' And decades ago, someone brought in a plant from Australia or Malaysia because they wanted a fast-growing timber crop or a good windbreak."

Susan recognized a hint of the spirit she had seen when he was leading the revival singing. She felt a jolt of electricity as his energy filled the piney air between them. He scrolled through the list of other invasive trees with his index finger. "Brazilian Peppertree—red berries, watch out for Florida's version of poison ivy. Australian Pine. Sure, it's an evergreen but it doesn't belong here and will take over where the natives have been. The noxious camphor tree—toxic to animals and humans."

Susan looked at him, unsure of what to say or what would happen next. He snapped the tablet shut and quickly set it on the truck seat. Then he slammed the door.

"Okay. Enough of that already," he said. "Hands-on is always the best way to learn. Let's do some real field work." Luke strode toward the jungle, and Susan walked quickly to catch up, trying to match his pace. He pushed aside branches as Susan stepped into the wild, overgrown thicket. She took a few steps, and the sandy soil felt squishy beneath her feet. Luke kept walking until he reached a large tree casting a canopy of shade over them. When Susan caught up, he said, "Botany test: Do you recognize this one?"

Susan looked at the tree trunk and then up to the leaves, studying their shape. "I think it was in one of the pictures. I forgot the name. The one with the bottle brush flowers."

"You're right. This is a melaleuca. It's gotta go." Luke pulled an aerosol can from his coverall pocket and shook it vigorously. "Rattle can." He held it up. "When we find something that needs to be cut down, we mark it with this." He sprayed an orange stripe onto the tree trunk at eye level.

Susan trudged behind or alongside Luke as he methodically made his way through the brush. The heat intensified as the morning sun rose higher in the sky. Luke marked several trees with orange spray paint and instructed Susan when they encountered a native. "We have these at home," she said, pointing to a banana plant, "but they can't survive the winter outside."

"A lot of tropical plants are your favorite houseplants in cooler climates," Luke said. "I'm not opposed to tropical plants in Ohio if they stay indoors and in their pots. Outdoors, they'd never survive the winter."

"Back in Ohio, we like to plant a row of canna lilies beside the house. And those elephant ears? Our neighbor has a couple of them growing all summer on her porch."

"See, you know Florida plants." He nodded approvingly, then wiped his forehead with a red bandanna he pulled from his pocket. "Eva knew what she was doing when she gave you this job." His quick smile sent a little shiver of joy down her spine.

When they'd marked several trees for removal, they headed back to the truck for the spool of orange plastic ribbon they would use to mark shrubs that needed to be cut. Sweat dripped down Susan's back as she reached for the tape Luke cut into foot-long pieces. Before long, Susan was making her way through the jungle, evaluating plants and tying ribbons.

He recited a familiar rhyme as he bent over and tugged at a clump of green pushing through the sandy soil. "Sedges have edges, Rushes are round, Grasses have nodes all the way to the ground."

"I learned it differently," Susan said. She watched as Luke pulled a few blades from the clump. "We say: 'grasses have knees that bend to the ground.'"

"Or how about this one," Luke said. "Sedges have edges, rushes are round, and grasses have joints...even when cops are around." Susan recoiled at the mention of cops. The old guilt pressed up and she brushed it away.

Her eyes shifted back to Luke, who held up a green blade. "The 'knees' of grasses are joint-like nodes along the round, hollow stems. In this area, we're more likely to find rushes or sedges. Their stems are solid." He took a few steps forward, searching for more examples.

Susan bent down to look at another cluster. "Sedge," she said.

Luke walked a few paces and stopped. "Rushes," he said. "I don't know about you, but I'm ready to rush out of this jungle for a lunch break. What do you say?"

"It's plenty hot out here. I'd be ready to sit in the shade for a while," Susan said.

They walked side by side back to the lawn area where the dump truck was parked. Susan waited while Luke retrieved his lunch cooler from the cab. She looked down at the skirt of her pink dress, now streaked with dirt and green stains. Her feet felt hot and tight inside the bulky boots. She unknotted the long-sleeved T-shirt she had been wearing to protect against the jungle and quickly pulled it over her head.

"We could sit over there for lunch if you want," she said, pointing to the Adirondack chairs under the tall pine tree. "Eva usually has some lunch stuff for us in the fridge, so I'll grab something and meet you back here." She hurried off, as Luke settled into one of the chairs.

At the back entrance to the kitchen, she kicked off her boots and stuffed the damp socks inside. She found her flip-flops and went inside. "How was your morning?" Eva asked. "Did you learn a lot?" She grinned mischievously at Susan. "Here, I made you a sandwich. And you can take this pitcher of tea out to Luke." She pointed to a colorful pitcher sitting on the counter. "If you'll excuse me, I'm going to enjoy my new dining room while I eat my lunch."

Ruthie came in carrying a spray bottle and cleaning cloths. "I've been washing windows all morning. That should have burned a few calories," she exclaimed. She fixed herself a plate of cold meat and cheese topped with lettuce and tomato slices. She filled a glass with water and added a lemon wedge. Ruthie was on a new low-carb diet, avoiding bread and sugary drinks. "What's he like?" she stage-whispered, even though no one was around to hear them. "He's cute. Did he ask you out yet?" She bumped her hip against Susan's, then stepped back. "You have leaves in your hair. What have you been up to out there in that jungle?"

Susan gave her a big smile. "I think I finally found a job I like. And people I like working with." She didn't bother to whisper but smoothed the scarf covering her hair and brushed off a couple of small leaves that had stuck to it. "Do I look okay? I mean, except for these leggings?"

"You look great. I hope you don't mind if I eat inside today. Like they say, 'Two's company. Three's a crowd.'" Ruthie squeezed past her friend and headed for the dining room.

Susan grabbed a tray for the two glasses and the pitcher. She pushed her plate to the edge, trying not to think about the pie incident. That bad experience was behind her, and today, a handsome stranger had come into her life. Things were about to be different from now on.

Luke was scrolling through his phone and stood up when he saw her approaching with the tray. "Here, let me get that for you." He grabbed it and set it down on the ground between them. When he was seated, he poured each of them a glass of iced tea.

"Is it okay if I pray before we eat? Or maybe you'd like to pray."

Susan blushed at this unexpected suggestion. "No. That's okay. Of course, we should pray," she stammered. She bowed her head, and Luke reached over and placed his hand on hers, which was resting on the wide arm of the chair.

Susan felt her fingers tingle as Luke's voice filled the space between them. "Creator God, thank You for this beautiful world You've given us to enjoy. Forgive us for thoughtlessly spoiling it and taking it for granted. Bless our efforts to repair and restore it. Just now we also thank You for rest, for nourishing food, for fresh air, and for good company. May we be enriched and sustained by Your gifts as we strive to love as You love us. Amen." Luke pressed his palm gently into the back of Susan's hand before he withdrew it. They sat in silence for a bit until Luke reached down to open his cooler.

"I saw you at the revival meeting," Susan blurted out. "You were the song leader. Is that your church?"

"Oh, at Harvest Home, on Thanksgiving weekend? Were you there? I didn't see you," Luke said. "We had huge crowds there every night."

"I came into the church at the last minute and sat in the back corner. I left right away when it was over. I had never been to a revival meeting before. I was just curious, I guess. Ruthie and I went there last week, but I didn't see you. Were you there?"

"I was in the fellowship hall most of the time, setting up for a fellowship dinner. You should have stuck around a little. It's an interesting group, but not as many young people as I'd like. They got me into leading singing there, so yeah, it's my church. What about you? Are you—were you—Amish back in Ohio?"

"My family is Amish. I was raised Amish, but I haven't joined the church yet."

"That's okay, you know? When you're Amish, you get to choose. It's not like you're born into it and have to stay. It's believer's baptism, right?"

"Well, yes. I guess so. But there's pressure, even so. Maybe coming to Sarasota was my way of taking a break. Giving myself time to think, to decide." As she said it, Susan realized the truth about her Sarasota trip. Until now, she hadn't admitted that she was here for something other than escaping from Amos and all the trouble he'd caused her.

"It's a hard thing," Luke said. "I've dealt with it, too, but in the end, I couldn't completely give up on being part of the church. I'm not as conservative as my folks. They were raised Amish. I guess some would say they jumped the fence." Susan laughed. She recognized that expression from back home, and it told her Luke understood Amish life.

"For me, it's not about how I dress, whether I drive a car, or if I have a college degree. I like to think of myself as a follower of Jesus, which is what Caleb, Eva's husband, used to say about himself. It's more about how you live your life than about following a specific religion."

"I wish I had known Caleb. Eva talks about him a lot."

"They were a dynamic duo," Luke said. "I sure miss that guy. He helped me think about a lot of things, especially my spiritual life. We had some deep discussions about God and faith. But in the end, the Plain group at Harvest Home felt more comfortable to me than their Mennonite church. Most everyone at Harvest has some Amish or Mennonite background. Their focus on outreach and evangelism drew me in, I guess. And their singing. I've always enjoyed singing in parts. I learned it in my old youth group. Now, my parents have started coming to Harvest, too."

"I have so much to figure out," Susan said. "I guess it takes time." She liked how she and Luke discussed these things. That's what she'd always hoped to find in a man. Luke was a stark contrast to Amos.

"It's a process," Luke said. "Maybe you and Ruthie can come back to Harvest next Sunday. There's a group of us that has a potluck and talks about stuff. We'd love to have you join us."

Susan's heart raced at the thought of spending more time with Luke and meeting his church friends. "Thanks for the invite. I'll see what Ruthie thinks." She didn't want to sound too eager, but she was already thinking about a dessert she could bring to the potluck.

"Do you like chocolate?" Susan asked Luke. "I could bring a dessert to the potluck—Death by Chocolate."

"Sounds like a hit," Luke said. "But if you bring it, promise me you'll take the first bite." He looked at her sideways with that smile that already made her feel more at home than she'd ever felt here in Sarasota.

"I promise," Susan said.

CHAPTER 17

The next day, before leaving Eva's house, Susan found some garden clogs. She wore leggings under her dress and grabbed a hoodie to wear in case she had to work in the thicket again. Eva and her two helpers arrived at the inn for work shortly after eight.

"You can stay out here and watch for Luke and the crew. They should be here soon," Eva told Susan. "Luke will let you know what's on the agenda for today. They'll have things for you to do. But if not, you can start cleaning out these flower beds." Eva motioned to the weed-infested beds surrounding the inn.

After a brief wait, Luke arrived. "I came straight from home. Wanted to give you a heads-up about what's happening today." Susan greeted him and noticed he was driving a mud-splattered Jeep. Luke went around to the back of his truck and wrenched open the creaky window and tailgate. He was wearing a fresh EdenKeepers shirt and new-looking jeans with the same work boots. Susan's pulse skipped a beat as she watched him prepare for the day.

Luke shouldered a loop of heavy log chain and reached for a long-handled saw-blade trimmer. "I came to warn you that you'll have to stay clear of us today while we're in there yanking stuff out and hauling away the mess." Luke started walking to the edge of the jungle, and Susan strolled beside him. His thick black hair was slicked back neatly, revealing comb marks along the sides.

"I get it, I'll stay out of your way," she said. "Can I help with anything before the rest get here?"

"Yeah, thanks. Could you grab the hard hat in the truck? Also, the to-go coffee that's in there. Gotta have my coffee."

She'd hoped to do more than just fetch coffee. But if it meant lingering a bit longer, she'd carry his coffee. Besides, his hands were full, and he didn't send her away. He set the tools at the edge of the overgrowth and leaned against a longleaf pine. She handed him the coffee and placed the hard hat on the brown pine needles beneath their feet. The evergreen scent of morning hovered around them, signaling a new day. Everything seemed to shine in the morning sun. Quietness enveloped them. Susan reveled in the beauty of the morning. Did Luke see it, or was he thinking about the workday ahead of him?

As if he'd read her thoughts, he spoke. "I love this time of day. Everything is fresh and new." He took a deep breath and exhaled audibly, reinforcing the thoughts circling in Susan's mind.

Luke's voice grew quiet and reverent. "God is with us. With us right here at the start of this new day. That God-presence. Here." He spoke slowly, his words punctuated with pauses. They inhaled the earthy scent. Luke's dark chocolate eyes fixed on Susan's blue ones. She returned his gaze, a brief glimpse of what she'd hoped for someday—understanding, connection, something real and truthful, a spiritual bond. How easily Luke had guided her into God's presence on what had started as an ordinary day. She matched her breath to his and took in the wonder of it. And the wonder of Luke.

Just then, the EdenKeepers crew drove up the long driveway in their noisy trucks, and the sacred moment slipped out of their realm as quickly as it had come. Susan clung to the feeling, wishing it would last, trying to hold onto the memory for later.

Luke sensed it, too. "Coffee is cooled off now. I'd better drink it fast. Maybe I can catch you at lunch. I'll see what the guys are doing." His voice was clipped and had lost its reverent tone as he strained to speak above the noise of equipment being unloaded from the trailer.

"Okay, great," Susan said. She turned and headed for the inn, hoping that just like yesterday, he would join her for lunch under the pine tree.

"Get ready for some mayhem! Do you have earplugs?" Luke yelled after her.

"Have fun!" Susan shouted back. She covered her ears with her hands and grimaced. Jeff and a few other guys were walking towards her. She greeted them and then took one last quick look as the workers gathered to plan their strategy. The landscape at Saw Grass Inn would never be the same after today.

Susan approached the front entrance of the inn just as Eva stepped out onto the concrete slab. That concrete would soon be gone, too. It served as the old inn's patio and welcome mat, but Eva wanted a new hardscape terrace. The inn looked better each day as Ruthie and Eva polished the windows, and painting crews worked their magic. The kitchen had been completely remodeled and only needed boxes of cookware and utensils unpacked and stored away.

There was a lot of work inside, but Susan wanted to stay in sight of the crew, especially Luke. She grabbed the empty five-gallon bucket and a few garden tools left on the portico.

Eva stood beside the front door. "We still have cleanup around the inn foundation and in the center of the traffic circle. I take it you know what the bucket is for. You can dump your weed bucket over there on that pile near the truck. But stay clear of the crew. I doubt they want you out there with all that activity going on." She flung her arm in the general direction of the EdenKeepers' project.

"Luke mentioned that I won't be able to help. I'd probably be in the way."

"And we couldn't risk you getting hurt on the job. Let's do a walk around here, you and me. I think there are some plants in this chaos worth saving." She gestured toward the tangle of vegetation growing up against the outer walls of the portico and the inn itself. "We might keep a few of these but most of this mess will come out," Eva said.

"I'm still trying to figure out what's a plant and what's a Florida weed—an *invasive*—as Luke would say." Susan's face reddened at her mention of his name, but Eva didn't notice. She'd bent down to examine a shrub struggling to survive beneath an out-of-control sarsaparilla vine.

"I prefer hand-digging and pulling weeds over using weed killers. It's better for the environment," Eva said. "Your EdenKeeper out there would agree. How do you like working with Luke?" Eva asked.

Susan wondered whether to question the "your EdenKeeper" remark. But she also didn't want to take Eva's bait.

"From what I observed, you two were getting along fine yesterday. Did he tell you about his Ohio roots?" Eva asked.

Susan's eyes widened. "Ohio roots? No, I thought he was a Floridian. He mentioned that his parents were once Amish, and they live near Pinecraft."

"They do. Now. The whole family moved to Sarasota in the early 2000s. His father didn't have work in Ohio, but at the time, construction was booming in Sarasota. Luke's dad was a bricklayer, one of Caleb's regular contractors. That's how I first met Luke, but he was just a kid back then. When he was old enough to work, Luke joined one of Caleb's crews."

"What part of Ohio were they from?" Susan asked.

"I think it's somewhere in Holmes County or maybe Wayne County. I forget exactly. Even though I'm from the same general area, I'd never met them until they came to Florida." Susan held back the little quiver that went through her at the thought that he was an Ohio native. Their families could have once been neighbors or part of the same church district. But why did it matter?

Equipment in the nearby conservation area started up, forcing Eva and Susan to briefly shout back and forth while pointing at plants and examining root systems.

When they had finished circling the inn, they examined the center of the traffic circle. It featured a large concrete fountain overgrown with palm scrub, crabgrass, and weeds. After she assessed the mess, Eva left to handle other urgent tasks inside. She had recently announced plans for an open house on a weekend just before Christmas, which was now only eighteen days away.

Eva's absence and the monotonous task of pulling weeds with her trowel, shovel, and garden gloves gave her time to think, a habit she developed as a child helping in *Maemm's* vegetable garden. Here, the beds were overrun with crabgrass that had a spreading root system. When she loosened a clump, the sandy soil gave way, leaving a strip of cleared ground.

In Ohio, gardens were never allowed to become this unruly. Susan pictured the orderly rows of plants and the rich, bare soil between them. The perfect borders of marigolds and a wild display of zinnias caught the attention of both people and butterflies. Here, everything was chaotic and untamed. If left alone for a few months, the growth would overrun everything. But she didn't miss that predictable garden or the predictable life that went with it. More and more, Florida felt like home to her.

The whine of equipment stopped temporarily, and Susan

guessed that the EdenKeepers were taking a mid-morning break. She stood up and stretched her back. Using the motion to turn around, she strained for even a quick glimpse of Luke. Some of the men were walking to their vehicles, while others had dropped down in the shade. She couldn't spot Luke, so she entered the inn's front door and headed to the kitchen. A burst of cool air brushed against her face.

"There you are!" Ruthie exclaimed. "You're making quite a racket out there. Are you driving a backhoe or running the weed-whacker?"

"Neither," Susan said. "I'm clearing out the flower beds and foundation plantings this morning. What have you been up to?"

"I finished the last of the windows on the third floor. Now I'm going to give the kitchen a deep clean and start unpacking those boxes. I hope their dirt and dust doesn't mean I have to redo the windows," Ruthie said, gesturing to the outdoors.

"Here. Try this. It's cucumber water," Ruthie handed her a tall glass with a green slice at the bottom. To her credit, she was sticking with the diet and avoiding soft drinks altogether.

"I'll give it a try, if you say so." Susan took a few sips, then drank an entire glass. "Hey, did you know Luke is from Ohio, originally? Like, from our area?"

"Nope. What does that mean? You aren't about to write him off just because he's from back home, are you?"

"Probably not," Susan said with a mischievous smile. "Eva said the whole family moved here in the early 2000s. I had no idea. He knew we were from Ohio, yet he never said a word." Something tightened in her chest when she thought about him being from Ohio. She couldn't quite explain why, but it bothered her.

"That's great," Ruthie said. "I'm not that surprised, though. Pretty much any Amish person in Sarasota came from Ohio, Indiana, or Pennsylvania. You know that don't you?" Ruthie looked at her with a puzzled expression. "What's his last name? Do you even know it?"

"I think it's Rohrer. I remember it from church. When he led the singing," Susan said.

"I don't remember hearing that name much in Ohio."

"Me neither."

"You're in luck then. You can marry him. He's probably not your cousin," Ruthie said with a laugh.

Susan giggled. "He invited me to Harvest church again next Sunday. They have a potluck afterward. I think it's their young people's group. He invited me—us—to go to that, too. Should we go?"

"Of course we should go," Ruthie said. "I can bring a low-carb dish." Ruthie was taking this diet more seriously than Susan realized, even planning a potluck strategy for herself. "I told Luke I was going to bring Death by Chocolate," Susan said apologetically.

"Sure. Go ahead and ruin my diet. Why not?" Ruthie laughed her familiar, fake laugh, which no longer sounded fake.

"If you're trying to snag Luke, Death by Chocolate is just the thing," Ruthie said. "I'll even help you make it." Susan gave her a high five. Ruthie's comments made her feel hopeful about her prospects with Luke.

"Okay. You're on. I have to get back out there now. Break's over. I heard a chainsaw start up."

After another hour in the heat, Susan came inside and washed up. Ruthie and Eva were having Cobb salad and offered to share, but Susan wasn't in the mood for the physical effort of eating a bowl of lettuce.

She made a sandwich and scooped some mixed fruit into a large bowl. "We're in the dining room," Ruthie said. She carried a salad in each hand. "You can eat with us unless you have other plans."

"I'm heading outside. I like those Adirondack chairs under the big pine tree," Susan said. She didn't want to miss another potential lunch date with Luke. As she walked toward the chairs, she noticed the stillness that had settled over the Saw Grass Inn grounds. Luke's truck and one of the EdenKeepers pickups were making their way up the driveway—probably heading to a nearby restaurant or pizza joint.

Susan's heart sank. The thought of having another conversation with him over lunch had kept her going all morning, but now he'd left to eat with his crew. She'd either eat alone or go back inside with Ruthie and Eva. In the end, her need for conversation won out, so she took her sandwich and fruit to the dining room, expecting the banter about Luke that she knew Ruthie would throw her way. So be it. She could handle that.

"Oh, good. You're eating with us," Eva said. "I was hoping we could find time today to discuss the open house and what we need to do before the 20th. You girls better not have any big pre-holiday plans because I'm going to need you for every minute you can spare." She sounded worried, and her voice grew intense as she laid out all the work that still needed to be done. Susan's disappointment about not having lunch with Luke disappeared as Eva explained her plan.

They would serve a charcuterie board, whatever that was. "I was on the phone just before lunch, looking for a catering service that could do our open house. With the holidays upon us, I'm way behind. It's impossible to schedule it for only three weeks out. I found a bakery that can do fancy cupcakes, but we need something more. I don't want it to feel like an old-fashioned baby shower or something." She grimaced and stabbed at the remains of her Cobb salad with her fork.

"Susan could make Death by Chocolate," Ruthie said slyly. "She's planning to practice that one this weekend." Her laugh echoed throughout the large, empty dining room.

"Oh," Eva said. "That's yummy. But not what I have in mind for our open house. How do you make yours?"

Ruthie began listing ingredients. "Whipped cream, pudding, crushed candy bars, cake, syrup...."

Susan chimed in. "We make it in a trifle dish. Do you have one we can borrow, Eva?"

"Sure. I know exactly where it is, but I haven't used it in a while," Eva said.

"There you go, Susan. You've got the dish, and you don't even need to look up the recipe," Ruthie said.

"Back to our plans for the open house," Eva said. "I was thinking about taking one of our smaller refinished tables and turning the entire tabletop into a giant charcuterie board. What do you think?"

"I have no idea what a char...char....How do you say that word? What are you even talking about?"

"It's simple, really. I read somewhere that it's a French word meaning 'cooked meats.' It doesn't sound quite as elegant as 'charcuterie,' though, does it? We'd probably just call it a meat and cheese platter, or an artfully arranged snack tray." She picked up her phone. "Here, let me pull one up on Pinterest."

Just like before, when Eva showed them the chair painting demo, she found a video. "Ach! This is too small. Let me get my tablet." Eva took her plate to the kitchen and came back with her device. She started a video, and they watched a hostess preparing elegant skewers of tomato and mozzarella balls, pepperoni roses, and piles of olives, along with containers of fig jam, berries, and lots of fancy crackers, as well as cascading sliced meats.

Even though lunch was over and they had eaten enough, the three of them sat there drooling over the feast that gradually appeared before their eyes.

"What do you think? Would you two help me make this for the open house?"

"That doesn't look hard," Ruthie said. "I think we could handle that as long as you are here to help with it. What do you think, Susan?"

"I like that we can do it ahead and just put it there for the guests," Susan said. The image of herself juggling a large tray in a tiny restaurant kitchen flashed through her mind. "This might be a little harder than making Death by Chocolate, but it would definitely give Ruthie more diet options." Susan flashed Ruthie a big gotcha smile, and Ruthie gave her a thumbs up.

"Great!" Eva said. "I knew you girls would come through. We can talk more later. Now, let's go check the progress out there."

CHAPTER 18

Susan's muscles ached after two days of raking, digging, lugging pots and flats of new seedlings, and squatting to plant them. All the pain was worth it for the joy of working outdoors in the sun with Luke, who was becoming more sun-kissed each day they spent together. And Susan was, too.

Now it was late Thursday night, and Susan had trouble falling asleep. Ruthie was breathing softly in the twin bed on the other side of their small room. Susan's mind whirled with thoughts about Luke, repeating words he'd said, imagining his muscular body, his smile.... The cell phone beside her bed rang. She sat up quickly. *Maemm* was calling. It was late—close to midnight. Something was wrong at home.

Maemm called every week on Saturday with Benville news. So, this late-night call must be important. "Hello?" Susan answered, hoping she didn't sound too sleepy.

"Susan? Did I wake you up? I'm sorry. I know it's late. I was thinking about you and wondered what you've been doing. Also, I thought I should call and update you on *Dawdi.*"

Susan swallowed hard. "What's happened? Is something wrong?" She knew *Dawdi* had a serious heart condition. In fact, before going to Sarasota, she'd gone next door to his place and fixed his breakfast nearly every day. He always thanked her for helping him. Many days, he shared a Bible verse with her before she left to help *Maemm* or someone else in the family.

"We took him to the doctor today. He's had so much trouble breathing and he's not getting around well. We make sure someone looks in on him several times a day."

"What did the doctor say?" Susan asked.

"He has heart failure. We knew that a long time already. He's been taking all his medicine but there isn't any cure. On the way home, *Dawdi* was asking about you. He wondered if you're coming home for Christmas. He wants to see you. He might not live too much longer. We just don't know."

Susan absorbed *Maemm's* news. So far, she hadn't made plans for the Christmas holidays. She knew they expected her to come home, but she hadn't made any promises.

"I don't know what to do about Christmas. I think Ruthie has a ticket to come back for Old Christmas. That's when her big family gathering is. Maybe I'll ride back to Ohio with her." The January sixth date that some call Epiphany is a popular time for yet another Amish family get-together in the new year.

Susan thought about the upcoming open house at Saw Grass Inn. She wanted to help Eva with that and the inn's grand opening. Eva needed her to help prepare and serve the food. She hadn't mentioned all of this to *Maemm,* though.

"I'll try to come," Susan whispered, hoping not to awaken Ruthie. She got out of bed and took her phone into the bathroom.

Maemm continued. "It would be nice if you could come back for a week or two. Or maybe just come back home to stay. We do miss you; you know?" *Maemm's* voice softened.

Susan felt a surge of love when her mother declared it, even as her mind flashed back to recent conversations she and Ruthie had with Eva.

"I'm sorry. We've been so busy here. I have a lot to tell you. Eva's having a big open house at the inn. I helped with a lot of the outside work. This guy, Luke Rohrer from a landscape company, was helping me plant seedlings and learn how to take care of them." Susan's words tumbled out.

"Working in a garden. I see. That might be better for you than working in a restaurant. You like the outdoors. Who is this Luke, someone special? Is that why you aren't making plans to come home?" *Maemm's* intuition was accurate.

"No. Just busy. I do like the work better. It's a lot different than gardens back home, but it is outdoors. Luke's a nice guy. He goes to a Plain church down here. He's a song leader. I think you'd like him."

Susan hoped she had reassured *Maemm* that she was interested in someone other than Amos. The problem was, she and Luke hadn't gone on a date yet.

"It's so different here without snow or cold. You can almost forget about Christmas." Her excuse for not making Christmas plans sounded weak. "How bad is *Dawdi*?" Susan asked.

"He has his good days and his bad days. He gets these coughing fits. I was worried he might have Covid. But the doctor said it's common for people with his condition to cough like that. Do you think you'll come? The bus runs a couple of times a week. *Daett* and I could pay for your ticket."

"No. That's not a problem. I have a good job with Eva. We have a big open house at the inn right before Christmas. She needs our help with it." As soon as she said that she felt guilty. Seeing *Dawdi* before he went to heaven should mean a lot more than her job or Luke. And Eva would understand if she had to go home.

She could hear *Maemm* breathing on the other end, as if trying to measure her words for the best effect.

Susan kept going. "I'll figure something out. Maybe I'll come at New Year's, when Ruthie comes. I do miss *Dawdi*—everyone really." Susan meant it when she said that.

"There are all the usual dinners and gatherings planned here. Family get-togethers. It would be nice to have you home before New Year's if you can make it."

The guilt intensified. Susan had learned to be an obedient daughter. To her credit, *Maemm* was doing her best to respect Susan's independence as an adult. She'd stopped short of demanding Susan come for Christmas.

Here in the sunshine, she could almost forget everything—the cozy Benville community where everyone knew, or thought they knew, what everyone else was doing. The weight of responsibility that pulled you into baking pies and caring for your elders. The loneliness you feel when you wish you were married but aren't.

"I'll talk to Ruthie, *Maemm,* and let you know. I do want to see *Dawdi*. Tell him I said hello. Tell him I miss him."

"Okay. I will. You let us know when to expect you. We love you and miss you."

"I love you, too," Susan said. She ended the call.

Susan stood in the bathroom, examining her tanned face in the mirror. It was late, and she was exhausted. Would going home take away precious time she could spend with Luke? She was just starting to get to know him. But *Dawdi* was dying, and he wanted to see her. She walked back down the hall to the bedroom.

"Susan?" Ruthie's whisper came from across the room. "Is everything okay? What's going on?"

"*Dawdi* isn't doing well and is asking for me. *Maemm* wants me to come home for Christmas."

"So, are you going?" Ruthie was fully awake now, but she continued to whisper.

Susan sat on the edge of her bed. "I know I should. It's just that...." Her voice trailed off. It was difficult to express her feelings.

Susan sighed. "But we promised Eva we'd help with the open house."

"Eva would understand. You know that. I get it, though, you and Luke are getting close. This is bad timing."

"Let's sleep on it and talk about it tomorrow." Susan yawned.

"Maybe it's not as bad as you think. We'll figure something out," Ruthie said. "Good night."

"Good night." Susan crawled under the covers and tried to stay calm, but questions raced through her mind. Why did *Dawdi* have to be getting worse now? Just when she thought she might have a chance with Luke.

———————

Worries about *Dawdi* kept running through her mind on Friday. She and Luke sat on the porch together during a brief rain shower, but Susan didn't tell him about *Maemm's* call. The Eden-Keepers project was nearly finished, and Luke would move on to the company's next project. Susan didn't want to ruin her last day working with Luke by discussing things happening in Ohio.

Luke and Susan had planted all the native seedlings, carefully watering and mulching them to give them the best start possible. They had fallen into a smooth rhythm. Luke marked sites for different varieties and dug holes for the larger shrubs. Susan scattered natural fertilizer into the holes. Luke placed the plants and covered the root balls with dirt while Susan prepared another bag of mulch. Luke was easy to work with. The first day's jitters had worn off as Susan joined him in cleaning up after removing the old plants. They raked and talked. Sometimes, they remained silent, and Susan felt no need to fill the silence. At noon, they stopped for lunch and sat under the pine tree, eating together.

"I guess this is my last day here," Luke said. "After this, you're on your own. Do you think you can handle it?" He gave Susan his sideways smile that made her heart flip-flop.

"I'll try. If there's trouble, I know who to call," she shot back.

"Seriously, try to check the new plants every day or two. If you notice something isn't thriving, give me a call. I'll stop by at the end of the day. Be sure to keep them watered if there's no rain. We needed that morning shower, but a good soaking would be even better." They stood together, surveying the area that had been nearly razed in some spots and then replanted with young seedlings, freshly mulched and watered.

"I hope Eva doesn't keep me too busy inside. She has so much to finish up before the open house. Do you think you'll come?"

"I don't know. Is she serving food?" Luke grinned.

"Of course she is. But don't tell me you're just coming for the free food."

"Well, maybe not *just* the food." Luke flashed a smile and pushed a lock of black hair from his forehead.

Susan would miss their lunch breaks, the banter, and the rhythms of working with him. Yesterday, he gave her a small lesson on pruning as they worked on the evergreens planted along the foundation of the inn. Then they added new plants around the edges of the stone patio. They even planted a large pot with herbs that Eva's chef could use in cooking. And the fountain in the traffic circle was working again, thanks to an EdenKeepers staff member.

At breakfast on Saturday, Susan told Eva about *Dawdi*. Eva looked concerned. "Thanks for telling me. I'll be sure to put it on the prayer chain at church," she said. "It's good that Christmas is coming. I imagine you'll want to go home to see him. And you, too, Ruthie. Your parents surely want you home for the holidays." Susan and Ruthie nodded their agreement, but inside, Susan wished she didn't have to think about going back to Ohio, which would remind her of everything she wanted to forget.

"I was planning to go to Ohio for New Year's and stay for Old Christmas. We have a big gathering with all my cousins on the sixth," Ruthie said.

"You two can travel together," Eva said. She looked back and forth between the two young women who had become like daughters to her by now. "What do you think, Susan?" Eva asked. "How sick is he? Do you think you need to go home right away, or can you wait a little longer? I wanted to take you to our church's Christmas Eve service. It's by candlelight, I'm in the choir, and it's always so beautiful. I'd love for you to experience it with me."

"I think I can postpone going a little longer," Susan said. "It's only a few more days. I'd rather travel with Ruthie." She pushed aside thoughts of *Dawdi*. She wanted to stay in Sarasota as long as possible.

With breakfast finished and a few holiday plans settled, the three women at Eva's house quickly took care of the house chores. Ruthie was an efficient cleaner, and Susan handled the laundry. Eva offered to buy supplies the girls would need for their potluck dishes, but they declined, preferring to do their own shopping.

They walked to the small grocery store and bought all the ingredients for their contributions to the potluck, which was scheduled right after the church service on Sunday. Eva had already found a fancy glass bowl on a high shelf. It sat on the countertop, waiting to be filled with Death by Chocolate. Ruthie's dish would be a mixture of chicken breast and low-calorie vegetables that she was allowed to eat on her diet. "We'll help each other make both dishes," Susan told Ruthie. She suspected that Ruthie might be jealous of Luke. Even though they were both working at the inn, they had barely seen each other.

On Sunday morning, they packed their dishes for the noon potluck into an insulated carrier. Ruthie's dish could be reheated in the oven. "It's going to be a challenge to carry this to Harvest Church," Ruthie said. "Be careful not to spill my dish. It wouldn't look good to have tomato juice all over your dessert topping." She laughed at the thought, and Susan grimaced.

Eva came out of her room ready for church, wearing a floral dress with a long skirt and a sweater over it. Her hair and makeup were done, unlike her usual simple look when she worked at the inn. Susan and Ruthie had also spent time getting ready. Susan wore a favorite deep red dress that fit her perfectly and flattered her newly acquired tan. Ruthie's bright pink dress had a subtle sheen that flattered her fairer complexion.

"Let me drop you off at Harvest," Eva said. "It's too far to walk with your potluck dishes, Bibles, purses, and all. It's on my way to the Mennonite church."

When they arrived at Harvest Home, they noticed a couple of young women carrying picnic baskets into the side door near the back of the brick building. "Looks like we should take our food in there," Ruthie said.

In the kitchen, a woman was organizing the potluck. She greeted them. "Hi! I'm Mary Rohrer. These must be for the young people's potluck." She put Susan's dessert in the fridge and popped Ruthie's dish into the oven. "You're new here, aren't you?"

"We've only been here a couple of times," Susan answered. "Are you possibly related to Luke? He's the one who invited us to the young people's potluck."

"Oh my, yes. I'm his mother. I agreed to help him set up today," she paused. "Now I realize who you two are. The girls from Ohio who are staying at Eva's place, right?" Her smile broadened as she made the connection.

"Yes, that's us. We're working at the Saw Grass Inn, helping her get it ready for the grand opening."

"I'll take care of serving your dishes. Now, if you go through that door," she pointed toward a hallway, "it will take you to the front of the sanctuary." Mary glanced at the clock. "The service hasn't started yet."

As they entered the door, an older man, the minister, recognized them from before and greeted them with a firm handshake. They walked down the center aisle and sat on a bench where two young women, who looked about their age, sat on the opposite end.

Susan looked for Luke and saw him sitting with his back to her on the opposite side. She studied the women in front of them. They wore plain dresses and head coverings, but they were of different types. Some had a small lace circle or a sheer white lace-edged oblong secured with white bobby pins. She recognized a couple of Lancaster Amish head coverings. One woman had a small strip of brown lace that blended into her hair, which she wore twisted into a bun. Susan and Ruthie wore their Ohio Amish coverings made of stiffened voile and shaped into a bonnet style by a multitude of tiny pleats. Despite the differences, the coverings and dresses set them apart as members of a Plain community. Some of the men, like Luke, wore store-bought shirts and pants. Others wore homemade black vests or had haircuts and beards that identified them as members of an Amish church.

Luke stood to open the service. "Everyone is welcome at Harvest Home. We're glad you're here to worship. Let's begin with some singing," Luke announced the number of the first hymn. He looked handsome in a pristine white button-down shirt open at the neck. He used a pitch pipe to find the right key and hummed the starting notes for the four parts. He directed as if he were leading a choir, using his entire body to keep the time. Susan's soprano blended easily with Ruthie's alto as they sang.

I'm pressing on the upward way, new heights I'm gaining every day.

Still praying as I'm onward bound, Lord, plant my feet on higher ground.

When they came to the refrain, Susan dared to look directly at Luke. His dark eyes lifted from the hymnal and held her glance.

Lord, lift me up, and let me stand, by faith on heaven's table land, a higher plane, than I have found, Lord plant my feet on higher ground.

Susan's heart pounded as her voice soared heavenward. She felt the hymn in every fiber. After the darkness of her recent past and the hours working the soil outdoors, she felt grounded. She'd come through the worst and was finally here in a place where she knew she belonged.

The service was lengthy, lasting nearly two hours. After the singing ended, there were announcements, prayer and sharing time, and an offering where they passed a basket down the rows of pews. One last song preceded a sermon that was just as long as one in an Amish church back home. Susan felt herself growing sleepy in the warmth and contentment of the morning. She tried to focus, but her mind was on Luke and the upcoming potluck, where she hoped they would sit together and talk. She was also eager to meet the other young people. It had been a while since she felt at home among peers, and Harvest Home filled that void.

People mingled after the church service, greeting each other and standing in small groups, talking. The two girls at the other end of the bench approached and introduced themselves. They invited them to the young people's potluck, and Susan and Ruthie assured them they planned to stay. "Susan made Death by Chocolate," Ruthie announced. "You have to try it. It's heavenly!" She laughed at her joke, and the two young women laughed with her.

In the fellowship hall behind the sanctuary, Mary was joined by Luke's father. "Susan and Ruthie, I'd like you to meet my husband, Richard," she said. "He usually helps me in the kitchen on potluck Sundays." Mary and Richard arranged the food on a countertop with a window that opened into the kitchen. The gathering room was simple, with tan vinyl floor tiles, pale blue walls, and white mini blinds at the windows. A circle of chairs had been set up at one end. Not far from the counter where the buffet was placed, several long, folding tables were pushed together, with chairs on each side.

Luke's mom had poured glasses of lemonade and made a pot of coffee. When everything was ready, they stood in a circle, and Luke led them in a grace that they sang together. Susan didn't know the words but recognized the tune.

The young people weren't shy about filling their plates with everything available. There was quite a variety of noodle casseroles, Mexican rice and beans, a slow cooker filled with meatballs, fresh vegetables and salads, and another entire section of desserts.

"Look at those desserts," Ruthie said to Susan. "Peach pie, brownies, German chocolate cake. Plates of cookies and bars."

"Don't you dare break your diet. You're doing so well," Susan told Ruthie.

"Cheat day," Ruthie said slyly. "I'm allowed a cheat day, but I'll go easy and just have a taste of one or two."

Luke was standing directly in front of them in line. He headed straight for Death by Chocolate and piled his plate high with the creamy, gooey sweetness. Ruthie noticed it first and nudged Susan with her elbow while Luke's back was turned. By the time most people had filled their plates, Susan's dessert bowl was nearly empty.

"Looks like all you have left is a Mennonite morsel," one of their new friends said. "Your dessert was a success. Of course, no one ever finishes it off. They're too polite to take that last piece."

Luke hadn't started on the main course, but he scooped up a big spoonful of Susan's dessert. "This is awesome," Luke said. "Bring this to every potluck from now on." The group around the table chatted casually as they ate. Most of the young men went back for seconds.

When the dishes were cleared and everyone had their fill, Luke's parents closed the kitchen window and began cleaning up. Luke invited everyone to join him in a circle of chairs across the room. Once everyone was settled, he said, "At Harvest Home, we come from different places and traditions, but we are all one in the Spirit. We started this potluck to give young people a place to connect with others who are visiting or have moved here permanently. This is our biggest potluck yet."

He looked around the circle as if counting. "Eighteen here today. At least five of you are new. Welcome," Luke said. "We hope you'll feel at home with us and come back. We meet for potluck once a month to share prayer concerns, update each other, and, of course, eat together. We understand the importance of community.

This is a place of support for you as we gather as friends and learn to know Jesus."

They went around the circle and introduced themselves, sharing background details such as where they lived or worked, whether they were visiting, or if they attended Harvest regularly. Susan fidgeted as she waited for her turn. She wasn't used to speaking to a group and anxiously rehearsed in her mind what to say. In the end, her introduction came out a bit flustered and garbled, but she managed to tell everyone her name, that she was here from Ohio for the winter, and that she was working at Saw Grass Inn, which was being renovated by Eva Good. Ruthie then introduced herself and also mentioned that everyone was welcome at the open house, which was now a little more than a week away.

When the introductions were over, Luke said, "I think this is the start of something good. We've been meeting for a few months now, and this is the biggest crowd we've had yet. We plan to start a young people's Bible study, so I hope you'll continue coming to Harvest Home. Consider this group your home away from home." He flashed a big grin toward Susan. She blushed and smoothed her skirt.

"Now that we all know a little about each other, I hope you feel comfortable sharing your prayer concerns with the group. We believe that praying together can bring hope and healing to our lives and the lives of others. Feel free to share your personal requests as well as concerns for family members or friends you've met at work. Who wants to go first?"

The circle of people grew silent. They lowered their eyes, and Susan wondered if the prayer had already started, or if they were just shy. Then a young man, Thomas, shared a concern for a coworker who had fallen from a ladder and was recovering from a broken femur and a dislocated shoulder. A woman asked for prayer for her young brother, who was recently diagnosed with cancer back in Indiana. Susan thought of *Maemm's* late-night phone call. Should she ask for prayers for *Dawdi?* She held back, waiting to see who else would share.

There was silence for a bit, and Susan took a deep breath. If Eva's group was praying for *Dawdi* surely Susan could share her concern with this group of new friends.

"My mother called late last night saying that *Dawdi*, my grandfather, isn't doing well. He's elderly and has heart failure, and they're concerned he might not live long." She paused and then added, "I'm concerned about him. I worry I won't see him again if I don't go home soon, but I've also got a life here now. I don't know what to do."

As he'd done after each request, Luke responded. "We know *Dawdi* is in God's care. He's being held in the palm of God's hand." He cupped his hands and looked at them. Susan's eyes rested on those hands that had become so familiar to her over the past week. She even knew why there was a bandage on his right thumb. Luke continued, "And God is holding you, as well."

Susan felt a lump rise in her throat. She fought back the emotion and tears that threatened to spill over. Susan looked at him across the circle. "Thank you," she said.

The group was silent for a moment. "Are there any others who would like to share?" No one spoke. As if it were an afterthought, Luke said, "We'll soon go to prayer, but before we do, I'd like to share a request. On Friday afternoon, my mom received a call from my uncle back in Ohio. My aunt Jane, mom's sister, was admitted to a mental health facility this week. She's been suffering from severe depression for weeks after losing her son. He was my favorite little cousin, Ray. He had a heart condition and he died of alcohol poisoning at a country music festival in Ashland County last fall."

Susan felt lightheaded and sick to her stomach. Luke's voice continued, completely unaware of the wave of remorse that hit Susan. "I'm going to suggest that some of you lead in spontaneous prayers for these concerns," he said. "We will end our time by reciting together the prayer that Jesus prayed." Susan was puzzled for a moment, then realized he meant the Lord's Prayer.

The room grew silent. Then someone started praying, and others joined in. Susan sat still, overwhelmed with grief. How could Luke ever forgive her?

CHAPTER 19

Eva was probably invited to dinner somewhere because she still wasn't home when Susan and Ruthie returned to the small house on Searcy Avenue. They decided to spend the afternoon reading and took books to the lanai, which was fragrant with bougainvillea blossoms. But they ended up talking instead.

Susan jumped in because she knew she needed Ruthie's friendship and understanding more than ever. "Ruthie, can we talk about something that's been bothering me?"

"Of course. I hope you're not mad at me. Eva's kept me so busy. Maybe I haven't been a very good friend lately. What's up?"

"No, I'm not mad. Far from it. But I have a huge problem."

"I'm all ears." Ruthie set down her latest cozy mystery and turned the plastic wicker chair so she faced Susan.

"Do you remember the last request this morning, right before we prayed?"

"You mean at the potluck? Didn't Luke mention his aunt having depression? Do you think his cousin was the one who died at the Red Hawk Country Fest? His family is from Ohio. That could be the same person."

Susan slumped in her chair and fidgeted nervously. "Remember that morning when I showed up at the end of your lane wearing jeans and we went to the thrift store?" Her voice was strained. "You got me a dress. I think you realized I'd been out running around all night, but you didn't press me for information." Susan felt her face flush as she realized she would need to come completely clean now that she'd started down that road.

Ruthie looked at her closely. "I thought you'd stopped seeing Amos. You told me you were done with him."

"I made a huge mistake. I agreed to go with him one last time. He took me to Red Hawk Country Fest. He and the crowd he was with were drunk, and one of the young guys died, probably from alcohol poisoning. His name was Ray. Same as Luke's cousin's name."

"Wait," Ruthie said. "What are you saying?"

Susan's chin trembled. "I didn't know Ray, but I was there when he died, Ruthie." Susan let out a deep sigh and continued. "It was awful. And now I find out that Ray was Luke's cousin. There was a lot of drinking that night—IPAs with a higher alcohol content than regular beer. And Ray was so young. Much younger than us. Maybe only fifteen." She paused and took a shaky breath. "We saw him lying there, then realized he wasn't conscious when officers came around checking IDs. Most of the group we were with took off, but Amos and I stayed—of course, Amos was out of it. Drunk. We didn't realize at the time that Ray was dead." She paused, taking another shallow breath.

Ruthie's hand covered her mouth. Her face twisted as she felt the terror her friend must have gone through that night.

"Amos and I were taken in for questioning. They arrested Amos for serving alcohol to minors. Of course, Amos had to sober up before anything else happened to him," Susan said, clenching her jaw as she waited for Ruthie's reaction.

"That's terrible. But you weren't arrested, were you? It wasn't your fault."

"I only had one drink, a wine spritzer. But a social worker talked with me for a while. I was told to go to alcohol education classes, just because I was there when it happened. I was screened for a substance abuse problem, but of course, I passed. I don't have a drinking problem." Her chest felt heavy at the memory of that night. "I'm sorry, Ruthie. I wasn't honest with you. Or with anyone. That's why I wanted to come here. With you." The truth was out.

Ruthie leaned forward and patted her friend's knee. "No. You didn't, you don't have a drinking problem. You just had a boyfriend problem. An Amos problem. Thank goodness you're here," Ruthie said.

Susan smiled, her face relaxing slightly. "I was so relieved to get away from all of it. That night, when the social worker offered to drive me home, I asked her to drop me off at the end of your lane. I didn't want anyone to know what happened or that I had been at the scene everyone read about in the newspaper." Every word of her confession eased the pain caused by Susan's heavy secret.

Ruthie gave her friend a searching gaze. "Honestly, I wondered what was going on, since you told me you were done with Amos. I can't stand that guy." Her voice rose.

Ruthie had been right all along. Why had it taken her so long to realize Amos was such a loser? "When they told me in the sheriff's office that Ray had died, I was shocked." Tears welled up, and Susan swiped her eyes in frustration. She didn't want to cry in front of her friend. "Now I find out Ray is Luke's cousin. It's my fault that Luke's little cousin is dead, and his aunt is suffering because of it. Luke will hate me if he ever finds out."

Ruthie faced Susan, their knees nearly touching. Her voice softened. "What happened isn't your fault. Ray is the one who drank too much. And Amos. You never needed him in your life. Luke is so much better for you." Her voice was full of understanding and acceptance.

Susan gave her friend a sad smile. "But don't you see?" Susan asked. "If Luke finds out, he'll never speak to me again. Our relationship will end before it even gets started."

"It's not your fault Ray died. I don't think Luke would blame you for what happened, would he?" she gave Susan a searching look.

"I'm not going to tell him. But I'm not going to talk to him anymore either. We're done. It's all over. Luke's history." Her voice had an air of finality.

"Not so fast," Ruthie cautioned. "Surely, we can come up with a plan. Maybe you can just tell him the truth. If he's the kind of Christian that he seems to be, he'll be able to forgive you. Don't you think?"

Susan wiped more tears with a balled-up tissue she had found in her dress pocket. "He can't know. He'd never forgive me. And what about the rest of his family? His mom? Everyone would know the truth about me and my past." Her breath came out in shudders, as if she had been crying.

"I thought it would go away now that I'm in Florida. So far, people back in Ohio don't know I was at the scene. If I told Luke, he might tell his Ohio family, and then it would spread, and everyone at home would find out I was involved. I'm so ashamed." Susan dropped her chin to her chest.

Just then, they heard Eva's car pull into the driveway. In unison, they stopped talking and picked up their books as if to resume reading, but Susan couldn't concentrate.

Eva stepped out onto the lanai. "Well, aren't you two just the picture of contentment?" she said. "I got a spur-of-the-moment dinner invite from the Gerbers. Some of Caleb's cousins are visiting, and they invited me over. I've been working so hard lately. It's been a while since I've had some fun." She sat down in one of the empty chairs.

"Good for you," Ruthie said. Susan exhaled, and everything she had been feeling gradually returned to normal.

If Eva noticed the tension or the tears that had recently spilled, she didn't show it. She cheerfully kept talking about her morning, her relatives, and the Dutch Blitz tournament her team had won. Then she asked about the potluck. Ruthie did her best to give an enthusiastic review of Death by Chocolate.

Inside, Susan winced at how casually death could be associated with a name of a rich chocolate dessert. Maybe it should be called something else. Luke had told her she should bring it to every potluck, but now she wasn't sure she'd ever attend another one. Or if she'd ever talk to Luke again.

Monday marked the last full workweek before Saw Grass Inn's grand opening, scheduled for the following week. Eva, Susan, and Ruthie sat at a dining table, reviewing a work plan. Eva's extensive experience as a hotel manager contributed specific ideas about guest comfort. The top priority was a comfortable bed. Eva had ordered high-quality beds and linens for each room. The beds had been delivered and set up as soon as the carpet was installed.

Eva's voice was passionate as she described her vision for their work in these final days. Everything was coming together. "We're going to have white on white bedding—all shades of white, cream, or beige," she crowed. "I've always dreamed of warming up the stale décor found in the places I used to work. Those chain hotels are so pedestrian." Eva swiped at a few strands of hair sticking to her cheek.

"I have loads of things stashed away. New stuff, perfectly good tables and lamps from secondhand stores and yard sales." Her face flushed even though the air conditioning at the inn kept the dining room slightly cooler than it needed to be with no guests present. "Nothing bland and boring," she pronounced. "Every room will be different and have its own unique vibe."

Susan and Ruthie listened and caught a whiff of her excitement. "I have a kind of mental sketchbook," Eva told her two accomplices. "I'm going for a bohemian look, but not heavy. Bright-colored chair cushions and lamps, luxurious, comfortable bedding, the softest sheets, cotton matelassé coverlets, scalloped-edged quilts, tufted chenille, and serene hand-quilted organic cottons. Mixed with wicker and rattan. I call it sunshine boho."

Susan had no idea what the things Eva described might look like, but it sounded perfect.

"I'm so done with Amish quilts," she said with a smirk. "No offense, girls, but it's been overdone. Don't you agree?"

Susan nodded. "In Ohio, my aunt Fannie owns a quilt shop. She doesn't sell many. She always says people like to look at them and talk about them, but she isn't sure people actually sleep under them."

"Exactly what I'm saying. Now, let's get back to what we're doing this week. I have a storage unit on Tamiami Trail—Route 41. It's packed with furniture I've collected from Habitat Restore and World's Attic on Beneva. Yard sales, too. And you know me; there's even the occasional roadside rescue.

"The plan is to clean all thirty rooms within the next two days. Ruthie has already cleaned all the windows, and each bathroom was given a quick once-over when the plumbing renovations were finished. Now that the carpet is installed, we'll do a thorough deep cleaning of all the surfaces in every room." Eva caught her breath.

"Goodness, that sounds like a lot of work. Should I hire a cleaning service? I thought about it, but I'm never satisfied with the results. I want things done right." She paused to catch her breath.

"We know how to clean," Susan said. She was thinking she'd enjoy cleaning something different instead of at home, where it was always the same.

Ruthie chimed in, "It's going to go fast. I predict we can get that out of the way in a couple of days." Ruthie made every move count when she was cleaning. Together, they'd sail through the inn in record time.

"That would be great because the furnishings in the storage unit are scheduled to be delivered on Wednesday, the day after tomorrow. I have Two Guys and a Truck coming around 11:00. The guys agreed to unload and carry the dressers, bedside tables, wicker chairs, and armoires to the rooms and place them where I want them to go."

Susan and Ruthie were carried away on the wings of furniture deliveries and creative imagination. Eva's dream-come-true had taken a lot of hard work in a short time. The restoration and repair work were finished. Now for the fun part. Susan hoped all the excitement and activity would keep her from thinking of Luke.

But she *had* thought of him, so Susan said, "Don't forget, I need to check on the plants every couple of days. Otherwise, I think most everything is done outside."

After a bit more planning, the three women gathered cleaning supplies from the organized, well-stocked cleaning closet and headed to the second floor. Eva vacuumed while the others tackled the bathrooms and wiped down baseboards and windowsills. Sunshine glinted onto the floor in patches.

They took a break at noon and ate their lunch on the patio, where several new sets of sturdy iron tables and chairs had been delivered over the weekend. As they sat there enjoying the view of the freshly landscaped grounds, Susan let her eyes rest on the reclaimed area she and Luke had planted together, with the fountain surrounded by red and yellow croton petra plants and sparkling landscaping rocks. Blue and white chinoiserie pots filled with succulents were spaced around the edge of the terrace. Susan remembered planting them with Luke—the camaraderie and lighthearted banter between them was a sweet memory. But she was determined to move on.

Eva exclaimed, "It's all so beautiful. Just the way I imagined, only better. You did a wonderful job, Susan. I can only hope the inside will turn out this well."

Susan wanted to remind Eva that it was mostly Luke's work, but if she said that, she'd have to mention his name, and that might make her cry. Instead, she said, "I guess I should go check on things while I'm out here. That way we can continue cleaning after lunch." She stood and stepped down off the patio. "I'm going to see if anything needs water."

She walked to the end of the inn and around the side, passing under the big pine tree and the Adirondack chairs, glad to be away from the other two and alone with her thoughts. If only things could be different. If only she had stood up to Amos. If only she hadn't finally found Luke. She thought he might be the love of her life.

She filled a watering can and went through the motions of checking each seedling, and watering those that appeared dry. The new plants looked happy and content, as if they wanted to send down deep roots and hold on.

After her walk, she put away the watering can and washed her hands. She joined Eva and Ruthie, who had moved into the kitchen. Eva was still talking about decorating and describing some of her thrifted treasures.

"I found a perfect mid-century blonde dresser and matching nightstands—1950s era pieces. That's what boho style is about: mixing different influences—antiques, mid-century, contemporary. It all comes together with the wicker and rattan. Baskets. Lots of texture. Metal and glass."

"I don't know much about it," Ruthie was saying, "but you're making me want to get everything cleaned so I can see what it's going to look like."

"By early next week, we'll place the smaller tables, lamps, and other décor in the rooms," Eva said. "Creating that eclectic mix will be the most fun of all.

"I'm planning to take a couple of trips to an outlet store for throws and anything else that catches my eye. You girls are coming with me to pick out all that new stuff. That's going to be the shopping trip of a lifetime. And a lady at church is making us three dozen throw pillows out of thrifted fabrics and upholstery samples. I can't wait to see them."

Susan and Ruthie grinned and simultaneously performed a high five for Eva's benefit.

After lunch, they returned to the cleaning project. Eva's chatter subsided as the loud vacuum moved with her from room to room, down the hall, and finally to the lower level, where she worked on the large, empty lounge-slash-meeting room.

Susan was in the stairwell, heading for the supply closet, when she heard a familiar voice. She stopped, caught in the perfect spot to overhear Luke and Eva's conversation.

"I know it's just been a couple of days," he said apologetically after greeting Eva. "But the first days are important for new seedlings."

"Definitely," Eva said. "You're going to want Susan to look

them over with you. Let me get her. I think she and Ruthie are upstairs cleaning the guest rooms."

Susan heard what sounded like a chair scraping the floor. "I think she watered some things at noon, but I'll go get her. After all, she's going to be taking care of the grounds long term."

Susan quietly crept back up the stairs and leaned against the hallway wall, still listening.

"Hey," Luke said, "you're busy. I'll go get her. You keep working."

"Like I said, they're on the second floor. They're probably down at the end by now."

Susan ducked into a guest room as Luke approached her. Her heart pounded. She hadn't expected to see him so soon. Now he was there, and she'd have to face him and find a way to let him know things had changed between them.

Luke spotted her and entered the room. "There you are. Wow! This place is huge." His voice echoed in the emptiness. "I thought we should check out the plants. Inspect everything. Are you about done for the day?" He offered his usual grin.

Nothing had changed. For him. Susan felt sick thinking about what she needed to do. "I'm kind of busy right now. Just go do it yourself. Okay?" The words sounded clipped and irritable.

"Hey, I can wait a few minutes until you finish up. No problem," Luke said.

"I already checked on the plants at lunchtime," she said. She wanted to avoid walking around in the garden with Luke. She needed to figure out how to let him know they were done but she wasn't ready. Didn't have the words. She crossed her arms defensively, as if to protect herself from the difficult conversation she knew was coming.

If Luke sensed something was wrong, he didn't show it. "Eva mentioned that you watered earlier. FYI, watering at noon isn't the best idea since it's so hot. It's better to water in the morning or evening."

He wasn't judging her, was he? Susan grasped at his criticism. He always seemed to know more. And let her know it, too.

"Yeah. You're probably right," she said. She wasn't going to argue with him. Her goal was to interact as little as possible.

"You just go ahead. I'm helping Ruthie," Susan said as she stepped past him and walked down the hall.

"Okay. Whatever." Luke sounded disappointed.

Ruthie was working in Room 215 and looked up from the sink she was wiping down. "I thought I heard you talking to someone out there," she said.

"Yeah. Luke stopped by. Wanted me to go inspect the plants with him."

"You should go," Ruthie said.

"No, I shouldn't. I'm done with him, remember?"

"Even so, you need to learn about the plants from Luke. That's your job here. Just go out there and handle the Luke problem already. Tell him the truth, or something. You can't avoid him with no explanation. That's just not right." Ruthie was a voice of reason.

"Not today," Susan said. "Not ever." Despite her brave words, Susan knew Ruthie had a point. As she finished polishing the mirrors on the second floor, she watched herself and practiced starting a conversation with Luke, who was still wandering around somewhere out there.

I'm really sorry to hear about your cousin, Ray. I believe I met him once....

I have something to tell you. I'm not sure how to say this...but....

I wish things were different, but I need to tell you something....

No matter how she phrased it, she couldn't imagine telling Luke the truth about who she really was or why she'd run away to Sarasota.

CHAPTER 20

The clean east windows of Saw Grass Inn sparkled in the sunshine. "I can't believe the transformation. This place was a hopeless mess, and look what we've accomplished," Eva said.

A feeling of satisfaction washed over Susan as she thought about that day in early November when she and Ruthie arrived on the bus, tired and disheveled. Eva had just purchased the inn, a run-down building surrounded by neglected grounds. It had completely transformed. She remembered that first day in Sarasota, and a wide grin spread across her face. Eva had brought them here and joked that this was their new home. At the time, the inn seemed far from civilization, the picture of neglect. "Remember how you told Ruthie and me this was where we'd be staying? At first, I thought you meant it," Susan said.

Eva laughed. "I can't believe I said that. This place was in no shape to handle guests back then. Far from it. Besides, you two needed time to get used to life on your own here in Sarasota." She paused for a moment and looked back and forth between the two young women. "But things are different now. I thought you and Ruthie might want to live here, share that suite at the end of the east wing. I have jobs for both of you if you want work—front desk, cleaning, and serving in the dining room. We'll start small, but if we work together, I believe we can make it for a few months. What do you think? Room and board included?"

Ruthie grew quiet and looked away. Was something wrong? She usually responded to Eva's proposals with enthusiasm.

"I'd be fine with that," Susan said. "I mean, if it would help you to have us stay here. Don't you think so, Ruthie? It's not scary at all now."

Ruthie hesitated then nodded in agreement. "But I'm going home for Old Christmas. Remember? You, too, Susan."

"Yeah, we're going back for a visit," Susan said. They'd been so busy that she hadn't had much time to think about a trip that was still more than two weeks away. Not long ago, she didn't want to leave, even for a short visit, because of Luke. Now, it didn't matter. And *Dawdi* wanted to see her. For now, it was fun to be here with Eva, putting the finishing touches on the inn. Something seemed off about Ruthie's reaction to Eva's offer of the new living quarters, though. Eva was so generous, and she'd hosted them for weeks in her home. If she wanted them to stay here, they should.

Eva said, "We'll talk more about this later."

A box truck pulled up the driveway, signaling the start of their busy day. Two Guys and a Truck backed up to the main entrance. Eva gave Susan and Ruthie their instructions. "We'll help unload. I'll tell them where to go with the heavy dressers and armoires, along with the overstuffed chairs and loveseats. You two can handle all the end tables, lamps, baskets, and wall decorations. We'll clean and sort those here in the foyer. Just stack them off to the side." Eva's eyes gleamed with anticipation. What would Eva's daydream look like? Her mental sketchbook was about to take shape before their eyes.

Eva opened the front door and greeted the movers. Susan and Ruthie moved quickly back and forth, carrying lamps, small tables, baskets, rugs, and various décor items Eva had collected from her regular stops at thrift stores and yard sales. The truck drivers slid heavy pieces onto a lift, a few at a time, lowered them, and then, using dollies, pushed them down the hallways to their destination. When the truck was empty, Eva handed the haulers a check, and they took off, leaving the three women standing in the foyer surrounded by scuffed tables, dusty bamboo chairs, and grimy ceramic lamps. To Susan's eye, it looked like a pile of sad, neglected leftovers. But when she looked more closely, she could see signs of value beneath the dust and dirt.

What was Eva thinking? She stood under the arched doorway surveying the loot she'd scavenged from all over town. "Well, 'beauty is in the eye of the beholder,'" she said. "Let's eat lunch. Then we'll get started."

Eva pushed a cleaning cart into the foyer. It would take time to clean this pile of wicker baskets, wall sconces, framed artwork, and mirrors. Eva handed each of them a bucket filled with warm, soapy water and a couple of soft cleaning cloths. Her cart also contained a small hand-held vacuum, dusting brushes, and a set of furniture oils and grease pens for covering scratches. She had some tacky glue, a screwdriver set, fine steel wool, and sandpaper. She brought light bulbs for the lamps, as well as some hardware, including drawer pulls and knobs. "Feel free to use your imagination and change out some of the knobs," she said.

"I'll help you get started. Once we clean a few things, I'll start staging some of the rooms on the first floor. We have several bookings after Christmas, but we can keep the second floor closed for now. First floor is the priority. Feel free to set aside a few things you'd like to keep for your suite. Anything's fair game."

Susan looked over the rows of stands and tables. She wished Eva's mental sketchbook was a real sketchbook. None of this looked appealing. Ruthie sneezed, probably from all the dust.

Eva wiped down a small pine table with a soft cloth and demonstrated how to use the pens and polishes. The dusty, scratched table looked completely different when it was clean and free of scratches. Eva had an eye for quality. She quickly replaced the tarnished metal knob on the table's one small drawer with a white ceramic one.

"Okay, I'm going to take this to Room 120. I'll start at the end of the hallway on each wing and work my way back to the rooms just off the foyer. We will do your suite later," Eva said. "Grab a few things and come with me. Whatever you want. Take your pick." Ruthie picked a large woven palm fan and two smaller matching ones that she'd just wiped down. Susan looked around the room until she spotted a clean wicker chair and a tall bronze vase. She picked up the vase and wiped it with a dust cloth until it shimmered, then placed it on the chair seat to carry it. Eva nodded approvingly. "Perfect," she said. "Those will work. It's 'old Florida' so far, but we'll add a splash of color on chair pillows later."

They carried their selections down the hallway and entered the room. The king-sized bed was already set up, with its upholstered headboard bolted to the wall. Creamy linen curtains hung at the windows and pooled on the floor. Eva placed the pine table under the window. Susan positioned the chair beside it. "The vase can go in that corner," she said. "I'll add some dried grasses later. Which wall is best for the palm fans?" Before Susan could think about it, Eva continued. "I guess just prop them there against the wall for now. I'll have the handyman take care of hanging some things later." She clapped her hands, admiring the result. "This is just what I'd imagined. What do you think?"

"It looks nice," Ruthie said.

"Trash to treasure," said Susan.

Eva led them back to the foyer and laid out a plan for the rest of the afternoon. "If you two are okay with cleaning and touching up the rest of these smaller things, I think I will unpack the linens before I continue staging more rooms."

"That's fine, Eva. We can handle it," Susan said.

Eva moved to another part of the inn. Susan couldn't wait to talk with Ruthie about the suite Eva had offered them. She grabbed a soft cloth and sprayed it with a little of the golden-colored restorative polish, then knelt in front of a wide-armed bamboo chair. It was sturdy but needed cleaning.

"Eva wants to give us a suite. That's a great idea, don't you think?" Susan kept her eyes on her work and hid her internal uneasiness with external enthusiasm. Maybe she'd misunderstood Ruthie's hesitancy earlier. She hoped so.

Ruthie didn't respond. Instead, she methodically polished ceramic vases and lamps with a damp microfiber cloth. They were lined up on a few long benches. She cleared her throat nervously and continued wiping down the piece she was working on.

Susan stole a glance at her friend and nearly gasped at the change. How had she not noticed before? The Ruthie she'd known since childhood had always been thick around the middle. But the Ruthie bending over now was someone different, someone with a trim waistline and graceful movements.

"Wow, Ruthie. You look amazing. I just noticed a big change in you. That diet must be working. When we go home for Christmas, nobody will even recognize you." Ruthie deserved some praise. She'd given up many treats and had cut most of her portions in half. It had paid off.

"Oh, I'm sure they will recognize me," Ruthie said. "But thanks. I'm glad someone finally noticed." She flashed Susan a smile.

Ruthie lowered her voice and looked down at her work. "Also, I wanted to talk to you about when we go home. And about us living here after we come back from Christmas." She sounded tense.

"I've been talking on the phone with Ben Troyer lately. I was keeping it a secret from you, but I shouldn't have. I just didn't know how to tell you," Ruthie said, keeping her eyes on the bright aqua lamp base she was buffing to a shine. "I know you and Ben were neighbors and used to be good friends. And your sister Leah is married to Ben's brother. It feels a little awkward...." Her voice faded.

Susan was still kneeling in front of the bamboo chair, a tremor running through her at her friend's surprising revelation. "You never admitted you even liked him when I teased you," Susan said accusingly. "Why keep it a secret? He didn't propose to you or anything, did he?"

"Not yet. I mean. No," Ruthie stammered. "You had so much to deal with yourself, with Luke and all. I didn't want to make you feel worse. But he said when he comes home at Christmas, he wants us to talk, spend time together. He wants me to stay in Ohio in January. Or maybe for good." She rubbed the back of her neck with her hand. "I hope you'll understand. I'm just not sure I'll be staying in that suite with you, Susan. I might not be in Florida that much longer."

Susan tried to stay calm. This was all so unexpected. She'd thought they would be discussing how to furnish their suite, and instead, Ruthie had blindsided her with this big news.

"But I thought Ben was in Maine at some organic farm. Isn't he going back after Christmas? It all sounds kind of fast if you ask me. Why don't you give it some time? Absence makes the heart grow fonder. Isn't that what they say?" Susan's unfiltered thoughts rushed out. She swallowed, hoping Ruthie would buy her argument. She couldn't imagine being here in Florida without her friend beside her.

Ruthie stopped polishing and straightened her back. "Ben wants to start farming, and we think my father will be interested in renting him some land or even having him take over my parents' farm."

Susan sat back on her heels and examined the musty-smelling cushion of the chair she was cleaning. "Hold that thought," she said to Ruthie. "This needs to go in the dumpster. I'll be right back." Susan carried the faded cushion to the bin, giving herself a moment to gather her thoughts. All along, she'd suspected Ben might be interested in Ruthie, and she'd been right. Ruthie was her friend, and this was good news, even though it might mean leaving Florida. Ruthie deserved to be happy. Susan tossed the cushion, and the dumpster lid clanked shut in response.

Back in the foyer, Ruthie waited, her face pinched with worry. Susan smiled at her and closed the gap between them, giving her friend a big hug.

"Ruthie, I think it's wonderful that you and Ben got together. Right from the start, I believed Ben was coming over to your place because he was interested in you. You didn't believe me. At least you acted like you didn't." Susan smiled at her friend.

"At first, I didn't," Ruthie said. "But you were right."

Susan took both of Ruthie's hands in her own. "I would miss you if you stayed in Ohio. But I can also understand if you decide not to come back after Christmas. I thought it would be fun for us to have our own place here for a while. So, yeah. I'm disappointed." She dropped her hands to her sides.

Ruthie smiled back at her best friend. "I'm sorry, Susan. Maybe it will end up working out and I'll come back for a few more months. But maybe not. I should have told you before, but you were all about Luke when he was working here. You and I barely had time to talk because we were both working so hard at the inn. And then, after Sunday and what Luke said, it was even harder to tell you about Ben. I wish things were going better for you and Luke."

"Luke. Don't remind me of Luke," Susan said. A bitter taste formed in her mouth.

"Susan, don't give up on him," Ruthie pleaded. "You need to talk to him about everything. That's what happened between me and Ben. One day, after we'd talked a few times, he just told me what he was thinking. Said he wished he could turn my parents' farm into an organic farm, make it more profitable. And from there, well, we just started daydreaming together. I feel like everything is falling into place." Her face flushed.

"I'm happy for both of you. I really am, Ruthie. Everything came together so smoothly. I only wish the same could happen for me and Luke," Susan said. Her shoulders sagged as she looked at another project that needed some TLC.

"You're going to figure it out," Ruthie said. "Give yourself some time and you'll know what to do." Ruthie swished a cloth in water and wrung it out before tackling another vase.

Her friend was so wise and steady. If only Susan could find that kind of confidence and resolve. They kept working on their cleaning projects while talking. Maybe their tasks made it easier to share deep things.

Susan resumed the conversation. "It's wrong not to tell Luke the truth. I'll admit that. I need to let him know why I can't see him anymore. I need to be honest. But if I tell him, it will be all over between us. I mean, it is already over. But until I talk to him about it, I can still pretend there's hope for us."

"You'll do the right thing," Ruthie said. "I know you will."

"I'm glad you think so," Susan said with a resigned tone. "At least something is going right for somebody. You and Ben are perfect together. I'm glad you've finally found each other."

The lobby was finally cleared of tables, chairs, artwork, and lamps. Everything had been moved to one of the first-floor guest rooms. Each room featured a tasteful blend of modern and quaint styles, arranged for maximum comfort. Susan and Ruthie were now focused on cleaning the lobby, where guests would first see the refurbished Saw Grass Inn during the upcoming open house.

It was late afternoon on a weekday, the usual time Luke stopped by after work to check on the plants with Susan. She tried to stay busy and avoid him as much as possible, yet she knew she needed to tell him she'd been at the festival where his cousin Ray died. But she dreaded it. Avoidance seemed easier.

Now, working in the lobby, an encounter was unavoidable. Maybe Eva had planned it this way. She seemed to enjoy pairing Susan and Luke whenever possible. He pulled up just as they began polishing the slab of steel-gray granite. Eva had saved the piece from the old kitchen and repurposed it as the front desk countertop. Susan watched and kept polishing as Luke unloaded a huge potted plant from the passenger side of his front seat.

This wasn't the first time Luke had shown up with a plant, whether it was a succulent in a plastic pot, something leftover from landscaping cleanup, or an indoor plant—a palm or fern someone no longer wanted. Eva's vibe, her sunshine boho style, needed plants, and here was a tall fiddleleaf fig to fill the corner.

Eva heard his truck and appeared from down the hall.

"What have we here?" she asked.

Luke stepped inside, carrying a plastic pot with slender stems and top-heavy foliage. "The folks we worked for today didn't want this," Luke said. "I thought it might fit in the lobby. The fiddleleaf fig loves a west-facing window and a good, regular soaking."

Susan groaned inwardly at the all-knowing Luke, who assumed Eva wouldn't know how to care for the plant. Susan knew she had a fiddleleaf fig at home. Eva grimaced at the tall, lanky apparition. A giant, veiny, oval-shaped leaf fluttered to the floor. She swept it up with her hand. "That ugly pot isn't going to work. Let me see if I can find a basket." Luke stood there, still holding the plant. He raised an eyebrow and watched for Susan's reaction.

Susan dropped her eyes and her shoulders sagged as she thought about the inevitable conversation she needed to have with Luke when they were alone. Now wasn't the time or place. Ruthie must have sensed Susan's thoughts. "We're extra busy this afternoon, trying to get everything ready for Friday. You might need to water the outdoor plants on your own today. Eva has a mile-long list for us to finish before the open house."

Luke nodded. "Guess I can do that if you need Susan in here. Eva should hire me to help after hours. I'd be available, you know."

Eva returned to the lobby carrying a couple of large wicker baskets. "I heard that Luke. Great idea. I keep finding things that are too heavy for me to lift. I have ladders to climb, concrete to power wash, stuff like that. What do you charge?"

"Not much," Luke answered. "Just hanging out in this beautiful place makes it worth it for me." Susan nervously smoothed her skirt; Ruthie's words from another conversation taunted her. "You need to talk to him. Tell him the truth." Her friend was right, of course. It shouldn't be this hard. But it was.

———

Thursday before the open house, Luke arrived on schedule, carrying a huge, long, skinny box over his shoulder. He held it as if it were a broom or a shovel, but it was much larger.

Susan had just finished soaking the colorful clusters of coleus, gerbera daisies, and lantana that surrounded the patio. Now, she used the leaf blower to clear twigs and seed pods from a nearby tree. She turned off the blower and prepared to put it away. Luke greeted her as usual, and she responded with a clipped "Hello." He eased the box onto the patio. "Did I just see what I think I saw?" he asked. Susan couldn't avoid answering him. The question was directed at her.

"I'm not sure. What did you see?"

"Mimosa pods. Where did those come from?" He picked up a handful of the long, brownish seed pods and waved them in the air. Susan pointed to the offending tree, a low, spreading tree with multiple branches. Susan's youngest brother would have an easy time climbing that one. Ugly pods hung everywhere, replacing the previous pink flowers.

"It's called the silk tree sometimes. *Albizia julibrissin,*" Luke said. "Invasive! I'd like to send them all back to China. Only it's too late now. They grow everywhere. The puffy pink flowers turn into this." He held up the pods and scowled.

Susan couldn't believe she hadn't realized it earlier. By now, she should be good at spotting invasive plants. But she'd been distracted by other things.

Eva stepped onto the patio and set down the large plastic tub she'd carried from her station wagon. "Great, you brought it," she said, gesturing to Luke's box. "I hope it wasn't too much trouble. I just started thinking we needed some holiday cheer around here."

"No problem. But Eva, you have a bigger problem."

Does he ever. Look out, Eva. You're about to get a lecture on invasive plants.

Susan stepped back, and Eva addressed Luke with her good-natured wit. "What did I do now? Over-water a succulent? Cut the grass too short?" Was she making fun of Luke's ever-present landscaping advice?

Earlier, he'd warned Eva and Susan about both infractions.

"No. Not that. But how did we miss this mimosa when we were culling the invasives?" He gestured toward the offender.

"I didn't realize it was invasive," Eva said. "I like the flowers. But I've noticed the seed pods are making a mess on the new patio."

"Those pods can stay dormant for years and be carried and spread by water and wildlife. But watch out. Years later, they can still sprout wherever they land. I don't think you want that here, no matter how pretty the flowers are. And they spread disease in other trees—mimosa wilt." Luke got philosophical. "Like life sometimes. Evil spreads and consumes all the good that gets in its way. Invasion and devastation."

A rock settled in Susan's stomach. Does he know something? Does he suspect the truth about my involvement in Ray's death and his aunt's depression. She struggled to keep her gloomy thoughts at bay, but they swirled as Eva and Luke continued their ecology lesson.

"In that case, we should get rid of it. I wish we had noticed it earlier. The open house is only two days away," Eva said. "But if we're presenting ourselves as conservationists, we can't have a known invasive in our landscape beds—or anywhere."

Eva gave the tree a long, despairing look. "Susan, you've been so quiet. What are your thoughts on this? Should Luke cut it down now or wait until later?"

Susan swallowed and understood the tree had to be cut down. "I know it's inconvenient, but there's no point in keeping it, no matter how pretty the flowers are," Susan said.

"Okay. Let's get this out of here. Luke, do you have a chainsaw with you?"

"In the truck. Give me a minute, and she'll be gone. Cut to the ground and hauled off to a burn pile within the hour."

Luke went back to the truck to grab his chainsaw.

Eva turned to Susan. "I know the Amish don't usually have Christmas trees, but Luke brought this one from EdenKeepers Floral and Gift Shop. I thought you and Ruthie could decorate it for me tonight. I hope you don't mind."

Susan looked at the long box Luke had left where he'd set it down a few minutes earlier. "I've never decorated a Christmas tree. But Ruthie worked in a tourist gift shop back home. I think she knows how to decorate a Christmas tree."

"Great," Eva said. "It will make a big statement in the lobby when our guests come for the open house. Do you mind grabbing the tall ladder from the storage room?"

"Sure. I'll be right back."

"If you see Ruthie, let her know she can stop making up rooms on the second floor for now. Getting this tree up is more important."

Susan went inside, relieved she could avoid Luke and his chainsaw that was removing evil from the garden. *Trees. Good and evil. It's all too real. Why can't I escape these constant reminders? What was it he'd said? Something about evil spreading, consuming all the good.*

She met Ruthie in the hallway as she was coming down from the second floor. "I saw Luke's truck out there. Is he looking for you?"

"No. I don't think so. He brought a fake Christmas tree. Eva wants us to decorate it. I hope you know how. I don't have a clue," Susan said.

"Great! That will be fun," Ruthie said. "I learned how when I worked in that shop in Charm. Remember?"

"I figured as much. I told Eva you'd know what to do."

"I can do the lights. I picked up a good trick from the store owner I worked with. Is Luke going to help us?"

"Ugh. I hope not. I don't think so. Eva has him cutting down a tree in the yard. Turns out that messy tree is a mimosa, and it's invasive. Somehow, we missed it when he was here marking what needed to come out."

Susan and Ruthie carried the box with the Christmas tree into the lobby.

"Fake pretty tree, nasty real tree. Take your pick," Ruthie laughed. Her clever humor and positive attitude made Susan smile. *Do you have any idea how much you mean to me, Ruthie? I know you love Ben, but please, don't leave me all alone here. It wouldn't be the same without you.*

Outside, the chainsaw whined. Susan found Eva's tall metal stepladder. It was surprisingly lightweight. She lifted it, tilted it to the side, and followed Ruthie to the lobby, where she set it up. Ruthie stepped out with Eva to see what Luke was up to while Susan stayed inside and unpacked the Christmas tree. She heard the fatal crash—the mimosa was down.

After it was felled, Luke took care of the branches, and Eva and Ruthie returned to the lobby to work on the Christmas tree. Eva orchestrated the setup, fitting the sections together as Susan and

Ruthie handed them to her. When it was up, she stepped back to look. The tree was at least nine feet tall and overshadowed the fiddle-leaf fig they'd moved to a space behind the front desk counter.

"Decorating is going to take a while," Eva said. "How about I order us some takeout? I was thinking of Thai food from that place up the road. I can run and get it while you two decorate." Eva pulled a phone from the pocket of her khaki capris and scrolled through the menu. "What do you like?"

Neither answered at first. Finally, Ruthie said, "I've never had Thai food. Is it spicy? I hope not."

"It is spicy," Eva said. "Otherwise, it's like some Chinese food. But if you don't like a lot of spice, I can tell them to make it milder. How about I order three of my favorites so we can share? They give big takeout portions."

"Okay," Ruthie said. "Do they have something low-calorie? Chicken and vegetables, maybe?"

Although she didn't mention her food plan, Susan knew Ruthie was sticking to it, even when she ate restaurant food. Her determination was admirable.

"Sure. I'll find something for you," Eva said.

While she tapped her phone to place the order, Ruthie plugged in the strings of lights that lay in a tangled mess on the floor. Miraculously, there were no burned-out bulbs. Susan watched as Ruthie began winding the long string of tiny white lights into a ball, starting with the end opposite the plug. "This makes the whole thing a lot easier. You can roll the next string. Just be sure to start at the end opposite the plug."

Susan followed Ruthie's instructions. Eva finished her order and helped out. Soon, six big balls of string lights were on the floor. "That's about fifteen hundred tiny white lights. Now what?" Eva asked.

"We start at the bottom of the tree and slowly unroll the ball, weaving in and out of the branches as we go around," Ruthie said. She plugged the first ball into a power strip and began tucking and twisting the lights as she moved. Susan and Eva stood back as the magic unfolded.

"That's genius," Eva said. "Now, if you two can handle it from here, I'm leaving to pick up our dinner. Let's hope it's ready by the time I get there. We might need to take a dinner break and then finish up. A tree this big is going to take a long time."

Susan watched as Ruthie bent and twisted gracefully while winding the string of lights in and out. Gone was the plump Ruthie of the past. She had lost weight and become more self-confident. Susan envied Ben and her for the future they had ahead. Although she tried to avoid it, she still experienced moments of self-pity. *Why can't things be easier for me? Why am I the only one still waiting for love?*

At church, she learned about Advent, a time of waiting before Christmas. A period of darkness. She looked out the west lobby window at the fading evening and watched Luke load branches from the evil mimosa tree onto his truck bed. He was everything she wanted—handsome, smart, capable, a hard worker, fun to be around, a spiritual leader. But the chance of them falling in love seemed impossible once he found out she had been at the scene when Ray died. She could have stopped it.

Susan let out a soft sigh and watched as Ruthie climbed the ladder, wrapping the top of the tree in lights. Christmas and lights would arrive as they did every year. Ruthie would have this tree lit before supper, but for now, darkness clung to Susan like the black woolen cloak of the simplest Ohio Swartzentruber Amish grandmother sitting in her dim kitchen.

Enough! Pull yourself together. Susan was learning to stop the negative thoughts when they came. A minute or two of silent self-pity was all she allowed herself. God had a plan for her, and she had to trust it would be revealed when the time was right. She began unpacking the fragile-looking ornaments from the boxes waiting in Eva's storage bin. It didn't take long to realize that the shiny round balls were all plastic. The decorated tree was beautiful, but Susan suddenly missed their simple Amish Christmas back home. She missed *Dawdi, Maemm, Daett,* Leah, her little brothers, and Leah's family. She missed baking and candy making. Shopping trips in a crowded van with relatives. Clipping evergreens to encircle the red candle *Maemm* always placed in the center of the table at Christmas.

"Ta da!" Ruthie stepped down from the tall ladder and paused to admire her work. Her exclamation brought Susan back into the light. "Look! The lights are finished."

"It's beautiful," Susan said. "I like how the tiny lights seem to twinkle from the very center of the tree."

"I know. It's pretty. Maybe it's not simple or plain like Christmas at home, but I kind of like Christmas trees, don't you?" Ruthie asked.

"I guess so. I just got a little homesick, though, thinking about that very thing."

As if the lights had been his cue, Luke ambled through the door and paused to admire the tree. "Wow! That looks great. I figured you'd need a guy to put the lights on it. Guess I was wrong," he said.

"Everything's under control," Ruthie said. "Glad you like it."

"I noticed that Eva left. Do you two need help with the rest of the decorations? I can stay and help you, then drop you off at Eva's place. We can grab burgers or pizza. It's past dinnertime."

"Eva's picking up Thai food for our dinner," Susan said.

"Maybe another time," Ruthie added.

"Okay. Well, let me help with the rest of this, then."

He's sticking around. Oh no. Maybe he's hoping for Thai leftovers.

"Where's your music?" Luke placed his phone on the front desk and opened a streaming app. He turned the volume all the way up. "Best I can do for now. Let's decorate." He grabbed a box of silver ornaments and started hanging them on the branches. Susan did the same, beginning on the opposite side of the tree. She wanted to stay as far away from Luke as possible.

Luke seemed unaware and started humming along with the season's songs. Soon, he was singing, filling the room with deep tenor notes that contrasted with the tinny voices from his phone.

When "Blue Christmas" came on, he switched to the melody. He leaned back and looked up to the top of the tree, singing at the top of his lungs and holding an oblong silver ornament as if it were a microphone. He looked sidewise at Susan, who ducked her head, hiding a smile. She couldn't help herself. Luke was a charmer. As much as she wanted to, she wasn't sure she would ever escape the hold he had on her heart.

Ruthie hip-bumped Susan. "We didn't know he was an Elvis impersonator, did we?"

"Learn something new every day," Susan said.

Could there still be some light in this darkness she felt inside? The starry lights of the tree blinked at her, and "O Holy Night" spread its hope around them. If only she could find the path. If only forgiveness were as real as Christians always say it is.

CHAPTER 22

Eva had learned to make a charcuterie board at the Mary-Martha Circle, her church women's group. She said it was the latest fad. "We Mennonites tend to appreciate simple, no-fuss spreads, which this is, but if it looks a bit elegant, so much the better." One evening, she brought home fancy cheeses, cured meats, and a package of assorted crackers. "I'll need to get much more for the actual open house. Tonight, we're going to make one for practice," she said. She found pictures she'd taken at the Mary-Martha Circle and propped her tablet on the table for Susan and Ruthie, pointing out skewers of tasty combinations, pepperoni roses, cheese wedges, grapes, crackers, and small bowls and jars of jam, olives, and relishes.

At home, they often assembled plates for weddings and gatherings of young people. Someone always brought local Trail bologna, made in the nearby town of Trail. They added thick slices of local Swiss cheese. In contrast, Eva's pictures showed smaller bites and much more variety.

"I got a few basics at the deli." Eva gestured toward a stack of containers. "We'll play around with this and try our hand at assembling a charcuterie board." She pulled out a large natural wood slab from a kitchen cabinet. "After we've experimented, we can eat it for dinner."

"It's pretty, but I don't think I've ever tasted some of the things in your pictures," Susan said. Fancy food made her a little nervous.

"Then, you're in for a treat." Eva demonstrated how simple it was to make a pepperoni rose by folding thin slices over the rim of a juice glass.

Ruthie grinned. "My mother used to tell me not to play with my food," she joked. "Now you're asking me to do that very thing." Ruthie had already taken on the challenge and was layering pepperoni slices, trying to copy Eva.

Susan examined the picture and tried to arrange something that resembled ham but was different, into a cascading ribbon along one edge of the board. She used her fingers to pinch hills and valleys into the thin slices. "How does this look?" she asked.

"You girls are good at this. Look at you. That prosciutto looks like it was arranged by a pro." Eva unpacked a tray of neatly sliced cheese squares. She spooned some fancy olives into a small bowl and arranged some skewers and crackers in the empty spots. In a few minutes, the three had artfully assembled a tray starting with cold meats, filling spaces with cheese wedges and slices, and tucking small bunches of grapes alongside the cheese.

Susan stepped back and felt a wave of delight at their handiwork. "This looks a lot like your pictures, Eva. I wasn't sure, but it wasn't too hard. Of course, our table at the open house is much bigger." Susan remembered the table Eva had pointed out earlier. It was huge compared to this board. How would they ever fill it?

"That's true, but the principle remains the same. Just remember to start with the meats and cheeses, then add the other items. We'll have a lot more food to work with that day." Susan filed Eva's advice away for Friday afternoon.

"Here, try this." Eva assembled a tiny skewer, layering a basil leaf between a fresh mozzarella ball, a red grape, and half of a small tomato. From a small bottle, she drizzled dark liquid over the ingredients and handed her creation to Ruthie. "Just eat it all in one big bite," she said.

Ruthie eyed the combo for a moment. She'd become more cautious about what she ate. "Looks perfectly harmless," she said. She popped it into her mouth. Her eyes widened, then she swallowed. "Yum! What is that sauce? That's delicious."

"It's balsamic reduction. I bought it at a gourmet food outlet. Now it's your turn, Susan. Tell me what you think of this." Eva picked up a cracker, spread it with soft cheese, and topped it with a dab of thick, dark fig jam. Susan took a bite and swallowed. "That's so yummy," she said. The jam reminded her of the syrupy date pudding served at Amish weddings. The cheese was creamy and white, with a mellow taste.

"Brie with fig jam," Eva said. She assembled another one for herself and smacked her lips after taking a bite. Finally, she opened the bag and added a few wrapped chocolates as a finishing touch. "This salty spread wouldn't be complete without something sweet now, would it?"

"*Maemm* told us our *Grosmammi* used to say a good meal should have seven sours and seven sweets," Susan said.

"I've heard that. It's a Pennsylvania Dutch saying. It does make a good balance, although I'm not sure it's good to eat that many sweets," Eva said. "But a bite or two of chocolate never hurt anyone." She laughed as she unwrapped a dark chocolate-covered caramel and popped it into her mouth. She tossed one each to Susan and Ruthie. Susan followed Eva's lead, but Ruthie found a place for hers on the board.

"As for the seven sours and seven sweets, I think that's just a saying," Susan said. "But some Amish do have to have their pickles—and Amish or not, everyone likes chocolate."

"But not at the same time," Ruthie added with a giggle.

When the board had final approval, Eva placed it in the center of the table. "Susan, if you'd get some bowls and spoons, I'll serve the soup. It's just from the deli. I hope it's good. Today's special was corn chowder. And, Ruthie, we'll need some plates for our charcuterie. We'd better enjoy this now because I'm hoping that when we serve up the real one, our guests will keep us too busy to stop for even a bite."

When everything was in place and the steaming soup was served, Eva said, "Now, let's pray so we can eat." They bowed their heads. Eva's appetizers must have done their job. Her prayer was unusually short. "Creator God, we're grateful for all good things before us. May this food bless us with the strength to do Your work. Amen."

They had been planning the open house for weeks. Now that the day had finally come, Susan felt a mix of emotions. The thought of talking to strangers at the open house—people so different from her—brought back memories of Sugar N Spice and made her feel uneasy. A mental picture of broken plates flashed through her mind, and she pushed it aside.

On Friday morning, they left Eva's house around eight thirty. Susan and Ruthie wore their favorite church dresses, while Eva wore a new teal dress, small gold earrings, and low heels. On the way, Eva discussed last-minute chores. "While I do the food shopping, you can do touch-ups and tidying, spread tablecloths, and place poinsettias on the guest tables. After I get back with the food, we'll assemble the charcuterie and set up the beverage fountain on the buffet."

"What is a beverage fountain?" Ruthie asked.

"I forgot to tell you. I rented it so you won't have to serve the punch—cranberry and papaya. It looks like a fountain with basins, and the punch flows nonstop. It's very simple to operate. We can add two gallons at a time and then forget about it. It's powered by electricity and can even be set to change color."

Eva was a beautiful and kind woman, but Susan could do without some of her fancy impulses. The charcuterie table was challenging enough. This sounded like extra trouble and fuss. She glanced at Ruthie, who shrugged and gave her a questioning look.

"The open house is scheduled from four to seven. Luke will be here before four. He'll be outside, guiding people around the property." At the mention of Luke, Susan felt the familiar weight settle into her core. Today, with all the activity, she could at least postpone the unavoidable conversation she knew was coming. Susan watched as the car passed by familiar homes and businesses.

Eva's overview continued. "I want our guests to see both the outdoor areas and the inside. Our conservation focus is one of the unique features of Saw Grass Inn. It's something I'm highlighting. Luke can guide the camera crew. I've got WWSB, Suncoast TV, coming to cover us."

"Don't you dare put me on TV," Ruthie said.

"Me neither," said Susan. Her parents had always disliked taking photos, even though they were slowly becoming more accepted within their Old Order community. The idea of being on television was unimaginable.

"I'm sure you'd both do fine, but I already told them that my Amish girls are camera-shy," Eva said with a bright smile in the rearview mirror. Susan and Ruthie sat in the back seat this morning. The passenger seat was filled with paper goods and utensils for the open house.

"They're just planning a quick outdoor interview with me. It will probably be edited down to about a minute on TV, but every little bit helps right now. I'll be in the lobby greeting people and handing out information packets. Besides the ads I purchased, we are hosting the Chamber of Commerce After Hours. I also sent special invitations to all the service clubs in Sarasota. I'm excited to see who all shows up."

Susan's stomach growled. She wasn't eager to dodge TV cameras or be around the important people Eva said would visit the inn. She was familiar with feeling out of her element, and she suspected that today would be no different.

"If you two keep an eye on the refreshments, we should be in good shape," Eva said. "When I pick up the charcuterie foods, I'll also stop by the rental place and pick up the beverage fountain. I'll help you set it up and make sure it works. Just have fun with everything. Keep the tables neat and greet guests. Be your pleasant selves, and everything will be fine."

Susan and Ruthie's eyes met, and Ruthie made a silly face. Susan rolled her eyes, and they both stifled giggles. Maybe Eva's positivity and excitement were rubbing off on Susan. Just a little.

Eva pulled up to the back door and unlocked the inn. She pointed out baskets and ceramic crockery on the top shelf of the pantry. "You can tuck the poinsettias in those. Keep it simple. Use the white tablecloths." She walked into the lobby and lit the Christmas tree, even though it was still morning. She looked around, then back and forth between Susan and Ruthie with a glowing smile.

"When I think about all you two have done, I am so grateful. I couldn't have achieved any of this without you. I hope you realize how much you both mean to me." Her eyes welled up with tears. "God brought you into my life at just the right moment. You are exactly who I needed to make a fresh start. If only Caleb could see what we've accomplished here together."

Susan felt a surge of love for Eva. She was almost like a second mother—a spiritual mother—to her. She nodded at Eva, unsure how to respond. Ruthie took Eva's hand. "We were glad to help. You helped us, too. We needed an adventure, and we've definitely had that here. Haven't we, Susan?"

Susan nodded. "It's true, Eva. I've learned so much. I never imagined two months ago when we left Ohio that we'd be doing all of this." She swept her arm in a circular motion around the lobby.

"Look at me now. Crying. But seriously, thank you. Now, let's launch Saw Grass Inn and have fun doing it. Group hug." Eva wrapped her arms around each girl and pulled them close. The warmth of their friendship grew. Christmas lights twinkled. Sunlight filtered through the tall windows and reflected off the polished front desk. Satisfaction filled Susan's chest, and her problems with Luke faded. Somehow, someway, she would get through all of it— the open house and the eventual talk she needed to have with Luke.

After Eva left, Ruthie cleaned the floor and dusted while Susan arranged poinsettias. She found a large silver container for the gigantic white poinsettia that a florist delivered and placed it on a stand near the dining room doorway. Later, more floral arrangements arrived. Susan and Ruthie thanked the delivery people and set them on the front desk. The last-minute tidying, decorating the tables, and receiving gifts made the morning hours fly by.

When Eva returned, they greeted her and carried everything from the station wagon into the sparkling kitchen. "Some surprises are waiting for you," Susan told her. "Take a look at the lobby." They left the unpacked bags and followed Eva to see her reaction.

"Goodness, I never imagined all of this. Aren't they beautiful?" Each arrangement was a seasonal bouquet. There were live planters decorated with glittery deer, red berries, and fancy ornamental picks. Eva opened the cards from local merchants, the Chamber of Commerce, and close friends. She read every word aloud. Susan and Ruthie admired them with her. Eva was a remarkable woman, and it was an honor to work for her.

"If you two want to start unpacking the food and prepping the produce, I'll make the rounds and place some of these in the rooms," Eva said. She glanced at her watch. "I brought some deli sandwiches and chicken salad on croissants for when you're ready for lunch."

———————————

The guests arrived in waves with brief pauses in between. Susan and Ruthie heard Eva's voice in the lobby, and when it grew quieter, they knew she had stepped outside onto the patio. Guests wandered in and admired the charcuterie, and a few looked at the two Amish women with curiosity. Susan naturally fell into the role she had once imagined when she wanted to be a food server in a restaurant. The feeling she had as she greeted people and offered refreshments reminded her of long-ago school programs when she went up front to say her piece. Back then, she pretended to be confident even though she was shaking inside. Now, years later, that tactic paid off. When she focused on others, it became easy. As if she had always been out there talking to strangers, saying hello to women with dyed hair and dangling earrings, and greeting men wearing ties and loafers without socks.

Susan remained in the dining room, managing the charcuterie table and making sure the fountain didn't run out of punch or ice. Soft music played in the background. Ruthie periodically returned to the kitchen to fetch another tray of snacks or a gallon of punch. It was all easier than Susan had expected. When needed, they put on plastic gloves and rearranged and freshened the table.

Eva's laughter echoed through the lobby. From time to time, she brought someone into the dining room to meet Susan and Ruthie. A few people reconnecting with old friends stayed longer than usual at a table in the back. Finally, after a couple of busy hours, the pace slowed down. "We've been working nonstop without a break. It's time for some fresh air," Ruthie said to Susan. "When you get back, I'll take my turn."

Susan poured herself a glass of punch and stepped out into the humid air. She walked the length of the inn, heading toward the Adirondack chairs under the big pine tree, all the while fighting off melancholy memories of sitting there with Luke a couple of weeks ago. As she rounded the corner of the inn, Luke charged toward her, unaware. He body-slammed her, knocking her to the ground.

They lay there, chest to chest, for a moment. Then Luke jumped up, his face reddening. "Oh, sorry! I didn't see you. Are you okay?" He was as handsome as ever. In the heat of this afternoon, his cologne clung to Susan's dress, and she breathed it in as her body curled forward, trying to catch her breath. Luke reached out his hand. She winced but took it, and he pulled her up. He brushed grass clippings from her back, and his touch sent a shiver up her spine. "Are you hurt? I didn't see you." Fortunately, the flimsy punch cup flew from her hand and spilled on the ground, not her dress. She picked it up. "I'm not hurt. But watch where you're going." Her voice sounded too shrill.

"I'm so sorry. I have an emergency out there." He indicated the wooded area he and Susan had worked to restore. "Someone fell and got hurt. I need some first aid supplies."

Susan pulled away from him. "I know where we keep the first aid," she said. She turned back to the inn and grabbed the kit from the pantry shelf "Here." She thrust the kit into Luke's hands as he entered the back door. "How bad is it? The person who got hurt?" she asked.

"Might be serious. She's bleeding. That's why I was in such a hurry," Luke said. "It's a woman. I might need your help. Can you come?" He was worried, and because of her, he had lost more precious time. She hesitated, then followed Luke, who was practically running down the path.

"The woman is right over here; she fell down a small embankment. I just saw the blood and ran." He veered off the woodchip path and pushed through the palmettos. A woman in her twenties, wearing a fitted, light-colored dress, stood leaning on her friend, holding a high-heeled sandal. They laughed as the friend brushed leaves from the injured woman's hair.

"I'm back. I brought the first aid kit and reinforcements."

The woman gave Luke a flirtatious smile. "I'm fine. Really. Just a little scrape. And maybe a bruised ego." Luke stayed professional and opened the first aid kit.

"I've got some antibacterial wipes here. Some bandages." He handed over the supplies. The injured woman's friend wiped at the scraped kneecap and placed a large adhesive bandage. The injured woman put on her sandal.

"The path is that way. You'll be fine if you stay on the path." Luke and Susan watched as the two women climbed the embankment, laughing as their high heels sank into the sandy soil. Susan felt her athletic shoes firmly underneath her, grateful her feet were well grounded, even though her insides were still shaking from her mishap with Luke.

The women turned and waved. "Thanks! You're a lifesaver," the flirty one said.

When they were out of earshot, Luke said, "Sorry. That was a false alarm. Maybe I panicked. I got worried the way they were yelling."

"It was just a scrape," Susan said.

"I don't know why they ever went down there. And wearing high heels, too," Luke said.

For the second time, in a few minutes, Luke took Susan's hand and led her up the embankment.

She pulled away when they reached the path. Luke walked a few paces and then sat down on a large stump. "Sit here with me a minute." He patted a spot beside him. Susan stayed where she was. Luke stretched his long legs out in front of him, and Susan wavered. She was tired and a little sore from the fall. She sat, willing herself not to let her body touch his. Her dress skirt flowed in a blue puddle around her.

"I wanted to talk to you," Luke said. "Now's as good a time as any."

Susan felt her heart pounding at his nearness. She looked out over the landscape. "I can't talk now. I should get back to the dining room. It's Ruthie's turn to take a break."

Luke ignored her. "You've been avoiding me, and I want to know why. Did I do something wrong? I thought we were friends, maybe heading toward something more. But you've done nothing but give me the cold shoulder lately." He was staring at his boots as he talked. Did Susan hear a quaver in his voice? Did it bother him that much? And what did he mean by "maybe something more"?

"I can explain it," Susan said. She slightly turned to face him. Her heart pounded, and she took a deep breath. The words swirling in her mind for days were finally ready. She owed Luke an explanation.

"Good. I want to hear it," he said. He looked away. "But you have a point about Ruthie. How about we postpone it for a day?" If Luke saw Susan's anxiety, he didn't show it. "Tomorrow's Saturday. I'd like to take you out to Siesta Key. Walk the beach. We can talk then. We'll have a heart-to-heart, okay?"

Susan felt herself drawn into the dark chocolate depths of Luke's searching gaze. Everything softened inside from the warmth of being with him, out in the jungle again. He was right to demand an explanation, but now he'd offered a welcome pause. Tomorrow would give them what she wanted: time, space, and privacy.

"I'll come by at five. We can watch the sunset out there," Luke said. "Now, how about I walk you back to the inn? Looks like the party is about to end. Let's hope there are some leftover snacks."

CHAPTER 23

Susan matched Luke's stride as they headed back toward the inn. Her insides quaked as she tried to figure out what had just happened. Luke was quiet, as if content to wait until tomorrow to talk. Or maybe he was tired, like she was.

A walk on the beach. Even though she and Ruthie had been in Sarasota for nearly two months, they had never made it to Siesta Key. Weekdays at the inn were busy, and Eva had things on her mind besides entertaining Susan and Ruthie. Now, Susan's first trip to the beach would be without Ruthie. Had Luke asked her out on a date? If it wasn't a date, Ruthie would have been included. But he didn't mention that. Luke said he wanted to have a "heart-to-heart," something Ruthie had been encouraging Susan to do.

It was nearly seven. All the guests had left, and the open house had been a major success. As they entered the inn, Susan went into the dining room looking for Ruthie, while Luke stayed in the lobby with Eva.

Susan and Ruthie had been too busy to eat. But now, they placed a few snacks on small plates and returned to the lobby. Eva looked exhausted and lounged in an overstuffed chair with her shoes off, drinking bottled water. Ruthie eased into the leather chair behind the front desk. And Susan sat on a wooden bench beneath the big window. Luke stood by the door.

"Luke, grab a container and help yourself to whatever is left in there," Eva said, motioning toward the dining room.

"Thanks, Eva. But I need to head out. I had no idea it was so late."

"Of course. I won't keep you. Tell your parents I appreciate them coming out this afternoon. I barely had a chance to say hello to them. And thanks for all you did today," Eva said.

"Okay. Will do." Luke shifted from one foot to the other.

"I heard many positive comments about the landscaping. EdenKeepers—and you—deserve all the praise. You too, Susan," she added.

"Thanks, I had a great time this afternoon," Luke said. "See ya' later." He headed toward the Jeep, then stopped, turned around, and waved at Susan. "You. Tomorrow. At five." Then he was gone.

Ruthie gaped. "Tomorrow? What's happening tomorrow?" Ruthie asked.

Eva smiled knowingly.

Susan had just taken a bite and nearly choked, swallowing a chunk of dry, peppery water cracker. She coughed as Eva and Ruthie waited, giving her a moment to gather her thoughts, which still didn't come out very clearly.

"Earlier, Luke and I were talking when someone fell off the embankment by the path. He was helping her, and I grabbed the first aid kit for him." A shadow crossed Eva's face.

"What happened?"

"It wasn't much of an injury. She was okay," Susan said.

Ruthie's eyes were riveted on her friend.

"Anyway, afterward, he confronted me about avoiding him," Susan's voice grew lower with each word. She hated admitting this to Eva.

Ruthie smirked.

"Were you?" Eva asked. "Avoiding him?"

"I think she was," Ruthie said.

Susan glared at her friend.

Eva's eyes widened. "He's a long-time friend of Caleb and me. I was hoping to get you two together. Did he do something that made you want to avoid him?" Eva fanned her face with an inn brochure and waited.

"It's kind of complicated," she paused. "I like Luke. I do. He's always polite and thoughtful. It's just that we need to talk about some things. And after I went to check on the injured woman—it was just a scrape—Luke asked me...well...he said he wanted to take me to the beach tomorrow to see the sunset." A crimson blush started at her collarbone and crept up to her forehead. She took a long sip of punch. *Please don't ask me why he wants to talk to me.*

Finally, Eva broke the silence. "It's okay. I don't need to know all your business. But if he did something wrong....He didn't hurt you or anything, did he? I can't imagine he would, but if you were avoiding him...."

"No. Not at all." Susan's cheeks flushed deeper.

"That's wonderful, Susan." Ruthie's enthusiasm was over the top. "You said you wanted to go to the beach. Maybe he read your mind." She flashed her funny Ruthie smile.

Eva looked back and forth between the two. "That's great, Susan. You're going to have a wonderful time at the beach with Luke. Which beach?"

"Siesta Key." *Please. Can we change the subject now?*

Eva's face lit up. "It's beautiful. And it's the perfect place to go when you need to talk things over." Susan gave her a thin smile. Eva would be disappointed if Susan and Luke didn't end up a couple. But it was a relief when she didn't ask more questions.

Eva had recovered somewhat, and the conversation shifted to a recap of the open house. "This all turned out even better than I expected," Eva said, sweeping her hands to take in the floral bouquets, the brochures, and the Christmas tree. "And it looked like you got along fine in the dining room. I wish I could have helped you more, but I was busy every minute. We'll tackle the mess in there shortly."

"I was a little scared at first," Ruthie admitted. "But the refreshments were so easy once we were set up."

"When you first mentioned that beverage fountain, I wasn't sure about it," Susan added. "But people enjoyed being able to serve themselves. Everyone was having a great time."

"I'll admit it," Eva said. "I always get a little nervous before a party. Especially when I'm the host, but I couldn't be more pleased with how this went. People loved the décor and took cards and brochures to give to friends. Saw Grass Inn is off to a great start. I even have a full house booked for two weekends in March."

"Sounds like we need to prepare that second floor," Susan said.

"Right. But first, we're going to celebrate Christmas, and you two will spend a few well-deserved days back in Ohio with your families," Eva sighed. "Ruthie, I know you have that special beau waiting for you when you go home to Ohio. Whatever you decide about coming back for the spring season is okay. Looks like I'm going to have to hire extra help no matter what."

"I'll decide soon," Ruthie said. "Maybe I can come back and stay through the end of April. I'll know more after I talk to my parents and Ben." Now it was Ruthie's turn to blush. The room grew quiet. The long day, aside from some cleanup, was finally over. Saw Grass Inn was officially launched.

As she went through her Saturday chores—cleaning and laundry—Susan thought about the upcoming evening with Luke. She rehearsed a few words in her mind, considering how she would start. "I'm sorry. I should have told you earlier." But....Her thoughts drifted to Luke—the sensation of his hand when he helped her up after the fall, the way he pleaded for an explanation, his energy and enthusiasm for his work, and his unwavering dedication to the church and his family. Eva had pictured Susan and Luke as a couple. *I like your thinking, Eva. But I'm afraid it's impossible.*

At three in the afternoon, the house chores were done, and Ruthie announced she was walking over to Pinecraft to do some shopping and drop her latest letter to Ben at the post office. Thankfully, she didn't tease Susan about her upcoming date. They were alone in their room, putting away the clean laundry. "I'll be praying for you," Ruthie said. "I know you're worried, especially about telling him you were at the scene when his cousin Ray died. But God has a plan for you. I'm sure of it."

Ruthie didn't often talk about spiritual things, so her caring words made Susan feel reassured. Somehow, she believed she'd find the strength and resolve to be honest with Luke.

After Ruthie left, Eva appeared in the doorway of the bedroom. "Tonight's a big night," she said, smiling brightly. "Your first date with Luke."

And probably the last. Susan blushed as her hand moved to her face. Eva's calling it a "first date" triggered the jitters she'd felt all day.

"I'm planning to read and nap on the lanai for a while," Eva said. "Why don't you get ready in my bathroom? You can use the jetted tub."

"What is a jetted tub?" Susan asked.

"Come here, I'll show you." Eva led Susan into the private bathroom attached to her bedroom. She demonstrated how to operate the tub, filled it with water, and retrieved fluffy white towels from a shelf. She added bath salts to the water. "I know you're a little nervous about this evening," Eva said. "That's understandable. This will help you re-lax." She lit a scented candle. "You go get your things and take your time. This is a great way to unwind before your big date. Enjoy!"

"...big date," was it really?

Eva picked up a magazine from her nightstand and left Susan in the unfamiliar room. Lavender-scented fragrance wafted from the tub. Susan undressed and sank into the deep tub. The slanted back supported her as she rested her head on a rolled towel. The water bubbled around her, and she took deep breaths, letting her fear swirl with the water. Ruthie's words echoed in her mind. "God has a plan for you. I'm sure of it." As Susan rested, her fears and doubts began to fade. Whatever happened tonight, she would accept it and move forward. She might have witnessed Ray's death, but she was no longer the same Susan she'd been that night. Whatever Luke said or thought when she told him the truth tonight, she knew she would always carry within her God's forgiveness and peace.

Luke didn't seem in any hurry to have that "heart-to-heart" he'd mentioned on Friday afternoon. He arrived in a car Susan had never seen, a white convertible. "I hope this is an acceptable ride for this evening," he said. He bowed slightly as he opened the passenger door for her. "I can put the top up if you prefer."

"No. This is fine," Susan said as she slid in. She tucked her pale aqua dress beneath her. The shiny interior smelled of leather cleaner. Luke came around to the driver's side and slid in beside her. It was a small car, and Susan felt nervous with him so close. She'd never been in a convertible. "This is nice," she said. "I didn't know you had a car. I always saw you driving a truck."

"This is my brother's car. It will soon be a classic. It's a 2006 Saab. S-A-A-B. He calls her Wasabi—you know, like the hot mustard. It even has a vanity plate that says WASABI."

Susan nodded, even though she had no idea what wasabi was. She filed the word away for further research, and she'd never heard of a Saab car.

"Yeah, it might have made my brother *sob* a few times," Luke said with a chuckle. "But he's been driving it around and told me to take it for a spin tonight."

The wind whooshing around them made it hard to converse. Susan was glad she'd fastened her *kapp* with extra bobby pins. Otherwise, it might have already blown away.

They managed to say a few words at stoplights and while traveling through the less busy streets. Soon, they reached the narrow bottleneck where the city gives way to the Intracoastal Waterway. Luke pointed out the bridge they would cross. "Let's hope we don't have a long wait," he said. "If there's a bridge lift, we might miss seeing the sunset on the beach."

It was the longest bridge Susan had ever seen.

"Traffic is heavy. It might take us some time." Wasabi was creeping along, giving Susan and Luke the luxury of conversation. She glanced at him as he studied the traffic. He smelled of that woodsy cologne she'd noticed at the inn on Friday. His straight, black hair was windblown. After avoiding him, it felt good to be with him again. All the resistance and fear she felt melted when she was around him. *How does he do this to me?*

Their eyes met. "I'm so glad you agreed to come tonight. I've been meaning to bring you here since the week we worked together. You're going to love it."

The traffic started moving again. "You know, Siesta Key is an island. This bridge opened in 1917. Before this bridge, people had to take a boat to get there. Like everywhere, people left their mark. Before the bridge, the whole island was filled with wildlife and greenery." Susan looked over the land ahead, where a few palm trees stood among tall buildings.

"A second bridge was built to connect the southern part of the county to the island. That's the Stickney Point Bridge."

Susan tried to concentrate, but being so close to Luke and hearing his voice made her feel a little dizzy. Luckily, the traffic started to move, and soon they were cruising across the bridge. The air had a tangy seaside scent new to Susan, but it seemed as if she'd always known it.

Luke was trying to tell her something. His voice carried over the breeze. "They called it Clam Island, Little Sarasota Island, or Sarasota Key. I'll tell you a little more when we get there. Just go ahead and enjoy the view."

Soon they were back on land, and Luke started looking for a place to park. "There's a place I like around here," he said. He pulled into a parking lot and found a spot. "Stay right where you are a minute," he added.

Susan smoothed her *kapp* and tucked in a few tendrils of hair. The air was warm and salty. Luke came around to her side and opened the door. He stepped back. "Here we are," he said.

As they approached the beach from the parking lot, Susan noticed rubber mats that created pathways to the water. The beach was expansive, and even though the parking lot was full, it wasn't crowded. "You can take off your shoes if you want to. Or just walk the beach in sandals," Luke said. "Even on the hottest days, Siesta Beach feels cool underfoot. It has to do with the type of sand. It's millions of years old, they say."

"But how would anyone know how old the sand is?" Susan mused.

"I'm not sure. And honestly? I don't care that much. God's creation is full of mysteries. And doesn't it say somewhere in the Bible that for God, a thousand years are like a day?"

Luke reached for Susan's hand, and a tickle ran up her arm. He laced his fingers through hers, and she felt his rough calluses against her softer skin. He led her to the water, which was crashing in waves on the sand. The constant soft rush of the ocean, the twittering of small birds, and the glistening sand filled her with wonder.

"It's so beautiful," she said to Luke. She inhaled, trying to calm her nerves, and tasted the salty air.

"I thought you'd like it," he said. "Let's just walk a little bit, shall we?"

They walked along the shore hand in hand. Susan forgot to be nervous about the heart-to-heart she knew was coming. The rhythmic sound of waves, punctuated by the screeching gulls, lulled her into a surreal yet perfectly normal state. Luke stayed silent. Maybe he recognized she needed to breathe in the salty air and take in the beauty of her first visit to the ocean. The white, sparkling sand and aquamarine sea stretched lavishly around them on every side.

When they reached a spot where rocks jutted into the water, Luke led her to a flat area on the rocks where they sat down. "This is where I like to watch the sunset," Luke said. "It's almost time now." Susan fixed her eyes on a spot where the sky met the ocean. An orange-pink glow stretched across the horizon. "It happens fast," Luke said. "Don't look away for long." They watched the golden orb slowly dip, then become a half circle, a crescent, and finally a golden sliver resting on the water.

Susan realized she'd been holding her breath. She inhaled deeply, feeling the evening coolness intensify. The sky was far from dark; they could still see everything clearly around them. Luke turned to her. "About that heart-to-heart we need to have. What is going on? We worked together at Eva's, and everything seemed fine. Then, you came to church and the potluck, and since then, you've been avoiding me. Why?"

Susan took another deep breath. Her insides quivered, and a sour taste rose in her throat. Luke waited, fixing his eyes on the water. Perhaps he hoped it would be easier for her to talk if he wasn't watching.

"I'm sorry. I didn't know how to tell you something, and I need to. I didn't know you were from Ohio...."

"Long ago," Luke said.

"I didn't know your cousin was Ray."

Luke shifted his gaze from the ocean and looked at her. "Wait. You know—knew Ray? I thought you were from Holmes County? Ray's family is in Ashland."

"I didn't know Ray. But I was there the night he died. I'm so ashamed. I'm not the same now that I'm here in Sarasota. Back in Ohio, I was running around with a guy—Amos. He wasn't a good influence. He took me places in his car—places I wish I hadn't gone. The night Ray died, he took me to Red Hawk Country Fest, a big country music festival. There was a lot of drinking in our group, and Ray, well, I think he overdosed. I think he died from drinking too much. Some thought he had a heart condition. I don't know what really happened. But I could have stopped him from drinking like that and I didn't."

Luke's face turned pale. His jaw clenched, and his eyes darkened.

Susan caught his glance. "Luke, I'm so, so very sorry. I was sitting there, and suddenly, I saw this young boy on the ground, passed out. A lot of the guys in our group were drunk by then—not me. I just drank a wine spritzer. The officers came around to check IDs, and he didn't respond. It was so scary."

Luke looked away; a fixed stare dropped from the water to the sand. He said nothing.

"There were EMTs on the grounds, and they were called. Most of our group left the concert, but I stayed. I didn't know he was gone at that point. I'm so sorry, Luke."

Luke stood and began pacing back and forth, finally walking away from Susan toward the water. Susan watched him go, his footprints leaving a trail behind. Tears welled up at the corners of her eyes. If only she hadn't gone to that concert. Things would be so different now. Would Luke even try to understand? Could he forgive her?

✳

CHAPTER 24

Susan kept her eyes on Luke, who walked along the shore, head bowed. He drifted farther from her down the beach. Tears welled up and spilled onto her face, mixing with the salty air. She wiped at her cheeks and looked again toward the ocean, but her vision blurred. Now Luke blended into the scattered shore walkers until she couldn't spot him anymore. Was he the man there, bending down as if he'd found a shell? Or was that him in the pale blue shirt, striding quickly? So many solitary figures out there, each in their own world, searching for something on their walk along the Gulf. Her eyes fixed on a blurry figure with dark hair. That must be him.

An older Amish couple, barefoot and holding hands, walked past her as she leaned against the rocks, wiping away her tears. Concerned expressions crossed their faces when they saw her. "You okay?" the man asked. His thin denim pant legs were rolled up just below his knees. The woman held her skirt hem bunched in her hand along with her sandal straps.

"I'm all right," Susan sniffled, and her breath came out in a little shudder. She managed a tepid smile. "I'm waiting for someone. He's out there." She motioned toward the shore.

"Well, you take care then," the man said.

The woman smiled and nodded.

The couple headed toward the parking lot, leaving Susan to reflect on what she had said. *I'm waiting for someone. He's out there.* Her mind was a jumble of scattered thoughts. *What was wrong with me...back then? Amos....How did I get so tangled up?* She wrapped her arms around herself and leaned forward, letting her eyes rest on the soft, pale fabric of her dress. It was the color of the ocean and had been her favorite dress last summer in Ohio, but she'd only worn it a few times. She'd been such a different person back then—so confused and unhappy.

A tiny brown bird with long legs caught her attention as she straightened up. It stopped hopping and looked at her as if it had absorbed every word in her mind. *"You're waiting for someone? Are you sure he's coming back?"* Its soft, white breast heaved, and its squeaky little voice seemed to mimic hers. *"Waiting for someone? Waiting? Waiting? Coming back? Coming back? Squeak!"*

Her mind drifted again. Susan felt the sand shift beneath her and suddenly wanted to be barefoot. She removed her sandals and let her feet sink into the cool, silvery sand. It cradled her as if God were holding her, despite life's shifting sands. She had taken the hard path, made the tough choice. She'd told the truth. God would guide her, no matter what came next. The sandpiper scurried this way and that, gained speed, and headed toward the water.

Susan watched until the bird was a speck on the sand, then lifted her eyes to see Luke walking toward her. Her heart raced. She curled her toes into the sand. *I'm waiting for someone. I'm waiting for someone.* She clenched her hands and forced herself to stay calm. Tears prickled her eyes, and she swiped at them. She didn't want Luke to see her crying.

Now he was standing in front of her, his eyes shining. Susan looked away. His compassionate gaze was more than she had ever hoped for. She looked back, and Luke wrapped her in his arms but said nothing. She felt his strong body support her smaller frame. The top of her head reached his chin, and his jaw rested gently against her forehead. She melted into the comfort of Luke's arms. This was what she'd always wanted but never thought possible.

Neither spoke for a moment as they stood, holding each other. She surrendered herself to Luke's deep embrace. Its warmth absorbed all the sadness, despair, and fear she'd been carrying since the day she heard Luke's prayer request for his aunt that Sunday at church.

Finally, Luke stepped back and took both her hands in his. "I'm sorry, I shouldn't have walked off and left you here like that," Luke said.

"You had every right." Susan's voice wobbled.

"I had no idea. I admit it took me by surprise. But what a burden you've been carrying, Susan." His sorrowful yet knowing look was so kind.

Tears, this time of release, welled up and spilled over Susan's cheeks. Luke gently wiped them with his thumb. "Luke, I wish I could go back and live that time over again. I don't know why I was so caught up in that life, hiding from the truth about who I was. I was so unhappy and confused. So lost."

"Let's sit here on the rocks for a minute. We need some time to think about this," Luke said.

They sat again in the same spot as before Susan's confession. The sky was darker now, and stars appeared, with the reflection of a full moon shimmering on the water. Susan fixed her gaze on it and listened to Luke, whose voice was soft and comforting.

"It's not your fault that Ray died. You do understand that, don't you?" Luke took her hand. "Honestly? People in our family, especially those back in Ohio, rarely talk about how he died. But I guess I've always believed it had something to do with his heart. No one really knows if the drinking was to blame. Although some did say it was a factor."

Susan felt a tingle run up her arm as Luke held her hand. "When I was with Ray after it happened, I didn't know he'd died. I just knew something was wrong." Her knees felt weak, but she kept talking. "Most of the guys in our group were so drunk, and some of the girls were, too. If anything, people in our group thought he'd passed out. After the officers came around, our group just dissolved, and I was left there with Ray and Myron, and of course, Amos, the guy I went to the concert with."

"You did the right thing by staying there. I'm glad you did that. I'm glad you were there watching out for my little cousin, even if it was too late," Luke said.

Susan let his words into her mind. It was true. She hadn't left the scene like most of the rest. She'd tried to comfort and reassure Myron, even though she didn't know either of them.

"I wish I'd been paying more attention to how much everyone was drinking. But there was so much alcohol, loud music, and confusion in our group." Susan shivered in the cool evening air as she replayed the horrors of that night. She turned so she could see Luke's face in the growing darkness.

The Susan she'd become in Sarasota was a different person from the one she'd been that night. Back in Ohio, she'd gradually let her unhappiness lead her into the evil that caused Ray's death. Here, with Eva, Ruthie, and Luke as her guides, she was returning to the strong woman she was meant to be.

The waves lapped against the shore, their rhythm providing a soothing backdrop to the difficult conversation. "Luke, I am so sorry for what happened. I'm sorry I was there, and sorry that you have to know this about me. About my past." She had been so afraid to tell him the truth. But he wasn't angry at her.

Luke wrapped his arm around her and held her close. His

body was warm, his voice gentle. He turned slightly, and his eyes met hers. "I can understand why it was hard to tell me, but honestly, Susan, I'm glad to know what happened. We can't go back and change that tragic situation anymore. All we can do is lean into God's forgiveness, knowing that if we confess our sins and are sorry for our wrongdoing, God's grace is sufficient. God will supply our every need."

Above the distant chattering of shore birds, Susan recognized the words Luke was saying—church words. She had heard them in various forms, week after week, since she was a young girl sitting beside *Maemm* on a bench listening to a sermon. Until now, they had been familiar words that floated in and out of her mind. But now, she understood their meaning. God's grace met her deep need. She was no longer trapped in a past she could never change.

"You're forgiven, Susan. God forgives you. I forgive you." They sat silently for a moment. Then Luke stood and helped her to her feet. In the glow of the full moon, he turned to face her. Peace washed over her. He looked at her, his dark eyes filled with compassion and love....

Wait, love? He didn't say the word "love," but still, Susan felt it. She let that inner knowing wash over her. Whatever it was, something of God, it was much richer, deeper, and more substantial than the romance she'd hoped for when she daydreamed about a young man who would one day walk into her life. She curled her toes in the sand and felt it shift, yet still hold her.

Luke looked down at her feet. "You took off your sandals. I did, too. Who walks on the beach in their sneakers?" He laughed, and the deep spiritual conversation seemed to come to an end.

"Luke?" Susan's voice whispered. "Thanks for understanding. I was so afraid. I wanted us to stay friends."

Luke reached for her again and held her, gently stroking her back. "Let's move on from this after tonight," he whispered. "Let's move on to what's next. Something better than just friends."

Susan's heart did a triple somersault. Had she heard that right? "I will. We will. Thank you, Luke, for understanding and accepting me. I will never forget tonight. Never. I feel...forgiven."

Luke watched her, his eyes resting on her face, then glancing over her body with a quick, affectionate look. He reached into his pocket and pulled out a small, perfect seashell. It had an elliptical shape and tiny, brown, evenly spaced spots. Luke held out the shell for Susan to see, opening his palm.

"I found this out there," he said, gesturing in the direction he'd walked right after Susan had told the truth she'd been holding inside for all those days.

"It's beautiful. So perfect," Susan exclaimed.

"It is perfect," Luke said. "It's also rare. It's a Junonia shell. When I first went out there, I was upset, and I was walking along, trying to process what you'd just told me, praying to God and asking for help. Because, you know, I liked you and I had even been praying that tonight would be special."

Susan's heart pounded as they started the long moonlit walk back up the beach.

Luke continued. "Anyway, I was just walking along, and right there in front of me, I saw this shell. I've looked for them plenty of times and have never found one. But tonight, without even trying, it washed up on the shore in my path." Luke took a breath and rubbed the shell with his finger, brushing grains of sand from the surface.

In the moonlight, they walked slowly, making their way back to the mat in the sand that would lead them to the parking lot and the car. Everything on the beach had quieted except for the waves, which kept their musical rhythm. Luke stopped, turned to face Susan, and held out the shell to her. "I want you to have it," he said. "It's yours."

"Oh, no, Luke. You just said you've been looking for one for a long time. Now you have it. You should keep it for yourself."

"Really. Take it. I want you to have it."

Susan took the shell. "Thank you. It's beautiful and I will cherish it always." The shell sat in her hand, fitting into the creases of her palm.

Luke said, "There's a story about the Junonia, about its name."

"A story? Jun-on-i-a." Susan said the shell's name slowly, letting herself savor the strange and beautiful-sounding name.

"It's just a snail," Luke said. "But they live deep in the Gulf, in water sixty to one hundred twenty feet deep—offshore. Out there on the ocean floor. Believe it or not, they're carnivorous. A meat-eating snail. We don't know much about them. Maybe that mystery makes finding one the prize it's become."

Susan opened her hand to get a better look. It gleamed in the faint moonlight. Luke kept telling his story about the shell.

"I heard you say the name: Junonia. It's beautiful, isn't it?"

"It is," Susan said.

"We happen to know where it comes from," Luke said. "Like many things in nature, the names come from long-ago languages, Latin and Greek."

"Is Junonia Latin?" Susan's Amish eighth-grade education didn't include much about other languages, but she knew the Bible they read had once been written in Latin. And the New Testament was first written in Greek.

"The name Junonia comes from a Roman goddess, Juno. If you're like me, you never put much stock in learning about Roman and Greek gods and goddesses. That's not something we Plain folks think much about. But hear me out," Luke said.

Susan smiled at this. Luke was a teacher, excited to share his knowledge, just like those first days in Eva's jungle when he seemed to know the names of every tree and bush on that little plot of land.

"You're going to like Juno," Luke said. "She was the wife of Jupiter and was known as the queen of the gods." Luke glanced at her. "You look a little skeptical. It's just a story. Okay?"

Susan smiled and wondered if she'd dare tell Ruthie about her shell, which had the name of a Roman goddess. Maybe not. It seemed a little wrong for a Christian to talk about gods and goddesses. But even so, she liked hearing Luke's story.

"Here's the sweet part, though." Luke gently held Susan's hand, the one that held the Junonia. "Juno was the protector of women. She was a strong, incredible woman who stood out among all the rest—kind of like you." Luke gave her hand a soft squeeze.

Susan considered what Luke said. *Kind of like me?*

They had reached the mat leading to the parking lot, where Wasabi-the car—was waiting for them.

The black mat gave way to a boardwalk they followed, along with the last of the other beachcombers, up to pavement and civilization. Bright streetlamps shone overhead. Luke led Susan to the faucets where people rinsed the sand off their feet. Susan stood near the water, holding her skirt to keep it from getting wet. The shell felt warm and snug between the creases in her palm, as if it belonged there now. What had he said? Something about being a strong woman. "Kind of like you," he'd said. She clutched the Junonia and let its mystery, God's mystery, fill her with hope.

CHAPTER 25

"It's still early," Luke said. "We'd have time for a sandwich or dinner. In Sarasota, we eat dinner at all hours," he grinned as he fastened his seatbelt and started the car. "What do you think? Are you hungry?"

"Sure," Susan said. Until now, the excitement of being at the beach for the first time and the high emotions of the evening had taken her attention. But Susan realized it had been a long time since her last meal. "I missed supper," she told Luke. "Eva was just starting to make it when I left."

"Perfect," Luke said. "Where should we go?" Wasabi idled in the parking lot. He placed both hands on the steering wheel and considered restaurant choices. "I know a place downtown, a fun spot with a wood-fired oven. They have great pizza."

"That sounds good, now that you mention it." Susan smiled at Luke.

Their eyes locked. A sense of calm washed over her. The tension she felt while traveling to the beach disappeared, along with the painful emotions before and immediately after her confession. She squeezed the Junonia shell and looked at it again, nestled in her hand.

They merged with the traffic leaving the beach and crossed the bridge. Cool sea breezes brushed their faces as Luke drove the convertible through the downtown streets. "It's on Lemon Avenue," Luke said. After looping around the block, he found a parking spot.

"Just a short walk from here. Sit tight. I'm coming around to open your door."

They made their way up the sidewalk, passing a coffee shop, another restaurant, and boutiques with lit holiday windows. Christmas music filled the air, and the aromas of yeast bread and fried food mingled and shifted as they strolled along. Susan slipped the smooth shell into her pocket—she always sewed a hidden pocket into the side seam of her dresses.

"The wood-fired oven at Stone Hearth is great for pizza and sourdough bread," Luke said. He took her hand, and a shiver ran up her arm. "Are you cold?" he asked. She wasn't. Even so, he dropped her hand and wrapped his arm around her shoulder. He pulled her close, and she felt his warmth against her. They walked comfortably like that as he matched his long strides to her shorter ones. She let herself lean into him, feeling safe and secure.

When they arrived at the restaurant, a host in a crisp white shirt greeted them. "Good evening. I'm Marco. Welcome to Stone Hearth. Two for dinner?" They nodded.

The Stone Hearth had a cozy outdoor patio with wrought iron chairs and tables covered in white tablecloths. This was a step above the Ohio restaurants Susan knew—the western-themed Black Steer or Village Pizza with its hard plastic tables and benches.

"Do you have an outdoor table?" Luke asked. Strings of white lights crisscrossed the open-air dining area and spiraled around the trunks of palms in the tree lawn. Music played in the background. The atmosphere was festive, and Susan felt everything inside her surrender to this moment. It seemed like a page from a story, not her actual life.

"Sorry, those are all taken at the moment." Marco shrugged apologetically. "I have a couple of tables inside, or you can wait here for one to open up." He looked from one to the other. Susan saw how his eyes lingered on her a little longer than necessary. Her home-made Amish dress and *kapp* weren't a common sight at this restaurant. Luke was Plain, too, but his gray dress pants and pale blue short-sleeved shirt let him blend in.

Luke may have noticed her discomfort and the unnecessary attention. "We'll take one of the indoor tables. Might be a little warmer in there, too." He squeezed Susan's shoulder, then dropped his arm and signaled for her to follow the host.

They weaved between the outdoor tables to the door, which was designed to look like a barn door but was stained and polished to a shine. They followed Marco into the dark interior, where he stopped and seated them at a rustic booth near the wood-fired oven. She could feel the heat even from a few yards away. It was behind a barricade of rustic rails and steel hog fence, something she'd never expected to see here.

"I had the best pizza ever in my life at this place," Luke said. "They smother it with so much cheese that all the vegetables and meat toppings are sealed inside. It steam cooks under the cheese blanket. Are you hungry for pizza?"

"I am now," Susan giggled. Any self-consciousness she might have had before was gone. It felt so right to sit across from Luke. "Thank you for this. For everything tonight."

He smiled back. "Glad you like it," he said.

A waiter came to take their drink orders. "I'll take a raspberry lemonade," Luke said.

Susan followed his lead. The drinks arrived at the table, along with a small basket of hot-from-the-fryer house-made potato chips and small cups of dipping sauce. "You ever fry potato chips at home?" Luke asked as he dived into the basket.

"No. Did you?" Susan took a chip and dipped it into what looked like ranch sauce. "Yum!"

"No. My mom's afraid of grease fires. I think there was one when she was a little girl, and she's avoided deep frying her whole life."

"I can understand her fear," Susan said. "Back home, our shop caught on fire a few years ago. You worry a lot more after something like that happens. If she doesn't deep fry, then your mother probably doesn't make *Knie blatza*," Susan said.

"Knee patches?"

"They have many names—*Kuchli*, nothings, elephant ears, funnel cakes. And they're deep fried and covered in powdered sugar. We usually make them at Christmas."

"I think I've had them. Elephant ears. But no, she never made them."

The waiter came back and took their medium sausage pizza order, topped with peppers, mushrooms, and onions.

They continued talking, allowing the conversation to drift as they explored similarities and small differences in how they were raised. Susan's favorite pie was rhubarb. Luke's was shoo-fly pie. They both enjoyed biking and disliked going to family reunions. When the pizza arrived, their chat paused as they dug into the greasy cheese, enjoying the mix of sauces and toppings.

"Speaking of Christmas," Luke said, stopping to wipe his mouth with a fresh napkin from the stack on the table. "We have our Christmas program tomorrow at church. I hope you can come. I put together a chorus. We're doing 'Star of Bethlehem' and a couple of other hymns as special music. We missed you the last couple of weeks; we could have used you and Ruthie in our young people's chorus. Too late now." He winked at her, trying to keep the moment light.

But Susan dropped her head. She'd gone to such lengths avoiding Luke that she even convinced Ruthie to skip church. "I'm sorry Ruthie and I weren't at church. It was my fault. I was avoiding you."

"I know," Luke said. "And now I know why."

"I'll join next time for sure," Susan said. "Having a chorus sing on Sunday morning is different from church back home. On Christmas Sunday, we sing traditional German hymns from the *Ausbund*. The young people have a special singing group, but my *Daett* wouldn't like it if they sang on Sunday morning. He'd say it's 'just for show.'"

Luke nodded. "My parents were Amish growing up in Ohio. I was too young to remember much, but I've heard my parents talk about it. There are some differences in how we do things at Harvest Home, but underneath, we still share the same core beliefs. The important ones."

"I know," Susan said. "I like Harvest, especially the singing." The first time she saw Luke was at the revival meeting, and she couldn't take her eyes off his black hair. She loved his energy, the way his body moved as he led the singing. Was that love at first sight? She felt a flush rise in her cheeks.

If Luke noticed, he didn't let on.

"We'll be there tomorrow," Susan assured him. "You know, I almost forgot tomorrow is Sunday and that it's almost Christmas. It doesn't feel like it outside when it's as warm as summer. And Eva has kept us so busy. I guess we got a reminder when Eva had us put up that Christmas tree in the lobby."

"You and Ruthie did a great job with that," Luke said.

By now, they'd completely decimated the pizza. A passing waiter grabbed the empty pizza pan and collected the pile of messy napkins. He returned with the check, and Luke handed him a credit card. While they waited for it, they sipped the last of their lemonade. Luke reached across the table for her hand. "Before we go, Susan, there's something I want to say. Or ask."

Susan's insides quivered. Would he want more details about his cousin Ray? Did he have concerns about how easily she'd skipped church? Maybe questions about her drinking friends back in Ohio? Whatever was coming was serious, and he was taking his time. Susan held her breath, waiting to see what would happen next.

"Susan, I like you. I like you more than any of the few girls I've dated off and on over the years. Honestly, I'd given up on ever finding someone. Just quit looking or thinking about it. Then you came along. I wasn't expecting anyone, let alone an Amish girl, but here you are." There was a hint of awe in his voice. He looked across the table at her, tears starting to brim in the brown pools of his eyes.

"I—I don't know what to say, Luke." She paused, trying to absorb what he'd just said, what it meant.

Luke let go of her hand. "We haven't known each other very long, but I don't think I've ever been happier with anyone than when you and I worked together at Eva's inn. You're so strong. So capable. I feel so...happy when I'm with you."

Luke continued. "When you showed up at church and stayed for the potluck a few weeks ago, I hoped we might get together as a couple. Then, afterward, when you avoided me, I was frustrated, even angry. My emotions have been all over the place lately." Luke stopped talking and looked at her directly, expectantly.

The waiter came back, and Luke added a tip, signed the receipt, and put his card in his wallet.

"I've been so upset about all of this for the past two weeks," Susan said. "I was afraid to tell you about being at the concert and what I knew about how Ray died," Susan said. "I knew I had to tell you, and I assumed I'd lose you as a friend. I didn't want you to know what I used to be like."

"I'll admit it. At first, it was shocking. I didn't picture you being like that—going to places where there was drinking and partying. That's not the way I imagined you," Luke said.

"I was struggling at home. My friends and even my younger sister had gotten married, leaving me behind. But running around and hanging out with rough friends didn't make me any happier."

Luke's eyes held hers. "The thing is, Susan, I want us to be more than friends. Maybe God meant for us to be together as a couple. Maybe forever." Luke looked serious. "I don't know if you have anyone back in Ohio. If you do, I'll try to understand," he said.

"No. I went with Amos, but he wasn't right for me. I broke up with him before I came to Florida."

"Then, would you go out with me again? I want us to get to know each other better. See what happens."

"I'd love spending more time with you, Luke," Susan said. Her heart was pounding. "The reason I was so devastated when I realized Ray was your cousin was that I already liked you so much and was hoping you'd ask me out. I figured you'd be done with me after you knew the truth," Susan said.

"Done with you? How could you think that?" Luke asked.

"I guess I thought you'd blame me for Ray's death. I felt guilty. It seemed like it was my fault because I kept thinking afterward that I could have stopped him from drinking so much." Susan paused, reflecting on how different this evening was from the one she first envisioned—and feared.

"Guilt by association," Luke said. "I get it. But, like I told you, it's not your fault he died. Ray shouldn't have been drinking like that.

He should have known better. Maybe he didn't. It was more like an accident. Not something you could have prevented."

Susan let his words sink in. "I know," she said. "If we're supposed to be together, I believe God can work out the details." Susan thought about her parents, her sister, and her brothers. They'd be disappointed if she stayed in Florida. And if she left the Amish. "I think somehow, we'll know the right thing to do when the time comes, don't you agree?"

"I do," Luke replied. "We'll take it one step at a time. Get to know each other better. I already know one thing: You're a strong woman. A wise woman. And you have a strong faith."

Susan gently touched the shell through the soft fabric of her dress. It still rested safely in her pocket, a keepsake from that special moment she and Luke shared on the beach. She hadn't considered herself a strong woman—unless it was physical strength, like gardening. But she knew her weaknesses well. "Thanks. I know that hasn't always been true, but I'm getting stronger now that I'm here in Florida and I've had time to think."

"We can save that for another time," Luke said. He looked at his watch. "It's getting late, and we have church tomorrow. I'd better get you home."

When they arrived at Eva's, the house was dark except for the solar lights lining the sidewalk and a light above the front door. Luke held Susan's hand as he walked her to the door. When they reached it, he turned to face her. "I guess this is where we say goodnight," he said.

Susan felt butterflies fluttering inside her chest. *Will he kiss me?* she wondered. She hoped he would. But he was such a gentleman, and it was their first date. He reached down and wrapped her in his arms, pulling her so close she could feel his heartbeat against her cheek. "Thank you for everything, Luke. It was a wonderful evening," she whispered.

"Yes," he said. "It was." He let go of her, held her at arm's length, and looked at her with tenderness. "I'll see you tomorrow at church. Sleep well."

"You, too," Susan said. She reached for the door, but Luke did, too. He opened it, and she stepped inside. "See you tomorrow."

He closed the door gently, leaving Susan alone in Eva's foyer, feeling strange, weak, and wonderful all at once. She reached into her pocket and took out the Junonia. It sparkled in her hand under the faint foyer light. She looked at its brown markings and felt the smooth surface. What a long journey that shell had taken—from the depths of the ocean, out into the deepest waters, to the shore, into Luke's hand, and now safely nestled in hers. The small shell would remind her of the strength she'd found to do the right thing. Outside in the driveway, she heard Wasabi start up as Luke pulled away and headed home.

In the quiet house, Susan went to her bedroom, debating whether she preferred Ruthie awake so she could tell her everything, or asleep so she could sneak in, put on her nightgown, and relive each moment of tonight in her mind.

Ruthie was sitting up in bed with her cell phone pressed to her ear. "I have to go now," she said into the phone. "Susan's back from the beach, and I want to hear all about it. I'll see you back home in Benville. Soon. Can't wait. Love you." Ruthie snapped her flip phone shut and set it aside.

"Talking to Ben?" Susan asked.

"*Yah*, I had a phone date while you had an in-person date,"

Ruthie smiled. Her face was flushed from having her cell pressed against her ear. "How was it? Tell me everything."

With a sigh, Susan sank onto the bed. "Whew! I'm glad that's over with." Her voice carried a teasing tone, and she paused, letting the suspense hang in the air.

Ruthie scrunched her pillow behind her back. She gave Susan her full attention. "So, what happened? Did you tell him? What did he say? Was he surprised? Angry?"

"Yes. Both, at first. It was terrible. Right after I told him, he just took off and started walking down the beach. I was so scared," Susan said. Ruthie's face twisted into a worried frown.

"It must have been a huge shock for him to realize that you were right there when his cousin died."

"I'm sure it was. I don't know what I was expecting, but not that he'd just get up and walk off." Susan felt a surge of gratitude for Ruthie—a friend who cared and listened.

"He must have come back eventually. You didn't walk home, did you?" Ruthie giggled.

"He did. He apologized for leaving me there, hugged me, and said he forgave me. He talked about God's forgiveness. It's such a relief to know he doesn't hold it against me." Tears threatened to spill as she recalled Luke's words to her.

Ruthie jumped out of bed and hugged Susan tightly. "I knew you could do it. You're stronger than you think." She stepped back and gave Susan a tearful smile.

Strength. That word again.

Ruthie wiped her eyes, and Susan dabbed at her own.

"I know you still carry trauma from that night. But, Susan, remember you didn't kill Luke's cousin. You just happened to be there when Ray died."

"That's what Luke said. But I've always felt guilty. For being there."

"It's all in the past, now," Ruthie said reassuringly.

"I'm so sorry I didn't listen to you back then, Ruthie. I knew better. You were right."

Ruthie hugged her knees to her chest, wrapping her arms around her pink, flowered nightgown. She gave her friend a long look. "Tell me everything."

Susan pulled the shell from her pocket and placed it on the dresser, relieved that Ruthie didn't notice. The shell carried the weight of her newfound strength, which still felt significant and personal. Susan grabbed her nightgown and hairbrush. "I'm getting ready for bed. If you're still awake when I come back, I'll tell you what else happened."

"Of course, I'll be awake."

Susan brushed her teeth, washed her face, and put on her nightgown. She had a lot to tell Ruthie. But some of it might need to wait until tomorrow. She was exhausted. And sleepy.

CHAPTER 26

When Susan returned to the room, Ruthie had the covers pulled up to her chin. "Goodnight," Susan said as she crawled into bed.

"Night," Ruthie answered softly.

Susan turned off the lamp on the stand between their twin beds. They remained quiet for a few moments.

"What else happened?" Ruthie whispered.

"What else?" Susan whispered back. There was no reason to whisper except that it was nighttime and dark. Still, the conversation continued in hushed tones as Susan gradually filled in the details before and after her confession—the confession, which had once seemed like the whole purpose of their sunset walk on the beach. As she told Ruthie about riding in Wasabi, the sunset on the water, and the Junonia shell Luke had given her, the evening sounded beautiful and romantic. "It was wonderful. I felt so comfortable with Luke. It's like we've known each other a long time, but it's only been a few weeks."

"That's just how it is, when it's the right person," Ruthie said.

"Right person? Like you and Ben?" Susan asked.

"Yeah, maybe," Ruthie said. "But go on. I want to hear everything."

Susan snuggled under her blanket. "We had pizza downtown, baked in a wood-fired oven. So much better than the stuff from Village Pizza back home. We talked about our families, Christmas, stuff like that."

"So, convertible ride, beach, pizza, and anything else?" Ruthie asked.

"Anything else?"

Was Ruthie waiting for her to describe Luke's good-night kiss? "Sorry, Ruthie. No kiss yet. Luke said he wants us to date." Just hearing herself say this made her heart flutter. "Ruthie, I can't believe it turned out like this. I was prepared to forget all about him—although that would have been so hard—but instead, we will be seeing a lot more of each other."

"I'm so happy for you. Can you believe it? When we left Ohio, we both felt so bored and alone. Now here we are—you're starting to date Luke, we both have jobs at Saw Grass Inn, and I'm in love with Ben, and who knows, maybe getting married next year." Her voice was quiet and filled with wonder.

"Getting married? Really?" Susan caught her breath. She knew Ruthie and Ben were serious, but she hadn't expected this mention of marriage.

"Tonight, he told me he's going to talk to *Daett* and *Maemm* at Christmas. I'm sure it's about us getting married." Ruthie took a deep breath. "He didn't ask me yet, but that's because he wants to ask me in person, not on the phone. I can't wait to get back to Ohio to see him. The sooner the better," Ruthie sighed. "Don't tell anyone—about the marriage part—that is just between you and me. Cause you're my best friend."

"Of course, I wouldn't. And thank you for being such a good friend to me, Ruthie. I can't imagine going through what I've been through without your support."

They were quiet then, as Susan absorbed Ruthie's news and its implications for their future in Florida. "When did you know Ben was the one?" Susan whispered to Ruthie.

"Probably a long time ago, when he came to talk to my *Daett*. He was asking about our draft horses, how we feed them, and so on. But he kept looking at me, trying to include me in the conversation."

"See, I was right about you and him all along," Susan said triumphantly. "I knew it."

Ruthie ignored Susan's remark. "We should get to sleep. Tomorrow is Sunday. And church," Ruthie said. "I guess we'll be going to church, now that you're not avoiding Luke anymore."

"Definitely. Luke wants us to come tomorrow. It's Christmas Sunday, and he's leading a young people's chorus. He wondered why we hadn't been there the last two weeks. I had to apologize for that, too," Susan sighed.

"Well, everything's been made right now," Ruthie said.

"Yes. Thank goodness. We'd better get some sleep. I don't want to be late for church tomorrow."

"And Luke," Ruthie said. "Goodnight."

"Goodnight." Susan wrapped the quilt around herself and smiled as each scene of their date replayed in her mind.

***

For a long time after Ruthie fell asleep, Susan lay on her back, her head turned toward the window, her thoughts scattered. She watched the full moon shining through the bedroom window. It slowly moved, obscured by drifting clouds, then reappeared. Her mind floated to Luke, to her family at home, to Eva's inn, the garden, thoughts of Christmas—both at home and here. She was tired but also restless. She wished it were time to get ready for church. Time to see Luke again. How would she feel when she caught sight of him? Would he give her another one of those looks, like he had tonight?

Or, with all the people around, would he pretend they were still only acquaintances who met at Eva's inn?

Finally, she fell asleep. But she shuddered awake to a garbled scene of sand, Christmas trees, and then her family, their faces flickering in and out of lantern light, peering at her through a crack in the door, then disappearing. Luke took her hand, told her not to cry, comforted her, and led her away from them. Her heart pounded with anxiety. What had happened? It felt like something bad. Something she couldn't stop. Susan opened her eyes and looked toward the window. It was still dark. She took a deep breath and realized this was only a dream. *Only a dream.* She concentrated on breathing and told herself to think good thoughts. She took several deeper breaths, trying to summon the strength she knew she had. No matter what happened.

When Susan woke up, Ruthie was standing by her bed. She touched Susan's shoulder and pointed at the clock on the dresser. "Better get up or we'll be late for church." They took turns in the bathroom, then Susan and Ruthie both brushed their long hair, twisted it, and pinned it securely with clips and barrettes before placing fresh *kapps* and securing them with bobby pins. Susan put on a pair of thin, dark knee-high hose and her plain black leather shoes. It was such a relief not having to wear the thick leggings under their dresses like the ones they used to wear in winter back home.

For breakfast, Eva set out bagels, pumpkin cream cheese spread, and juice. "Good morning. I have the coffee ready," she said. They accepted the filled mugs and sat down at the table. Eva bowed her head, and they joined in a short silent prayer.

"I need to hurry. I'm helping with Christmas brunch at church. I signed up to serve the food, rather than make it on this busy weekend." She took another sip of coffee. "Susan, I'd love to hear all about your date with Luke, but I'm afraid I must run. I might be late as it is."

"You'll be happy to hear that we had a great time," Susan said. "We're off to church, too. We can catch up later."

"Sounds good. See you after church." Eva grabbed her purse and Bible and left for church. Susan and Ruthie weren't very hungry and shared an everything bagel before walking to Harvest Church. They'd been in Florida since early November, but they still constantly compared Florida weather with winter in Ohio.

"I can't believe it's almost Christmas, and it's what? Sixty degrees?" Ruthie said. "At home, we'd be bundled up in heavy coats, freezing our faces. We've had some frosty Sunday morning buggy rides in December."

"Yes, we did. This is so much better," Susan said. "I'd rather not think about Ohio. But you're going back to it, maybe for good." They hadn't spoken about Ruthie leaving Florida, but after last night, when Ruthie revealed that she and Ben planned to marry, Susan did not doubt that Ruthie would stay in Ohio after Christmas. "I'm dreading the cold up north when we go back for Old Christmas. I'd rather stay here. But I need to see *Dawdi.* He's not doing well and keeps asking for me."

"Your *Dawdi* is such a dear, sweet man. You have to go if he's asking for you. And you want to see your parents, your little brothers. You must miss Leah and Aaron, and their children."

"I do," Susan said. The unsettling dream from last night returned to her mind. Was it trying to tell her something about *Dawdi?* Was Luke trying to pull her away from *Dawdi,* from her family? She had enjoyed being apart from all of them and appreciated her newfound independence. It felt like a fresh start in life. How would it feel to be back with them again? Even just for a visit?

What would they think if they knew she loved someone who wasn't Amish?

"I just thought of something," Ruthie said excitedly. "When I marry Ben, with your sister Leah married to his brother, Aaron, you and I will be at some of the same family gatherings."

"Maybe," Susan said. She was already imagining a life with Luke here in Florida. She might not be able to attend those family gatherings up North.

They were close to the church, and Susan let the subject drop. But questions nagged at her. If she were to marry Luke, would he be willing to leave Sarasota? Would she? She set the thought aside for now. There was enough time later to figure things out.

They entered the church's front doors only to find it was almost empty. Two older men with short, neatly trimmed beards stood talking seriously near the pulpit at the front. A woman was arranging pinecones and boughs on the windowsills, but apart from that the place was deserted. The distinctive scent of cinnamon filled the air. By now, the church should have been filled with people.

The woman finished with the pine and walked their way. "You must be visitors," she said. Her blue eyes crinkled in the corners when she smiled. She brushed away a few strands of white hair that had escaped from the sheer black triangle scarf, her prayer covering, tied at the nape of her neck. "Welcome. I'm Rosa Zook. And you are?"

"I'm Ruthie Miller, and this is Susan Troyer," Ruthie said. "We've been here once before, but it was a couple of weeks ago."

"Well then, you probably missed the announcement last week. Before today's service, we're having a coffee hour with freshly baked cinnamon rolls in the fellowship hall. Follow me, I'll show you the way."

Susan and Ruthie followed Rosa through the double doors at the front of the church and into a hallway leading to the room where they had gathered for the potluck and prayer circle. Today, the place felt warm and inviting, filled with laughter and lively conversation, as mostly older men and women greeted each other and caught up with friends at tables covered with white tablecloths decorated with red poinsettias. A few younger people mingled with the pale snowbirds and deeply tanned locals.

Susan and Ruthie fit in, even though they were younger than most. The women wore long dresses, some with an extra panel above the waist called a cape dress. They wore black or white head coverings of different sizes and shapes, depending on their traditions and where they were from.

The men wore either blue or white long-sleeved shirts, and some had on plain jackets or vests. "Go help yourself to fresh cinnamon rolls and coffee," Rosa said. "Most of the young people are sitting over there. I'm sure they'll be glad to see you." She pointed toward a large round table off to the side in one corner.

"Thank you," Susan said. "We've met some of them." She smiled and felt her face flush as she looked toward the table. Luke was already making his way to them, weaving through the crowd. He was handsome in a white dress shirt and black trousers. A look of embarrassment crossed Luke's face, but he greeted them with a handshake. At his touch, Susan felt a tingle run up her arm, and his smile brought a flush to her face. By now, Rosa had wandered off.

"Susan, I'm so sorry. I completely forgot to mention the coffee hour before church today. The coffee and cinnamon rolls are a fundraiser for one of our church projects."

"It's okay. We noticed something was going on when we arrived, and no one was in their seats. It smells delicious," Susan said.

"Some of the young marrieds came in at six. The guys set up while the ladies made the rolls." Susan saw a basket near the end of the serving station. It was overflowing with cash and folded checks. Luke continued. "Donations from today go to fund the next mission trip to Guatemala, where we're helping to build a church in a small village. But don't feel like you need to donate," he assured them. "We have a big crowd today. I'm sure they met their goal, and they're about to clear things away."

"I'm going back for seconds. Those cinnamon rolls are incredible." Luke looked between them. "You hungry?"

"We already had breakfast, but they smell so good, I have to have at least a taste," Susan said.

"No thanks," Ruthie said. "But they do smell delicious."

He led the way as they grabbed refreshments, then found seats. Luke and Susan shared a sticky roll. The coffee had cooled and wasn't very good, but Susan took a sip anyway. People kept talking. Some moved between tables to greet friends. As Susan and Luke finished their roll, a few people started moving into the main part of the church. The three of them stayed at the young people's table, watching the crowd slowly flow through the doors. "I need to get in there; it's almost time to start pre-service singing," Luke said, standing up. "Let's talk after the service, okay?" He grinned, and his eyes met Susan's knowingly.

"Okay," Susan said. She felt a blush gradually spread across her cheeks.

Luke picked up his Bible and left. Susan and Ruthie soon followed, but in the hallway, his mother, Mary, stopped them. "You two are Susan and Ruthie, aren't you? The girls staying with Eva? We met at the potluck a few weeks ago."

"That's us," Susan said.

"Luke told me you were coming today. And to look out for you," she said. But she didn't mention last night's date. "I'm so glad you came back to Harvest. I want to ask you something. I'll make it quick; I know the service is about to start." She smiled warmly, her glance lingering longer on Susan's face. "Did Eva tell you about the women's gathering tomorrow? We're making Christmas cards. I hope she invited you to join us. You're certainly welcome to come with Eva."

Susan glanced at Ruthie, who always made the prettiest cards of anyone. "Eva told us, and it sounds fun. We all have the week off. Eva decided to take a break and didn't book any guests at the inn until after the holiday. We'll come, won't we, Ruthie?"

"Sure, what time?"

"Come at ten. We'll be in the fellowship room. I'm making a big pot of chili for our lunch. Eva promised to bring her card-making supplies and some cookies."

"Thanks for inviting us," Susan said.

"You're welcome. You can follow me. Richard saved us a seat halfway back." Mary hurried down the side aisle, with Susan and Ruthie following closely behind. Just as they took their seats, Luke stood and walked to the side of the pulpit.

"Welcome to Harvest. Let's start our service this morning by turning to number two-forty-one. 'O Come, All Ye Faithful.' Please stand." Susan was delighted to see Luke back in his song-leading role. He looked across the congregation and caught her eye.

Susan smiled at him.

Mary opened a hymnbook, and Ruthie reached for the last one in the rack. Mary moved closer to Susan, holding out the book and inviting her to share. Susan took it, feeling a little self-conscious. She fidgeted. How had she managed to sit right next to Luke's mother? Luke blew the pitch on the silver pitchpipe he'd pulled from his pocket. He placed it on the podium, then lifted his arm in readiness.

For a moment, Luke's voice stood out above the rest. Then, the congregation joined in. Music filled the space, bouncing off the plaster walls, the bare wood floors, and the high wooden ceiling. Mary's rich, steady alto blended with Susan's thin, hesitant soprano. By verse three, "sing, choirs of angels," Susan's breath deepened, and her tone became more confident and resonant. Deep down, she felt the exultation that uplifted and held her in this chorus of voices—people singing their hearts out in this place where she knew, without a doubt, that she belonged.

CHAPTER 27

The service ended with a closing hymn as the ministers walked down the center aisle. Luke's mother, Mary, turned to Susan and Ruthie. "I'm glad you came today, but I'm sorry my son forgot to tell you about the coffee time. I'll get you a newsletter with the schedule of upcoming activities."

"Thank you. That will be helpful," Susan said.

Susan and Ruthie followed Mary to the back of the room, where she picked up newsletters from a stack on a long, narrow table and handed one to each of them.

The table held various pamphlets, Gospel tracts, and a stack of *Upper Room* devotional booklets. "You're welcome to help yourself to anything here," Mary said. "They are for visitors and members alike." Susan looked at the small *Upper Room* booklet with a colorful nature picture on the cover. The sunset behind mountains in the distance reminded her of the sunset she'd witnessed the evening before. She picked one up and examined the cover more closely.

"We had these back home, but I never read them," she said to Ruthie. She thought of *Maemm* and *Daett* sitting in their rocking chairs at the end of the day, reading the little booklets, each with a Bible in their lap. While she'd been hiding her true self from her parents, they were reading the Bible and silently praying for those in need, including their children and grandchildren. Susan was sure of it. A mental image appeared—her and Luke sitting together like her parents, reading and praying. A warm glow spread through her at the thought. But, knowing Luke, they'd be speaking their prayers aloud.

Near the wide-open double doors, the ministers shook hands with people in line. Men exchanged a few words of appreciation for the sermon. The women stood by patiently. Susan suspected they were thinking about the Sunday dinner they would be preparing within the hour. Often, there would be guests from church or visiting relatives. Harvest didn't serve a meal at the church like the Old Order congregation back home. But either way, a Sunday dinner required extra planning to make sure it appeared quickly with little fuss after the service.

Richard met them near the door, and from the front of the room, Luke came to join them. His dark eyes sparkled. Susan gave a small wave, then blushed.

"Looks like there's no way out of the building except here," Luke said. He sounded jovial, as if he was suggesting the ministers kept them detained for as long as possible. He stepped into line beside Susan. "Mind if I join you?" he asked.

"Not at all," said Susan. The thought of greeting the minister made her nervous because she wanted to make a good impression on Luke and his parents. She had met one of the leaders on her previous visit to Harvest, but he was busy talking with someone. What should she say when the minister greeted her? Susan's mind had wandered during the long sermon. Now, at last, it was their turn, and Luke stepped forward. "Shepherd Eli, I'd like you to meet Susan Troyer. She's a friend of mine, here from Ohio for the winter. Maybe longer."

Susan cheered inwardly at the "maybe longer" comment. Eli's handshake was firm, yet his palm felt soft. He wore a steel gray long-sleeved shirt with an open collar. The sunlight streaming through the doors cast a metallic gleam across his shoulders, and his smile was just as striking. "Glad you could come today. Are you working in the area?"

"Yes. I've been working at Eva Good's inn, Saw Grass Inn," Susan said. The minister's eyes were a deep blue, and his short beard was completely white. "I'll be helping in the kitchen and doing some cleaning, along with answering the phone sometimes."

"Good for you. I know Eva. Knew her husband, Caleb, too. Fine people."

"Yes. Eva's been good to us." Susan turned to include her friend in the comment, and Eli greeted Ruthie.

"I'm Ruthie Miller. Susan's friend." Ruthie stepped forward, sounding as confident as ever.

"Troyer, Miller, of course. Say no more. I could have guessed you're from Ohio with those names."

"I suppose you're right," Ruthie said.

Susan hoped the minister wouldn't start the name game. That happened too often. You told an Amish person your name, which then sparked a long conversation as they tried to find a connection. "Do you by chance know Lyman Troyer?" the person might ask. Or "Are you from the Robert Yoder branch—well, I guess that's back a couple of generations. That was way before your time..." And so, it went.

Thankfully, Eli didn't play the name game. "Ruthie and Susan, please come back again. We'd be happy if you decide to make Harvest your church home."

"Okay, thank you," Ruthie said, knowing she would stay in Ohio after Christmas.

"Thank you," Susan said. "I will."

The words "church home" echoed in Susan's mind as she continued down the steps into the sunshine. She appreciated the idea that a church could feel like a home for her in Florida. And there was a sense of home at Harvest that wasn't just because of Luke and his family, although that helped. Harvest was a place where she could be herself, even among strangers. A place where she was accepted and welcomed, no matter what.

Richard and Mary stood waiting for them on the sidewalk. Susan and Ruthie were saying goodbye to them under a huge palm tree as the sun shone through the leaves, casting shadows across their faces. "I'd ask you girls to join us for Sunday dinner, but we're invited to the Martins' place today. We'd better get going. I don't want to keep them waiting," Mary said.

"That's fine. Eva's expecting us back at the house," Susan said.

"Maybe another time, then. Don't forget, the card-making party is tomorrow morning. Eva will bring you. She always shows up."

"Should we bring some cookies or something?" Ruthie asked.

"That would be perfect. Eva mentioned she could bring cookies. There's going to be a potluck for lunch," Mary said.

Luke's brother joined them, and the four members of the Rohrer family headed to their cars, as Mary called out, "See you tomorrow."

Susan and Ruthie began walking back to Eva's. "It looks like it could rain," Ruthie said. "We'd better hurry or we might get wet."

Eva had the table set out on the lanai when they returned. She was warming an egg casserole in the oven. "We had so many casseroles leftover from church that they sent one home with me," Eva said after she'd greeted them. "I hope you're hungry."

"I know I'm hungry. I'll let Ruthie speak for herself."

"Me, too," Ruthie said.

Eva's Sunday dinner wasn't fancy, but she had plenty. Besides the casserole, which included bread, milk, cheese, eggs, and sausage, there was a bowl of fresh-cut fruit and a basket of warm blueberry muffins from the bakery.

A brief rainstorm passed quickly as the three women sat on the lanai talking. Susan mentioned the card-making party and Eva's invitation. Then, Eva wanted details about Susan's date with Luke, so Susan shared a detailed account.

Ruthie mentioned that when she went home, she would be seeing Ben, the guy she had been talking to on the phone lately. But she didn't mention the possibility of marriage or the part about not returning to Florida after Christmas.

Eva listened carefully and contributed her comments and exclamations at all the right moments. "I've been so busy at the inn, I haven't had a minute to think about Christmas. Thursday and Friday will be here before we know it. I'm really glad I didn't book any guests until mid-January. That gives us time to catch our breath and prepare for the holiday. I'm so happy you both will be here. With Caleb gone, Christmas is a difficult day for me."

Susan nodded, and Ruthie reached out to take Eva's hand, giving it a squeeze. "We'll plan a good dinner and cook for you, won't we, Susan?"

"As long as you help me, I think I can make most of the dishes. But I've never cooked a turkey," Susan said. She thought about *Maemm,* who always got a fresh turkey from Uncle Aden. Last year's was so huge there wasn't room for anything else in the oven, and her sister Leah's husband, Aaron, had to be called into the kitchen to lift the roaster with the gigantic bird when it was finally cooked.

"We always have ham for Christmas," Eva said. "Is that okay with you two?"

"Sure. That's way easier, too," Susan said.

They kept talking about the menu, with Eva asking for Amish date pudding. "I haven't had that in years. Caleb insisted on pie and ice cream, and of course, I usually went along with him. If we ate at one of the Amish restaurants during the holidays, I'd order date pudding, but it wasn't as good as when I was a little Amish girl." Eva looked wistful, and Susan tried to picture Eva as a young girl wearing a *kapp* and eating date pudding. She would look like Leah's little one did last Christmas, her face covered in whipped cream.

After they had made their Christmas dinner plans and Eva told them more about the Christmas Eve service at the Mennonite church, they cleared the table, and Susan and Ruthie did the dishes.

Eva returned to the kitchen as they were finishing up. She had changed out of her church dress into a loose Christmas T-shirt and capris. "Do you want to play some games this afternoon?" Eva asked. "I have Dominoes, Chase the Rat, and Uno. Or maybe you'd like to play Dutch Blitz." She yawned.

"It's nice of you to suggest it, but I think we're all tired today," Susan said. "I know I am. Maybe we can play games on Christmas Day."

"You're right. I am tired," Eva said. "I just don't want you girls to be bored staying here with me."

"Don't worry about that," Susan said. "We can take care of ourselves. You go take your afternoon nap. We'll be fine."

———————————

Susan and Ruthie got up early the next morning and made Molasses Crinkles and Thumbprint cookies to take to the card-making party. Then, after breakfast, Eva showed Susan and Ruthie her craft supplies. She climbed onto a step stool and lifted clear plastic storage boxes from the top shelf of a closet. Susan and Ruthie carried them to the dining room table. Many of Eva's supplies came from garage sales or thrift shops. Some items were new and still in their original packaging, and everything was neatly sorted and labeled. The girls opened the boxes, and Eva showed them several large rubber stamps and colored ink pads that could be used for making cards. Some featured Christmas designs such as stars, bells, or Christmas stockings. Others included words, Christmas phrases, and greetings.

Susan poked around in the boxes, admiring Eva's stash. "This looks like fun, doesn't it, Ruthie?"

"I'm already getting ideas, just looking at some of this paper," Ruthie said. She was leafing through a pad filled with assorted background papers in festive colors, some metallic or embossed.

"We can take all these items to the party to share and trade. There's always a demonstration, too. This year, someone is bringing a machine that does die cutting and embossing. She can make samples for us, and later we can use it to create our projects," Eva said.

"We made cards at home sometimes, but we used old greeting cards," Susan said. "*Maemm* collected them from neighbors, and we reused parts in our new designs. But, I've never tried stamping."

"I worked in a gift shop for a while, and we sold craft supplies. We even made a few cards that we sold to customers," Ruthie said.

"You make beautiful cards," Susan said. "Maybe you can finally give me a few pointers today. I still keep every card you've sent me in a special box in my bottom drawer at home."

"There will be plenty of card-making options this morning," Eva assured them. "I'm keeping mine simple because I need to mail them immediately. The party is late this year because of me. Mary waited until after the open house at the inn.

"Making cards will help us get into the Christmas spirit. Let's pack these supplies now. I don't want to be late," Eva said as she found some cloth shopping bags, and she and Susan packed the craft supplies. Ruthie went to the kitchen and arranged the cookie platter.

Eva entered the kitchen. "Ready to go?" she asked. "I can't believe you two—getting up so early to bake. I wish I had half your energy."

They were finally in the car and buckled up. "Wait. I forgot to bring my phone. I was charging it earlier." Susan unbuckled her seat belt and opened the car door. "I'll be right back."

In a minute, she came back. "I know I'm acting like an *Englischer* who can't go anywhere without their phone," Susan said. "But I don't want to miss a call from *Maemm* about *Dawdi.*"

"Oh, Susan. I didn't think about that," Ruthie said. She was sitting in the front seat and turned to Susan. "Don't worry, he's going to be okay until you get there. Just a few more days, and we'll be back in Ohio. When we get back, you can go see him first thing."

Eva gave Susan a reassuring smile as she looked at her in the rear-view mirror. "Susan, I can imagine you're feeling anxious about your grandfather. I've been praying for him ever since you first told us about his condition. What's the latest on him?"

"The last time I talked to *Maemm,* she said he was doing a little better. Everyone is hoping he will be well enough to celebrate Christmas Day with the family. They're planning a small gathering— my three younger brothers and Leah's family. The big Troyer gathering isn't until Old Christmas, but he can't go. The doctors warned him to stay away from large groups. It wouldn't be good for him to be exposed to COVID or the flu with him having heart failure."

"We'll keep praying for him to get better. And for you. It's tough being so far away when he's been such an important part of your life," Eva said.

"I like Florida, but out of all my family back home, I miss him the most. He's lived in the *Dawdi haus* ever since I was little, always nearby, doing what he could for us, teaching us stuff," Susan's voice faded, and she swiped at a couple of tears. It was only a short drive to Harvest Church, and Eva was parking the car and didn't notice Susan's tears. It was just as well. Any more kind words and she'd be crying for real.

They carried the bags and cookie tray into the fellowship room. Mary was organizing card stock, scissors, colored pencils, stamps, and ink on a long table pushed against the wall. Susan and Eva handed over their craft supplies while Ruthie took the cookies to the kitchen. Mary looked inside the bags, smiled, then set them aside to give each of them a big hug. "Great. You two can help me organize this. We have so much stuff to work with here," she said. "I hope you're ready to get creative."

Ruthie rejoined them, and Mary hugged her, too. "Wow! Look at all this. I love to make cards," Ruthie said.

Susan and Ruthie worked with Mary and Eva to organize the supplies. Susan hoped her creative skills would shine today. From the looks of it, some of these women were experienced card makers and crafters.

Susan surveyed the scene. Most of the tables formed a large U-shape that served as their workspace. Off to the side, a tall woman wearing skinny jeans and a fitted buffalo check Western shirt was setting up a machine. It was about the size of a sewing machine but had a crank on the side. She took paper and sheets of clear plastic from a box and laid them out on the table. A Craft Lobby badge identified her as "Lisa." Susan tried not to stare at her oversized, dangling Christmas tree earrings. Everyone else in the room was Plain, except for Eva and one other woman.

Soon, all the supplies were in place, and Mary clapped her hands to get everyone's attention and welcome them. The women jostled to find seats at the tables. "Eva, you and your girls can sit by me," Mary said. "You'll have a good view of the demonstration from here."

Susan tucked her purse with her phone inside under her chair. When everyone was settled, Mary introduced Lisa, who started explaining the machine. As she put it together, she held up different parts. The Veevik Manual Die Cutting Embossing Machine had a crank on the side. It included a base plate, various cutting plates, dies in familiar Christmas-themed shapes, and came with a dozen patterns. It could be converted to embossing with a simple change in the plates. Lisa picked a bright red sheet from her stack of card stock and showed how to insert it into the machine.

As she turned the crank, the red sheet emerged, and Lisa lifted it, placing a sheet of white paper underneath the red one. An intricate, perfectly cut manger scene became visible. The audience erupted in applause, and Lisa thanked them with a triumphant smile. When the room quieted down, she explained how the machine worked, holding up various Christmas designs. The women watched as Lisa switched a plate and started making a new design.

Suddenly, a cell phone rang, and Lisa stopped speaking mid-sentence. Everyone looked around to see who had forgotten to silence their phone. Horrified, with her heart pounding, Susan grabbed her purse and hurried into the hallway. *Maemm.* She never called during the day. This could only mean one thing.

CHAPTER 28

As she rummaged in her purse for the phone, Susan hurried past the restrooms into the children's wing of the church, where she hoped her ringtone wouldn't disturb the group. She looked at a large, framed, old-fashioned picture of an angel watching over two young children, then sank down to the floor beside it.

She flipped open the screen of her small cell phone and pressed the green button.

"Susan?"

"Hello, *Maemm*?" There was a question in her voice, as if she hoped it might be someone else. She was breathless and shaky as *Maemm's* voice spilled out.

"Susan, I'm sorry if this is a bad time and you're at work or something, but I wanted to call right away. It's *Dawdi*. We took him to the doctor this morning; he was having such a hard time getting his breath. The driver dropped us off as close to the door as she could, but *Dawdi* barely made it to the first chair in the waiting room."

Susan felt weak. She studied the pattern in the rough green carpet on the floor, then lifted her eyes to the picture of the angel.

"I'm afraid I have terrible news, Susan. We all knew this was coming. It's been a few years now since he was first diagnosed with heart failure. Today, the doctor told us most don't hold on for as long as he did...."

A garbled sound came from the other end of the call—*Maemm*, choking back a sob. Oh, no! *Dawdi* died. In the few seconds *Maemm* took to compose herself, Susan's imagination spiraled. *I missed seeing him and saying goodbye. Now it's too late! Why didn't it matter more? How could I be so self-involved? Why wasn't it a priority?* The excuse about the open house and Eva needing her, the drama around herself and Luke, and finally the beach date—all felt so selfish. Every time they talked, *Maemm* said *Dawdi* was asking for her. He wanted to see her. Now it was too late.

Maemm's voice broke through again. "The doctor told us he doesn't have long now. They suggested hospice. I don't know if we'll call hospice or take care of him ourselves. He's not in much pain. But Susan, if you want to see him...."

Maemm paused in the middle of her sentence and waited.

"So, he's still alive?" Susan lifted her chin, and hope flooded inside her. There was still time.

"Oh yes. He is now. It's just that the doctor said it won't be long. Maybe a week, maybe less. We hope he holds on at least until Christmas Day, but there's no way to know. It could happen at any time. The doctor said some wait to go when there's a holiday to look forward to. Christmas might mean he'll be with us a little longer." *Maemm* sniffled, and Susan knew she was probably crying. *Dawdi* was so dear to all of them.

"I was planning to come on the bus soon after Christmas," Susan said, avoiding the fact that she had scheduled her trip for January third, nine days after Christmas. "I really want to see him."

"He wants to see you, too. In fact, on the way home from the doctor's office that's one of the few things he said. He asked if you were coming for Christmas Day. I told him I thought you would. I hated to disappoint him by saying you wouldn't be here until New Year's." Susan knew *Maemm* thought Susan would change her plans now that it had come to this.

Eva stepped through the fellowship room doors and hurried over to Susan, a worried look on her face. She knelt down beside Susan, who sat uncomfortably hunched on the floor, clutching her phone.

"I'll figure something out and try to get there soon," Susan said. "I'm at a women's meeting at Harvest Church right now. I'll try to change my bus ticket. I think there's a bus leaving for Ohio tomorrow."

"So, you'll come then? Soon?"

"Yes. As soon as I can. I'll call back when I have it figured out, so you know when to expect me."

"Oh, Susan. You don't know how much this will mean to him. He misses you so. We all miss you." There was relief in *Maemm's* voice.

"Yeah, I know. I'm sorry. I should have listened to you earlier."

"Just get here as soon as possible. I'll tell *Dawdi* you're on your way. He's going to be so happy."

"Eva's here with me now *Maemm*. I'll call tonight, okay?"

They said goodbye, and Susan slid her phone into her purse. By now, she'd forgotten all about the embarrassing interruption she'd caused during Lisa's demonstration.

Eva extended her hand to Susan and helped her up. "Did you get some bad news?"

"Yes. *Dawdi*. He doesn't have much time left. If I want to see him, I have to go back to Ohio right away. *Maemm* says he's asking for me." Her voice broke, and tears rolled down her cheeks.

Eva pulled Susan into a deep hug. Susan surrendered and wrapped her arms around Eva. She felt the softness of age beneath her warm hands and absorbed Eva's compassion. The angel in the picture hovered just above the children, who seemed unaware of her shimmering presence. Moments passed as Susan surrendered to deep sobs. Unlike those children, Eva's angelic presence rubbed Susan's back and murmured, "Don't worry, Susan. Time is in God's hands. Everything will work out."

Susan hoped she was right. How could Eva be so sure? Susan stepped back and dabbed her eyes with the clean tissue Eva pulled from her denim skirt pocket. "I need to call the bus company to see if I can get on the one going out tonight," Susan said.

Eva squeezed her arm. "I'll help you with that when we get home. And I'm sure you don't feel like making Christmas cards anymore. I don't either. Why don't you go to the parking lot? Sit on one of the benches out there under the palm trees and take some deep breaths. I'll tell Ruthie what happened and let Mary know we're leaving." Eva led Susan to the exit door at the far end of the hallway, and Susan stepped out of the building into the sunshine.

The concrete bench was warm in the noontime sun, and Susan let her mind drift to *Dawdi* memories. His wiry hair and how it sometimes curled beneath his hat. She'd be heading to the compost pile with a pan of potato peelings and discarded watermelon rinds, and he'd be leaning on his cane, looking up into the apple tree branches. "Shhhh!" he'd whisper. "There's an oriole's nest." He'd lift his cane and point to it. Susan never resented *Dawdi's* interruptions.

In the evenings, they sometimes sat on the creaky porch swing until after dark—just sitting in silence. Or she'd bring him a slice of cake she baked. He'd always split it, claiming the piece was too big for him to eat alone. She'd stay and eat it with him while he shared a story or two. It was hard to believe those moments would never happen again.

The palm branches rustled above her as Susan looked up, almost expecting to see an oriole's nest. But of course, there was none. Was Luke's love of nature one of the things that drew her to him?

Because he reminded her of *Dawdi*? Luke expressed it differently, yet he, too, noticed things she might miss if he didn't point them out.

At the thought of Luke, her heart sank. She'd hoped to spend this Christmas with him, maybe take another walk on the beach, be invited to his house for dinner, exchange gifts, or at least give him a handmade card. But she hadn't made a single card today, and there was no time to shop or see Luke if she was leaving tonight. Just when there was hope for time together, she had to leave Florida. She pushed aside thoughts of Luke. Right now, her main concern was getting home and seeing *Dawdi* before it was too late.

Eva and Ruthie emerged from the church and hurried over to Susan, who stood up from the concrete bench. Sitting there hadn't helped; she felt weak and shaky. Ruthie threw her arms around Susan's shoulders in a tight hug. "I'm so, so, sorry, Susan. When I heard your phone ring, I knew right away it was your *Maemm*. Eva says he's gotten a lot worse." Susan nodded and sniffled. She didn't dare say anything, afraid she'd burst into tears.

The car was quiet on the short ride back to Eva's place. When they arrived, Eva went to the fridge and pulled out a leftover breakfast casserole from yesterday's brunch at the Mennonite church. "I'm going to heat up a little something for us to eat since we missed lunch at Harvest. I should have thought of bringing back take-out—some of Mary's chili. We should plan to be at the bus park by 3:45. I'll get lunch started and give them a call to change your ticket. Ruthie, why don't you help Susan pack?"

In their room, Ruthie found a suitcase, gathered Susan's clothes from the closet, and put them on her bed. Susan sat on the other bed, confused and unable to move. Ruthie hurried around, opening drawers. "You should take your best church dress, but it's in the hamper in the laundry room. I'll get it. You might want it."

She's probably thinking I'll need it for the funeral. Susan wiped tears from her eyes, but Ruthie's back was turned to Susan, so she didn't see.

"Do you want to take these?" Ruthie held up a fistful of lacy under things. She made a silly face, and Susan couldn't help but laugh. After that, Susan went into the bathroom for her toiletries, and the two of them finished packing the suitcase and a tote bag for the long bus trip home. "I wish I were going with you, but I think it's going to be challenging to get even one seat on that bus. The Monday bus is always full, and it will be even more crowded this time of year, with Christmas just a couple of days away."

"I hadn't thought of that. What am I going to do if I can't change my ticket?" Susan swallowed back this new fear.

"We just have to trust it will work out," Ruthie said. "I'm sure it will. It has to."

"Eva might have friends at the bus company. She said she'd call and get my ticket changed," Susan said.

"Could be. She'd pull a few strings if she needed to," Ruthie snapped the suitcase shut and placed a fleece throw on top of Susan's tote. "Hand me your pillow. It's a lot easier to sleep on the bus if you have a pillow," she said.

Susan tossed the pillow, and it landed on the suitcase.

They wandered into the kitchen where Eva had set the table for lunch. One of the open-house centerpieces sat in the middle of the table, and there were Christmas-themed placemats and matching napkins. The casserole reheating in the oven gave off aromas of sausage and melting cheese. Susan saw Eva through the sliding glass doors that led to the lanai. She was talking on the phone. She must have succeeded in changing the ticket because, when she finished the call, she was smiling.

"Have a seat," Eva said. "I'll get that casserole out, and then I can explain everything."

Her words might have made Susan worry, except Eva didn't sound troubled. If anything, she seemed in good spirits. Eva grabbed a potholder, placed the dish from the oven on the table, and then sat down, bowing her head.

Susan and Ruthie did, too. "Creator and all-knowing God, we thank You for Your abundant blessings, for this food, and for this time of the year when we remember Your coming into the world. We ask You to be with Susan, her grandfather, and her entire family as they go through *Dawdi's* final days. I pray especially for Susan as she travels home to be with loved ones. Grant her traveling mercies and a blessed homecoming. In Jesus' name, Amen." Eva lifted her head and reached for Susan's hand. She gave it a gentle squeeze.

They took turns serving themselves a piece of the steaming breakfast casserole that had been cut into squares. Susan picked at her fruit cup. She wasn't sure she felt like eating, but she'd try. Supper on the bus would probably be a cold sandwich and snacks.

Eva took a few bites of her food. Ruthie and Susan did the same. Then Eva said, "Susan, I tried my best to change your ticket so you could go on the bus tonight, but it just didn't work out. The person I spoke with, an old friend of mine, said they're full, and most have had their reservations for weeks. People are heading back to Ohio and Indiana for family gatherings. It is Christmas, after all."

Susan's fork stopped midair, then she set it back on the plate. Her face turned white. "B-b-but what am I going to do? I'm all packed and ready to go. Is there a bus tomorrow? I need to get home. *Maemm* said...*Dawdi*, he's expecting me...." A lump formed in her throat.

"Oh, I know that my dear. I know you need to get home. I figured Mary might know someone going to Ohio that you could travel with. She couldn't think of anybody, but then she remembered that Luke's off work all this week. She checked with him, and he said he'd be happy to drive you back to Ohio. In fact, you can both go with Luke. You, too, Ruthie!" Susan's fork clinked onto her plate, and she felt the blood rush to her cheeks. Never could she have imagined such a thing.

"Goodness!" Ruthie exclaimed. "I'll have to pack, too!"

"It's so much easier to sleep in the car than on that bus," Eva continued. "You'll arrive rested and ready to spend time with your family. Luke's an excellent driver, so there are no worries on that front. I hope you're okay with this. It seemed like the best way to go on such short notice. Unless you'd fly," Eva said.

Okay with this? Are you kidding? Of course I'm okay with it.

"Flying would scare me, and I'm worried enough as it is," Susan said. Her parents would be okay with her flying since *Dawdi.* was dying. But, in her opinion, driving with Luke was much better.

"You'll arrive in Ohio hours before the bus does, and Luke can take you directly to your place instead of ending up at five in the morning in German Village in Berlin, or wherever their drop-off is."

"Drive all night? In a car?" Susan asked. After saying it, she thought it sounded silly or even stupid.

"Oh, people do that all the time. The trip is much quicker at night. Caleb and I have driven through the night more than once on our trips. When he got tired, we switched, and I took the wheel," Eva said. Then she caught herself. "Of course, you don't drive. But Mary assured me Luke's a coffee drinker and loves to drive. You'll listen to music. If he gets too tired, he should just pull over and take a quick nap. You'd be amazed at how much that helps." Eva had worked out all the details.

She paused and took another forkful of the bread-egg-cheese-sausage square on her plate. Susan picked a grape out of the mixed fruit cup. It was easier to eat something than to decide what to say to Eva. Susan couldn't believe what had just happened. But according to Eva, she didn't have any other options.

"Oh, I forgot. Mary said Luke will be here around two-thirty." Eva glanced at the clock. "You're packed and ready to go, right?"

Susan nodded. "Yeah. I'm all packed."

Ruthie took her dishes to the sink and hurried to her bedroom to pack her belongings for the trip.

The reality of spending the rest of this day and the upcoming evening—night—with Luke finally felt real. "I'm sure my sister, Leah, and her husband would have room for him to stay at their house when we get back to Ohio," Susan said. "I'll ask *Maemm* when I call her."

"Yes. You should go ahead and call your mother. You can tell her the bus was full, but your friends here in Sarasota found you a ride to Ohio." Eva shot Susan a big smile, and Susan wondered if she should tell her mother that she was dating Luke. Maybe she'd wait until she got home.

"As for staying with your sister's family," Eva continued. "Luke will have lodging at a relative's bed and breakfast in Berlin, not too far from where you live, if I remember right. Tourism is slow there this time of year, and your family might have other guests coming to visit *Dawdi*."

"That's true," Susan said. She thought about spending hours in the car with Luke. Eva had said she would be sleeping most of the trip, but would she get any sleep if Luke sat next to her?

"My phone's charging in my room," Susan said. "I'll go call *Maemm*. She's going to be so happy to know I'll be there tomorrow morning," she said. "And they don't have to find someone to pick me up from the bus."

"Tomorrow you'll be home in Ohio, having breakfast or lunch with your *Dawdi*," Eva said. "Now you'd better help your friend pack. Tell her I canceled her bus ride."

CHAPTER 29

Susan dialed the Troyers' cell phone, hoping to leave a message or talk to *Maemm*. Thoughts raced through her mind while she waited for someone to answer. Back home, everyone was busy working. The phone was probably in *Daett's* desk drawer at the shop. She'd leave a message. But then *Maemm* answered.

"Hello, Susan?"

"*Maemm,* we got it worked out. I should be home tomorrow morning sometime. I'm leaving here soon."

"What a relief. I've been waiting for you to call back. I stepped outside for a minute. I was with *Dawdi,* but I didn't say anything to him about you coming. I was so afraid you couldn't change your ticket. I kept the phone with me, hoping to hear from you." Susan pictured *Maemm* leaning on the porch railing, shivering in the Ohio winter.

"Eva called the bus office, but they didn't have room for me."

"But you said you're coming."

"I am coming to Ohio, but not on the bus. Eva found someone to bring me. And Ruthie, too." Susan's heart pounded as she thought about telling *Maemm* about Luke. "It's a boy—I mean, a man, a young man," Susan stuttered and felt her face flush with embarrassment.

"A young man, you say?" *Maemm* sounded curious.

Susan hurried on. Might as well say it—*Maemm* would find out soon enough. Susan had decided to be honest from now on, not secretive like she'd been before leaving Ohio.

"Luke Rohrer is driving me up. He's the son of Eva's friends, Rich and Mary. We met at Harvest Church, where his family, Ruthie and I go. It's near Pinecraft." Susan stopped and held her breath, waiting for *Maemm* to say something—she had no idea what. But *Maemm* just listened or maybe was impatient to get back to *Dawdi*. "Their family used to be Amish and lived somewhere around Ragersville. They moved to Florida a long time ago. You'll like him."

"It doesn't matter if I like him or not. Is he a good driver? That's what counts." *Maemm* didn't comment on Susan's lengthy explanation. Her direct tone was a hint that she needed time to form her opinion.

"He's a good driver. I rode with him Saturday evening. We went to the beach. Eva said not to worry about him staying with us, or with Leah and Aaron. He plans to stay with his cousins, who have an Airbnb near Berlin."

"I'm glad of that," *Maemm* said. "We have too much going on here with Christmas around the corner and *Dawdi* doing so poorly."

"I know. Of course." There would be time once she was in Ohio to tell *Maemm* about the trip to the beach with Luke. He was an important part of her life now. If *Maemm* understood, she didn't let on. She was probably cold standing there on the porch or worried about *Dawdi*.

"Well, be safe on the way home. What time do you think you'll be here?"

"Eva thought we might make it sometime tomorrow morning. I don't know for sure how long it takes to drive overnight in a car. I'm sure Luke has it figured out."

"Okay. We'll see you soon. It's freezing here. Be sure to bring your warm coat."

"Okay, bye." Susan shivered at the thought of cold wind and snow. She hadn't even brought a warm coat with her to Florida.

Ruthie zipped her bag shut. It was so full that she had to press the lid down. "I just stuffed everything into my suitcase. If I left something, it's yours. I probably won't come back after Christmas."

Susan nodded. She knew Ruthie would stay in Ohio. "Luke's here. Are you ready to go?"

"Already? That was fast. I'm ready. Let's get going."

They walked single file, dragging their suitcases, and opened the front door.

Luke stepped out of his parents' silver sedan and waved, flashing her a big smile. Susan suddenly realized how important this road trip would be for them. It was the perfect time to get to know him. Finally.

Luke popped the trunk as Susan and Ruthie dragged their suitcases down Eva's brick sidewalk. The luggage thumped across the surface as if to punctuate their departure. Luke reached for Susan's suitcase. Their hands touched, and her heart quivered with anticipation. He grabbed Ruthie's bag with his other hand and took them to the car.

Ruthie turned to Eva, who had followed them out the front door. "This is so sudden. I wish we had more time to say goodbye." Her voice cracked, and she couldn't hold back her tears. She gave Eva a long, tight hug.

"I was looking forward to spending Christmas with you Eva," Susan said. "But I guess it wasn't meant to be." Sarasota felt like home now, and she didn't think that would change when she got to Ohio.

"It's okay. I'm invited to Mary and Richard's house on Christmas. You need to go. I'll be praying that you arrive safely."

Eva cared about them. She had been a good listener and a wise guide. Susan was eager to settle into the front seat with Luke and hit the road. But Ruthie was still saying her goodbyes. "I might not see you for a long time. I'm going to miss you, Eva. I'm going to miss Florida and the sunshine."

Eva wiped her eyes. "There's sunshine in Ohio, too—sometimes. And someone is there waiting for you. Bring him to Sarasota next winter. You can stay at Saw Grass Inn."

"We just might do that," Ruthie said. She sounded like her usual jolly self, but her face looked sad.

"I'll be back soon," Susan said. "After Old Christmas. As soon as I can get here. You'll need me when the inn opens for the winter. You can count on me."

"I know I can, Susan. I'll be praying for you and your family so you can celebrate despite *Dawdi's* condition. It's in God's hands. Take all the time you need in Ohio. That's more important than the inn. I have people to help me until you return."

It was a quick drive to I-75. "We're going to be on this road for quite a while," Luke said. "And I've brought songs for the trip. The Weiler Singers will make these miles fly by. You heard of 'em?"

"Sorry. No," Susan said as she half-turned to see if Ruthie knew something she didn't.

"I don't think so. Are they a Florida thing?" Ruthie asked.

"Nope. Indiana Amish group, but they've been here for concerts once or twice—Gospel bluegrass." Luke briefly took his eyes off the road to cue his playlist, then adjusted the sound. The car felt like a small concert hall, filled with guitar, fiddle, mandolin, and voices. "This world is not my home; I'm just a passing through...." The twangy, soulful mountain music made it impossible for Susan to stay still. She tapped her foot, starting gently and then with more enthusiasm. Luke kept time with his hand on the steering wheel, adding his voice to the song.

Susan kept glancing at him. She'd be stuck in a car with Luke beside her for hours. It felt too good to be real.

One song after another carried them up the highway as signs alerted them to exits for Tampa and announced the miles to Ocala. It kept playing on repeat during the long stretch to Gainesville. Luke added new nuances to his performance with each replay. Ruthie started humming along before they reached Tampa. Soon, she was singing full throttle, and Luke had shed all inhibition, mimicking the characteristic twang—even exaggerating it. "Will the circle be unbroken, by and by Lord, by and by...."

Susan sang, too, but not as loudly as her two companions. She was thinking about how the words didn't quite match the cheerful fiddle and the trill of the mandolin. She felt the music in her body, but also deep in her soul. And those two feelings didn't match. As if reading her mind, Luke lowered the volume. "That's Bethany on the mandolin. She's good. I'll show you the YouTube videos sometime. They play in their kitchen or dining room, just tearing through these old bluegrass songs. Maybe you've heard of Ralph Stanley or Ricky Skaggs. Ever heard of the Carter sisters? They were the originals. The Weilers sound about the same to me. Maybe even better."

Susan hadn't heard of those singers but knew some of their songs. The instruments and the husky, nasal voices, accompanied by guitar and banjo, made them sound completely different from the slow tunes they used to sing at youth group singings. They sang about death and heaven, but there wasn't much sadness in the sound. Unfortunately, that didn't stop Susan from thinking sad thoughts.

Sadness built inside her as she absorbed the words. Her toes stopped tapping, and her mind took over, trying to picture the "glory land" that was "brighter than day." One song talked about a son watching a hearse come up the driveway—words that reminded her of when that exact thing happened after *Mommi* Troyer's death. And yesterday, *Maemm* had told her *Dawdi* was dying. She swallowed the lump in her throat.

Luke had the playlist set to repeat. The sad question kept coming back: "Will you miss me when I'm gone?" Even before the song ended, Susan knew she'd had enough.

"Can we please stop playing this music for a little while?" Her voice sounded sharper than she intended. Right away, she felt bad for being so negative.

"Of course, we don't have to listen to music. Enough already!" He turned the knob until it clicked. He glanced at her, and she swiped at the two big tears falling onto her cheeks. "Susan, what's wrong?" Luke's question was quiet and soothing, barely above a whisper. He reached over, took her hand, and gave a gentle squeeze of reassurance.

"I started thinking about *Dawdi*. He's the whole reason I'm going home. And I'm scared. I don't want to lose him, but I know he's going to heaven. Maybe he already has. Who knows?"

"I'm sorry. I never considered how those songs could affect you, given your worries about *Dawdi*," Luke said. "Your mother will call your cell phone if *Dawdi* passes, don't you think?"

"Yeah, she would." Susan gave Luke a weak smile.

Ruthie leaned forward and patted Susan's shoulder to show she understood.

"I know what they say is true. Like the song says, 'If on earth we meet no more, we will meet on heaven's shore,'" Susan said. "We *will* meet again after we die, don't you think so? *Dawdi* always told us we have a hope of heaven after we die."

"I've heard preachers say that sometimes," Luke said, "...a *hope* of heaven...I'm *sure* we will meet again—in heaven. The songs aren't wrong to call it Glory Land. I think it will be glorious!"

Everyone grew quiet. Susan thought about Glory Land and hoped Luke was right. She wanted to be sure of heaven. For now, though, she prayed *Dawdi* would stay in this world for at least a few more days. She needed to see him, talk to him, and see his smile. She needed to tell him she loved him before it was too late.

"Here's the exit I was looking for," Luke announced. "We've been driving for three hours. It's time to grab something to eat and do some last-minute Christmas shopping in Micanopy."

"I'm ready for a break and some supper," Ruthie said. "My *Daett* always stops for a hot meal when we travel. Besides, I need to get out of the car and walk around some."

Susan was glad about the rest stop, too. She realized neither of them had thought about packing snacks for the trip like they did when they rode the bus. The music had kept them from thinking about food.

"You two might want to buy a bag of oranges to take home. I'm going to grab some for my cousins. Northerners will expect you to bring them fresh oranges from Florida."

"I didn't think of that, but you're right, Luke. And I don't have any presents so far," Susan said.

"Caleb and Eva took us to Micanopy once when I was a kid," Luke said. "It's Florida at its best. I'm sure there's a citrus market. It's too cold to grow citrus here, but they know enough to cater to tourists. I'm guessing the town will be decorated for Christmas, too."

In a few minutes, they passed a sign announcing they'd arrived at "The little town that time forgot." Luke parked in front of a charming restaurant called Sweet Orange Café. Climbing roses, a weathered picket fence, and a large old door painted bright turquoise greeted them. They got out of the car, and Susan looked down the street, taking in the mix of old brick buildings, overhanging porch roofs made of corrugated tin, and comfortable-looking painted wooden rockers.

And sure enough, next to the Sweet Orange Café was a small open-air market with handmade signs listing the prices of fruit displayed in bushel baskets and wooden crates. Susan's mouth watered just thinking about juicy oranges and grapefruit.

———————————

"Good morning, sleepyhead," Luke said. He was singing the Beatles this time. "Here comes the sun. Here comes the sun. It's all right...." He sang softly; his eyes were fixed on the highway. Susan pulled her head away from the pillow she'd wedged against the car door and stretched her sore neck. She rubbed her eyes. Now fully awake, she sat up, fixed her hair, and tucked a few stray strands beneath the scarf she'd worn for the trip.

They saw a sign saying they had entered Virginia. "What time is it?"

Luke pointed to the car's dashboard. "Four in the morning. How do you feel? You and Ruthie slept right through the night. Good for you."

There was no sound from the back seat. Ruthie was either still asleep or pretending to be asleep.

Susan kept her voice to a whisper. "I feel okay, a little groggy. How about you? Driving for such a long time," Susan said. "How did you manage to stay awake all that time?"

"It was rough around 2 a.m., but my Yeti was full of hot coffee. I listened to podcasts, drank my coffee, and kept driving. Oh, and I sneaked a few looks at you over there." He grinned at her. "With all that, I managed to stay awake and on the road." Luke's eyes twinkled. He reached for her hand, and her heart flip-flopped. How wonderful to wake up and see Luke right beside her.

Susan's hand moved to the Junonia shell he had given her at the beach just three days earlier. To remind her of her newfound strength, she had tucked it into the pocket of her quilted jacket, the warmest coat she had with her in Florida. The smooth shell twirled, symbolizing strength for a new day—in Ohio.

"When Ruthie wakes up, we'll find a travel plaza and get some breakfast," Luke said. "Stretch our legs. Get some hot coffee."

From the back seat, Ruthie's muffled voice emerged from the pillow and fluffy fleece she'd cocooned in overnight. "What? Did I hear someone say something about me?"

"Luke said we're going to stop when you wake up. I guess you are—awake. How did you sleep? Are you hungry?"

There was a yawn, then a rustle behind them as Ruthie shifted herself and her belongings. "Oh goodness! Is it morning? I'm ready to stop whenever you are," she said.

For a few miles, they listened to music and watched the morning's hazy purple-pink color overshadow the landscape ahead. "We'll be in the mountains for the next while. Ohio, here we come."

Susan felt an uneasy gurgle in her stomach. Was it hunger or the mention of Ohio? She wasn't sure.

"But first, how 'bout some breakfast?" Luke guided the car onto an exit ramp and stopped near the brightly lit, almost empty travel plaza parking lot. "You go on inside. I'll fill the gas tank and meet you in there."

Susan and Ruthie stepped out and stopped on the curb, regaining their legs and clutching their coats. They were wide awake in the brisk air, inhaling that familiar, bone-chilling dampness. Susan shivered.

"Oh! It's cold," Ruthie exclaimed. "But it's so worth it to be on our way home. I still can't believe I'll be in Ohio on the same day Ben comes home. Tomorrow—I mean tonight. Ohio can't be too far away now."

"Yes. Unbelievable," Susan said. But she didn't feel as excited as Ruthie sounded. Restlessness churned inside her at the thought of Benville—its potential for pain and discontent—whether due to *Dawdi's* fragile condition or her worries that Luke wouldn't meet her parents' approval. But he was the man she'd never dared hope for, until now.

CHAPTER 30

After coffee and breakfast, they hit the road again. Memories of palm trees and bougainvillea faded, replaced by fallow fields and rundown barns under gray, overcast skies. Now and then, the dormant landscape was dotted with evergreens resembling frosted Christmas trees. A small pine tree by the highway was decorated with tinsel and a few red and silver ornaments, a seasonal touch. Already, Susan missed the Florida sunshine. The clouds, brown fields, bare tree branches, and a light dusting of snow made Susan feel melancholy.

When they crossed the Ohio River, Ruthie exclaimed, "Back in Ohio at last!" Of course, Ruthie was happy. She would soon see her parents and Ben. And the life she'd been dreaming of would be underway. Susan kept her thoughts about the landscape to herself—no need to dampen her friend's high spirits.

But as Luke drove up State Route 77, getting ever closer to the Strasburg exit and Route 250, discomfort and fear simmered inside Susan. She had left Ohio as a dishonest, confused, and unhappy woman. Dissatisfied with her place in the community—or at least with the place she imagined herself to have—she was a lonely, unmarried, childless woman ready to take over Aunt Fannie's quilt shop or find some way to support herself. She would be the one her parents looked to for help in their old age—an old maid, a spinster.

Now that she'd met Luke, that unfortunate future had been

replaced with something and someone else. While she wasn't as sure of the future as Ruthie was, Susan felt life moving in a new direction. Living in Sarasota and getting to know Eva, Luke, and his family had changed everything. Should she tell her parents the truth about why she left? She knew they were relieved she'd ditched Amos and his bad influence. But what would they think of Luke? Would they accept him as they'd accepted Leah's Aaron? Luke was Plain, but he wasn't Old Order Amish. Would they understand her desire to live in Florida and give their blessing?

Huge snowflakes splattered on the car windshield, and Luke turned on the wipers. "Getting some snow. Just in time for a white Christmas. It's been a while since I've had one of those." He glanced toward Susan.

"Hey, why the sad face? You're almost home," Luke said.

"Oh, not sad. Worried, I guess. It's been so long since I've seen everyone. And *Dawdi*....I feel like a different person now from when I left. Will anyone know, or will they still see me as the old Susan?" Luke and Ruthie didn't respond right away.

"It's good you're going to see *Dawdi*. That will make him so happy," Ruthie patted Susan's shoulder. "Just be yourself, and they will soon see that you've changed."

"I have changed," Susan said. "I'm much stronger now and know what I want—and what I don't want."

"You can trust God to help you find the right words to say," Luke paused, "and to know what is okay to leave unsaid."

Susan's fingers twirled the Junonia shell inside her pocket. "I know you're right," she said. Her voice was nearly a whisper.

Luke reached across the seat for her hand. She didn't let go. The warmth of his fingers curled around hers. And she knew everything would be okay.

They rode for a few miles while it snowed. Then the snow fell so quickly that they were driving through wet slush. Luke stayed in the right lane with the slow traffic, but cars and trucks rushed past. A station wagon went by, splashing slush. The car was full of Christmas gifts. The driver wore a Santa hat and was eating a red apple.

Luke pulled into a service plaza at the Cambridge exit. "This will be our last rest stop. If you want to freshen up before seeing your folks, this would be the time."

"Good idea," Ruthie said. "I didn't think I'd need rubber boots, though." She laughed as she carefully navigated the sloppy parking lot to the salted sidewalk.

At Mount Eaton, they traveled south along a narrow, snow-covered township road. The wet flakes had built up, and Luke concentrated on driving. His hands gripped the steering wheel so tightly that his knuckles turned white. He pressed the brakes to check for ice under the snow. Luckily, the snow was wet enough, and the temperature high enough, that ice had not yet formed.

"Our place is the next one on the left," Ruthie said. "You can turn just by the mailbox there. Otherwise, we might get stuck."

Luke nodded.

The heavy snow and Luke's nervousness about driving in it made Susan's heart race as they pulled into Ruthie's driveway. Luke turned the car around and opened the trunk, while Ruthie, almost before the car stopped, opened her door. Ruthie's parents came out of the house without their coats. Susan quickly got out and hugged Ruthie tightly. "I'm going to miss you, girlfriend."

"Me, too. I'll call you. I'm praying for you and your family, and of course, *Dawdi*."

Luke retrieved Ruthie's bag from the trunk and handed it to her father. They shook hands. "Thanks for bringing her home safely. We appreciate it." He held out some folded bills.

"No need to pay me. And now she's here just in time for Christmas."

"Yes indeed."

Then Susan and Luke were back on the road, driving through the snow-covered landscape to Benville.

As the neighborhood homes and shops came into view and the car slowed behind a buggy followed by three E-bikes, Susan took a deep, but shaky breath. Luke looked at her and grinned. "You ready for this? You're nervous. I've been praying for you, you know?"

"I've been praying for you, too," Susan said lightly.

"For my driving? I'm not used to driving in snow."

"Well, yeah!" she admitted with a laugh. "And you did great. Thanks to you, we've made it to Ohio. I don't know what I would have done otherwise."

"My pleasure. Look, I won't stay long, but I'll be thinking of you and praying for you as you settle in with your family and talk to your *Dawdi*. I won't be far away, down at my cousin's place."

"I want you to meet my family, but since I don't know how things are with *Dawdi*, it might be best to spend some time with them first," Susan said. "And it's almost Christmas."

"Alright. When you get the chance, give me a call. You have my number."

And then they were there. Susan let her eyes rest on home: the snow-covered pasture out back, the white-blanketed kitchen garden with a few green parsley and sage leaves pushing up from the snow, the porch swing lifted to the ceiling to protect it from the elements, and the bird feeders filled with bright red cardinals, black-capped chickadees, and dark-eyed juncos. The scene reassured her. Luke squeezed her hand, and their eyes met. All would be well.

Luke waved to *Maemm,* who stepped onto the porch and wiped her hands on a dishtowel. Susan ran up the steps and dropped her bag. She turned briefly to watch Luke, who was already back in the car. "My goodness. I thought I'd at least get to say hello to your young man," *Maemm* said. She wrapped Susan in a tight hug right there on the porch.

After a moment, Susan took a step back. "I guess Luke's in a rush to get to his cousin's place in Berlin. He isn't used to driving in the snow."

"That makes sense. It's getting worse by the minute," *Maemm* said. They entered the warm kitchen that smelled of freshly baked bread and shared a warm hug.

"Susan, you made it! Come in, sit down. How was your trip? Are you hungry?" Questions, hugs, and exclamations kept coming as Susan's brothers appeared through the back entrance with *Daett.* They took off their snowy boots inside the door and headed to the table.

"We waited for dinner until you got here. You must be hungry after that long trip," *Maemm* said.

Susan was back in a world where the noon meal was dinner. Today, it felt more like one of Eva's lunches, with *Maemm's* dinner chowder—a special potato soup recipe. She set the large kettle of soup in the middle of the table, next to a fresh loaf of cinnamon bread from the line on the countertop. All the relatives had come to expect cinnamon bread from *Maemm* around Christmastime. It was so delicious with Uncle Daniel's apple butter. The meal was finished with a big dish of home-canned applesauce, one of the jars Susan had helped preserve before she left home.

The family bowed their heads together, and the room fell silent except for the ticking clock. *Thank You for bringing me safely home, dear Jesus. Thank You for my family, for this food, and for all Your good gifts. Be near me, Lord Jesus.* Those last words were from the familiar Christmas carol and felt just right for this moment and place.

The conversation around the table was lighthearted and not particularly focused on Susan. It was almost as if she hadn't left, except that Susan's brothers Jake, Andy, and Adam seemed more grown-up, and they bombarded her with questions about life in Florida. She wasn't sure whether to ask about *Dawdi*. Were they waiting to share bad news until the meal ended? Their chat revolved around community news they'd heard at the shop.

Maemm listened quietly. She placed dessert dishes on the table and took a glass bowl filled with vanilla graham cracker pudding from the refrigerator. She spread a jar of sweet cherry pie filling over the top. When they finished eating, *Daett* prayed aloud, offering a second prayer. Susan listened to the rhythm of his words, spoken in the familiar *Deutsch,* as he thanked *Gott* for her safe arrival. She sensed his and *Maemm's* love for her. Had his prayers always been like this? Why hadn't she noticed before? At the end of the prayer, he mentioned *Dawdi*: "...in his hour of need, be near to him and comfort him...."

Daett and the boys got up from the table and headed back to finish their workday at the wood shop. Susan collected the dishes and carried them to the sink, while *Maemm* started the hot, soapy water for washing. Susan grabbed a towel and dried the dishes.

"I'm sure you're wondering about *Dawdi,*" *Maemm* said. "He's holding on. I thought he was a little better this morning. Fannie is sitting with him right now. We'll go see him once the dishes are done. He usually naps around this time of the day, so there's no hurry."

With the dishes dried and put away, Susan wasn't going to delay visiting *Dawdi.* "It's okay. You don't need to come with me. I'm heading over right now," she told *Maemm.* She didn't need a coat to run across the porch to the *Dawdi haus.* The air was crisp and cold, and she took a deep breath, gathering energy to face this unfamiliar place at the edge of life and death. She tapped lightly on the door, and Fannie opened it a crack.

"Susan. Oh, it's Susan!" Fannie turned her head and whispered loudly into the room, then opened the door wider to let Susan in.

"I'm here to visit *Dawdi.* Is he awake?"

In the corner of the main room of the *Dawdi haus,* Susan's grandfather sat in a plush brown recliner. He was wrapped in an old afghan from when *Mommi* Ruth was still alive. A hospital bed near the wide window faced the large garden with *Dawdi's* grape arbor beside it and the pasture beyond.

"You came at a good time," Fannie said.

"Ah, my sweet girly, you've come," *Dawdi* said. His voice was thin and slow, but he still used the familiar greeting she'd heard since she was small. "Come. Sit. You're a sight for sore eyes. Let me get a look at you." His eyes were reddened and watery, and he didn't bother to wipe the tears that escaped and flooded his wrinkled cheeks.

Susan bent over to hug *Dawdi.* His thick white beard prickled her skin. She rubbed her hand across his shoulders and felt the coarse texture of his gray woolen sweater. An unsettling odor filled the air around them, something like cheese or decaying garden compost, but stronger and more pungent. She pulled back abruptly. Fannie brought a wooden kitchen chair so Susan could sit facing *Dawdi.*

"I missed you so much. I'm sorry you're not feeling well, *Daw-*

di. I've been praying for you. We all have. Ruthie, my new friends in Florida." The words sounded empty and insufficient.

"*Ach*, girly, my times are in *Gott's* hands. For now, I'm still here among the living, and I thank *Gott* for this blessing of seeing you before I die. They say you are happy and doing well, but I needed to see for myself." His voice rasped as he pushed out this long speech, then a coughing fit took over.

Fannie handed him a handkerchief, and he covered his mouth and coughed again. "Even talking wears him out now," she whispered to Susan as she left the room. Her face showed the sadness Susan felt deep inside. Fannie came back with a small glass of water. He took a couple of sips and handed it back.

Dawdi turned back to Susan. "They say you like Florida sunshine. I can see it's done you some good. And you've made friends there and found work?"

"Oh, I have good friends there, and a job helping run Saw Grass Inn, that's Eva Good's hotel. She's just starting out with it, and Ruthie and I helped get the place fixed up and open for business." Susan paused, trying to think of what to say that would keep *Dawdi* from another long speech and coughing fit. But he pushed forward.

"They said you go to a church down there near Pinecraft. Is that so? I hope you found a community to fellowship with there."

"I went to Harvest Church a few times and to the youth prayer circle. Luke started it for the young people, hoping to get more to join in." Somehow, Luke's name had slipped just as Fannie stepped back into the room from the kitchen, where her tidying up had been interrupted.

"Luke, you say? Who is this Luke fellow?" *Dawdi* asked.

"He's Luke Rohrer. He's the son of one of Eva Good's friends. Old family friends. We've only had one date so far." Susan felt her face flush.

"He's the one who brought Ruthie and me up to Ohio when the bus didn't have room for us." The blush spread across Susan's cheeks and down her neck.

Dawdi seemed to be soaking it all in. It was as if Susan's presence and her chatter about the inn, her church, and her new friends had given him renewed energy. His tired eyes still sparkled despite his poor health. "Ahhh! Luke is the someone special you've been waiting for; I can see that. Now, where is this Luke fellow? Bring him in here so we can meet him." With that the coughing started again, and Fannie repeated her ministrations.

Susan stood and wrapped her arms around *Dawdi*. "Maybe you would be more comfortable in bed," she said. "You don't have to sit up on my account."

"He's been sitting up for most of an hour. I think it's time to get him back into bed," Fannie said. Susan and Fannie helped *Dawdi* stand, and he slowly took a few steps to the bedside, which Fannie had already lowered and made up before Susan came to visit. They tucked him in, and he sighed deeply, closing his eyes—signaling that the brief visit had ended.

"I think it made him happy to hear you're part of a church and you have friends and a job. Even if it is far away in Florida," Fannie said.

"I hope I get to talk with him again. There's so much I want to tell him yet," Susan said.

Fannie and Susan moved to the front of the main room, where some rocking chairs and a couch had been arranged into a circle for visitors. "I'm glad you got away from Benville. I wasn't sure about it when you left, but it was the right decision. And you even met a young man—a good one this time." Fannie gave a knowing smile. Even if no one else understood, Fannie did.

There was a tap on the door, and *Maemm* and *Daett* entered and joined the circle. "How is he?" *Maemm* whispered.

"He was pretty good there for a spell," Fannie said. "He was happy to hear that Susan has a fellow. What's his name? Luke somebody?"

Susan felt her hot cheeks, as if to check whether she was blushing again. She shifted in the rocker and dropped her eyes. "Luke Rohrer. He's the man who drove us up from Florida. I had a date with him last week."

"*Dawdi* wants to meet him," Fannie chimed in. "So do I."

Susan shifted in her chair, relieved it was too dark for them to notice her blushing.

Daett raised his eyebrows and gave Susan a questioning look. "By all means. We all want to meet your Luke. Why didn't he stick around instead of just dropping you off and leaving?"

Susan stammered, "Well, I didn't know...it was snowing so much, and his cousins were expecting him. And with *Dawdi* sick and it being Christmas, it just all seemed like a lot. But I can call him and invite him if you think I should."

"It's going to be a different Christmas anyway. We're staying close to home, not knowing how long *Dawdi* has. He could go at any time," *Daett* said. His voice was soft but matter-of-fact.

Maemm said, "Leah's planning to have us all over on Christmas Day for dinner."

"I could stay with *Dawdi*—Luke and I could—while the rest of you go," Susan said.

"Oh no, we want you there. Besides, Rita, the hospice nurse, offered to stay with him while we have our Christmas." *Maemm's* voice held the anguish they all felt. "It's such a hard time right now, Susan. You're a bright spot in these dark days. We've missed you."

"And we want to meet your young man," *Daett* said. "You give him a call. Tell him he's welcome to come for Christmas."

It was only mid-afternoon, but the skies had turned overcast and dark. No one lit the gas lamp on the table. Susan had grown accustomed to electricity and overhead lights, but at this moment, it felt right to sit here in the dimness. The day before Christmas Eve was one of the shortest days of the year. The solstice had just begun to bring longer minutes of light. They waited for that light, *Dawdi* perhaps for a heavenly one, but in their waiting, they knew the peace and comfort of a dark, quiet room.

The conversation continued in hushed whispers so as not to wake *Dawdi*. The young people planned to come caroling for *Dawdi* later on. *Maemm* had baked some date nut bread, which she would serve to them with warm, spiced cider. There was an Old Christmas Day family gathering for *Maemm's* side. The children's school program was outstanding again this year, and Adam had given the longest recitation, the biblical account of the birth of Jesus from Luke 2—in German. Fannie had contributed to a gift basket for an *Englischer* family who needed help after the father lost his job.

Susan listened to everything, happy to be part of this close family circle. In another part of her mind, she pictured Luke sitting with them. She yearned for his strength to support her as she faced what was coming.

Out on the porch, footsteps could be heard. "Oh goodness! I lost track of the time," *Maemm* said. "The carolers are here!"

CHAPTER 31

The wood stove radiated heat as the group gathered in *Dawdi's* front room and listened to the carolers' footsteps. The young people clomped up the stairway from the ground level and shuffled across the long front porch that connected the main house to the *Dawdi haus.* Their boots crunched through the accumulated snow. "I should have had the boys clear the steps before they left," *Daett* said. "I did sprinkle some salt on the steps."

Susan stood and raised the roller blind covering the window on the front door. A flicker of flashlights glowed on the snowy porch where the singers gathered. She cracked the door open slightly to let *Dawdi* hear them better. He moved his hands over the old flannel comforter. Susan went to him and bent down. "*Dawdi*, are you awake? The carolers are here. They're going to sing for us now."

He nodded slightly and opened his eyes. "Susan. I'm awake. Carolers...." His thin voice drifted away, and he closed his eyes again as if keeping them open was too exhausting. Susan returned to the group at the other end of the room. "He's awake. He seems weak, but I think he understood me."

Someone on the porch started singing, and the others joined in: *O little town of Bethlehem, how still we see thee lie, above thy deep and dreamless sleep, the silent stars go by. Yet in thy dark streets shineth, the everlasting light....*

Susan hummed along as they sang about peace, the stillness of a dark town like Benville, blanketed in deep, wet snow. Bright stars floated above them as they listened to the old Christmas story and waited for the coming of that Everlasting Light.

When the singers finished with a shout of "Merry Christmas!" *Maemm* opened the door and thanked them. "That was beautiful. Would you come next door for some cider?" She led the way, and the rest followed, except for Fannie, who stayed to keep *Dawdi* company.

Susan greeted the young people and sipped a cup of spiced cider that had been simmering on the stove all afternoon and evening. The long trip, combined with an emotional day, had worn her out. She crept upstairs to her old bedroom and slipped into her nightgown. There was only one thing she needed to do before falling asleep: grab her phone from her bag and look for Luke's number. She couldn't wait to invite him for Christmas. They'd only been apart for a few hours, but even so, they had a lot of catching up to do.

Susan slept late and woke up feeling refreshed. Luke had agreed to join them for Christmas dinner and said he wasn't sorry to miss the Christmas his relatives had planned—he wasn't interested in trudging through the snow with them for the Christmas bird count.

Maemm had left a note beside the French press for Susan. "There's hot water on the back of the wood stove. When you're ready, come on over to Leah's place. I'm helping her make the turkey dressing, then we'll be baking cookies and pies for tomorrow." Susan made a cup of coffee and ate a couple of slices of date and nut bread from a plate on the sideboard. With coffee in hand, just as she had so many mornings before, she made her way to the *Dawdi haus* to say good morning. The hospice nurse, Rita, was there, along with Fannie. They were bending over *Dawdi's* bed but turned to greet her.

"How is he this morning?" Susan asked.

"About the same. He was up for an hour. We just got him back into bed. Rita gave him a breathing treatment. That should help," Fannie said.

"Hello. I don't think we've met." Rita was petite, with salt-and-pepper hair cut short. She wore plain, dark-rimmed glasses and leggings underneath a simple, long-sleeved maroon knit dress.

"I'm Susan. A granddaughter. I'm visiting from Florida."

"You're the one your grandfather was asking about," Rita said. "I'm so glad you came. Did you get to talk to him last night? I just told your aunt Fannie here; he might hold on until after Christmas."

Susan hoped so. Seeing the breathing apparatus and the oxygen flowing through the tubing across *Dawdi's* cheeks made it feel more real. Her eyes welled with tears.

"Don't worry. We're keeping him comfortable. And your presence here provides more comfort than you realize." Rita wrapped her arm around Susan's shoulders. Her warm hug reassured Susan.

"I'd hoped to talk to him more, yet. There are things I want to tell him, but it looks like I'm too late."

"I think you'll still have time with him. I'll be here all morning and can let you know if he wakes up. In the meantime, why don't you enjoy seeing the rest of your family? Your sister Leah was here earlier. I think she was looking for you." Rita gave Susan's shoulders a final squeeze. Susan wiped her eyes and kissed *Dawdi* on the forehead.

"Thanks, Rita. Bye Fannie. Let me know if anything changes. I'm going to Leah's place now."

The two women smiled. "Goodbye. See you later."

Maemm had found Susan's old gardening muck boots from last summer. She'd cleaned them and placed them by the front door. Susan pulled them on, thankful for thick socks and dry feet. The postcard picture snow crunched under her feet as she walked down the lane and along the roadside to the next driveway where Aaron and Leah lived.

When she reached Leah's door, Susan hesitated. Before leaving Benville, she would usually walk in and announce herself. But today, she felt more like a guest. She raised her gloved hand to knock, but before she could, one of the twins tugged the door open—Susan had to look twice to tell which one. The three-year-old girls, Rachel and Rebecca, stood there wide-eyed and squealing with excitement. Susan stepped inside, and the door whooshed shut behind her. Her heart swelled with love for the little girls she'd cared for so often before she left for Florida. She knelt down and wrapped one arm around each of them. "Your auntie made it back. How are my girls?" She looked from one to the other. "You've grown up. Look at you." Their cobalt blue eyes, inherited from their father, sparkled as the morning sunshine streamed through the windows in Leah's spacious front room.

Leah turned away from the stove where she was stirring something. Susan smelled the familiar blend of onions, celery, sage, and butter for tomorrow's turkey dressing. Leah wiped her hands on her apron and hurried over. Susan felt a surge of love for her sister and her little family.

They met in the center of the room and wrapped their arms around each other. "I missed you," Leah said. "You look great. Must be all that sunshine."

"Your *kinnah* are so grown up." The twins had followed Susan and Leah. They each wrapped their arms around one of the sisters' legs. Little Matthew toddled over and joined the group hug. Susan reached for him and tousled his blonde curls. "Goodness, Matthew has quite a head of hair."

Maemm stood up from the bentwood rocker where she was cuddling Leah and Aaron's youngest baby, Michael. He'd fallen asleep, and *Maemm* gently carried him to the bassinet placed just the right distance from the woodstove—warm enough but not too hot. Susan peeked at her youngest nephew's sleeping face. "He's so sweet," she said to Leah. "You sure do have your hands full."

"It's a little busy around here sometimes," Leah said. "Still, I'm so thankful for my *kinnah,* good health, and Aaron. There was a time when I never imagined I'd have this life. *Gott* has been good. But enough about me. How are you? How was the trip up from Florida? I wanted to come over so bad to see you last night, but with this crew, it's tough to get away sometimes."

"I'm doing well. I have things to tell you, but that can wait. Looks like we have work to do for Christmas dinner," Susan said. She'd wait for a long sister-talk when the time was right, but now there were kitchen chores to share with Leah and *Maemm.*

They spent the rest of the morning preparing food—Susan sliced stale white bread into cubes for the dressing, while *Maemm* was mixing pastry for several pies. "I thought we'd make two apple pies, a couple of pumpkin, and at least one pecan pie. I don't know what Susan's young man prefers. What do you think?"

Leah raised her eyebrows and gave Susan a searching look. "Susan's young man? I didn't know there was a 'Susan's young man,'" she said. "It can't be Amos Maust unless they let him out of jail for Christmas," she grimaced.

So Amos is in jail. Yikes! But he deserves to be. Susan pushed away the intrusive thoughts, feeling thankful for her new reality. She gulped and brushed away strands of hair that had fallen from her *kapp.* "No. He's history. I didn't know he was in jail." She paused. "It's Luke Rohrer, the guy who drove Ruthie and me to Ohio. We had a date last weekend. I met him at Harvest Church in Florida, and he worked at the Saw Grass Inn, Eva's inn, cleaning up the property."

"He's coming for dinner tomorrow?" Leah asked.

"*Daett* said I should invite him. He can come, by the way...." She looked at *Maemm,* who had a big smile as she watched this exchange between her two daughters.

"Well, that's wonderful," Leah said. "He's certainly welcome."

Matthew toddled over and babbled something incomprehensible. "This little guy needs a diaper change. Can you take over here?" Leah handed Susan the sturdy wooden spoon she was holding. "Go ahead and stir those bread cubes into the pan. I've got chicken broth here. You'll likely need most or all of it. I'll be right back."

The morning went by with friendly kitchen chores interrupted by toddlers' tears, diaper changes, hand washing, peeling apples, and peeling potatoes, as the scents of Christmas dinner filled the air. It felt and smelled just as Susan remembered. Soon, it would be Christmas Day, and Luke would meet her family. And they would meet Luke. Susan wondered...what exactly was she hoping for? Love, a family of her own, acceptance, forgiveness, and understanding.

After a quick meal of ham salad sandwiches, chips, and orange slices, Susan went back to *Dawdi's* house. "I can sit with him, Fannie. You've been here so much. What would they do without you?" Susan said.

"I'm happy to do it. Your *Maemm* and Leah have their hands full. Plus, Cozy Corner is closed for the winter. Your *Daett* wants me to shut it down for good, but I'm not sure. What am I supposed to do?"

"Knowing you, Fannie, you'll find ways to stay busy. You always do."

"*Yah,* I expect so. The store keeps me tied down, and I'm on my feet too much. I've got some arthritis in my hip now. Besides, if you return to Florida, Leah will need me sometimes. You are going back, aren't you?"

"I'm planning to, Fannie. I think Luke might be the one. But I'm worried. *Daett* and *Maemm*…what will they say if I stay there? And Luke, he's not Amish."

"He's Plain though, isn't he?"

"Yeah. He's Plain. He's staying with his Beachy Amish cousins in Berlin. They own an Airbnb. Luke's coming here for Christmas dinner. He decided not to join them. They're doing the Christmas bird count."

"You don't need to worry about your *mann*. Your family is just happy you aren't associating with that jailbird anymore. And plenty of our young people move away when they marry—maybe not so much the young ones in Benville."

Fannie was right. And she always seemed to understand and stick up for her niece.

"Fannie, you go home and rest up. I can stay with *Dawdi* this afternoon. I'm happy to. Just tell me if there's anything I need to do or be aware of."

Fannie whispered goodbye to *Dawdi*. She sprayed a homemade lavender-scented room spray to freshen the room, then sprayed a clean white handkerchief for Susan. "Here," she said, offering the cloth to Susan. "This helps with the odors in here. It will calm you, too."

Fannie pulled on her boots and wrapped herself in the thick shawl she wore over her quilted jacket. Susan settled into the up-holstered chair that someone had placed near *Dawdi's* bed. It hadn't been there the night before.

"I'm here, *Dawdi*," she whispered.

He opened his eyes and tried to smile. "Sus…" His voice drifted away.

Susan's heart pounded. She feared he might have just spoken his last words, but his uneven breathing soon reassured her. She sat quietly, watching him, letting her gaze linger on his face and savoring one of her final chances to hold onto a memory.

She sat by his bedside for the rest of the afternoon, listening to his labored breathing, sniffing the handkerchief, praying, listening, waiting, and hoping....It seemed as if *Gott* was whispering in her ear. *All will be well. All will be well.*

Near suppertime, *Dawdi* woke up, blinked his eyes, and moaned. Susan immediately stood and leaned in close. "*Dawdi,* are you awake?"

He tried to smile, to speak her name again. "Please, you don't need to talk if it's too hard right now," Susan whispered.

He closed his eyes. Susan took his hand in hers. "*Dawdi,* I love you. And I'm so sorry for how I acted before I left Benville. I was dishonest, and I hurt people. Please forgive me, *Dawdi.* I've found my way now." She squeezed his hand tightly. He murmured, then blinked again. Their eyes met, and Susan knew he understood. She felt the forgiveness he offered her in his eyes.

There was a tap at the door, and Fannie entered carrying an insulated mug. "I brought some broth from my noodle soup. My supper this evening. You'd best be on your way over to your *Maemm.* It's about time to eat over there."

After dinner, they gathered at *Dawdi's* house. It was Christmas Eve. Leah's family joined them shortly after, including the *kinnuh.* It was only a matter of time before *Dawdi* left for his heavenly home. They wanted to spend this special evening with him. Susan reached for baby Michael, eager to hold her sister's youngest.

Fannie lit the old oil lamps mounted in wall sconces. The

flickering light cast shadows as the family gathered around *Dawdi's* hospital bed, their muffled movements contrasting with *Dawdi's* ragged breathing. Bishop Maust had been summoned, and he entered quietly, greeting them. One by one, family members took turns whispering to *Dawdi,* touching his hand, or bending down for a hug. Leah stayed longer than the others, whispering something about his grapevines, the *kinnah.* Susan caught the word "love."

When it was Adam's turn, he looked at *Daett,* who nodded. "*Dawdi,* Adam's going to recite the Christmas story from Luke 2 for you, in German." *Dawdi* blinked in acknowledgment. Susan listened to the familiar words and admired her youngest brother's voice and his accuracy with the language they mostly knew from church.

After that, *Daett* led the family in singing *Stille Nacht.* They huddled around their loved one, feeling the weight of this sacred moment. Bishop Maust opened his book and used a small flashlight to read the words of an old prayer from *Die ernsthafte Christenpflicht.* Susan remembered it from years ago when he read it at the end of *Mommi* Ruth's life. If *Dawdi* could hear and understand it now, he must be eager for their sweet reunion in heaven.

A sob escaped Susan's throat as memories from the past flashed through her mind—*Dawdi* pruning grapes, faithfully keeping a list of the birds at his feeder, leaning on his cane at the edge of the garden, sipping his morning coffee in his rocking chair. Around the circle, others sniffled and wiped their eyes, each recalling their own memories.

Before they left, *Daett* asked them to join in singing one more hymn, the *Lebt Friedsam* (parting song) from the *Ausbund,* their German hymnal. Those words would stay with her, even as she moved on, serving as a reminder of her Amish roots and Ohio childhood. This time, Aaron led them. *Though I depart, my heart remains with you,/Until we enter into joy.*

CHAPTER 32

Susan awoke to family sounds in the kitchen below as the sun streamed through the window on Christmas morning. She smelled cinnamon rolls and bacon and heard *Daett's* footsteps approaching the wood stove—the squeak of hinges, the clunk of firewood dropping onto the grate. Luke would arrive in three hours. The thought brought a smile to her heart as she dressed quickly and hurried to join the family in the kitchen for breakfast.

"I checked in with Rita this morning. *Dawdi* is some better today. Maybe having the family together over there last night helped him. He doesn't have long, but I think we should go ahead and have our Christmas after all the work you women did to make us a good dinner," *Daett* said.

Susan hadn't realized there had been talk of waiting to have their Christmas dinner because of *Dawdi's* condition. She was glad it would still be happening.

When breakfast was finished, Susan said, "I'm going over to help Leah. I haven't had time to catch up with her yet."

Maemm nodded. "Go ahead. I'm sure she can use your help with Christmas dinner. I'll finish up here and bake my casseroles before I come over. Did your Luke say when he was coming?"

"I told him to come to Leah and Aaron's place around eleven."

"That's good. You and Leah can visit before he gets here."

At Leah's house, the twins and Matthew greeted her. She knelt down and fussed over them, admiring the new toys they held out to her.

"We let them open their presents from us," Leah said. "I was just as excited as they were."

Susan laughed. "Remember how we used to beg to open our gifts, and *Daett* made us wait until after Christmas dinner?"

"I do. Maybe that's why we took pity on our *kinnah* this morning. Besides, now they have something to do while dinner's cooking."

"Speaking of, what can I help with?"

"Everything's underway. The turkey's been in the oven for a couple of hours already. Aaron helped put the extra boards in the table and set up the benches and chairs. I even got the table ready. I thought Luke might be here by now."

"I told him to come around eleven. I didn't want him to feel rushed." Susan didn't mention that she was apprehensive. She wanted him to arrive just before dinner. Conversation was easier over a meal.

"We're planning to eat by noon. Maybe a little before," Leah said. "I can't wait to meet this guy."

Susan laughed. "I hope you like him."

Leah had spread a white tablecloth along the length of the oak dining table. She'd set the table with her good wedding dishes, embossed with a blue flower border. In the center of the table, she'd arranged an antique oil lamp with evergreen boughs and a few pinecones around it. "That's the perfect Christmas table," Susan said. She made a mental note to suggest white tablecloths and real pine boughs for next Christmas at Saw Grass Inn. Eva would have fun looking for antique oil lamps for the tables.

"Let's sit down and have some coffee. We haven't had a sister talk yet," Leah said. The baby whined, and she prepared his bottle while Susan filled their mugs. Leah settled into a rocking chair with the *boppli*, a picture of motherhood.

"Leah, it's hard to believe you're a *Maemm* to four *kinnah*. It seems like no time at all since you came home from Cleveland and started dating Aaron." Leah's peaceful countenance prompted Susan's misgivings. *Why isn't this me? She's all married and settled while I'm still figuring out God's plan.*

"Sometimes I can barely believe it myself," Leah said. "You and I are only a year apart, but so different. I always thought you'd be the one to get married, and I'd end up single. I mean, not that you won't get married someday," she added. "It's just that I thought you'd find someone way before me."

"I know. In Sarasota, I had time to think about what went wrong. I'll admit that before I left here, I was angry. About a lot of things. I was angry at God, even. But I'm learning to be patient. I know God has a plan, yet I sometimes feared the worst."

"The worst?"

"You know that I'd end up alone, like Fannie. I never imagined everyone would be married except me," Susan said.

"Fannie seems happy enough, even without being married. And, what about Ruthie? She's not married."

"She might be soon. But I'm not saying more than that." Susan smiled mischievously.

Leah nodded and rocked slightly. "Okay, then I won't ask. I'm glad you're home, and I hope you've gotten Florida out of your system. We missed your help around here. Not just me, but *Maemm* and *Daett*. Fannie needs you at the quilt shop, like before."

Susan winced at her sister's words and struggled to respond. "I-I-I'm not going to stay. I'm going back to Florida. I have a job waiting for me at Eva's inn. I'm only planning to stay here until *Dawdi...*"

Leah kept her eyes on baby Michael as they both finished the sentence in their minds rather than speak of *Dawdi's* impending death. "I thought you were just going to Pinecraft for the winter. And winter will soon be over."

Susan looked around her sister's home, feeling its comfort and security. Aaron had taken the older children to the woodshop to give Leah and Susan time to visit with each other. A wave of jealousy washed over her and broke, flooding Susan's mind. Aaron was a devoted husband and father, and he owned a family business. They lived close to *Maemm* and *Daett* in this community where they had both grown up. It was God's plan, and it felt so perfect for them.

Susan inhaled suddenly. She needed to explain that she had caught a glimpse of God's plan. She had been imagining that she and Luke would be together, living in Sarasota instead of settling down in Benville. As much as she loved Leah and her family, Susan felt deep in her heart that God was guiding her away from her sister, parents, brothers, nieces, and nephews, and away from Aunt Fannie and her quilt shop. "I think I'm going to stay in Florida. Like Eva did. When I first went there, I wanted to work in a restaurant. Eva found me a job, but it didn't go well, and I got fired."

Leah gave her sister a worried smile. "Yeah, that must have been awful. *Maemm* told me about it."

"It was a terrible day. But on my way home, I stopped at a nearby park, Locklear Park. I was crying, but then this Bible verse started running through my mind. It's about how God has a plan for us. God gives us hope and a future."

"I know that verse," Leah said. "You probably remember it from when *Dawdi* said it to you. I know he said it to me a few times."

"I kept saying the words, maybe in *Deutch,* I'm not sure. And, after that I felt better. As if God was telling me that things would work out, that there's a plan, even if I don't completely understand it yet."

"It's hard when we don't understand what God is doing. I know I felt that way for a long time before I had my back surgery."

Susan continued. "Then maybe you can understand what was going on for me. Back in November, I needed to get away from here and away from Amos. I'm so sorry for all the sneaking around. It was wrong of me, and I hurt people. I was lost. I felt hopeless. But things are different now."

"I knew you needed a change, and going to Florida with Ruthie was the right thing to do. You're on a better path now, I can see that."

Leah hummed an old lullaby as she rocked her baby. Affection filled Susan as they sat in the cozy sitting room.

Leah continued. "It must have been hard, though, living in a place so different from Benville. How did you handle such a big change?"

"After I was fired from the restaurant, Eva offered me a job at her inn. Luke was working there, too. Then Ruthie and I started attending Luke's church, and I feel like I belong there. Now Luke and I are dating—well, we've just had one date so far—but I already know him well since we worked together and he's the song leader at Harvest Church. I've met his parents and even sat with them at church."

"So, he's a song leader, like Aaron. But he's not Amish. I mean, I can see that. He *drove* you back here to Ohio two days ago. Would you leave the Amish if things got serious between you and Luke?" Leah looked troubled.

"I suppose I would. It's different in Sarasota. There are so many Plain groups, and everyone belongs, no matter where they're from."

"Are you going to drive a car, watch TV, and have air conditioning?" Leah seemed to struggle with the idea that Susan's life might be much different from what they'd both imagined.

"I don't think his group has TV. I'm not sure about air-conditioning. I know they have electricity in their homes. They dress Plain, though, and wear head coverings. But it's different from Old Order Amish. Being Amish is a lifestyle choice, the same as dressing plain. Following Jesus is the main thing, don't you think?"

"Of course, you're right about that. Whatever happens, I don't want to lose you. If Luke turns out to be the one, then I'll be happy for you. Our parents might be disappointed at first, but they aren't like some. They won't disown you."

"I know. If we end up together, they'd accept him."

Leah nodded. "It's just that I thought you'd come home now and settle down here, and we'd be neighbors, or at least you'd live close by—like *Maemm* and her sister." Leah's disappointment lingered in the air.

"Until I went to Sarasota, I never imagined living anywhere else. It's not that I don't feel at home here. My roots are here. I don't know yet what will happen. But God does." She smiled as their eyes met.

Leah moved baby Michael into a sitting position and gently patted his back, waiting for him to burp.

"I know what it's like to worry and feel uncertain about the future. I struggled so much when I was stuck in Cleveland that summer. But everyone was supportive, especially you. And after I had the babies, you were such a big help. I don't know how I'd have managed without you."

Leah's life had fallen into place after she underwent surgery to correct her spinal scoliosis that summer in Cleveland. If help hadn't arrived at just the right moment, her condition might have left her disfigured and disabled. At the time, from Susan's perspective, it seemed like an easy choice, but what had it been like for Leah? They hadn't spoken about it until now.

"I knew it was tough for you. You were so strong and brave. As for helping with the children, I'm glad I was here." Yes, she'd run around with Amos. She regretted that. But she wasn't sorry she'd been there to help her sister with Rachel, Rebecca, and her boys.

"You seem happy. Happier than before." Leah paused. "We'll have to trust God to work everything out for the best. No matter what, you'll always be my sister, and we'll stay connected."

"That's right. I promise. Letters, holiday visits, phone calls—we'll stay close somehow."

It was quiet for a moment as Leah rocked and Susan absorbed Leah's affirmation.

"This little guy is out. Let's hope he stays asleep for a while." Leah rose from the rocking chair and carefully placed little Michael in the cradle. "We have dinner to get on the table, and I see *Maemm* heading our way."

Susan met *Maemm* at the door and grasped the handles of the sturdy cardboard banana box, which held two steaming casserole dishes covered with foil and new Christmas kitchen towels. "I baked the sweet potatoes and dressing. You can keep them warm on top of the heating stove until dinner. *Daett* and the boys will be here soon. They're checking on *Dawdi*. The hospice nurse is staying with him this morning."

Susan glanced at the clock. Luke should be arriving soon, and there was still a lot to do.

Susan, Leah, and *Maemm* worked to put Christmas dinner on the table. The kitchen chores took on a familiar rhythm. They poured a half-gallon jar of pink Rome applesauce into *Grossmommi's* antique, cut-glass bowl and placed the cranberry sauce in one of the old glass dishes their family had used for years. *Maemm* must have passed these on to Leah. There was that twinge of jealousy again. Susan pushed it aside and sliced the pies, arranging them on the kitchen table alongside Leah's German chocolate cake.

Fannie arrived with a flurry of apologies for her lateness, her arms full of warm, fresh-baked dinner rolls, and some fried knee patches on a platter, covered with a towel. "The Yoders sent over some *knie blatza*," she said. "I guess they knew we didn't have time to make *nothings* this year." She pitched in to help, and the four Troyer women arranged all but the hot foods, placing the *nothings*, cake, and pies on the kitchen table, along with Susan's gift of Florida oranges.

Leah looked out the window as the women moved between the kitchen and dining room. "Susan, I think a car's coming down the lane. Is that Luke?"

Susan looked up. "Yes, it is!" She felt giddy, and her face flushed with excitement at being the center of everyone's attention.

"Just in time. Everything's ready here. You'd better go out and meet him." Leah sounded a little breathless. And why not? This was the first time Christmas dinner would be at her and Aaron's place, and now they were having a guest they'd never met.

Susan glanced in the small mirror by the door. Her face was flushed from the warm kitchen. She straightened her *kapp*. Her heart fluttered at the thought of seeing Luke and introducing him to *Daett*, who didn't speak more than necessary. *God, please let this go well. And thank You. I love You.*

She ran outside without a coat, warmed with the pure anticipation of seeing Luke.

He parked the car and stepped out, smiling his big, wonderful smile as he spread his arms wide, ready to give her a bear hug. Susan hurried to him, stumbling through the melting snow, forgetting to notice the cold, forgetting that her entire family might be watching.

Forgetting everything except Luke, who had entered her life by some miracle she could hardly understand. He was the plan, God's plan. God's plan for her good, and a still-mysterious future.

She slipped on a patch of ice on the downward-sloping lane. She was close enough to Luke that he caught her before she fell. He wrapped her in his arms and whispered, "My love. I've missed you."

Susan sank into him, burying her face in the soft, down-filled black parka with the green EdenKeepers' logo on the sleeve. "I missed you, too."

She pulled away just enough to see his face again, and their eyes met. Time stopped as they held one another in a gaze filled with volumes of unspoken love. Susan's heart pounded in anticipation of their first kiss. Forgetting the women in the house who might be watching, she tilted her face as Luke pulled her close. He bent to kiss her—long, slow, and soft.

"Merry Christmas, my love."

"Merry Christmas to you," Susan whispered. She was floating a few inches off the snow, flying with a snow angel into a glistening future, barely visible but belonging to them both. It was a memory she would keep in her heart forever.

They clasped hands and headed for the house. She shivered now as her heart raced from the excitement of their first kiss, her mind drifting in and out of reality as she willed herself back to earth.

Luke let go of her hand and wrapped his arm around her, pulling her close. "Where's your coat?" he asked.

She snuggled closer. "I forgot it when I looked out the window and saw you."

Luke laughed. Susan shivered again.

They entered Leah and Aaron's warm home, where everyone was gathered. Amid the noisy chaos, Susan quickly introduced

Luke somewhat awkwardly, then left him to fend for himself while she joined *Maemm* and Leah in the kitchen. Leah handed *Maemm* a small saucepan, then elbowed Susan. "He's cute! I approve," she whispered.

"I know," Susan whispered back. "Good to know."

If *Maemm* heard the exchange, she didn't show it. She kept her eyes on the mixture of flour and cold water as she stirred it into a saucepan of turkey broth. Her whisk clattered against the side of the pan, blending the contents into perfectly smooth gravy.

The women dished up mashed potatoes, carved slices of turkey, and scooped dressing from the enamelware roasting pan into a large bowl. When everything was on the table, *Daett* called for them to be seated. In her mind, Susan had imagined she'd sit beside Luke at dinner. She expected to feel his elbow against hers, his thigh against her own, as the family gathered around the dining table.

But Rachel and Rebecca insisted on sitting on either side of *Auntie* Susan. There was nothing she could do about it. Across the table, Luke had been claimed by Jake and Andy, Susan's two oldest *brüdah*, who elbowed him in the ribs as if they thought he already belonged to the family.

Daett welcomed everyone more formally than usual. He spoke of Christmas, Mary and Joseph, and of baby Jesus who grew to be a *mann* who taught His disciples to love one another and welcome the strangers among us. Susan blushed at what she took to be an outright nod to Luke, who listened intently and smiled at *Daett's* veiled promise of acceptance. After the prayer, they passed bowls of food to the left, starting with the rolls and ending with the cranberry sauce.

When the main meal finished, Fannie served desserts to those who weren't too full to enjoy them. The adults lingered around the table, chatting a little longer while the children wandered off to play, followed by their young uncles. Susan watched Luke, who sat across from her. Their eyes met as they shared a smile.

Luke was at home in their circle, as if he had always been part of it. Susan observed him. He was dark-haired, brown-eyed, and tan, a stark contrast to Aaron's fair hair and bright blue eyes. Yet, in other ways, the two men resembled each other—strong, self-assured, skilled in their trades, precise, and diligent. The awkwardness Susan had feared before never appeared.

The clock chimed one-thirty, and Leah started collecting the empty serving dishes from the table. *Maemm* stood up to help, and the others followed her example. Leah took the folded tablecloth to the porch and shook it.

"You take it easy, now," Fannie said to Leah. "Your *Maemm* and I can do the dishes. Besides, I don't know where you keep the Dutch Blitz cards."

Fannie turned to Luke. "I hope you know how to play Blitz. If not, we'll have to teach you."

"Of course, I know how to play Dutch Blitz, unless you Ohio people make up your own rules. We play by the rules on the box," Luke said with a teasing smile.

"*Yah!* We play by the rules. At least most of the time." She grinned at Luke before bustling off to the kitchen. Susan watched this little charade with a sense of satisfaction. Without question, Luke had found his place among the Troyer family.

Fannie returned with a damp cloth and swiped away any lingering crumbs. They needed a clean surface for slapping cards down as fast as possible in perfect order.

Aaron found two sets of Dutch Blitz cards, a notepad, and a pencil for scorekeeping. Finally free of the twins, Susan patted a chair beside her. She and Luke sorted and checked for missing Blitz cards while Aaron fed the woodstove and Leah changed diapers and put the little ones down for naps. Fannie and *Maemm* stacked dishes and wrapped leftovers in the kitchen.

Finally, everyone gathered around the table. They played a few rounds in two groups, with a foursome at each end of the table. Susan stayed close to Luke this time, her shoulder nearly touching his as they faced off against *Daett* and Fannie across from them.

In the middle of a noisy round, there was a knock at the door. Aaron hurried to answer, and Rita, the hospice nurse, entered the room. Susan froze, and Luke reached for her trembling hand beneath the table.

The game—everything—stopped, except for the mantle clock that chose that moment to chime four o'clock. They listened and waited, already knowing what Rita had come to say.

CHAPTER 33

"I'm sorry. Your *Dawdi* has gone to be with the Lord just a few minutes ago. I guess he's celebrating Christmas in heaven now."

Susan's brother Andy quietly gathered the cards and placed them back in their boxes. Aaron reached for Leah and put his arm around her shoulders as her eyes filled with tears. Luke moved to Susan's side and pulled her close. She leaned into him. A sob broke free, and Susan let it out, tears streaming down her face as she wiped at them. It felt so unreal after the festive dinner and lively game, even though they all knew this was coming sooner or later.

Maemm stood close to *Daett,* who reached out to grip his sister Fannie's hand. Their heads bowed, and *Daett* reached into his pocket for a handkerchief to wipe his eyes. Susan couldn't remember ever seeing her parents cry, but now they both were. Fannie, too.

It got dark early this time of year, but no one lit a lamp. They stood in the gathering darkness, knowing Christmas was over for another year. And they realized it would never be quite the same again; the memory of this evening would always stay with them on Christmas Day.

"There are things you'll need to do now," Rita said. "I can stay for a bit at *Dawdi's* place. Come over when you're ready. You can see him if you want to. I'll be happy to help with whatever you need me to do." She zipped her magenta hooded parka and pulled on her leather gloves.

Daett thanked Rita, and she slipped out the door. They sat back down around the table, everyone stunned and disoriented. "I knew this would happen," Fannie said. "I just didn't imagine it would be today, Christmas Day."

"None of us did," *Daett* said. "He seemed better this morning. I expected he'd at least make it through the day. I'll call the ministers and the undertaker. Boys, you go over to the Yoders and let them know *Dawdi* died this afternoon. When word gets out, people will start coming by to help with things."

Susan's brothers seemed relieved to be excused. They grabbed their coats and hurried away. Susan thought about the chores—caring for the horses and clearing the steps, which were still covered with snow. The neighbors would soon arrive and take care of everything for the Troyer family.

"We need to see to the *kinnah*. Get them to bed before too late. Tomorrow will be a long day," Leah said, looking at Aaron.

"Of course. I'll help with baths tonight."

Fannie blew her nose into a tissue, then got up and went to the kitchen. She turned on a lamp and continued cleaning the dinner dishes they'd left in the sink when the game started.

"Do you want to go see him?" Luke whispered to Susan. "I'll go with you."

She nodded and took her coat from a hook near the door. He helped her into it, smoothing it around her shoulders before he found his own. They left and walked together down the lane. Luke reached for her, and they continued walking hand in hand out to the road. Neither of them wore gloves.

"I'm sorry, Susan. I wish it hadn't happened during Christmas. Look, if it's easier for you, I can leave now so you can be with your family."

"No. Don't leave. I want you to stay here with me. I don't know how I'm going to get through this otherwise." Susan squeezed Luke's hand. Then he reached out to wrap an arm around her.

"I'm here for you. For as long as you want me to stay."

"Please stay." Luke's arm rested lightly on Susan's shoulders. She wrapped her arm around his waist, and they walked in step silently, minding the deep snow and keeping to the tracks where buggies and cars had packed the snow down into the gravel. On the road, they turned toward Susan's home and the attached *Dawdi haus.* Susan felt her stomach tumble at the thought of seeing *Dawdi* like this. At the very hour of his death. But she wanted to see him. To memorize his face, touch the wrinkled skin on the back of his hand, stroke his arm, and speak softly to him.

Luke gently tapped on the door, and Rita opened it. She had lit the wall sconces, and the soft glow of lamplight softened the sharp edges of the room.

"Go ahead," Rita said quietly. Susan moved across the room, propelled by her sadness and dread. She felt Luke's hand on her back, guiding and supporting her.

Dawdi lay still and pale, covered with a quilt rolled and tucked securely under his chin. An oil lamp on the table beside his worn Bible cast flickering shadows across his face. He looked peaceful and at rest. Luke pulled her close, then even closer, and they stood together in silence for a long while. Susan felt a sob rising from deep inside her. She didn't bother to stifle it but buried her face in the soft relief of his down-filled parka.

Finally, Luke guided her back into the snowy cold. It was nearly dark now. They leaned against the porch railing, hesitant to go into her parents' house where people were still doing the chores death required. They wanted to be alone, just the two of them, for a little while longer.

A few stars were visible. The planet Venus shone brightly. "Is he somewhere up there now?" Susan asked.

"Ah, I'm sure of it," Luke said. "He's left this world for a better place. Yet he will always be with you, his lessons and love guiding you, showing the way."

"If only you could have known him. You would have loved him," Susan said.

"You'll have to tell me about him sometime. Tell me what he meant to you."

"I will," Susan said. "But there's so much to tell. It will take a long time."

"That's okay," Luke said.

He turned to her as they stood together on the long porch between the *Dawdi haus* and Susan's parents' home. He gathered her in and held her tightly. "There will be plenty of time for you to tell me those stories."

Susan nodded wordlessly.

"This is just the beginning," Luke said. "It's just the beginning—for us."

THE END

ABOUT THE AUTHOR

Joanne Lehman's Amish-themed fiction is grounded in her rural Mennonite roots. Rich in descriptive detail, her lyrical fiction explores hope, healing, and forgiveness—always with a dash of romance. She grew up on a chicken farm in Columbiana, Ohio, next door to Appalachia, where she wandered the fields and woods barefoot and swam in the farm pond. Life revolved around church, cousins, and grandparents.

Joanne earned an MFA in creative writing and has worked as an adjunct English instructor, journalist, and community relations specialist. She is an award-winning author of three poetry chapbooks, a novel, *Kairos*, and a collection of creative nonfiction. Joanne has published poetry, essays, and articles in literary journals, religious periodicals, and local newspapers.

An incurable procrastinator, Joanne relies on a wide assortment of passions and hobbies to avoid writing. These include cycling on rail trails, doing Pilates and water aerobics, thrift shopping, traveling abroad, and baking desserts with zucchini or rhubarb as an ingredient. She is equally skilled at charcuterie and cheesy potatoes and can cut a pie into seven pieces. Joanne and her husband, Ralph Lehman, live comfortably in their *Dawdi haus* in Wooster, Ohio. They have two children, four grandchildren, and nine great-grandchildren.

BENVILLE COMMUNITY SERIES

 *Leah's Faith*

 *Susan's Hope*

 *Fannie's Love*

Word of mouth is crucial for any author to succeed. If you enjoyed *Susan's Hope* please leave a review online, wherever you are able, even if it's just a sentence or two. It would make all the difference and would be much appreciated.

Thanks!

Joanne Lehman